FEARLESS
in
Alaska

40 BELOW INK

Published by 40 Below Ink
Anchorage, Alaska

First 40 Below Ink Printing, 2011

The Library of Congress Cataloging-in-Publication Data

Ballard, Izzy.

FEARLESS IN ALASKA
Reluctant clairvoyant, Abigail Vertuccio, meets her match while running a small rural air service in Fairbanks, Alaska.

1. Alaska - Fiction. 2. Mystery - Fiction. 3. Romantic Comedy - Fiction.
4. Fairbanks - Fiction. 5. Chick-lit - Fiction 6. Women's - Fiction.
7. Airlines - Fiction. 8. Mothers and daughters - Fiction. I. Title

2011930179

ISBN: 978-0-9818267-1-4

Printed in the United States of America

FIRST EDITION

For

Amy and Dylan

To-Do-Before-You Die

You all know the standard To-Do-Before-You-Die list. Right? They pretty much all go like this:

1. Go to_____. Insert name of exotic or incredibly difficult-to-reach locale, namely Timbuktu, Bali or Tibet.

Hey. I already live in Alaska. (Translation: six months a year of cave-like darkness. Frozen fingers, nose and toes. Frozen spit. Frozen cars with frozen groceries. Six months of cabin fever, unless you're addicted to snow machining or have a death wish and just have to climb Mt. McKinley.) So, no way.

2. Try_____. Insert some activity that rates at least a ten on the It's-Likely-To-Kill-You scale, you idiot. Like jumping out of planes or wrestling with polar bears. All in the name of adventure and squeezing every last ounce out of life before you croak or fall off a glacier.

3. Sleep with_____. Insert name of some hot babe or hot guy. Your choice. Although he/she must be way out of your league. Obviously.

Did that. Regretted it. We got married. He cheated. End of story. He said he loved me and wanted me back. I say I've had enough adventure for one marriage, thank you very much.

This is *my* To-Do list. And please don't tell me it reads like a cross between a *Nancy Drew* novel and a self-help manual for the dysfunctional and deluded.

I already know.

1.   Escape the family business, namely Alaska Virgin Air, a small rural
air service located in Fairbanks, Alaska, that I'm currently running—
Grandma's orders. Really, I had no choice. Because when Gran tells you
to get your butt back to Alaska, you do it. When Gran says stay, you stay.
That's the Italian way.
   But it could happen. Escape, I mean.

2.   Keep my wits about me. Don't be talked into any number of dangerous
activities—like love, for instance, and this time I mean it.

3.   Never get so close to a man that you end up in a puddle of your own
tears like the Wicked Witch of the West. Okay, so the WWW never cried
a single day in her life, but you get my point.
   Here's the thing. I have Mac in my life, a God-like pilot (just ask any of
the pilot groupies around town) who never makes me cry; but hey, I'm not
taking any chances.

4.   Keep Big Ellie oiled, gassed up and ready to go. Big Ellie being my
ancient motor home. She may be decorated in early garage sale, but she's
my first and best escape route, should escape become possible, which goes
a long way to keeping me from dancing on table tops or bungee jumping
naked off the Cushman Street bridge.

5.   The real biggie? Don't let being clairvoyant fuck things up again. The
thing is, being clairvoyant is a noose around my neck. A monkey on my
back. A one-way ticket to someplace I really don't want to go, again.
   Did I forget to mention the clairvoyant thing before? Well, there it is.
And trust me. I'm not exaggerating. Being clairvoyant is truly a curse.

Prologue

I'm pretty sure everyone has at least one moment when everything is going exactly right. Perfect even. Although, you may not see it at the time, or may even forget about it later. You're about to be late for a job interview with Rolling Stone Magazine and someone pulls out of the only parking space within a three-block radius just as you pull up.

Or, picture the local coffee shop. You manage to dump a caramel frappucino all over your lap. The cute guy one table over dumps his espresso down the front of his shirt in solidarity. Soul-mates in the making.

For me, that one perfect moment involved a cloudless sky, a shiny Cessna 180 and a flight so amazing it made me wonder why I'd ever questioned my decision to return to Alaska in the first place. (Like I said: perfect.)

That is, until my life flashed before my eyes. I'm not talking about in some new-agey, alternative universe, reiki healer kind of way. I mean, I saw The End.

Well, fuck. There goes #5 on the To-Do list.

I wasn't kidding when I said being clairvoyant is a curse. It's bad enough seeing the future, worse when people find out. Then they want to know all sorts of things they have no business knowing. Lottery numbers are popular. Who's cheating is another big one. Followed by: Should they stay or kick him to the curb, and on and on.

Either way, I lose. Because depending on how things work out, they end up either hating me or treating me like some kind of God-like healer.

If I could change it, I would. Especially now, seeing my own worst fear in front of me, as clearly as I can see my breath on a frozen day in January. As clearly as you see your face each morning in the bathroom mirror.

Oh, God! Take a breath, Abbey. Breathe. I'd explain, but, oh, hell. I don't have time for this. I have to load up Big Ellie and get the heck out of here.

Really, you don't want to know all the gory details. I know I don't. Though I don't get a choice in the matter.

Truth is, being clairvoyant isn't just a curse. It's a life sentence.

Until yesterday, I'd convinced myself all I had to do was stay under the radar and keep to the list.

Today, I'm writing a new list.

Chapter 1

Countdown to Valentine's Day:
Seven days to go

Twelve hours later and here's the new list: 1. Start taking the previous friggin' list seriously! Twelve hours later and I had no clue what I was going to do. Ignore the vision. Option 1. I mean, being clairvoyant isn't a sure thing. Not even close. I can't even remember how many times I was wrong.

I once had a vision of our city mayor wearing Victoria Secret panties. And hey, we don't even have a Victoria's Secret in Fairbanks. In fifth grade, I told my best friend, Jo, that Freddie Costa was in love with her. Instead he lobbed a Twinkie at her head during recess. In sixth grade, I got everyone all excited because I said school was going to be canceled due to a blizzard. They made us go, anyway.

I sure as heck never knew my ex was sleeping with my former friend. (Suzette, in case you were wondering.)

One time I flashed on a kidnapping before it happened. Thanks to fast thinking and a lot of luck we averted that one. Still. That proves I'm not going to meet my end on February 14th at exactly 2:46 p.m.

Countdown to Valentine's Day:
Day Six

I don't know what time I finally fell asleep wearing nothing but my pizza-stained I Love NY T-shirt and raggedy pink bunny slippers, but when I awoke it felt like target practice was competing with a demolition derby for top billing in my head, thanks to too much vodka and too little sleep. So, except for the pain, so far so good. Except for Mac, the other half of the vision.

Okay. I'll tell you about the vision, and then we're not going to talk about it ever again. In exactly three thousand, one hundred, four hours and fifty-seven minutes from this date—on February 14th, to be exact—I am going to meet my fate. On February 14th, I'll be slipping into a one-use-only dress. Marching, marching, marching down a long, carpeted aisle. Smiling like I mean it. Until death do us part, no less.

Like I said. Oh. My. God!

I mean, I'm too young. I'm not ready. I'm not getting married. Do you hear me?

That being said, how, in good conscience, could a nice Italian girl like me keep stringing Mac along, knowing he wanted the whole red-carpet-buttercream-frosting-in-the-face-I-do thing. Followed by pink lines on pee sticks, PTA meetings, paper, silver and gold anniversaries. Death Sentence 101.

Me? I have no intention of spending a lifetime arguing over whose shoes were left in the middle of the floor for someone to trip over and whose turn it was to pick up the milk. I'm not ready for a batch of ungrateful teenagers making us wonder why we ever had kids in the first place. The idea of color-coordinated toothbrushes and matching bathroom towels makes me want to puke. No swaying on the porch together as we edge into old age. Although I have to admit, that one sounds okay.

Being clairvoyant may not be a sure thing, but I wasn't taking any chances. The whole thing made me realize I had to do the right thing and cut him loose. It was only fair.

"Hey, don't look at me that way," I snapped at my reflection in the bathroom mirror. That's the way it has to be. End of story. Fini.

One quick email, then I hit the kitchen, grabbed a handful of Frosted Flakes to eat on the way and headed for the office, not quite sure how I was going to pull it off—working with Mac day in and day out. (Because he's the pilot; I run Alaska Virgin Air. Too close for comfort.)

Either way, there was no time to dwell on it. I'd just have to think about it tomorrow. Sicilian Diversionary Tactic #40. And trust me. We came up with that one way before Scarlet.

"Nice outfit, Ab."

Great. It must have been pretty bad for Jaye, Alaska Virgin Air's other pilot and a true southern gentleman, to resort to sarcasm.

I glanced down. Yep. There I was, standing in the lobby of Alaska Virgin Air in my crumpled, pizza stained T-shirt and bunny slippers, made worse by the little bits of Frosted Flakes sticking to the bunny ears and bunny whiskers. It was amazing I hadn't frozen my toes off on the way over.

My hair resembled a hornet's nest. My breath? I didn't want to find out. But charming, I'm sure. On some level, I really didn't care. I dropped my backpack in the middle of the floor, spit out a breathy "humph" and slipped behind the front counter. I was trying to ignore the concerned look on Jaye's face when the vision came back to me.

I was at the University of Alaska's classic movie of the week with Mac, watching as Spencer Tracy waved a gun at a quaking Katherine Hepburn. My thoughts were on Mac and how everything felt so right, when suddenly everything rotated a quarter turn and I heard the words, like they were coming right out of Spencer Tracy's mouth: "Do you take this man?"

"Bloody hell. Who left this f'in bag in the middle of the f'in floor?"

Justine. The object of Jaye's affection—feisty, loud-mouthed, British, with a penchant for funky outfits, tattoos and body piercings and AVA's all around office guru—snapped me back to reality.

"I might of f'in killed myself, if anyone bloody well cares," she barked, all the while aiming an accusing look at Jaye; at least until she noticed me and shook her head, pointedly staring at my breasts. "Forgot your bib, again, Abigail?"

I humphed again, showing them how much I didn't care about the What The Hell Happened To Her? looks they were shooting over my head.

"Trouble with Mac?" Justine asked, with no regard whatsoever to whether she was treading on potentially vulnerable toes. Sheesh.

Jaye elbowed her, right before I showed them my back and began sorting a pile of already-sorted shipping manifests.

Justine tilted her sheared head, exasperated, and whispered to Jaye. "Where's Mac?"

Jaye said on a shrug, "Early flight to Kotzebue."

She tapped her foot impatiently. Arms firmly planted across her chest.

"And?"

"Then you arrived."

"Bollocks!" That said with a force she usually saved for customers who had the audacity to sneak extra baggage on a flight, change their reservations for the third time, or those unfortunate enough to comment on her adorable British accent.

Meanwhile, Jaye, quicker on the uptake than most (from years of experience, having apparently figured out which side his bread was buttered on) blushed all the way down to his armpits (a guess) before he whispered, "She showed up fifteen minutes ago, ran into the fire hydrant out front, tripped over José, dumped a box of donuts onto the computer and can't seem to remember where she put anything."

For the record, José is Jaye's inert lump of a hound dog and I didn't trip over him. He tripped me.

"Business as usual," Justine snapped. "What else?"

"She nearly shipped a thousand pounds of groceries to Nome that were slated for St. Mary's, right before she ate five donuts." If he were being interrogated by the CIA, he couldn't have spilled more. The rat!

"She's been picking things up and putting them down and walking around muttering, 'Gotta get a grip' and 'I've been wrong before.'"

"It's Mac." Justine nodded knowingly. As if man trouble was the only thing that could put a girl into a tailspin.

Jaye sneaked another peek at me before continuing. "Mac was in earlier, muttering something about an email and how it was for his own good, and then he took off for his flight.

I had to wonder. If I fired Jaye, how long would it take to find a new pilot?

Justine squinted through her pink John Lennon glasses and gave me the once-over before she shook her head and sighed. Like maybe I was a lost cause.

Weird that she didn't jump all over me, tell me how I was a total screw up or toss Ding Dongs at my head. Instead, she turned her back to me and pulled out her phone.

"Time to call Jo."

"I can hear you."

Any eavesdropping that I may or may not have been doing was absolutely unintentional.

Justine turned, gave me a hard look and headed my way. The phone rang and I snatched it up like it was the last peanut butter cup in Alaska. Sicilian Diversionary Tactic #41: Don't just sit there and wait for them to get you.

"Alaska Virgin Air," I said, going with my perky-but-let's-be-professional voice, all the while praying it was someone needing to ship 12,000 pounds of penny candy to Chicken, Alaska, so Justine would be too busy to worry about me and my bunny slippers.

"Abbey?" a distant voice said. "Sam here."

"Sam?" I shouted, as my elbow connected with Gran's AC/DC coffee cup sending it crashing to the floor. My third spill in a little under an hour. "I can't believe it's you."

Sam, aka Samantha Prewitt—not her real name, but the only name I've ever known her by—is my favorite British spy. She came into my life a year ago in pursuit of an international crook, and convinced me she was a flighty American student with a penchant for classic costumes and an Alaska Virgin Air pilot or two.

I should have been angry at her, and I was, except that she helped save Juliette, Justine's daughter, from being kidnapped last year, and almost as important, believed in me when I needed her to. Hearing from Sam was almost as good as escaping in Big Ellie—my favorite thing for when the world is spinning around and confusing the hell out of me.

She waited a beat. "How are you, Abigail?"

"Fine," I said, a little too quickly. I was so glad to hear her voice I could almost feel the tears coming on.

"Really?"

What? Was she a mind-reader or was she working some kind of secret agent trick on me?

I tried to keep the irritation out of my voice. "I'm fine," I said, with a finality that screamed, "So stop bugging me about it, already."

"Fine as in fine? Or fine like in 'The Italian Job'; FINE being freaked out, insecure, neurotic and emotional'?"

"I'm okay." I sighed. How many times did I have to lie?

When I didn't elucidate, she changed gears. "Brilliant. Because I have a favor to ask and I don't have much time."

That got my attention. British agents don't need favors, especially not from burned-out clairvoyants who are running from themselves.

"It's personal," she added. "I'm. Well, I'm out of town and it's my brother."

"Out of town" being code for undercover in one of those extremely exotic and dangerous locales from our To-Do lists, eight million miles from civilization and barely enough time for a brief but searingly hot fling with any number of enigmatic 007 partners named Sean or Ian.

". . . if you see that he doesn't get himself locked up or ravaged by a polar bear."

Okay. I admit I missed a bit. Lost in my fantasy of 007 framed by a flowing tent somewhere in a steamy desert, I may have drifted. So sue me.

"Forget it, Abbey," she said. "It's too much to ask."

"No, wait," I shouted, earning a round of pointed looks and raised eyebrows from Jaye and Justine. "Sam. Sorry. I was preoccupied."

Does dealing with the end of life as I know it in seven days—well, six now—and having a sex-in-the-desert-with-a-stranger fantasy count as preoccupied? God. I needed to focus if I had any hope of beating this thing.

"I'm back, Sam. What do you need?"

For the next thirty-six minutes and forty-two seconds (believe me, I checked) Sam, the cool, calm and collected tormentor of assassins and other reprobates, rambled on about the one case at which she'd failed miserably (her words)—talking sense into her step-brother, Ben. Ben, a university professor obsessed with ex-fiancé Rebecca (a TransLondon pilot who recently ran off with one Frank Merona, owner of Merona Air, an upstart bush air freight service right here in Fairbanks, Alaska). Coincidence? Hmm. Seems Ben got it in his head that Merona was using Rebecca to launder money from a highly illegal operation. Now Ben is determined to prove that Merona is a really a porn king by day and a drug lord by night.

"Abbey, don't believe a word he says; he's totally barmy. Bloody Nora, he sold his flat, took a sabbatical from university, all so he could go chasing after some beastly tart. Frankly, I don't have the time for his daft—"

"Take a breath, Sam," I managed to squeeze in.

"Bugger all. He's been driving me over the edge ever since he was six and he was convinced his rabbit, Sir Earwig, could speak. Take his work. After he got over the idea of being a mad inventor, he decided to become a minister. Brilliant. Right? But no. Too much hypocrisy. Then it was rocket science. Art. Then philosophy. I think religion as myth." She squeezed out a ragged breath before I could get a word in. "And now it's American cultural studies. Did you know the media is the root of all evil, Abigail?"

"Sam?" It was clear she was heading for a meltdown. I needed to put the brakes on this. Stat. "Sam?"

"Lord. He won't step into a Walmart. Don't ask him to, unless you—"

"Sam!"

". . . want to hear all about how big box stores are destroying the cultural landscape of America—"

"Sam!" I banged the phone down on the counter hard. "Did you hear that? You can stop talking now."

When she finally paused, I continued. "How do you know all this? About his flat, about Alaska?"

"I have my methods."

"What? Stakeouts? Bugs. Satellites?"

All I got for my efforts was a heavy sigh. "No drama necessary, Abigail. I have a friend who teaches at Oxford." Code for ex-lover, no doubt. I'm getting really good at deciphering this spy stuff.

"You've got to stop him before he does something totally nutters, Abbey. You'll understand him, what with you two being—"

"What? We're alike? You said he was barmy, Sam," I said as I shook Frosted Flakes distractedly from my bunny slippers.

"You're . . . different. Clairvoyant. He loves that kind of nonsense. I mean . . . well . . ." she stuttered, failing to redeem herself in the least.

"You think I'm crazy." Then I thought back to last night. I suppose she might have something there.

"Focus, Abbey."

"I'm focusing. You said I was crazy."

"Unique. Brilliant."

Right.

"So, will you?"

If I'd been less distracted and more on my game, I might have avoided getting sucked into her evil plot. If I'd felt less indebted to her for helping thwart Juliette's kidnappers, I might have told her to forget about it. If I'd had my wits about me, things would have been different. I wouldn't have said, "Of course, I'll help, Sam. I'll watch out for Ben. No. He won't suspect a thing." If I hadn't agreed to all of the above, I wouldn't be where I am today.

"So, you'll do it?"

"I already said yes six times. Is there some secret code I need to give you, because I said, yes. You want me to sign in blood?"

The Sicilian in me tends toward melodrama in situations like these.

"He arrives at Mt. McKinley Park tonight."

"Tonight?"

"You'll recognize him from the photo I'm faxing you."

"You have a fax in the desert?"

"What desert?"

Never mind.

"Just remember, you don't know me."

I grabbed a handful of stale Fritos from behind the counter and tossed them back. A half-eaten chip lodged dangerously in that place at the back of my throat between tongue and swallow and I tried not to make the ack, ack sound cats do when they're trying to yak up a fur ball.

When I could speak again, I wondered aloud. "And how do you suggest I get him to go with me if I don't tell him I know you?" I mean, I'm not Courtney Love, so he won't follow me for the sex and the drugs.

"Once he finds out you're clairvoyant, he'll stick to you like grits on eggs."

"Where are you, Sam. Georgia?"

"Stop worrying, Abbey."

Famous last words. I dropped my aching head into my hands and muttered a reply. "Barely breathing, and who knows for how long."

"What?"

"Nothing."

"Gotta go," she said.

"Camel waiting?" I asked. But she was already back in 007's manly arms, leaving me with the feeling that fate had hijacked me for some unknown reason. Because Ben and I were about to share a point in destiny—like it or not. That much I was sure of.

I tossed the receiver onto its cradle, watched as it rocked back and forth and briefly wondered if it would stay in place or cascade to the floor below, all the while patently ignoring Justine who was busy hovering over my left shoulder with a look that said she would not be deterred.

Her smoothly shorn head and ethereal style reminded me of a modern day archangel. At least until she opened her mouth.

"What was all that about?" she demanded.

Justine was also, if I haven't mentioned before, AVA's indispensable office manager; I was going to have to talk to her sooner or later.

"Justine, do you think you can run this place by yourself for a few days?"

"Is Jude Law a total dish?"

"Good. I'll call you when I can."

Before she could yank me back and put a stay-right-where-you-are hex on me, I snatched up my backpack, holding it to my chest like a shield, and shot out the front door, a woman on a mission. Abigail Vertuccio, unofficial British Intelligence.

Which would have made for a great exit, if Justine hadn't come running after me, shouting "Where the hell are you going," all the way out to my car, until I slammed the door and was safely inside, windows rolled up, doors locked.

Who cared what Jaye or Justine were thinking. I was a spy. I was Jason Bourne. Mrs. Smith. Wait, Lara Croft. Nothing was going to deter me from my mission. Bunny slippers and all.

Clearly it was a case of too little sleep and too much vodka, Fritos and fear. You can't believe how exhausting it is, trying not to think about all the things I didn't want to think about. Like wedding vows. About Mac and how he was going to freak out when he found us—me and Big Ellie—gone without any explanation or scrap of decency on my part, other than a quick and dirty email this morning about visions and ending things.

I didn't want to think about how Justine was probably calling Jo right this minute and blabbing her guts out. Don't think about failure. Just stop thinking. Or I should think about the trip. About Big Ellie. No, I can't think about Big Ellie, since it was Mac who'd had her totally refurbished last year after she was shot up, stolen and run into a drainage ditch on the Alaska Highway.

First things first. Packing.

Clothes. Spares on board.

Other essentials. Books, flashlight, tire chains. Check. Check. Check.

Food. 7-Eleven on the way. Check.

Mr. Peanut, Gran's two-ton cat. One phone call to the neighbor and check.

Alaska Milepost, lifesaver guide book, replete with descriptions of every highway, tree, brown bear and porta-potty between Barrow and the Canadian Border. Check.

What else? Nothing. I brushed aside my fear as I turned the key in Big Ellie and let out a half-hearted whoop.

Maybe going after Ben would tame any visions of impending wedding debacles. Only it didn't.

Even as I was planning my Great Denali Adventure, I couldn't escape the vision. A vision within a vision, really. There we were at the movie. Normal enough. Right? Mac was leaning his head against mine. He smelled spicy. A combination of garlic from our pizza dinner and pepperminty, from a shared piece of Wrigley's.

He'd just asked me something—I don't remember what—when I was bombarded with images of satin clad, oh-so-precious flower girls converging on me, while laughter from the neighboring theater seats accompanied my panic in a creepy, foreboding background melody.

"Open road here we come," I said to Big Ellie, as I shook it off. What else could I do?

Big Ellie's engine answered with a comforting whoosh, before we started the trip down the long, dirt driveway heading away from Fairbanks, toward the Parks Highway and Mt. McKinley, aka Denali.

I knew my phone at home would be ringing off the hook by now. The Fairbanks gossip network in full swing. The calls would keep on coming, no doubt about it. First from Gran, who was in Portland, stopping between band gigs with her lover, Al. Then Mom, at the Jersey shore, wondering why her daughter couldn't stay put, behave like a normal person and stop worrying everyone. (Like she worries about me.) Then Jo. Furious that I'd left her out of all the fun. And why didn't I tell her what was going on? After all, we're a team; we're Sassy Sisters Investigations. And I should remember how Tony, her husband of almost a year, was being Tony, as usual, with all this Italian stay-at-home, barefoot and when-are-we-going-to-have-a-baby stuff, and didn't I know she could use a break? And then there was Mac.

But forget about Mac. Because when a Vertuccio woman screws up—not that I was screwing up—we never look back.

Sicilian Tactic #42.

Chapter 2

According to the Alaska Milepost, we'd missed the last public outhouse for the next eighty miles. According to my keen sense of observation, we (me and Big Ellie, of course) had passed about a kazillion skinny, sun-starved trees. The Milepost warned we were coming up fast on a Dangerous Bear Area!—one of many between Fairbanks and Mt. Mckinley on the George Parks Highway, a wild and lonely road that makes you wonder how anyone could be this deep in the middle of Alaska without a dog team and sled. We weren't at the center of the earth, but at times it felt that way.

A dense ice fog was slowing me down to forty, where in the summer, I would have been pushing seventy, even in Big Ellie. What should have taken a couple of hours was edging into three with no Mt. McKinley in sight. To make matters worse, my cell phone kept ringing and ringing and ringing, until I had no choice. I threw it over my shoulder onto Big Ellie's green shag carpet where it landed with a mild, unsatisfying thud.

I drove on, straining to see through the fog, singing off key and trying to picture Ben. If the fax Sam sent meant anything, Ben was gray, with no definable features and a head a lot like Charlie Brown's. From her description, Sam's American half-brother—I'd have to remember to get more from her on that later—was 5'9" or so. Dark, wavy brown hair. "Not helped by his endless habit of running his fingers through it any time a stray thought crosses his mind."

A cross between The Nutty Professor and Dr. Who, with the addition of a pair of thick tortoiseshell rimmed glasses. The kind rock stars have taken to wearing, oh, and he's built like a wrestler because he rides his bike everywhere and forgets to eat." And let's not forget, "A dish, but can't keep a girl because he's too weird, once he starts talking about—"

I stopped listening. Typical sister/brother stuff. Although, I really don't get it. I would have loved having a brother. Someone to grab Richie Spellman by the shirt in seventh grade and shake him until he got the message: Don't snap Abbey's double-A training bra ever again, or I'll put a hit out on you. Sicilian Tactic #11.

Someone to show me how to keep my elbows up so I could get a line drive every once in a while. A brother to bring friends home for me to dream about, and someone to explain why Eddy Johnson kept pulling my hair and throwing spit wads at me all through fifth grade.

I didn't get a brother. Or sister. My dad died in Vietnam. I had Gran and Mom. I have Jo, Justine, and now Sam. My adopted family. Which makes Ben mine, too.

To recap, I have an insane wedding vision hanging over my head, a newly ex-boyfriend to deal with, Ben's mystery, Sam and worse—how I was gonna explain everything to . . . well, everyone.

I had no choice but to go with Sicilian Tactic #43: Family comes first. The rest you deal with if there's time.

Life Lesson #1: You can't believe a sister's description of her brother. When I arrived at the hotel at Mckinley and found Ben, he was nothing at all like Sam had described. Reginald from Australia, however, was.

Here's how it went down. I walked over to the one guy in the place who fit Sam's description and slipped right into my best secret agent routine: I accidentally on purpose tripped over his outstretched foot, where I landed in an unladylike fashion across both his dining room table and his jean-clad lap. Making the best of a bad situation, I peered up at him through seductive lashes and waved. Like I wasn't spread out before him like a naked sushi tray.

"Hi," I said, trying for casual.

"Hi, yourself," he grinned, before lifting me back onto my feet before the rest of his dinner hit the floor along with the salad and dinner roll that were already rolling around beneath us.

That was right before he asked me to join him. What a guy!

If he hadn't been so sweet and charming and welcoming, it would have been thirty minutes down the drain. The thirty minutes it took me to realize he wasn't Ben. True, his hair was red, not black, but hey, he could have dyed it. His accent was Aussie, but he could have been faking it. When I casually tossed in that I was clairvoyant and he broke out laughing, I knew. Not Ben.

If not a proficient spy, I was persistent. Keeping in spy mode, I ditched Reginald to surreptitiously peruse the dining room. One down, at least seven or eight to go. Seems I'd arrived in the middle of a climber's convention. My luck, hundreds of young, firm, hunky guys would be arriving at any moment—at any other time, a blessing from above.

With no time to waste, I set my sights on a lone table tucked back in the corner, one I'd missed earlier, where a compact, dark-haired man sat hunched over a thick book, mindlessly spooning red soup into his mouth. Nerdy tie. White shirt. Brown shoes. Professor material to a T.

I took a second to plot my next move, then slid past his table, empty coffee cup in hand, heading for the self-serve coffee pot at the end of the long counter. As inconspicuously as possible, I read a few words over his shoulder. Psychology. Well, Ben was into cultural studies. That included psychology. Sort of.

I circled back around, walked up to him and, with as much surprise in my voice as I could muster, said, "Oh. My God. It's been so long! I can't believe it's really you!"

He abandoned his book, adjusted his glasses and, to his credit, didn't ask who the heck I was. Instead he pushed his seat back, put out a hand and returned my greeting. That was all it took.

And there went an hour in which I learned more than I ever wanted to know about the University of Colorado, the psychology of climbing, his long, torturous trip getting up here, oh, and what a coincidence that we'd run into each other like this, because he'd never had the pleasure of bumping into any of his colleagues in Alaska before.

I never did ask who he thought I was.

I orchestrated at least three more failed meetings before I hit pay dirt. One. The dentist from San Louis Obisbo, who was certain we'd met in a previous life, and was I sure I couldn't stay and discuss it further over a whiskey sour? Two. Thor from NYC, here for a bit role in a movie he wasn't at liberty to discuss. *Get real*. And Roland, who, in a different time and place, given no Mac, no mission and more than five days of freedom left, might have been worth exploring. Unfortunately, as soon as I saw his Visa card, proving he was in fact Roland and not Ben, I made my getaway.

No time for flirting, playing with fire or fun.

In truth, I was exhausted. Trying to remember which lies I'd told to which guy was enough to make me crave a nap and an Excedrin.

I was hunched over a barely tasted and heavily picked-over pastrami on rye, with a steamy cup of hot chocolate pressed against my forehead, wondering what I was going to do next, when a gentle voice asked, "Can I help you?"

The voice didn't come from above, as one might have expected, but from the seat next to me. Caught off guard, I turned to gaze into a pair of soft-brown eyes, ones filled with curiosity and a whisper of a crinkle in the space between his eyebrows. One hand ran absentmindedly through his choppy hair, and I sensed him move closer, right before he reached over and took my hand. He held my gaze and, still, I didn't pull away.

"I'm Ben."

It was like something I'd never felt before. Two wrongs making a right. You know. A pot and a lid, a spoon and a fork, only with a touch of kismet tossed in to throw me off completely.

No, it was more like this. A missing part returned. Reality and desire meeting. The eye of the tornado. The absolute certainty that something was meant to be, mixed in with a fierce and decidedly dangerous amount of fear.

"I'm Ben," he repeated.

I looked back at him, wordlessly.

Sicilian Tactic #44: Keep your mouth shut when no other words seem necessary.

Chapter 3

Seriously. What was Sam thinking? For one, Ben was at least six feet tall. If he looked nerdy at all, it was in a Robert Downey Jr. sort of way. Maybe Sam never noticed, but Ben dressed like James Dean: black jacket, tight, worn jeans, chunky boots and enough self-confidence to have every waitress in the room looking for an excuse to drop by our table, like bears to a salmon stream.

"Looks like your coffee's low," one giggled.

"More cream?" asked another, making it sound distinctly dirty, as she shifted her weight from one foot to another and pushed her breasts up with two hands. In case he hadn't noticed.

"Anything I can get for you, handsome?" A third asked Ben. Never mind me.

When the stream of groupies finally slowed to a trickle and I'd run out of supplies for the sugar cube igloo I was busy constructing, I found my voice. "Ben?"

"Hmm."

"Not that I'm complaining, but what made you come over to my table?"

With a look that was one part bad boy and one part boy next door, he laughed. "From where I was sitting, you'd already approached most of the men in the room. I thought I'd save you the trouble."

Which would have sounded conceited coming from any other guy, but on him it just came off as honest.

"I figure you're either a reporter, a climbing groupie or a spy."

He released my hand in order to pirate a couple of fries from my plate, dipped them in the puddle of hot sauce that was sitting next to my wilting sandwich, popped them into his mouth and closed his eyes, savoring the spicy treat. He looked over and caught me staring. "So? Am I close?"

By the way, that's the exact way I eat my fries: with enough hot sauce to burn the tongue off a grizzly.

"Maybe," I said, considering my mission. Technically, I was a spy, if you weren't too picky about a little thing like the truth.

Ben continued to devour my fries like a half-starved teenager, while I tried not to stare. I'd stop myself, then before I knew it I'd be doing it again.

"What about you?" I asked.

He unzipped his jacket to reveal a black Einstein T-shirt—the exact mate of the one that was in my clothes hamper back home—and saved me the trouble. "A friend of mine is in with a bad lot up in Fairbanks, so I came to get it sorted."

In the face of such candor, guilt hit with a vengeance. I should tell him about Sam's call. Confess now before I got in too deep. Sicilian Tactic #51: Lies have a way of biting you in the rear when you get in too deep. Although you don't have to be Sicilian to know that one.

"I had a dream about Rebecca leaving and two days later she was gone."

I stuffed a fry in my mouth to keep from snorting.

"Fiona—our professor of mythology—has been working with me on my psychic abilities."

I couldn't help it, I snorted. "Like a psychic-in-training?" Stranger things have happened, but come on.

"Exactly. Brilliant," he said, flashing me his cat with cream smile. "Fiona says everyone has some psychic ability."

"Okay. Prove it." Sicilian Tactic #52: I'll believe it when I see it.

His eyes roamed the café and landed on a man in a suit and tie, two tables down. "See him. He's going to call the waitress over for a ketchup. Watch."

I didn't need spy school or clairvoyance to see that he was right. For one, the guy had a salmon burger with home fries sitting in front of him. For two, the mustard stood like a lone sentry guarding the salt and pepper. No ketchup in sight. And three, he was wearing a Rolex. No way would Rolex guy get up and snag a ketchup from an adjoining booth or table by himself.

I didn't recite the list, but I did a hand wave. "Ben, he's got fries," just as Rolex guy called the waitress over.

"See," Ben said. Triumphant in his victory. "Ketchup."

I rolled my eyes, then caught myself. "What else do you know?"

"Abbey, it doesn't work that way. I don't know everything. Like what you're thinking, for instance."

I was thinking maybe I should jump him. Right on the table. Get it over with. Okay, briefly. The thought was gone in a sec.

He looked at me and this time it felt like he was seeing parts of me that even I couldn't see. Like I was an unexpected gift. The one he'd wanted but never thought he would get.

"Ben. I. "

I wanted to tell him all this. The other half thing, the gift thing, (not the jumping him part) and about Sam, too. Especially, about Sam. But I didn't know where to begin.

"I was wondering what brings you to Alaska," was what fell out of my mouth, instead. Stupid. I get that.

He reached for my hand, and I knew. Even if this was the eye of the tornado, I could stay here forever.

"I feel like I just met my best friend," he said. "Is that weird?"

He looked so earnest, I had to laugh.

"Yeah, it's weird," I said, and reached out and held his hand right back.

I caught the twinge of relief on his face as his forehead relaxed into contentment. Then, just as quickly, things changed.

Call me clairvoyant, but I knew trouble was coming.

Chapter 4

"Well, well, well."

Jo? It couldn't be. No way. Jo was in Fairbanks, not McKinley. Denali. What the heck?

"What's going on here?"

Her tone couldn't have been more chilly if we'd landed on an iceberg a mile off the coast of Barrow.

How did she get here so fast? Hands on hips, she radiated a silent command: Straighten up, Abigail Vertuccio. Lucky for me her green Lucky Charms T-shirt clashed with a pair of pink plaid bell-bottoms and red hair, making the whole Judge Judy act a bit hard to take seriously.

Oh, no. Tony came? And doing a pretty good impression of a mafia godfather. What next?

Jo turned to Ben. "Sam's brother. Right?"

Rats! Double rats. To put it politely. I froze as Ben tilted his head, grabbed a handful of hair and squinted, the wheels turning as he held out a hand to her with welcoming eyes.

"Tony, meet Ben. Jo, Ben," I said, telegraphing Jo a message: Keep your mouth shut. But no such luck.

Question? Did this call for a "son of a bitch" or a "what the fuck?" Come to think of it, I was pretty sure the situation called for both.

"What?" Jo snapped.

"Nothing. Just nothing," I replied.

Great! Now Ben knew that Jo knew Sam, and since I knew Jo, how long would it take your average Ph.D. to figure out he'd been had?

I jumped out of my seat, sending a batch of congealing fries and my creaky chair crashing to the floor, giving me enough of a head start so I could latch onto Ben's sleeve and edge him past Jo and Tony (while they were brushing ketchup off their Adidas), until we rounded a corner and were out of sight. Quickly, I scoped out the lobby for possible getaway options. A. The pond outside. Dive in and hide like they do in the movies? Hmm. February. Alaska. 20 below zero? Forget about it.

There was Option B. Ben's hotel room. But if Jo and Tony knew that Ben was Ben, then going to his hotel room would be like leading a moose to a cabbage patch. Plus, there was the bed part, so not a great plan.

The only other choice was right in front of my face. I pushed open a door, and with Ben following along like the puppy dog I'd previously mentioned to Sam, we ended up in a puke-green room lined with urinals on one side and toilet stalls on the other.

I'm absolutely certain our arrival had nothing whatsoever to do with the gentleman with the comb-over and plaid polyester pants almost peeing himself in his haste to zip and rush out of the room, which he did while muttering something about being late and wanting to give us our privacy.

Ben was unusually silent. Not that I knew what was normal for him. Maybe he made a habit of hiding out in rest rooms with strange women.

Me. I was thinking about Sicilian Tactic #4: Take the offensive in any defensive situation. For example, "What're you looking at?" Only that didn't seem like the right attitude to take with someone who, after all, had let me drag him unceremoniously away from the only two people who might have had the answers to his most pressing questions, i.e. how they knew Sam, how they knew me, how we all ended up here at Mt. McKinley, and to top it all off, how he wound up in a men's room causing a perfectly respectable-looking gentleman to think we were in here for a quickie?

Maybe Sicilian Tactic #37 would work. Stall. (Being Sicilian, we have many, many tactics—an entire trunkload—for handling the little problems that crop up on a daily basis in the life of your average Sicilian. Feel free to borrow them.)

I pressed one hand against Ben's chest—to keep him from escaping, naturally—opened the door a crack to check for signs of Jo or Tony, pulled a crumpled piece of Wrigley's from my back pocket (no worse for wear if you didn't count the little bits of tissue fluff sticking to one end), popped it in my mouth and turned to Ben. Time to face the music.

"I knew we'd end up in here," he said, as he took in the overflowing trash can and "Harry loves Jimmy" graffiti carved into the stall behind us.

I gave him a shove. "Don't give me that." I was close to my breaking point with all this psychic stuff. "You did not."

He lifted an eyebrow and gave me a look. Probably the same one he reserved for students who argued with him in class. "So, tell me."

Rats. I walked right into that one.

"No? Okay. I'll start. You wanted to meet me. The question is why?" He ruffled his hair slightly. "Of course. Sam."

That he didn't look disappointed in me only served to add fuel to my defensiveness. He was the one who was worrying his sister half to death. He was the one going off half-cocked, leaving a perfectly good job and flat and country. He was the one landing me in the middle of his harebrained scheme. Not to mention forcing me to tell a batch of out-and-out lies to both friends and family.

I tried for a shocked and unfairly accused look. Sicilian Tactic #38.

"So, you didn't mean to meet me?" He waited patiently while I sputtered a reply.

"I didn't want to meet you," I said, then gave it up. "But I meant to meet you. Sorry."

One second I was confessing my horrendous behavior, the next Ben's powerful arms were holding me for all I was worth. After a calming minute, he brushed the hair from beside my ear and kissed my cheek.

"Sam always gets her way, Abbey. Don't feel bad," he whispered.

Did I mention he smelled delicious? Like coconut cupcakes and lemon pie. That was before a vision of Mac flashed in front of my face and I stepped back, tripping over nothing.

If Ben hadn't grabbed the front of my T-shirt, I would have landed in a dubious puddle on the floor; as it was, his hand was on my breast for less than a second and my heart was pounding in my chest, just under the place where his hand had touched, the image of Mac far, far away.

Could I get away with one kiss without winning the Tart-of-the-Year or Rotten-Cheating-Girlfriend award? Maybe not.

We kissed anyway. Don't ask who started it. All I can say is, thank God we were still in the men's room. I draw the line on dropping trou and jumping guys up against the urinals. I also draw the line at having an audience, so when Jo pushed her way into the bathroom and hit me on the head with a rolled-up newspaper, I was doubly glad my pants were still up, up, up, where they were supposed to be.

"Son of a bitch," Jo said, aiming her best evil eye at me as she grabbed a fist full of my T-shirt (which Ben had recently released) and pushed me against the bathroom sink where a warm pool of what I hoped was water seeped into the seat of my pants. Beyond her shoulder, I caught Tony signaling Ben, right before they disappeared. Chickens. The two of them.

Once Jo ran out of evil eye (it's harder to maintain than you'd imagine), she turned her back on me. "I. Can't. Even. Look. At. You."

This called for desperate measures. Sicilian Tactic #24: The Truth. "I'm dying, Jo. Well, getting married, but it's like dying, isn't it." I said, more a statement than a question, in as pathetic and miserable a voice as I could muster. I tried to squirt a little tear out of each eye. Sicilian Tactic #39. When that didn't work, I dabbed a drop of water—unobtrusively, I hoped—from the puddle I was sitting in, dribbled it onto my cheeks and gave her puppy dog eyes.

She turned and demanded, "When?"

Wouldn't most friends at least start with something like "really?" or "bullshit!"? But not Jo.

"February 14th, 2:46 p.m."

"So, you kept that news from Mac; and now, instead of maybe thinking you're nuts or you got it all messed up, he thinks he did something wrong."

I got up, pretty sure she was too busy to push me back into the puddle, pressed paper towels to my rear and searched for something to say. But she wasn't done. Not by a long shot.

She pointed at me like I was the Wicked Witch of the East and she was ready to land a house on me. "You couldn't have called and said, 'Jo, I had a flash.'"

"But—"

"Shut up, Abbey. You don't want to get me started."

Started?

"Justine told me everything."

Okay. No need to race out and do something crazy. Like seek revenge and whatnot.

"The corn flakes, the backpack, Sam's call."

"Not the bunny slippers?"

"The bunny slippers, too. And now you're cheating on Mac." She wrinkled up her nose, like I was moldy salad.

"Did you forget the dying part?" I asked, a little insulted that it had slipped her mind so easily.

"Marriage is not death. And, by the way, I'm married. You were the Maid of Honor. Remember?" she shouted. "Besides, Dumbo, what are the chances? I mean, you said we'd have a blizzard that time. And we still had to go to school."

See?

"And you said Jesse James was going to marry me some day. I even knew what I was going to wear."

"I was eight, Jo. And Jesse James was dead already." For crying out loud.

She gave me an ah-ha look. "The Seven Shades of Death! You said we were going to be a big hit and we'd all be rich."

The Seven Shades of Death was our high school band, and we stank. "Wishful thinking, Jo."

"And—"

"If I'm so wrong, why do people keep bugging me for advice all the time?"

She leaned against the counter, forgetting about the puddle, then jumped back up.

"Okay. So, there's a 50-50 chance. At 2:56 sharp, we make sure we're glued to my TV, watching Gilmore Girls on DVD. Easy."

It was 2:46, but what's ten minutes here or there when you're about to die, get married, whatever. Anyway, I wanted to believe her. I shrugged as she hugged me to her chest, then pulled me back, her hands resting on my shoulders, one finger playing with a curl nesting behind my ear.

"Now tell me exactly what's going on with Sam and Ben, Abbey. And don't leave out a single thing."

Strange how no men were coming into the bathroom the whole time Jo was beating the story out of me. Well, not the entire story. I left out the part where Ben was supposed to be bonkers. About the whole porn king/ drug lord thing. About psychics-in-training. About the instant attachment, other-half feeling I had with Ben. And about the fear that the vision was real. The uncertainty. The anxiety. Oh yeah, and about the kiss.

She got the Girl Scout version. The one you'd tell your mom, but instead of the Girl Scout hand thingy that I can't remember, I kept two fingers crossed behind my back like a true Sicilian.

Sicilian Tactic #25: Never Disappoint a friend in need. Ben needed me, maybe more than Sam knew, and I wasn't going to rat him out to anyone, not even to Jo, my very best friend in the world. Mac was another story. Back to Sicilian Tactic #40 on that one.

I thought I was in the clear. I really did. I had one foot over the finish line, the keys to the gold Mercedes in one hand, the handle to the men's room door in the other, when a bony hand gripped my shoulder and jerked me back.

"Right, and I'm Gandhi," Jo said.

I sighed. Some days I wonder why I don't stick to the simple truth, considering my success rate with little white lies, withholding and deception of any shape or form.

"I *said*, bullshit," Jo said, raising her voice, in case I'd gone deaf in the last six seconds.

"No. You didn't," I said, as the men's room door pushed inward and decanted a 20-something, 6'2" stoner, who eyed us then eyed the urinals. I could see the wheels turning for a half sec before he shrugged, unzipped, peed, shook, zipped and left again, without benefit of the sink.

Jo's and my eyes met and we burst out laughing, bending over and holding our stomachs. She went into a stall to take care of business, since we were here already, but that didn't stop her for long.

I folded my arms across my chest and glared at her through the open stall door. "That's all I have to say."

"Well then," she said, "I'll talk." So, what else was new? "You had a vision, got a call from Sam, dumped Mac and ran away to rescue someone you don't even know. Did I leave anything out?"

When I didn't answer, I guess she took that to mean go right ahead. "Except why would Sam's brother need help? He's a nutcase, isn't he? I mean, he looks normal, but—"

"Who said anything about a nutcase?" I asked, sounding guiltier than I'd hoped.

"You just did."

"Sam's being protective of her little brother and I—"

"Was looking for an excuse to run away, like you always do."

"Past tense. Did. Not do."

"So, you came to help a perfectly normal guy that you don't know get his girlfriend back, and to do that, you broke up with your boyfriend."

I turned on the tap and splashed warm water on my face in a futile attempt to drown her out. The toilet flushed and the water turned icy cold. I turned to face her.

"What would you have done if Sam needed you, Miss Perfect? Would you help, or would you go on with your happy life and forget all about it? But wait, I'm dying in five days, so, that's not really the same thing, is it?"

If looks could kill. "Getting married, dufus. That's not dying. I'm married. Remember?" She looked up at the ceiling and sighed. "You're not dying."

"And if I am—"

"You're not getting married or dying."

"I don't want to bring Mac down with me."

"So, you leave without a word?"

"I emailed him."

"Let me see, um. 'It's over. It's better this way.' Does that about cover it?"

How'd she get the details so fast?

"Abbey, half of Fairbanks knows. How long do you think it'll be before the other half finds out you left Mac to meet a great-looking guy for a lovefest at Mt. McKinley?"

"I didn't." I shook my head. But wait. "Who knows?"

"I saw Lanie Hartman in the lobby talking on her cell phone as if she'd just discovered do-it-yourself liposuction."

"Shit."

"Exactly."

The damn door of the damn men's room popped open again. Tony this time. "How long you ladies' going to be in here?"

Jo pushed him out with a squinty-faced look. He lifted his hands in surrender, "I'm going. I'm going, but—"

"Out!" Jo pointed at him and his head disappeared as the door shut behind him. She glanced at her vintage Power Girls watch. "That was twenty minutes ago, give or take a little. In thirty minutes Mac will know, 'cuz someone is bound to tell him. You know, for his own good."

"It's all perfectly innocent," I whined. "You know it is."

She put a finger to her lip, tilted her head and gave me an appraising look. "I'm not so sure."

I stood up taller and tried to look insulted.

"I can see how you'd find him sexy as hell. The devil in cowboy boots."

"They're not cowboy boots."

"Ah, ha! You noticed his boots. That means you were looking down." *If you get my drift*, her eyes shouted. "What else didn't you notice? Cause it looked like he had more than enough to go around in the jeans department."

"You were looking, too?" I demanded. *Shut up, Abbey.*

"Too? Hmm? Is he a good kisser?" She gave me a conspiratorial smile, bumped my shoulder with hers and laughed.

"Maybe," I said. Double shut up.

"Of course," she sighed, the conspiratorial air gone. She makes a much better spy than I do. "See, you've done it. Kissed him and now you're all thinking he's your soul mate or something. Weren't you?"

Guilty as charged.

She checked her reflection in the mirror before she turned to leave.

"Jo, wait," I said. This time I was the one stopping her with a hand to the T-shirt. "It wasn't the kiss."

Her look was the same one our third grade teacher, Mrs. Johnson, used on me when she caught me with a cigarette I'd sneaked from my cousin Jimmy's jacket.

"It was like kismet."

Jo put up a hand. "I can't listen to this, Abbey. You're an idiot." And she walked out before I could stop her.

Okay, Plan C. Call Mac, because I am an idiot. Make that plan D. Plan C? Find Jo before she blasts Ben's head off.

At the moment, February 14th was beginning to look less and less scary compared to the wrath of Jo. Trust me on this one. I know.

Imagine Morning-After Barbie and you have a pretty good picture of me. My pants were damp, my hair was sticking up all over the place—I must have picked up on Ben's hair thing—and I felt like hiding, even if it meant squeezing my butt under a stinky urinal. (Wishful thinking. No way I'd fit.)

I hit the button on the wall hand dryer, rear end aimed high, hands on knees and prayed no one would barge in on me. After Jo's tirade, I was less spellbound than before, thinking about Mac and how he was taking the news of my running off like this.

Not that my running away was news. It was a wonder he put up with me at all.

I couldn't stay in the men's room forever, no matter how much I may have wanted to. Men less intrepid than our previous stoner friend kept coming in and backing out with apologies, as if *they* were the intruders.

When I finally had the nerve to come out of my self-imposed bathroom exile, I found the world beyond the lodge a blur of snow. And it was still coming down. Great! Just friggin' great. A blizzard. Here's the thing. If you've ever driven the Parks Highway in Alaska in February you know two things. One, make sure you're not going to break down along the way. And two, you'd better have a cell phone, survival gear and food on hand, in case you do break down. With the storm in full force, driving back to Fairbanks would be only a little bit better than navigating the frozen road to hell.

I trudged over to the hotel desk to do what I knew every person in the lodge with half a brain had already done—book a room for the night, or at least until the storm slowed enough to make going home not look like an act of suicide.

The room was for Tony and Jo, of course. No way was I sleeping with the enemy.

When I caught sight of Jo and Tony, they were arguing in urgent whispers across a coffee table strewn with shredded paper napkins and gesturing wildly.

"You said you would." – Jo

"I would have offered to sky dive naked if it would have kept you from going off on this wild goose chase alone." – Tony

"You lied . . . (I didn't get the middle part) . . . belly." – Jo

"I did what I had to do." – Tony

I edged closer.

"You sound like the Mafia. I did what I had to do," Jo mimicked, in her best wiseguy voice.

"Don't go there." Tony, one New York Italian who was none too tolerant of stereotypes, said with more than a hint of danger in his voice. All I could say was, Jo had better watch out.

Jo stood, hands on hips. "Make me!"

Oh, brother. Jo, usually the voice of reason, seemed to be the surefire winner for the Miss PMS 2011 crown these days. Not the right time to give them the bad news. There was no room at the inn.

From what I heard of the argument, it was all because Jo had decided to track me down and beat some sense into me. Alone. Tony apparently promised her something to let him ride shotgun.

Maybe he promised to tell her she was right after every fight they had for the next six months. Okay. Obviously not. Or maybe he promised to let her make all the family decisions for I-don't-know-how-long. Equally ridiculous.

What would Jo have asked for? She hates his Italian guys-bring-home-the-bacon-gals-cook-it-up-in-the-pan bit. (I really should have warned her, being Italian and all, but I love Tony, so sue me.) She hates what she feels is pressure to cut back on her hours at her thrift store, The Second Chance Blue Moon, and start a family, which she sees as the picture of the little-woman-barefoot-and-pregnant mentality. No way was she going there. Her words, not mine.

The only other clue I had was that she'd said "belly."

He promised to eat chocolate cheesecake off her belly? No. He'd like that one.

He promised to shave his belly? No. Perfect as is.

He promised to, what? Sign up for belly dancing classes? Hmm. Or to get a belly ring? Or to let her . . . I mean, not scream, if she got one? That fit. Maybe.

What else goes with belly? Belly liposuction. Belly shirt. Belly tattoo. Pregnancy belly? If she got him to say he'd wear a pregnancy belly, it'd be a miracle, and fat chance he'd go through with it even if he did promise. Achy backs, sore ankles, clothes that don't fit, dragging around an extra thirty pounds all day, every day.

Actually, it was a pretty good idea. Just the kind of thing Jo might pull out of her—.

"Abbey?"

I turned toward the voice, like a needle to magnetic north.

"Mac."

An treacherous drive, a mélange of men, bathroom hijinx, a blizzard, and now Mac.

What else could possibly go wrong?

Chapter 5

First of all, any fool knows you never tempt fate by saying, "What else could possibly go wrong?" Not out loud or without your fingers crossed. Secondly, I get that I am a miserable, rotten brat for implying that Mac's arrival was another wrong in a long list of wrongs. I knew it as soon as the thought popped into my head. Because Mac is better than taco pizza with avocados and cream cheese on top. Which is yummy. Really!

He's the pasta; I'm the Kalamata olives. He's corn chips; I'm picante salsa. Mac is the parking meter, I'm the hot air balloon tied to him, and if from all of that you gathered I'm a bit of a gypsy, so be it. If you assumed I'm the hot one—not so. Mac is heat, spice, a fever. I want to be.

But then there's Ben. Ben is flaky. Mac is solid. Ben sells his flat and chases his dreams. Mac is reliable. Ben is a matching puzzle piece. Mac accepts the puzzle that's me. Ben is sensitive. But Mac's sensitive too, and as he stood there with a question mark in his eyes, I couldn't, or didn't, want to resist.

"Mac," I shouted as I threw myself at his chest, bawling like a little baby.

I didn't know if he was there to tell me off and dump me or to put me on probation, which only made me cry harder.

"Mac, I'm dying. I was in the men's room with Ben. Jo yelled at me. I gotta help Sam. Justine saw my bunny slippers, my mom's going to kill me and I sent you a crappy email."

I sniveled and sniffed and rubbed my nose on his sleeve. "Did I mention I kissed Ben and that I'm dying?"

I was scraping the front of Mac's shirt with a soggy tissue I'd dragged out of my back pocket, when Ben found us.

"You must be Mac," he said. "I've heard all about you."

No way. I hadn't said a word to him about Mac. I'm certain. Meanwhile Mac said nothing.

"From Tony," Ben added.

Ah, Tony. All I had to say to Tony was: Just you wait. You're going to regret it! I'm not Sicilian for nothing.

"We spoke when you were in the loo with Jo."

Right. The blasted men's room, again. It just keeps getting better and better.

Ben was being so nice. Still. Under all that rah-rah, let's-get-along exterior, was he silently adding up the score? Three betrayals by Abigail Vertuccio in less than three hours. One. Failure to mention Sam. Two. Failure to mention Mac. And three. We can't forget The Kiss.

Finally, Mac reached over and shook Ben's hand, and, swear, it felt like someone was walking on my grave. I shivered. Two voices asked as one, "Cold?"

"Dead cold," crossed my mind, but I thought better of admitting it. "I'm fine." Sam's words came back to me. "Freaked out, insecure, neurotic and emotional." A perfect fit. "I mean, I'm not cold," I said, even as I continued to rub the goose bumps on my arms.

"Well, we can't stay in Big Ellie. It's freezing out there. I'll get a room." Mac hesitated. "If that's good for you."

"The hotel is full."

"I have a room," Ben said.

"Big Ellie's warm enough for me."

"We'll have to stay with you in Big Ellie," Jo said.

"Where the hell did you two come from," I snapped. Were they trying to give me a heart attack, sneaking up on me like that? "Oh, and about staying with me? Like hell you are."

I held my head, suddenly exhausted.

Ben touched my shoulder. I jumped and looked at Mac guiltily. "I have a room," he said.

Jo snapped. "Congratulations, Ben."

Patience thy name is Ben. "I meant, Tony and Mac can share with me. My room, I mean."

"Oh, no. No!" I could see the conversations between those three, more specifically between Mac and Ben. Not in a clairvoyant way. More like in an I'm-a-woman way. "No way," I insisted, as Jo said, "Good idea."

I punched her arm, hard. I was putting my foot down and that was that. "One sec," I said to the boys as I pulled Jo aside. "What are you thinking, Jo?"

She shot me the witchy look I've come to know so well. "I'm thinking it's better the guys bunk together than you try to remember which guy you're supposed to be with. Am I right?"

I opened my mouth and closed it again, then re-opened it. Nothing came out. As opposed to before, when I couldn't shut up. She had a point, even if it was a bit insulting and rude. But of course, there was always Sicilian Tactic #26: When you've painted yourself into a corner, get out. What's a little paint on the soles of your shoes anyway?

"Screw you," I snapped as I walked off in a huff.

I guess Mac and Jo know me well enough to get when I need time to calm down and make sense again. Ben, however, the newcomer on the Abigail Vertuccio show, silently carved a path behind me in the snow.

"What are we doing?" he asked, rubbing his hands together in an attempt to keep them from turning into ice pops.

Holy moose nuggets. He nearly scared the next five days out of me.

"We gotta get the power on. Now." I pulled open the metal door where the heavy power cord was coiled up like a frozen snake and fumbled it. It took two of us, with stiff, bulky gloves and frozen fingers, but in the end, we did a five-minute job in twenty, finally getting Big Ellie connected to power and a reliable source of heat.

"Damn, I dropped the keys, Ben. No wait, I have them."

I'd lost all feeling in my fingers and barely managed to get Big Ellie's door open, then jump inside with Ben right behind, turn up the thermostat and throw a comforter over our shoulders, where we huddled together like two kids in front of a bonfire. All we needed were the marshmallows and hot cocoa.

I caught Ben's smile and beat him to the draw. "If you say you knew this was going to happen, I'll—"

He bumped my shoulder. "You'll what?"

His I'm Utterly Adorable and Innocent smile didn't fool me. I could only imagine how many girls he's made senseless with that smile. "I mean it. Don't say it."

"I wanted to say, I knew who you were all along."

I shot him a skeptical look. "Not that psychic business, again?"

"No. From Sam."

Impossible. Wasn't it Sam who'd insisted I keep my mouth shut?

"She's been talking about you for months."

Damn, damn, damn! See? You can't trust a spy. Spy/trustworthy. Oxymoron. I am so stupid.

"What did she say, exactly?"

"That you're bonkers and you need me."

"Great. Just great."

"Forget about Sam. I overheard you say you're dying."

"You didn't pick it up on the Psychic Friends Network?"

"Nasty habit, that sarcasm."

Humph!

With Big Ellie now as warm as a hot muffin, I felt myself drifting off in Ben's arms, inhaling his cologne; except that he wasn't wearing any. It was just him. I closed my eyes, and mumbled, "Not actually dying. Just as bad."

The cold and heat and stress, the kiss, Mac, Jo and Tony. Every guy who'd walked into the men's room and stumbled back out again. It was all too much. I tried to shove the thoughts aside. But I couldn't help asking myself what it was about Ben. Why had I let him help me with Big Ellie, as if I had nothing to lose with him. Not so with anyone else.

"Abbey?" Ben whispered, his mouth next to my ear. "You're going to have to tell me about this thing that's as bad as dying. And I have to tell you about Rebecca."

"February 14th," I murmured as I fell asleep firmly snuggled against his shoulder.

Chapter 6

Countdown to Valentine's Day:
Five days to go

What the hell? I woke up to a big toe this close to my mouth. Uck.
"Have I frozen to death yet? Cause it feels like I have?" I
recognized that voice. Jo.

"I don't remember saying you could spend the night," I moaned, as I
shoved her foot aside. (I didn't ask about Ben. I was sleepy, not stupid.)

"What *do* you remember?" she asked. Decidedly smug.

Too bad what I remembered was nothing. I thought about it some more,
my head firmly tucked beneath two heavy quilts and a down comforter.
When I peeked out, I could see my breath. It couldn't have been a degree
above 40. Oh, God. Now I remembered. "Holy Shit, Batman."

"Exactly, Robin."

Rats. Last night was a certified natural disaster. So bad, it might mean
hiding out in Big Ellie forever. Miss Havisham does Alaska. Only leave out
the wedding dress.

This called for a Sicilian Tactic, only I couldn't think of a single one
that fit.

"Out of party tricks?"

Why was Jo still here? The ticking time bomb in my head was
threatening to detonate. Someone was moaning and groaning. Oh, yeah.
That was me.

"Not exactly the vodka queen, are we?" Jo sniped, making me want to smack her upside the head. Okay, not particularly clever, but effective, albeit also loud. So, no.

I remember waking up after falling asleep on Ben's shoulder, hungry and wanting something besides Fritos and chocolate milk, all that was left in Big Ellie since I'd forgotten the scheduled 7-Eleven stop on my way out of Fairbanks yesterday. Which meant that at approximately 11 p.m. last night (what chance could there be that Mac, Ben, Jo or Tony would still be running around?) I may have walked into the lodge wearing my flannel robe with the polar bears on it, and found all of the above engaged in a game of bridge. I may have, at some point, dumped a glass of water over Tony's head when he said how I should go ahead and get married now before it was too late. In my defense, this wedding thing was turning me into a lunatic.

When I told Jo the bits I remembered, she almost peed herself laughing. "That's not the worst part, cookie."

I groaned. It wasn't fair. Hangover? Fine. But humiliation, too? The way Jo was grinning and nodding like a bobble head doll told me I was in deep do-do.

"Go away. You're dangerous to my mental health," I complained. Then I thought better of it. "No wait. Make yourself useful, go find me an extra strength Excedrin; a bunch of them." I pulled the covers back over my face and stuck my fingers in my ears, muttering "La, la, la, la," when she started up again.

"But you have to hear this, you'll die laughing."

If I could have made evil eyes at her without my head cracking open like a dried up, old wishbone, I would have.

"Get out," I hissed. Ouch. "And don't come back without the drugs."

I don't drink. One ounce of liquor and every thought in my head goes straight to my mouth.

The rest was coming back in snippets. I'd not only baptized Tony, but I told him he should go back to the 6th Century, because the battle of the sexes was over and he'd lost. I may have told Jo that marriage was a crutch, entered into by women who were too scared they couldn't make it on their own.

There may have been a kiss and or two. I'm pretty sure I told Mac and Ben I loved them. About the only truly embarrassing thing I didn't do was give away lap dances.

Definitely an Oh, Fuck moment. Ouch! My head hurts.

Big Ellie's flimsy metal door rattled open and I looked up in time to see a pill flying at my head.

"Here. You don't wanna know what I had to do to get this," Jo said, shaking her head.

Great. Now all I could think was, "Whose nasty pocket did the pill come from? The bottom of which purse?"

"Take it," she said, when she caught me turning the pill over, checking for stuck-on crumbs and used bits of tissue. The idea of downing a glob of Grandpa Jones' snot held no appeal. I spit on two fingers, ran the juice over the pill and wiped, hoping she wouldn't notice. Before I popped it into my mouth, I added a little wordless prayer for good measure. Too bad I hadn't thought about protection prayers before the brilliant vodka idea last night.

"Okay, Jo. I give up. Where did the vodka come in?"

"Right after Ben told Mac about Sam's plan to set you two up. You grabbed Tony's drink and knocked it back in one."

"What are you talking about?"

"Something wrong with your hearing? Sam was fixing you up with Ben, dummy. It was a trick."

"No way. Ben left his job, sold his flat—"

She leaned back, resting against my knees and curled up like a kitten. "She thought that once Ben met you, Rebecca would be history."

I sat up, dumping her on the bed unceremoniously. "But she knows I'm seeing Mac."

"Get real. Everyone knows you're never going to marry him. You don't live together, you wouldn't take the ring when he offered it. What's she supposed to think?"

"What do *you* think?" It had never occurred to me to ask before; I always thought she had my back. Viva la différence, free choice, sister solidarity and all that good stuff. "What do you think?" I repeated.

"I think you're nuts. Now do the world a favor and get up, get dressed, comb your hair and eat a mint, because your breath smells like the bottom of Mr. Peanut's litter box.

An hour later, after the mystery pain pill had kicked in, my teeth were brushed and my clothes Frosted Flake-free, Jo casually mentioned that Ben had taken off.

If looks could kill. I shot to my feet. "When?"

"A couple of hours ago, maybe."

I clicked into high gear, folding blankets and stowing them in the cabinets above the bunk, getting ready to hit the road. "And you're letting me know now?"

She pulled the neatly folded blankets out of the cupboard, ruffled them up and tossed them on the floor. "I wouldn't have told you at all if I didn't know you'd find out anyway."

I kicked a blanket. "Don't talk to me anymore. Traitor."

"You'll thank me later."

"Rat." I tossed the blanket on the bed.

"Trust me."

"Crackhead!" I said.

"Crackhead?" She burst out laughing. "You know I'm right, Abbey. Ben is no good for you."

"At least he's not planning on marrying me in four days."

"God, Abbey. You're so weird. Just because you have a vision doesn't mean it's gonna happen. You know that."

"I knew you were going to marry Tony."

I'd seen the whole thing the very first time we met him. It was his first day in Fairbanks; we were in a hole in the wall coffee shop and he asked for directions he really didn't need.

"You did?" she asked, her voice softening.

"Yeah, and I saw it working out. Forever."

She was off in la-la land, grinning like an idiot.

"You two, old and happy, with lots of kids, grandkids, the whole thing."

She took my hand. "You're not so bad. Really."

We got to work folding the blankets, putting them back in the cupboards and getting Big Ellie ready for the trip home to Fairbanks, like old times. Me and Jo, back on the same team again.

"By the way, he left this for you." Jo pulled a slightly crumpled envelope from the back pocket of her jeans and tossed it to me.

"Why didn't you just wait until Christmas to show me? Or maybe shred it? For all the good it does me now."

No answer.

I ripped it open, cut my finger in the process, glared at Jo and sucked the blood as I read from the raggedy piece of paper torn from a loose-leaf notebook. "Dear Abigail, blah, blah, sorry, blah, blah, blah. I'm sure you understand. Love, Ben."

"So, Rebecca and Merona didn't show and he left," Jo said.

"That's it?" I said, throwing the offending page on the bed. "I'll understand?"

"Now you know how Mac feels." No sympathy whatsoever. "Me? I didn't even get a note. I had to hear about it from Justine. And you know how she likes to Lord it over—"

"Jo. This isn't about you," I said. "It's about courtesy. He could have told me."

"Yeah. Think about that the next time—"

"I get it." I was working on matching Jo, evil eye for evil eye, when my cell phone rang. My mom. Great. Vincenza Vertuccio (aka Vinnie), a Sicilian force of nature, 55, looks 40, non-stop energy, a vamp, a flirt, completely self-absorbed. The only mom I've got. "Hi, Mom."

Jo, who learned a long time ago to run when Mom was in the vicinity, even by phone, escaped out the side door into the cold.

"Abbey. I'm finally doing it—writing the definitive Alaska travel guide."

My mom writes travel books about everything you never wanted to know about the most exotic places on earth.

"What do ya think of this? 'Fairbanks in February is a freakin' icebox. Spit and it'll freeze before it hits the ground.'"

"Lovely, Mom." Her last book, *Irritable Bowel in Bologna*, was a best seller. Although she's still receiving threats from the Bologna Board of Tourism.

"And what about this. 'In July, be sure to pack ten cans of Cutters, two boxes of Kleenex and a net. The mosquitoes are so big that when you hit one, it's like smashing a ripe, Bing cherry.'"

Yuck. "Mom—"

"Wait. What if I say, 'Be careful not to smack one on your forehead or it'll look like you're bleeding from the head.' Better?" Hmm.

Lost as I was in the imagery of cherries and big globs of mosquito goo, she caught me off guard.

"I hear you're at Mt. McKinley." From Fairbanks to Jersey in two minutes flat. Ah, the wonders of cell phones. "That you had a vision and ran out on Mac."

I waited for the explosion that had to be coming.

"You did good, Abbey."

What?

"Listen to me. Are you listening?" I nodded as she continued. "You don't need the cow to get the milk. Don't go signing your life away. 'Cuz marriage is the devil's hot tub. Get my meaning? "

I was picturing the devil leading a cow to a jacuzzi when she continued. "Besides, Mac's too safe for you. You need. Well, I don't know what, but not safe."

She might have a point there. Oh, God. I just agreed with my mother!

"Gotta go. Gotta write down about how the mud flats of Anchorage can suck you down and kill you before you can hit 911 on speed dial."

And just like that, she was gone. Whew! I'd have to check with Jo, but I think that was the first time I'd agreed with my mom since I was fourteen and she'd just given me the tampons versus pads talk.

And where was Jo, anyway? This called for a meeting. I slipped into my down parka and Bunny Boots, thinking I'd find Jo somewhere nearby, sneaking one of the weekly cigarettes she doesn't think any of us know about, and ran instead into a sheepish-looking Ben.

I wanted to hug him. "Damn it. You left me a note," was what I finally managed.

"I know." He touched the top of his head to ruffle his hair and only got cap.

I looked him over for a minute. He looked back.

"So, what're you doing here?" I admit it; I wanted to pull him inside Big Ellie and forget all about the note, and yet, pride is a crazy thing. "Forget something?" I snapped.

He laughed. Seems I don't do outraged very well—at least with him.

"Don't think that smile's gonna get to me, either." It was totally getting to me.

"I'm pissed and one thing you better remember is you don't mess with a Vertuccio woman when we're pissed."

He held his hands up in surrender, the grin changed into a take-me-I'm-yours invitation.

"That's right. You blew it." I crossed my arms and glanced at him, making sure he knew I meant business.

"Can I come in?"

I stepped backward into Big Ellie. Well, it's not like he'd kicked my cat or put hot sauce in my toothpaste or ratted me out to my mother. It's not like he served 5 to 10 at Leavenworth.

"Enter," I said, truly hoping that didn't sound like more of an invitation than I'd intended.

And really, I wasn't mad at him. I was just so damn glad he was back. "Why'd you leave?" I asked. And before he could answer, "For that matter, why are you back?"

"You know why I left, Abbey. And you know why I came back."

We sat side by side on the edge of the bed without speaking, staring straight ahead, not touching. I did know why he left. Honor. And why he came back? Connection.

The next question was this: Now what?

Chapter 7

N ow what?" turned out to be a call on Ben's cell phone. "Lara Croft I presume," he answered.

"Sam?" I mouthed. He nodded and put a hand on my shoulder, I'm guessing so I wouldn't attack the phone, or take off for parts unknown. Maybe so I'd be quiet. I reached over, pushed the speaker phone option and Sam's voice filled the room. I bumped into Ben, accidentally letting out a squeak.

"Who's there, Ben?"

"Rebecca."

"Bollocks! What is she doing there? I thought—"

"You thought you had this all sorted, did you?" He raised an eyebrow at me. Even when he was busy putting the screws to his not-so-innocent sister, he looked delicious.

I elbowed him to cut it out. Sam may be nosy, bossy, sneaky and a bunch of other things, but she's also been like a guardian angel to me. I leaned into the phone. "Mission accomplished, Sam."

"Very amusing, Ben. Abigail. I nearly shot out my toe when Ben said Rebecca was there."

I stifled a laugh.

"I'm hanging up now, Sis. I had a vision of Rebecca in one of Merona's porn flicks and I have to find her before it's too late."

Oh. My. God. I am so dense. "You mean . . ."

"You believed her," he said, simply.

"Wait a minute. You never thought Merona was a porn king? Or a drug lord?" I shook my head. Because how could I have lived this long and still be so damn naïve.

"That part was all Sam. But something isn't right with Merona and Rebecca, and I intend to find out what it is." He gave me one of those soul-searching looks, the kind that can melt a woman's heart and make her forget all about #2 and #3 on her To-Do list. "Join me?"

I headed for Big Ellie's avocado green kitchen and began assembling items from the tiny cupboard above her sink: tea, tea pot, filter. Dropped the tea bag in the cup. Poured. All to keep my mind off Ben's sitting on my bed, asking me to join him.

"Join me in finding out why Rebecca dropped everything to follow Merona. To see if she's in trouble." His voice came from behind me as I fiddled with mugs, milk, sugar, napkins. There was no question as to my answer.

He wrapped his arms around my waist and rested his chin on my shoulder.

"Thank you, but I don't drink tea, Ab. Do you?"

"Nope." British. Who knew?

"Okay, then."

"Yes."

"Excuse me."

"I said, yes. I'll help you."

"Brilliant. As long as you keep the geisha costume at home."

Fine. You're going to find out anyway. Last year Justine, Jo and I went on a stakeout in disguise and the whole town is still talking about it. All because the Alaska State Troopers happened to catch us on film and are currently using the footage in their training videos.

"As long as you stop winding Sam up," I said. "All we need now is a freaked out British agent on our tails."

"It's like we're married, isn't it?"

All the color drained from my face and I slid down to the floor; Ben slid down beside me, his voice all comfort and concern. "Abigail, what is it?"

"I had a vision. I was getting married—February 14th to be exact."

"What a disaster!" He ran his hand up and down my back, until I relaxed, as happy as a kitten. "Don't worry, Ab. We won't let it happen. You can count on me."

Nothing to think about there. "You can count on me, too, Ben."

Ben and Abigail, the Two Musketeers.

Chapter 8

What is it that makes intelligent, ambitious, passionate women head for the altar like lemmings racing toward massive cliffs? You're married, so now you can be yourself? He isn't going anywhere. Normal politeness goes bye-bye. You can yell all you want. Not that you'd treat the clerk at Trader Joe's that way. And guys, now you don't have to call when you're going to be late. No worries about missing the toilet bowl or leaving dirty boxer shorts . . . wherever. She's not going anywhere, either.

No thanks. Anyway, I was married once already. My ex (Rob) was kind, sweet, and intelligent, a master in bed and my gran loved him. He also slept with one of my best friends and being clairvoyant didn't help me one bit. When he confessed, I left him and Alaska and didn't look back until I had no other choice. You remember Gran. But it was always going to be over. I know that now.

Now lust. Thank God for lust. I'm in favor of it. I vote yes to lust. With lust, you don't need to sign a lifetime contract. I'm not cynical. I'm practical. I don't need or want any guarantees, because are there really any guarantees in life? And what if you promised your life to someone and broke your word? (Me, for one.) Why would Husband #2 have any reason to believe you were going to stick around this time? Maybe in the vows we could say, "I hope to love you 'til death us do part," or "I hope to be with you for richer or poorer," or "I'll try; that's the best I can do."

As long as you don't let the lust cloud your head and confuse the hell out of everything, then lust is great. The whole world may not agree with me, but at least Ben gets it.

"Abbey?" Ben bumped my shoulder and interrupted my internal rant.

"Just to be clear. I believe in marriage."

"That's impossible," I stammered.

He got up and pulled me to my feet, kissed the tip of my nose and then the inside of my palm.

"What can I say? I do."

"I can't just sit here, I have to find Jo," was all I could come up with; but it was true. I'd completely forgotten about her since Ben came back. (See? Exactly the mind fog I was talking about.) And where was Mac? He had to be here someplace, wondering what I was up to, and that couldn't be good.

I stumbled out of Big Ellie clutching my unzipped parka to my chest, wondering how I kept finding men who thought marriage was a good thing, when I ran into Mac.

It was 30 below zero, at least; even so, when he saw me, he opened his coat and pulled me inside. I stretched my head back to look up at him and see exactly how mad he was and got a welcome home smile. Hmm. He pressed me closer, making me think about things I shouldn't be thinking about, until I was blasted back to reality. Mac pulled away, suddenly. I stomped the snow off my boots. He brushed his cheek against mine, so softly I almost missed it.

Hey! Wait a minute. I was supposed to be staying away from him. Cross. Garlic. Stat!

"Stay away from me," I shouted, as if *he* was the one who'd been thinking about hotel rooms instead of getting back to work. He took a step forward, shook his head, the devil in motion.

I took a step backward. "I mean it."

"Stop me," he challenged, turning the devil grin up a notch and moving in two steps.

"Come any closer and I'll—"

"Rip your clothes off and jump me?"

Unlikely. It was so cold, we'd freeze just thinking about it. Not that I was considering it. I took another step back, bumped into the lodge's big glass doors and stumbled as they opened, depositing me in a tangled mess at Jo's feet. Thank you. Thank you. Thank you.

"Where have you been?" I asked Jo as I hopped up, grabbed her and maneuvered her between Mac and me.

"What are you doing?" she asked.

"Yeah, what are you doing?" Mac repeated.

"Nothing. Nothing."

I glared at Mac. "Don't you have someplace you need to be?"

He reached around Jo and snagged my belt, drawing me into a kiss that was all tongue and heat, so much so that I could barely remember my name or stand on my own two feet. Then he slowly pushed me back, pure larceny in his smile.

I could have sworn I heard him say, "This isn't over, Bunny," before he turned and walked away.

Okay, this was war. He knows darn well Gran's the only one who calls me Bunny and gets to live. Okay, Mom, too. But definitely that's all. And that means you, too. Swear you won't repeat it, or I'll have to use Sicilian Tactic #32 on you.

"Wasn't the plan to stay away from him?" Jo asked, as we watched Mac drive off from the comfort of the hotel lobby.

"What just happened, Jo?"

"If you ask me, the dominant male bear marked his territory. And speaking of macho males, here comes Tony."

Tony, basketball coach for the University of Alaska Fairbanks men's team, with the look of a New York City boxer, (or biker, I can never decide) can't get through a crowd in the entire state of Alaska without shaking a dozen hands, and today was no exception. To make things worse, wherever he went, random women managed to offer him things no nice girls should be offering a married man. It was like watching a politician, the way Tony could tell a gal he wasn't available and leave her feeling like he'd just proposed. The only one it didn't work on was Jo.

He materialized between us and put a protective hand on her back. There was a definite chill in the air. "Jo. You ready to go?"

She dismissed him with a wave of her hand, as Ben came out of Big Ellie and headed our way.

"I can't leave, yet."

The "you idiot" was unsaid but understood, as she jammed her elbow into his side and jerked her head toward Ben, who was about to enter the lodge.

"You don't trust me?" I asked, pointing a finger at her beady little head. "You think I'm going to screw—"

"Screw what?" Ben asked.

I should join a convent and take a vow of silence. "Nothing." Sicilian Tactic #1: When in trouble, act innocent. "Nothing. Really. Nothing."

"So? Are you two getting ready to leave?" I asked, hoping Tony and Jo would take the hint. I didn't see any luggage; but, hey, I could dream, couldn't I?

"Yes." "No." Jo and Tony said, then glared at each other accusingly.

"I can't leave."

"I have to get back to work."

"Then go," Jo said defiantly. "I can come back with Ab."

"You came with me, you'll leave with me."

The hairs on my arms jumped to attention. Trouble on the horizon, folks.

"Really?" Jo put a hand on one hip and tipped her head to one side. "Says who?"

"Says me, your husband, who you promised to love, honor and obey."

"Only because your grandmother threatened to have a stroke if we wrote our own vows."

"Your point?"

"The obey part is invalid."

With the grace of a panther, I backed away. Really. Ben, no fool, followed right behind until we were well out of range. "Safe at last," he said, wiping imaginary sweat from his brow as we pushed into a corner booth of the hotel cafe.

"The classic fairy tale. The feminist princess is rescued by the all-powerful prince and she says no thanks, you just want to control me."

"A whole field of American cultural studies yet to be explored—revisionist fairy tales," Ben said.

"Stick with me and you'll be the next Grimm brother."

"Stick with you and something will happen," he said.

I brushed snow off his hair and snapped, "Wouldn't a psychic-in-training know?"

He mumbled something unintelligible. I strained to hear, bumping his hand. A touch was all it took and I was blasted into the wedding vision. Different this time. It was like I was looking through a keyhole or a telescope. All I could see was the back of a flowing white dress. No who, what, when, where or how. Odd.

"Abbey." Someone was shaking me. "Abbey? What happened?

"The wedding vision again," I said, absentmindedly. I could still see the beaded train of the dress, the place where the neckline dipped down to the gathered-silk waist. Then I remembered what I'd missed earlier. Frank Merona was there in a tux. What on earth would Merona be doing in my wedding vision, when I didn't recognize another soul? "Merona was there."

"Where?" He looked around, instinctively.

"In here." I tapped my head with one hand and answered my cell phone with the other.

"Miss me yet?" Mac! I held up a finger to Ben and slipped out of the booth and around a corner, like a sneaky snake or a villain in a B movie. "Do you remember the flight we took to Kotzebue," he asked.

I blushed furiously. I never did find my panties after that flight.

"I have something of yours, Abs. Blue with little yellow daisies. Remember?"

The blood left my face, because, oh, yeah, I remembered. I should be ashamed of myself.

"Don't forget me," he said and hung up.

I leaned back against the wall, working hard to calm my pounding heart and the tingling where I shouldn't be tingling, then I peeked around the corner to see if Ben had heard anything. Nope. A gal in spandex ski pants, two sizes too small, with silicone implants (I'm absolutely certain) had him cornered with what had to be two of her sorority sisters.

I stomped over. A woman on a mission.

"Benjamin Bradford. I haven't seen you in an age. Where's Harold? I heard you two were trying to adopt a baby? How's that going?"

Girl #1, with the kabuki makeup, suddenly remembered she'd left the water running in her room.

Girl #2, the one with the cat woman manicure, thought she saw an old friend across the room.

Silicone Girl said, "OOPS," and slipped away.

"OOPS," I said, imitating her lilting, valley girl tone. "Was it something I said?"

"Abbey, Abbey, Abbey."

"Ben, Ben, Ben."

"Ben, tell Tony you need me to help find Rebecca and Merona." Jo ordered.

Rats. Right after the three sorority sisters dropped Ben like a used condom, Jo and Tony found us.

"Go ahead. Tell him, Ben," she repeated.

I pitied Ben, but better him than me.

"I think you'd better ask Abbey," the rotten bastard replied.

"Oh no you don't," I said, my hand firmly planted on Ben's back, my face a twisted threat.

"See, they don't need you," Tony said. "And what about Amelia? She didn't agree to watch the store all week. Besides, I have practice. We need to head home before the weather turns again."

Jo's look softened a bit. She knew he was right. Her part-time sales clerk, hadn't signed on for this. Then Tony opened his big mouth again. "Come on, Jo. Be reasonable."

Didn't he know about Sicilian Tactic #27? Quit while you're ahead.

Jo lost it, starting with his macho behavior and ending with a pointed reference to his performance of late; right before she ran to the ladies' room in a storm of spitfire and tears.

There wasn't a thing I could say to Tony, because any man who's been married a whole year and hasn't figured out Sicilian Tactic #27, truthfully, is too stupid to live.

I found Jo in the ladies' room, brushing her curls angrily, as if they were the ones who'd told her to be reasonable, when in fact she was being completely reasonable. Any idiot could see that.

"Thanks for nothing," she said, avoiding my eyes. Then she sank to the floor and burst into big, heaving sobs; I'd never seen her like this.

I crouched down next to her, not quite ready to try the floor. Who knew what was down there? Although it couldn't be any worse than the men's room, could it?

I was plotting what to do next when a large-bosomed, 50-something woman in a wild paisley print shirt, teased hair and capri pants came out of a stall.

"Get up off that floor, Honey. There ain't no man worth screwin' up that pretty face for," she said, getting right to the heart of the thing.

Jo looked up and stopped quivering for a second.

"That's right. You're actin' like he's got all the power. What'd your mama teach you, Chil'? You're in control."

A tiny smile lifted one corner of Jo's mouth and I thanked my lucky stars for angels in spandex.

"Get up and brush off them tears. You hear?"

Jo leaped to her feet, wiped her face and went for some toilet paper to blow her runny nose.

"That's better. The trick is, you gotta go along when it don't matter to you and let 'em think it's their idea when you want 'em to do what you want."

She checked her teeth in the mirror and reapplied her cherry red lipstick. "Forget Oprah. This here is war. You lose a few battles, but in the end," a victorious grin crossed her face, "you win and they go along as easy as a puppy to a neutering. You got that?"

Jo nodded solemnly, like she was in church or something.

"Good. Take care now," our new hero said as she sashayed out of the ladies' room, flipping her hair like a prom queen.

"Wow," I said. "That's a little cold, don't you think?"

She waved me away with one hand. "You worry too much. Just tell me you and Ben are coming back to Fairbanks tonight, in two separate cars, and I'll go home with Tony."

"Jo, he's got a rental car; I have Big Ellie."

"Okay, but call me as soon as you get home."

And that's how I ended up waving to Jo and Tony as they pulled away, wondering if there was any marriage out there that wasn't built on a foundation of half-truths, trickery and outright lies.

Chapter 9

You've probably heard about how Alaska winters are so cold we have to plug our cars in to keep them from freezing. All true. We put a special electric heating blanket around our car battery and attach another heater to the oil pan. Any time it gets to 20 below zero, we plug the car in. Occasionally, people will wait until it drops to 30 below zero, but then maybe they don't mind being late for work or paying hefty towing fees.

In February, in every parking lot in Fairbanks you'll find cars running, because if you're inside more than an hour or two without plugging in (and there are no outlets for customers), you're probably gonna live to regret it.

Which explained why Ben wasn't going anywhere in his little frozen rental car.

"No one mentioned plugging the car in," he said, once we were back inside the warmth of the lodge, sipping hot chocolate and waiting for our hands and feet to defrost.

"It doesn't get as cold in Anchorage," I said. "Are you sure they didn't say anything about it?"

"I thought they were talking about music and headphones. I wasn't actually paying attention."

"Too anxious to see Rebecca?" I asked. A red hot devil was sitting on my right shoulder, apparently.

"Not the way you think."

I waited. My cell phone was ringing, but I ignored it.

"Your phone." The couple one table over must have been staring, because he persisted. "Aren't you going to answer it?"

I gave Ben a You're A Suck Up look and picked up.

"Abbey? You need get your arse back here. Immediately. Molly Everett is back."

"Justine?"

"Yes, Justine. Who did you think it was? The bloody tooth fairy?

Best to ignore her when she gets like this. "Who's Molly Everett?"

"Where have you been?" she demanded. "Mac's ex. She arrived today, with a bloody truckload of roses in hand. Seems she's completed a course to get over her fear of flying and is back in town, ready to make a new start. With Mac—in case you can't put two and two together."

"How do you know all this, Justine?"

"Girl talk. Now get back here before things really go pear-shaped."

Girl talk? Really?

"Take a breath. I'm coming home today."

"You'd better, because you know the blonde midget in 'Harry met Sally?'"

"Meg Ryan?"

"Well, they could be twins."

"Damn," I said.

"Anything wrong?" Ben asked as I hung up.

"No."

"Who looks like Meg Ryan?"

"No one. Mac's ex." He was going to find out sooner or later. "She's back."

"I can't say I'm sorry."

"Why not? You want Rebecca."

"We dated for about two minutes; mostly we were flatmates."

"But Sam said—"

"That I had a broken heart and came here to win Rebecca back?"

My remaining hot chocolate was now a warm, mucky mess in the bottom of my cup. Like my assumptions. "Something like that," I mumbled.

"What else did Sam say?"

"Other than making me promise to keep you out of trouble?"

"Besides that."

"That we were alike. Both crazy."

"She's part right," he said, as he took my hand and ran his thumb over my open palm.

"That we're crazy?"

"That we're alike."

"So, you didn't give up your job and flat to win Rebecca back?"

He sighed. "I was approved for my sabbatical months ago. I leased my flat to a visiting professor from Romania and decided to leave a few weeks early to see if I could help Rebecca."

Hmm. "Does she think she needs help?"

"Debatable."

"You do know she's not going to thank you if you find out Merona's a crook?"

"I know that. Psychic. Remember?"

"Then how does it end?" I asked, fighting to keep a straight face.

"I wish I could tell you, but I haven't seen that far."

"So, you're not in love with Rebecca, Sam's trying to set us up and you knew about it all along. Does that about cover it?"

He grinned sheepishly. I really do love that grin. "I think so," he said.

"Okay, then," I said and took back my hand so I could slurp the mucky remains of my hot chocolate, not tasting a thing.

We were debating what to do next—stay, in the hopes that Rebecca and Merona would show up, or catch up with them in Fairbanks—when they walked in. I can't say my mind was in the game. I kept thinking about Molly looking like Meg Ryan and about her being in Fairbanks with Mac.

Rebecca, on the other hand, looked nothing like Meg. More Parker Posey. Thick black hair, shoes that probably cost more than I paid for Big Ellie. A subtle look that whispered class and elegance. I couldn't drag my eyes away.

Ben whispered. "She has that effect on people."

I pulled an innocent look. "What effect?"

"Abbey, does Merona know who you are?"

"We never met. I've been meaning to go by, but—"

"Good, then we still have the element of surprise."

"It sounds like we're about to ambush them."

"I was thinking more like seeing what he's up to."

"Spying, you mean."

"Like you were doing yesterday?" he asked, pointing out the flaw in my argument against invasion of privacy.

"That was different."

"You were helping a friend, right?"

"Exactly."

"Exactly," he said.

"Fine, but what do we do? They're bound to see you eventually, then they'll know I'm with you and there goes the element of surprise."

My cell announced a text message from Justine. "Another truckload of roses arrived for Mac. I'm cutting their heads off and jamming the bits in the shredder. If you don't come home right this minute, I'm calling your mother. Don't think I won't."

Great. I'd just about decided that Molly's return was innocent. Now she was sending truckloads of flowers? What was that about? Okay. She wanted him back and wasn't beating around the rose bush. No time like the present. Take the moose by the horns. Antlers. Whatever.

On the other hand, Mac was a big boy. If he wanted Molly, my rushing back wasn't going to change a thing. Besides, jealousy is for those who don't know their own worth. Jealousy is for those who aren't trustworthy themselves. Okay. So I kissed Ben, but I didn't sleep with him.

"I'm trustworthy."

"I know you are," Ben said.

Did I say that out loud?

Luckily Rebecca and Merona stayed on their side of the restaurant, far from our little hideaway tucked into a dark corner by the kitchen.

So far, from Ben's newly developed waitress gossip network, we learned three things. One. Rebecca is high maintenance. Extra fudge sauce for her sundae. Sliced, not whole rolls. No ice in her Coke. Steak well-done but not too well-done. A clean water glass, when it was already clean. Two. Merona is smooth as ice. He touched one gal's thigh so innocently he almost had her believing it was an accident. Three. They were not spending the night. He had to get back to town for an important meeting.

"Time to hit the road," I said, but Ben, one step ahead of me, had already scoped out our exit strategy, thanks to Betty-the-waitress and a little used back door.

We were safely ensconced in Big Ellie by the time Merona and Rebecca exited the lodge heading for a silver Landrover, got in and pulled away, forgetting to unplug. Their long orange cord flapped behind them until it finally wrapped around a tire and snapped in two. (I can't count how many times that's happened to me.)

We pulled out onto the highway behind them. Luckily the one good thing about tailing someone on the Richardson Highway is that it's one lane in each direction. So, unless the person in front of you pulls off for a pit stop, you'll eventually be following someone. And in the colder months, it's a Godsend not being alone in the middle of an untamed wilderness at 40 below zero.

I was memorizing their license plate, just in case, when Ben said, "The rental company said they'd take care of the car. Nice people. I should have asked them where they shop."

"Good plan. Stalk Merona and get some research done in one." I was going for sarcastic, but wait a sec. "That's a good idea. Instead of saying you're on vacation, you're here for research. It's perfect."

"Would you like to hear what I'm working on?" He opened his backpack and brought out a hand-tooled notebook and beat-up Montblanc pen.

"Walmart, Sam said. Never mind. I'm an idiot."

"I complained to her once about mega-stores pushing mom and pop stores out of business and she took it from there."

"I'm starting to think maybe *she's* the crazy one."

"I'm actually researching trust and the eBay phenomenon."

"That's interesting," I said, not interested in the least, thinking he really should be researching the effect of manipulative family members on interpersonal relationships, until I remembered something unbelievable that Jo had told me ages ago.

"Hey, Ben. Did you hear someone once bought a ghost on eBay for $30,000?"

We were pulling into Fairbanks, when we got a call from Sam.

"Ben, Rebecca's staying at the Captain Bartlett Inn."

"The crow barks at midnight," Ben replied. (Spy talk 101. Which she patently ignored. No fun at all.)

"Not with Merona?" I asked, pushing Ben aside. "That's strange."

"Merona's address is 47 Goldhill Road," she added, all business.

"Good to know," I said. "Hey, Sam? Could you check out a Molly Everett for me?"

"What do you need to know?"

"Anything. Everything."

"I'll see what I can do." Then she was gone.

"She's like your eBay ghost," Ben said.

"Like God."

"A chameleon."

"Like silly putty," I said.

"Like string theory."

"What?"

"String theory? Quantum physics? Do you know how it works?"

"Does anyone?" I asked. "Back to Rebecca. Why would she be staying at a hotel?"

"She's not sleeping with him."

"You don't think so?"

"I never did."

Oh!

The road to my house came up fast, and as I made the turn heading for home, the where-are-you-staying question was heavy on my mind. I couldn't stick him in a hotel. Not when I had plenty of room. But then what would Mac say? And Jo? Maybe Mac could move in, too. That would work—or be weird. Or both. No. I was supposed to stay away from Mac, but with Ben there, it might be okay. Probably. And we could both help Ben, and I could watch out for Molly.

"Let's go home," I said, convinced I was on the right track. Sicilian Tactic #28: Never second guess yourself.

It only confuses everything.

Chapter 10

Countdown to Valentine's Day:
Four days to go

Alaska Virgin Air has operated out of Fairbanks, Alaska, since 1922 when great grandpa Noah got a loan from his father-in-law to buy his first Super Cub and started flying medicine and groceries to villages previously served by dog teams.

Great-gran got her two cents in and the fledgling air service was named Alaska Virgin Air after the disreputable side of the family, more specifically her great Aunt Mae, who made her living with goldminers in a none-too-respectable manner. Great-grandpa hoped people assumed the name came from Alaska's unexplored territories. At a time when women were meant to be seen and not heard, no one told Francesca Vertuccio what to do.

She passed most of her power down to Gran and Mom. I'm the watered-down Vertuccio, more prone to turning the other cheek than in-your-face diplomacy. Go figure.

On our first day back, I overslept, Ben didn't wake me and my cell phone seemed to be lost. I walked through AVA's heavy double doors, head down, searching through my pack, trying to do two things at once, as usual, and still couldn't find the damn phone.

"Lose something?"

Justine was giving me a look that was scarily close to the one my mom likes to use on me. One hip out, foot tapping, brow crunched up, sighing, like I was the disappointment of the century.

"I've been calling you for over an hour. I texted, called your home, your cell. Where have you been?"

Justine works for AVA, so technically I'm her boss. Not that you'd notice.

"I lost track of time?"

She grabbed me by the sleeve and pulled me behind the counter, pointing at my closed office door. "That's not all you lost. Mac is in there with HER!"

"Her, who?"

"Meg Ryan, you wanker. So what are you waiting for?"

I took a deep breath to calm myself, then noticed the trash can stuffed with bright yellow roses, their heads smashed to smithereens. "Another delivery?"

"Does she own the bleedin' florist? Where is her pride?"

"Does Mac know where his flowers are going?"

"Get real." She shoved me toward the office door—hard. "Go. Now!"

I gave her my, Who, me? look. She, on the other hand, looked like she was ready to carry me in there, if I didn't get a move on.

"Go on. Reinforcements are on the way, but there's no telling how long they'll take to get here."

The word "reinforcements" was still ringing in my ears when the office door sprang open and Mac surfaced, followed by a short little blonde who was laughing as if she'd just seen Seinfeld's Master-of-Your-Domain episode.

"Abbey!" Mac said. "This is . . . this is . . ."

Molly, I presume. Neither of us said a word, ready to let him swing in the noose for a while. As a former counselor, I've learned to keep my mouth shut at critical moments. I'm not sure where Molly learned it.

Justine, however, couldn't take it.

"Molly! It's Molly, Mac's girlfriend from ages ago. Molly, this is Abbey." She shot Mac a warning look.

"They're engaged," Justine said, "but you must have known that—with the flowers and all."

Molly took in the demolished blooms overflowing the trash can.

"A little accident," Justine said and shrugged. "Clumsy me. They fell."

More like a homicidal flower maniac got them, but prove it, I say.

Molly held her ground next to Mac. "Mac never told me. Congrats."

I slid between Justine and Molly. I mean, who knew? Justine might just leap up and rip Molly's throat out next and I didn't want to get blood on my Bunny Boots. I looked over at Mac. Was he enjoying all of this?

"Nice to meet you, Molly. But we have a meeting. Justine will show you out."

I have never been so rude to anyone in my entire life. Well, maybe once, but that was to my no good, lying snake of an ex, which doesn't really count.

I pulled Mac into the office and slammed the door. How to play it? I was the bad guy here. What with Ben sleeping under my roof and all. And yet, Mac was the one caught in a compromising position. So, the question became, what to do, what to do?

Unfortunately Mac saw the wheels turning and knew I was up to something. I went for Sicilian Tactic #29: Confuse them with honesty when they're expecting sneaky. A twist on #24.

"Mac, I want you to move in with me." There, the truth. Not all of it, but a start.

"Man, two offers in one day. It's like Christmas around here," he answered.

"Ben's staying there, too. But don't worry, you'll each have your own room."

As for Molly, I had to wonder if her offer involved black whips and tiny lace panties with holes in them. Like my mother always says, watch out for the innocent-looking ones.

The look on Mac's face said he wasn't thinking about whips and cuffs, at least not for Molly. I've never seen him mad before, but I think this was it. His face was cold enough to freeze Texas.

"He spent the night?"

I backed up a step, just in case. "In the spare room."

"I was kicked to the curb, but Ben's invited." He took a step forward.

"Didn't you hear? You can move in, too?"

"A menage-a-tois? No thanks."

"God, no. I'm not sleeping with either of you."

"Oh, good. That's better." - Mac

"I mean—" - Me

"You can't decide—" - Mac

"No, I've decided—" - Me

"So, you want us both there? Like reality TV?" - Mac

"No, more like for protection." - Me

"From me?" He moved dangerously closer.

"Of course from you."

His eyes flashed.

"Hmm."

"Really. I can't be near you." I looked around for a means of escape. "Something'll happen and we'll get married and I'll be miserable. You understand."

How could he not understand? Every married person I've ever known is miserable. Well, not Jo, but I say give it time.

"Thanks." He turned away.

"We don't need marriage," I said, hoping to gain some lost ground.

He turned back. "Who's asking?"

"What?"

"Anyone ask you to get married on February 14th? Have you seen a marriage license? A tux? Did anyone call your mom? Get down on one knee?"

"Well, no."

"Well, doesn't it work that way, generally?"

"Yes," I said. But I didn't really believe it. Being clairvoyant may be a curse most of the time, but sometimes it's a blessing.

"So, why are you so worried? And why do you want me to move in with you all of a sudden?"

I wasn't telling. He already thinks I'm crazy. He doesn't need to hear the whole convoluted who's-watching-whom thing.

I could tell from the way he was rubbing the back of his neck, eyes closed, that he was onto something. "I've got it. If I'm living at your place, you can keep an eye on Molly."

"You wound me," I said, looking six shades of innocent.

"You're worried," he challenged.

"Hardly."

"You're jealous."

"You wish."

I was up against the desk before I knew it, Mac's body hard against mine, his eyes hot, his breath warm. "The thing is, Abbey, you don't want a nice boy like Ben. You want a bad boy for some things." His mouth trailed along the ridge of my shoulder, leaving little bites behind. "Tell me what you want, Ab."

I closed my eyes and felt the heat spreading through me. I wanted him to . . . I wanted . . . shit!

"Let me go, you, you vampire. You sneak," I said. He backed up and suddenly I lost all my heat. "What do you think you were doing, anyway?"

"I think you know what I was doing, Abigail."

I held my arms out, widening the distance between us. His look could have melted stone. I yanked the office door wide and stood in the frame.

"Sex doesn't mean marriage, Ab." He yanked a condom out of his pocket and held it up to make his point.

"It'll break, it'll be past its expiration date, or fate will put a hole in it. I don't trust fate."

"We make our own fate," he said.

"Good. Then I choose not to flirt with danger until February 15th."

He shot me a look filled with meaning. "Does that include Ben?"

What could I say?

"Lucky for you, I'm a patient man."

There was no way I was going to talk about Ben. I crouched down to tie a shoe that didn't need tying.

"So. You're moving in?"

"I wouldn't miss it for the world."

Chapter 11

D amn, that was close," Jo said, right after Mac took off for a flight to Ruby.

"When did you get here?" I snapped.

Jo shrugged as Justine jumped in. "You're not doing very well in the stay-away-from-Mac department, are you?"

"Who asked you?" Apparently, my love life was an open book.

"Admit it. You guys were halfway to paradise a minute ago."

"What happened? " Jo asked. "Not that I don't know. You're in love with two guys and it's got you scared to death."

"Well, bollocks. She might as well go ahead and shoot herself," Justine said, "so we can all get the pain over with right now."

"Or become a nun," Jo suggested.

"Boring. And no men. Rotten plan."

Like shooting myself was a good one?

"It doesn't matter, because you're not in love with Ben." Justine waved a half-empty cappuccino in my face. "You're just—"

"I'm what? Please. Tell me."

"A spoiled brat who can't decide which toy she wants." This coming from a woman who, last year, had Jaye watching on the sidelines while she almost threw it all away with Grant (Juliette's father and the man who almost killed Mac and me in the process of trying to get AVA.)

"How did this turn into Bash-Abbey Day? And what about you and Tony?" I asked Jo. "That's not exactly working like peanut butter and chocolate these days, is it? Besides, I thought you guys were rooting for Mac."

"I'm rethinking my position on men. Last night, the bastard pulls out a condom and something in his eyes looks funny, so I stop in mid *you know* and ask what's wrong. He says nothing's wrong, but the more he denies it, the more I know something's up. I push him off and then I see the packet on the floor. Turns out it's the one he's been carrying around in his wallet. Since high school probably."

We gave her blank stares and she shouted. "He's trying to get me pregnant? I told him a thousand times I'm not ready, and now he's using old condoms. You get it?"

Justine and I shook our heads. "No. No way. Tony wouldn't do that. Impossible."

"Possible," Jo insisted.

"What'd he say when you shoved it in his face. I'm assuming you shoved the evidence in his face," I said.

"He said I was losing it." She looked away.

"And?"

"Nothing," she said, suddenly fascinated with her wedding rings.

"Not nothing. What?" I asked.

"Fine. He said I'd been hanging out with you too long."

"The bastard." I mean, really.

"Exactly. Now do you believe me?"

"Well, no." I stole a sip of her cappuccino and almost gagged on the sickening sweetness of it.

"The condom was expired."

"An accident," Justine offered.

"A mistake," I suggested.

"A trap to get me barefoot and preggers," Jo said.

I had to admit, it looked funny; funny suspicious, not funny funny.

"See my point?"

Maybe. "So, what're we going to do about it?" I asked.

Justine shook her scruffy head and rubbed the spot she sometimes calls her third eye. "I know you two; you're looking for trouble and I want nothing to do with it." She collected her backpack and stomped toward the door.

"Wait, Justine. I need you," I said.

She turned and tossed her backpack on the floor. "If you're planning on casting any spells on Tony—"

"Not Tony. Ben."

"You want to cast a spell on Ben?"

"Justine, I'm not a witch, I'm clairvoyant. Not the same thing at all." Like she didn't know. "Ben needs information on Merona Air and we thought maybe you could . . ."

"What?" she asked, looking skeptical, but she was still there. That was something.

"I'm still working on that part."

"Let me know when you formulate a plan that doesn't involve seduction, scandal or sabotage," she said, covering all her bases.

Hmmph. "Would I do that?"

"The real question is, what wouldn't you do, Abigail?"

"Forget about Ben. I'm thinking castration for Tony," Jo said. Then she looked off into the distance, like she had something even better in mind.

Justine and I threw her identical quizzical looks. "Just say no? Abstinence?"

"You might as well declare war, Jo."

"You've got to show him who's boss," Justine said.

"I'll get my tubes tied."

"If you want to get divorced, sure." I said.

"Too much?"

"I'd say. What about showing him what it's really like to have a child around the house?"

"Look you two drama queens, why not go with the obvious. Birth control pills?" Justine offered.

Jo twisted her rings and shook her head. "Birth control would only solve one of my problems. What about all the pressure he's putting on me? Hey. Maybe I could borrow Juliette for a while."

"Forget it. Juliette's too well-behaved," I said. "You need colicky babies, obnoxious teens and a set of ADD twins, like on 'Desperate Housewives.'"

"Okay, it's settled," Jo said. "We'll make a list of all our friends with beastly children and call them. Now what the hell are you going to do about Ben and Mac?"

"I don't know, but Mac's moving in tonight, heaven help us all."

"Sod it. The flower truck again."

Justine's heavy army boots hit the floor as she stomped over to AVA's entryway seconds before a young man, who looked barely old enough to drive, entered and jumped back in surprise as Justine ripped the flowers from his hands. He backed into the door, and let out a squeak, then turned and ran to his truck, racing off like Seabiscuit on speed.

Jo and I gaped after the delivery guy while Justine was furiously rummaging through the junk drawer.

"Where is the bloody thing when you need it?" she demanded. Then she apparently found the bloody thing, because she tossed the flowers onto the counter and proceeded to bludgeon them until there was nothing left but a paper sleeve that looked like it had been flattened by one of those giant, rolling pins that makes newly paved roads all hard and flat and even. Like the flowers.

Jo picked through the debris until she found the card. "To Abigail and Alaska Virgin Air. Nice to see you at McKinley. Frank Merona, Merona Air."

"Bloody hell," Justine said, stomping her feet again. "That Molly woman will be the end of me."

"Double bloody hell," I said. Molly was the least of our problems. "Merona saw us at McKinley, which means he knows I was there with Ben and that we tailed him home," I moaned. "Now what?"

"Well, the ball's in our court. That's for sure," Jo answered, turning the card over to see if there was something I'd missed.

My cell ringing interrupted my brilliant reply, not that I had one.

"Hi, Bunny," my mom said. "I hear you got into it over a bunch of flowers. Were they the wrong color? 'Cause I hate it when that happens."

I mouthed "Mom" to Jo and pointed to the flowers.

"So, Mom, should I ask? How'd you hear so fast?"

"Loretta Fucolli's son, Frankie, is the Floral Fantasies delivery boy. He told Loretta he was accosted by a flower terrorist at AVA, and when she heard AVA, she assumed . . . well, you know. You're getting a reputation up there, Bunny."

"It wasn't me, Mom. It was Justine."

Okay, maybe I should be ashamed of myself for throwing Justine under the bus, but . . .

"Whatever. That reminds me. What do you think of *Frozen Nuts* for the title of my Alaska book?"

"Do you think it's a bit suggestive?"

"So who's asking? I gotta go. Tell Jo I got ideas if she wants to get even with Tony for the condom thing. Tell her to call me."

I dropped the phone into my pocket and glanced over at Jo.

"She heard about the condom?" Jo asked, looking stunned.

Did she forget who we were talking about here. "Jo, she knows what color panties I put on each morning."

The phone rang, again. Gran this time. "Buns, I heard Justine pantsed the UPS guy." Gran always gets the gossip right behind Mom. Even when she's on the road with the band.

"You're completely cold, Gran."

"And that you have two guys living with you."

Getting warmer.

"And that you're driving them both crazy." (Code for not sleeping with either of them.)

Hot.

"You're your mother's daughter, Abigail Vertuccio."

My eyes and mouth popped open. It's not like Gran to be vicious. "You take that back, Gran. I'm nothing like Mom."

Jo pushed in, before I could say something I'd regret. (Sicilian Tactic #30: Distract Them Before Someone Ends Up Dead.) "Hi, Luna."

"So, Jo, what's this I hear about an old condom?" Ha! Jo's turn now.

"Luna, did you hear Molly's back?"

Okay. I forgive her. It was self-preservation, after all.

"Put Buns back on the phone, Honey."

"Now you did it," I hissed at Jo, the amnesty over.

Justine hijacked the phone next. "Hi, Luna. I wanted to talk with you about my new business. It's flower therapy. I deliver the flowers and then smash them all to bits. The flowers, of course. Or if the customer prefers, they can smash the flowers themselves. I bring the hammer. I can't decide between 'Smashing Blossoms or Squash Blossoms.' What do you think?"

I didn't know what was going on with Justine, but I wasn't going to be the one to ask who put the pea under her mattress, landing her in princess hell.

"Try not to take out any more delivery guys," Gran said and hung up.

"That's settled then," Jo said, tossing the rest of the flower bits in the trash.

I nodded a shaky agreement. But really, I was asking myself: What's the opposite of unsettled? Knowing full well that, with my luck, this was only the beginning.

Chapter 12

What with Vinnie and flower smashing and vintage condoms and two guys prancing around my house like the Doublemint Twins, I hadn't realized until now that something was missing. "So, where's Jaye these days?" I asked.

"So, where's Ben?" Justine mimicked as she fingered the fragrant flower petals Jo had missed in her clean up. "Jaye's working, of course, thank you very much."

"Right, so where *is* Ben?" Jo asked. "And what happened last night?"

It was a miracle she'd waited this long to ask, not being known as the Princess of Patience on a good day.

"You didn't shag them, did you?" Justine asked.

"That would have been a trick." I could see it now—Abigail Vertuccio, Queen of Never Doing a Wild or Impulsive Thing in Her Life (except leaving, but I don't count leaving) in bed with two men. At the same time! Ha! And let's not forget about the Fairbanks gossip network.

"If I'd slept with two guys in one night I'm sure you'd know it by now," I said, shaking my head in a What Were You Thinking way. "And are we forgetting the real issue here? Merona is on to us. Our cover's busted."

"Sleep being the operative word here," Jo said.

Justine eyed me suspiciously. "Snogging. Now that's a different story, isn't it? No sleep involved at all. And shagging. You don't sleep for that either."

"We talked."

She shook her head; her disbelief was as obvious as the flower bits sticking to her shoes.

"Really!" I insisted.

She ignored me like I was a cat box nugget. Something was wrong with this picture. Razor-tongued, opinionated, feisty Justine with no come back?

"Obfuscation will get you nowhere, Abigail. We want to know exactly what went on last night," Jo demanded.

"And I want to know what's up with Justine going on and on about snogging and shagging," I replied. Sicilian Tactic #4: Take the Offensive in Any Defensive Situation. "Wait a sec. You're not having sexual problems with Jaye, are you?"

"Stop right there. That's enough."

"Not nearly," I said.

Jo stepped between us. "Enough already."

"Fine," I said. "Now, what should we do about Merona? A head-on attack or a covert operation, eh?"

"We still haven't heard about Ben and I'm not leaving until you spill every last detail," Jo said, her attention in no way diverted or tempted by the offer of potentially dangerous and exciting covert ops.

When I glanced over at Jo, I noticed at least three grays hair I'd never seen before. Marriage related, no doubt. First a few grays hairs that you don't bother to dye, then thirty extra pounds, three kids and a Volvo station wagon.

Justine waved her rubber mallet in our faces menacingly. "Where is Ben right this minute?"

"Hold your hammer. He's meeting with a sociology professor who agreed to hook him up with students for his eBay research."

"He's researching shopping? If I'd known I could study shopping, I would have gone to college," Jo said, probably thinking of the hours and hours spent at the mall.

"Oy, did you hear about the ghost that sold on eBay for $20,000?" Justine asked.

"$30,000," I said.

"Shut up!"

"No joke. The seller claimed the ghost was living in her grandfather's old cane and scaring her little boy, so she sold it on eBay and wham—college education paid for."

"Ben's studying ghosts?" Jo gave me a He Must Be Crazy look.

"You know when you bought the handcuffs for Tony?"

"It was a joke, Abbey. And don't say that too loudly or we'll be getting a call from your mother wondering why we handcuffed the UPS guy to your bed."

"You bid on the handcuffs, you won, you sent a check and now they're under your bed. Who are we kidding?"

She ducked her head to hide the blush that was spreading across her face.

"And when you bought that massager for your back, same thing. Right? Bid, win, mail the check and wham, it's safely tucked inside your night stand."

"I have a bad back," she protested. "I do."

"And Justine, when you ordered the Martin guitar for next to nothing."

"I know. Bid, check, guitar arrives. Your point?" she asked.

"Trust. You sent money to total strangers before you even saw the merchandise. Ben is studying eBay's honor system. You have to admit, it's interesting.

"So then, where does that leave his investigation of Merona? If he's going to be busy studying eBay?"

I almost mentioned his sabbatical, adding that Merona shouldn't take much time at all. But that raised all kinds of sticky questions. Like, how long was Ben staying and where would that leave me when he left? So instead, I said, "That's where we come in. I'm thinking we could get Justine a job with Merona. She could do the whole spy thing: sneak into the files, listen to his voice mail, hack his computers, search the place. You know."

"And I'm thinking, I don't look good in bright orange jumpsuits and prison slippers. Of course, this could be my opportunity to try a new look, but no."

"What about Sam?" Jo asked. "She's a spy. She must have a few connections."

"Sam's no help at all," I said, thinking of how her main concern had been setting me up with Ben.

"Then we're screwed. Speaking of which, did you or didn't you? And how was it? And if you didn't actually do it, how many times did you sneak up to one of their doors and turn around and go back to your own room before you finally decided to stay out of trouble?"

"Question one? I already told you. I didn't. Question two. I don't know. Question three. Shut up and mind your own business. Happy?"

Thank God for Candi's Temptations, because before Jo or Justine could badger an answer out of me, Candi's truck slid to a stop just short of AVA's front doors. The none-too-intrepid delivery guy stepped out of the truck, looking around cautiously—I'm certain checking for any crazed Brits on the loose. He pushed the front doors open, barely enough to squeeze a largish, gold foil and beribboned box through and dropped it on the floor. "Delivery for . . ." He double checked his manifest. "Mackenzie Kerrigan." Then he ran like crazy back to his truck and drove away before any of us could shout "Boo" out the door at his retreating back.

A boo really did escape my lips, but floated into Ben instead. If I hadn't been distracted by the antics of the candy guy, Ben would never have managed to sneak up on me. But as it was, he did. And yes, Molly's motives were on my mind. Because Candi's Temptations sells high end, fancy-pantsy candy, and only people with bribery on their minds or guilty souls or people who are trying really, really hard to impress some poor sap or snag some unsuspecting sucker, patronizes Candi's.

Just how much did Molly want Mac, anyway, for heaven's sake.

"Boo, yourself," Ben said as he planted a tiny peck on my lips, catching me completely off-guard. I put my fingers on the spot where his lips had been and could have sworn my mouth felt warmer now and tasted like chocolate.

This was getting to be ridiculous. I was not supposed to be snogging, as Justine would say, new men while technically going out with Mac. Get a grip already, self.

I abruptly turned away and slammed my eye into the edge of the open door, stumbling backward two steps, while clutching my face dramatically and yelling. Damn, ouch, and double damn. I could feel my face swelling up like a dumpling on steroids. Ben reached for me—to check for brain damage was my guess—as the sound of heavy pounding emanated from the vicinity of the poor, unsuspecting AVA counter.

Justine, again. She had her hammer out and was bashing in one creamy chocolate after another. Vanilla, cherry and caramel candy guts stuck to her hair and eyelashes and were splattered all over her delicately embroidered peasant blouse and heavy, black army boots. Jo stood by watching, the way you do when you can't pull your eyes away from a disaster, even though you know better.

"Is this some Alaska ritual I should know about?" Ben asked, as if it were perfectly natural for someone to be blasting candies into eternity with a piece of equipment more suited for use on resistant plane engines and boyfriends.

"Candy smashing therapy," I answered. Pretty soon I was going to need some therapy if I stayed in this loony bin much longer.

Jo still hadn't moved. Or spoken. Probably shock. If she wasn't mobile and verbal in fifteen minutes, I was planning on checking her vitals.

"Have you vanquished them all yet?" I asked, as I peered into the box, found the one intact piece and popped it into my mouth.

"Don't eat that," Justine shouted, as she wielded another blow to the chocolate pieces that had not yet liquefied into chocolate goo. "You're consorting with the enemy."

I spit the chewy lump onto the counter, adding to the unsightly mess.

Jo finally spoke. "Charming. Ladylike, too."

"Good. You're alive." I didn't care about Molly sending Mac chocolate candy, 'cause one thing I know is this: Mac is not stupid. Well, two things I know. One, he's not stupid, and two, he knows a good thing when he sees it and it's not Molly.

Justine, on the other hand, considers ex's of all size, shape, sex and variety as lower than toe jam since her ex, Grant, came back last year and almost ruined everything between her and Jaye. Watch out, Molly!

So, my spitting out the candy (and it really tasted great) was an act of solidarity with Justine. Okay, maybe not entirely. In truth, keeping Justine happy is essential to basic survival at AVA and one thing you learn in Alaska is basic survival. Because when Justine's upset, you don't even want to think about it.

"So, Justine. You done yet?" I asked.

She was breathing hard, sweat dripping off her nose and forehead, and still she slammed the mallet down one last time for effect. "Maybe a voodoo doll is what we need," she said, looking as earnest as one can when seriously contemplating voodoo.

Ben put in, "Unfortunately, they only work when the subject believes in them."

"And you are?" Justine asked, all haughty, as if she didn't already know.

He stretched out a hand and took hers, sticky and all, and introduced himself. "Ben. I'm Ben. Justine, I presume."

Of course, she couldn't help but relax the tight muscles around her face and neck and flash him a smile, in spite of herself. She looked him up and down, taking in his dimple, the one that shows up when he grins, the recalcitrant hairs on his head he can never seem to tame and the way his jeans have a habit of slipping down on his hips. "Now I see," she said. "Definitely fanciable."

I think in England that means someone you want to do it with.

"Okay, moving on." I did what I always seemed to be doing with Ben and tried to steer him away from the girls. This time he resisted. Apparently, he wasn't done with Justine yet. Nor she with him.

"So, you're Sam's brother?" she asked, giving him her third-degree stance: arms crossed over chest, decidedly suspicious look.

"Step-brother, I was born here, actually. My mother married Lord Archer and moved us to London when I was five.

"I've had all my shots, I floss daily, I have no communicable diseases, I do my own laundry and cook my own meals. I cried when George W won, I vote religiously and I never kick animals or steal from old ladies," he concluded.

"What about cats?" I asked.

"Adore them."

"And children?" Justine asked.

"Love them."

"And if someone sent flowers to try to lure someone back who obviously didn't want luring, what would you suggest doing?"

He eyed the counter. "Demolish them with a mallet, of course."

"We understand each other."

"Perfectly."

"Good. Then understand that Abbey has Mac. You are her friend now and will always be. Nothing more. So you know."

"I get it," he said. "But Justine, Abbey's a big girl." He stood a little straighter and his voice sounded a bit firmer. Then he winked at me. "And so you know. I don't scare easy."

I didn't know who was more surprised. Me or Justine. For the first time since I've known her, Justine was speechless. We were all pretty much looking for a diversion when we caught Jo on her cell telling Tony, I presume, no, she wasn't sure when she'd be home, and yes, if he wanted dinner he'd better think about cooking it himself, and yes, that was right. There was nothing in the wedding vows that said she had to cook every friggin' meal for a husband who has two good hands and two feet and can fix his own damn food, and no, she didn't care if he told his grandma because she doesn't believe the old biddy can really put a curse on anyone, anyhow.

Then in an about-face faster than a politician the day after the election, she got off the phone, acting like she'd done nothing more dramatic than ordering pizza.

"Abbey. Can I use your computer? Ben's being here gave me an idea," Jo said.

Curiosity got the better of me. We all walked, single-file into my office where Jo took my chair and I punched in my password. We watched as she pounded on a few keys, the eBay screen opened and she typed "pregnancy belly" into the search box.

Justine rolled her eyes, and from the way she kept pressing her fingers to her temple and wincing, it looked to me like she was nursing a headache. Too many blows with the mallet, I suppose. Or possibly too many friends she couldn't control or set straight.

I leaned over Jo's shoulder. Oddly enough she had seven hits. I'd definitely have to look up Great Guy Who Isn't Obsessed With Marriage later, because if you could buy a ghost and a pregnancy belly on eBay, then who knew. Maybe Mr. Perfect for Abbey was right there waiting for my bid.

When Jo had found the one she was looking for (twin weight, because you might as well make it as painful as possible), she put in her bid. What I wanted to know was, who would have a pregnancy belly in the first place? Another irate wife who wanted to keep her husband in line? A pregnant gal who wanted her partner to share (code word for suffer) the experience with her?

"How do you know who the seller is?" I asked.

"You don't. Not until after you win." Ben looked on with interest. "Then they tell you where to send your check or money order and you tell them your info and that's it. Usually."

"What do you mean, usually?" Ben asked.

"There was that time where some guys in Illinois sold a bunch of stolen merchandise. But they were caught in Florida a few weeks later."

"Have you ever been—" Ben started.

"Scammed? Yeah, for two dollars once. I mailed a book and never heard from the buyer again. What about you?"

"I haven't tried it, actually."

What?!

"You haven't tried it?" Jo laughed

"Well. No," he said, casually. "But you don't have to be a chip to appreciate ketchup. Do you?"

"Or a nutcase to study nutcases," Justine said, looking at me. "Although it helps."

"You have to try it." Jo jumped up and pushed Ben down into the seat. "What do you need? Valentine's day is coming."

"How about a gift for a girl back home you want to impress," Justine asked.

"No." He gave her a Good Try look. "No girl. At least not in England." He shot a grin in my direction. God, I'll never get tired of that grin and how his eyes get all happy when he smiles, as if he knows something wonderful about the world and can't keep it in.

"What shall I look for? Maybe a love potion," he teased.

"Or one to ward off gift giving, veterinarian ex-girlfriends," Justine said as she shoved her skinny little butt into the seat with Ben, forcing him to hold on so he wouldn't be ejected, and started typing.

"One thing I'm certain is, I'm going to get rid of that twit," she said. "If I have to dip her in chocolate sauce and cover her in sprinkles."

"One thing I'm certain of is, I'd better check your temperature because you are acting even more bizarre than usual."

"Like my mum always says, 'You'll thank me later. See if you don't.'"

That remains to be seen. That's all I can say.

Chapter 13

Most days, all I need to keep me happy is a little sunshine, an interesting book and Mr. Peanut, my cat, to snuggle with. What I can do without are the usual: candy-whomping Brits on a rampage, husband-avenging maniacs and two men living in the same house. That said, Justine tossed on the final straw and invited everyone—Mac, Ben, Jo, Tony and Jaye—to my house for dinner tonight. Her reasoning? Most of us were going to be there already. It just made sense.

In truth, I'm pretty sure it was all part of her evil plot to ensure Ben and I were never alone for more than a minute at a time.

"Where's Juliette going to be while you're busy guarding me?" I asked.

"Juliette is on holiday with her grandparents in Inverness."

"Scotland? How did I not know this?"

"I don't like to dwell on it. And it will be brilliant for her. It will," she said, like she was trying to convince herself more than me.

Now I understood what all the gift smashing was about. Until Juliette was safely back home, I was Justine's mission in life.

"She'll love Scotland," Jo agreed.

"The UK in February. What could be better?" Ben said.

Really? Damp, gray, windy. Alaska with a Scottish accent.

The door slammed open and an intrepid, khaki clad UPS man walked in, dropped a package on the desk in front of Ben and stuck an electronic contraption under his nose. "Mackenzie Kerrigan?"

Ben sighed and signed without comment, after Justine impaled him with her elbow. As soon as UPS man hit the pavement she dropped the box into the middle of the candy goo and lifted her hammer.

"Whoa." Jo grabbed Justine's raised hand and held it in a death grip. "Let's wait to see what it is, at least."

"Right you are." She set the hammer on the counter and proceeded to rip open the bundle containing, of all things, a studded collar, leash and a bag of doggie treats, then grabbed the hammer and systematically whacked each doggie treat into dust.

Next she scoured the junk drawer, tossing aside broken pencils, crumbly rubber bands, dried up pens and glue sticks. "Ah ha!" She held up a pair of heavy duty scissors. Goodbye dog collar.

"You could have saved the treats for José," Jo reminded her, as she scraped kibble bits and candy goo into the trash.

"Not in this lifetime."

A small bark, more like a woof or an erk came from the vicinity of our feet.

"What the?" I peered out the front door, checking for signs of yet another delivery person and found none. Whoever it was must have beat the hastiest retreat on God's green earth.

Ben scooped the puppy into his arms where it gratefully licked his chin. No dignity whatsoever.

"Can't smash you, little fluffer nutter."

To some people a puppy is like a baby, binding two people together for eternity. Seems Molly was stepping things up.

"This is starting to annoy me," I said.

"Send him back," Jo suggested. She scratched the puppy's chin and bent to stick her nose in his coat and sniff his yummy puppy scent. "Of course, he is kind of precious."

"We can't send back what isn't ours," I said.

"Well, hide him," Justine suggested. "Mac will be back from his run in about twelve minutes and then our options will be—"

"Kaput," Jo finished, "Like your relationship with Mac if you don't watch out."

I was not going to start worrying about my relationship with Mac. I had a dog to worry about, because I can't have a dog. Mr. Peanut might do to a dog what Justine had done to the candy. Of course, it would have to be the most adorable puppy in the world, didn't it? Black, brown and white with a broad, friendly face that reminded me of a manatee, but in reality was a St. Bernard. The heart-shaped name tag read Butch. Ha! Cupcake was more like it.

"I'll take him," Justine said. "For Juliette."

So much for not touching anything That Molly Person sent. But I wasn't about to argue with her. I gathered up the leash and shoved it in her backpack.

"Go, already," Jo said, as she pushed Justine and Cupcake out the door. "And don't forget dinner. Dinner is very important."

They were up to something, those two. No doubt about it. But I brushed it aside as I peered through the window at Mac who was acing an elegant three-point landing.

"Ben, I need to go to the store for dinner supplies. Why don't you come along?" Jo asked. She put one arm through his to ensure his cooperation. With Justine and Cupcake on their way, it was Ben's turn, and no way was he getting out of Jo's iron grip.

"I'll drive. Abbey, see you at 7. Your place," she said as she dragged Ben out the door, leaving me alone with two hours to kill and no protection from Mac whatsoever.

Think, Abbey. Think. I just needed to keep away from him for four more days, then everything would be fine and we could all get back to normal. That is, after Ben figured out what Merona was up to, after Jo got Tony in line and after Juliette returned to Alaska so Justine wouldn't have the time or energy to worry about me. *Then* everything would be fine.

And you don't have to remind me what FINE means. I remember.

The front doors opened again and I steeled myself for the inevitable. My plan was to act busy, so busy Mac and I wouldn't be able to get into it. Jo's eBay screen glared at me like a seductress. I'd have to suggest Ben look into a connection between eBay and the Home Shopping Network. You know. The addiction factor.

Mac should have popped in by now. But no sign of him. No matter. I busied myself doodling a list of the most inconceivable items you never expected to buy or sell on eBay, or any other place, including: ear wax, belly button lint, bad luck baseball cap. I was up to chewed bubble gum wad, gnawing on my pencil and wondering if anyone was selling chewed-up pencils on eBay, when I glanced up and caught Mac standing in the doorway, a cup of coffee in hand. He smiled. I smiled. Like old times. Before my vision and Ben.

"Good flight?" I asked nonchalantly.

He nodded, telegraphing all kinds of unspoken messages I had no intention of pursuing. Not four days before V-Day.

Then the front door slammed and I jumped.

"Abigail, take this sodding creature right this minute."

Justine appeared in the office, holding Cupcake away from her body like he was congealed liver. "The bugger peed on me."

She handed the culprit over to Mac and started wiping her pants with a wad of soggy tissues. "He's yours. Good luck," she said before she dashed out, leaving a handful of pee tissues on the floor by Mac's feet.

Great. No leash, no extremely expensive doggie treats, squished or otherwise, and now pee tissues.

"She's missing Juliette," I said, by way of explanation, as Cupcake squirmed inside Mac's parka.

"Hey, Butch," he said, catching the name on the engraved name tag.

"Cupcake, actually," I corrected.

He raised an eyebrow and looked down at the wiggly pile of fur and nodded. Anyone with any sense could see the logic in it and Mac has good sense, if nothing else.

"Should I ask what this is about or chalk it up to Sicilian Tactic #8?" he asked. (Sicilian Tactic #8: If You Can't Convince 'em, Confuse 'em. My Mom's personal favorite.)

Did I mention that Mac is a patient man? He has a strong belief that the universe and all truths eventually reveal themselves, so why try to twist things into shape before they're ready. Meaning me.

"Any interest in going to Man's Best Friend for doggie supplies? I'll drive," I said, grabbing my gear. I wasn't about to be Cupcake's next victim. After all, Molly sent him to Mac, not me. So, if anyone was going to get peed on, it shouldn't be me. Even if I did participate in a dognapping and candy/flower smashing.

"I'll drive. You puppy sit," I repeated as I headed for the driver's side door, keys in hand.

Okay, so I wasn't supposed to be getting in a car alone with Mac, but what could go wrong in broad daylight?

Mac set Cupcake down on the ground before getting in the car and let him sprinkle little yellow puddles in the snow until he had no sprinkle left. "That should do it," he said, as he snuggled Cupcake against his neck and cooed, "Good job," and "Good boy," while I steered us slowly through the ice fog toward Man's Best Friend, where every pampered pet in Fairbanks shops.

The sheer size of the place amazed me. How much stuff could any one pampered pet use? Mr. Peanut, for example, needs cat food and litter. The rest he provides. He bathes himself. He makes his own bed, whenever and wherever he chooses. Toys are a few balls, a scratchy box and all of my possessions: keys, lipsticks, and especially pens. Low maintenance.

The array before us included everything from puppy Prozac to kitty nail polish. "What about this?" I asked Mac, as I held up a contraption you apparently fill up with milk and lay on your belly so the puppy can feed. It's supposed to trick them into thinking you're their mommy. Doggy psychology.

"Pass," Mac said, shaking his head.

"What about this?" I held up a doggie monitor. Something like a baby monitor, only affixed to a collar, so you can tell how your puppy's doing from anywhere in the house. Only $69.99.

"Are you planning on picking up every overpriced, unnecessary piece of equipment in here?" Mac asked, "Because if you are, we're going to be late for dinner."

"Who told you about dinner?" I forgot about dinner.

A perky sales lady sprang up behind me. "You've got the doggy monitor. Good choice. I can't tell you how much trouble it saved me last winter, when my little Fernando got stuck in the basement. I heard his whimper and went right to him. It has a tracking device."

She turned her sugar on Cupcake next. "Ooh itty oody oody bitty babies like to get into trouble, don't you."

"Get me out of here," I begged Mac telepathically. To the sales lady, I said, "We're really looking for a dog home," then rattled off a long list of necessities that included two stories, indoor-outdoor carpeting, heating and cooling and a bunch of other things that only Ivana Trump's dog house would have. "So, if you could please look into it for me, I'd really appreciate it." She aimed her perky little tail toward the office, doggie mission in hand.

It wasn't as mean as it sounds.

"You're terrible," Mac said as we hastily gathered the few supplies Cupcake really needed.

"You knew that already," I replied. Because, really. If he knew me at all, he'd have to know that. Wouldn't he?

My house, really Gran's—the house she gave me when she and Al had enough cold and dark, enough of AVA and not enough rock and roll—is a work of art. Al and Gran got the musician's life on the road and I got a four-story Architectural Digest home in the middle of an Alaska spruce forest. Solar energy, a gray water recycling system, floor-to-ceiling windows surrounding my octagonal bedroom perched on top of the house like a crow's nest, reached by a hand-carved spiral staircase which traverses all four stories. And the frosting on the cake? A Bosendorfer grand piano.

Having Ben and Mac living together under one roof was becoming a balancing act rivaling the best of "Lost" and "The Survivor", and it'd only been one night. The honeymoon period. Fortunately for me, last night Ben's jet lag caught up with him and by the time Mac arrived with armloads of take-out, Ben was in his PJs (at least I imagined him in his PJs), safely tucked in for the evening.

Night 2: Ben will be arriving any minute. Hell. They could end up surprising me, like Mr. Peanut, who hasn't eviscerated Cupcake, yet. On first introduction, Cupcake cornered Mr. Peanut under the grand piano, and for several hairy minutes we weren't sure Mr. Peanut was going to come out of it with his self-esteem and manhood intact. Luckily, he managed a brilliant escape up the stairs. Since then, he's whizzed past Cupcake at every opportunity, nails bared, just so Cupcake wouldn't get too cocky.

I could only be so lucky if Ben and Mac got along as well.

The house smelled great. A mixture of roasted coffee, spicy eggplant parmesan and chocolate chip cookies, thanks to Mac's slaving in the kitchen ever since we walked in the door and he shrugged out of his parka.

Jo and Ben pushed into the entryway moments later, shaking snow from their boots, stripping off layers of winter gear and mirroring each other the way old friends sometimes do. When Jo wasn't looking, Ben glanced over at Mac, busy in the kitchen, and handed me a package no bigger than my hand. One corner of his mouth lifted into a half-smile and he asked, "What's for dinner?"

I slid by him and hissed, "Not funny."

In the end, Mac, who's a great cook, burned everything. It was during Jo's tirade about how pissed she gets when people (i.e. men) say the fight for equality is over when really we've moved into a backlash against feminism, that I first caught the familiar scent of charcoal wafting from the kitchen into the foyer where we all stood either transfixed by Jo or too chicken to move.

Truth is, I'm the one who usually drops, spills or burns things when I'm nervous, in a hurry or distracted. Not Mac.

The eggplant parmesan resembled volcanic rock. The pasta was unrecognizable; the pan melded to the burner. The chocolate chip cookies charred buttons of steel.

The fumes and smoke were threatening to send us running for cover when the front door opened. Tony came in and sniffed the burnt air. "Jo cooking again?"

Sheesh. Something must have petrified the man's brains if he hasn't figured out how to keep his foot out of his mouth by now.

Jaye and Justine arrived behind him, squeezing past the little group crowded around the piano. Justine sniffed the air, held her hand out to Jaye and said, "Five quid."

Jaye blushed; then, as if by way of apology, held up two bags from Fidelo's, the best Italian food in town.

"Doesn't take a genius to hope for the best and plan for the worst when Abigail's cooking," Justine said.

"I didn't," I stammered. Although I understood how they might come to that conclusion.

Still. They had a point. Because Mac doesn't burn things. It was an easy guess that his mind had been on Ben's arrival when the food was changing from juicy to molten. Then again, he could have been thinking about Molly. About how natural it felt to be with her again. About how sweet she was to send all those thoughtful gifts. (The Fairbanks Gossip Network would have tipped him off about the gifts, even if most of the them were in the dumpster behind AVA.) And maybe he was wondering if it was worth trying things with her again, what with Ben invading his territory.

"Abbey?" Ben bumped my shoulder and leaned close to my ear. "Would you like me to go to the market?"

I inched us over to the sun room, where we wouldn't be interrupted or overheard.

"I'll be happy to go out for dessert if you point me in the right direction."

I caught Jo checking us out. Actually glaring from across the room, so it seemed like a good idea to get him out of the line of fire.

"You know where the mall is?"

After he said he'd find his way and don't wait supper because he'd had a late lunch, I sent him off with a list long enough to ensure his absence for at least an hour and sighed in relief as I heard his latest rental car head down the driveway.

With Ben out of the way, Jo's mood lightened; across the room, I could hear Tony laugh in a way that told me things were back to normal. I was helping Jaye and Justine lay out the hot food containers, paper plates and napkins, when Jo popped up behind me. "Where's Ben going?"

"He decided to step aside. He's on a flight to London tonight."

"Where'd he go? Really."

I recited the grocery list: blueberry cannoli, chocolate chip cookies, New York cheesecake, fresh baked bread.

"Dinner's served," Mac said, as he did a mental head count. "Where's Ben?"

"He had to go meet 007. Very hush hush. Can't talk about it," I answered.

No one moved. "Okay. Okay. He went for dessert, now shut up and let's eat."

"Abs, I'm having a T-shirt made for you that says Fettucini Alfredo Slut," Jo said.

Don't think she wouldn't. I was on my third serving and wracking my brain for an equally scathing comeback when Ben called.

"What's taking so long?" I asked, skipping the usual pleasantries.

"Small problem with the rental," he said.

"How small?"

"Frozen, I'm afraid."

Okay. Here's the thing. I almost wet my pants from laughing so hard, but in my own defense, I covered my mouth first. When I had the hysterics under control, I asked, "You sure?"

"Rent-an-Oldie has confirmed the diagnosis."

"You rented from Rent-an-Oldie?"

"Abbey, are we really having this discussion?"

"Where are you?" In his defense, he had no way of knowing that at 40 below zero he'd have to leave his car running while he did his shopping, a little detail I'd forgotten to mention during the McKinley plug-in lecture. "I'll be right there," I said as Mac, Jo, Tony, Justine, Jaye, Cupcake and Mr.

Peanut, from his perch atop the refrigerator, looked on. "Ben's car is frozen. I have to get him."

"I'll go," Mac offered.

"No!" I said, too loudly, even for me. "That's okay," I added, in a voice bordering on insanity.

"I'll go with you," Jo said, with a firmness that assured me I wasn't going anywhere without her. And if that wasn't enough, she grabbed my car keys, tossed them to me, and with more glee than was absolutely necessary, said, "Get a move on. We have a cheechako to rescue."

Luckily, Ben was stranded a quick ten minutes away. We found him huddled in his too-thin jacket, stomping his feet, icicles already forming on his eyebrows and nose hairs, as he forlornly stared after the tow-truck.

"Hey, Ben. Need a lift?" I shouted, as we came to a sliding stop in front of him.

He'd no sooner jumped in the car when Jo snapped, "See those cars, Ben?" as she pointed to the parking lot full of idling vehicles.

"Give him a break," I said. "He's new."

"This is the second time."

"So he lost track of time. Remember when you were flirting with the meat counter guy that time and—"

"I get it," she said. "Hey. Where are you going? Don't we need to follow that tow truck?"

"They're dropping it at the rental company," Ben said. "I can pick up another tomorrow."

I steered the car toward the bridge that would take us over the Chena River and into downtown Fairbanks. As we passed the old St. Joseph's Church and railroad station, I saw what looked like Merona's car. I squeezed Jo's arm in my excitement. The car was a silver Landrover and the person in the passenger seat looked a lot like Rebecca. I did a U-turn, cutting off an RV in the process.

"What are you doing?" Jo screeched, as she grabbed for the dashboard.

"Put your seat belt on before we get a ticket, already."

"Abbey, slow down right now. Or, swear to God, I'll call Vinnie," Jo threatened.

"Ben. Ben. Is it them?" I yelled, as I tried to keep the car in view.

Turns out, keeping a discreet distance when tailing someone isn't as easy as it looks in the movies. For one, you have to stay so far back you can't always be sure you're tailing the right culprits, and for two, I kept losing them.

"What are you going to do if you catch up with them?"

Weird. Jo was hanging onto the door like her life depended on it or something. I shot her a look. "I'm just going find out where they're going. No big deal."

The U-turn had us heading toward the outskirts of town.

"This is insane," Jo said, as I navigated a 15 mph turn going 40.

"What happened to Sassy Sisters Investigations and ninja outfits? I thought you loved this stuff," I said.

"Tony's gonna kill me. If you don't first," she screamed.

"Why?" Tony was used to Jo's antics, so this was news to me.

"For taking Ben's side. Not that I'm taking his side."

The Landrover turned left, toward Anchorage and the Parks Highway. I snapped on my blinkers and hit the on-ramp. Ben leaned forward and rested his hands on my shoulders. "Maybe we should stop, Abbey."

"Look. They're turning into The Whaler," I said, as I made the turn and skidded down the gravel driveway. "Jo, call everyone and see if they can meet us down here."

"This is a waste of time," she muttered as she flipped open her phone and dialed.

"It'll be fun," I said. Famous last words.

When we were driving back from McKinley, Ben had given me the intel on Rebecca. Apparently she came from a long line of crooks, con men and criminals. Her father once served time for grand theft auto. Not that one auto was the extent of his criminal career. Rather, he'd only been caught once. Her brother opened a chop shop to process the boosted autos and only escaped capture thanks to a friend who overheard someone in a bar bragging about a big bust going down the next night at a local garage. Sheer dumb luck.

Her other brother was the point man for selling the altered vehicles. He placed ads in different newspapers every Sunday and met prospective buyers in suitably respectable attire at suitably respectable locales. If it wasn't for a larcenous soul and the heart of a devil, he could have been a preacher.

Rebecca's sister—Margolyn, married, two babies, husband, a security guard at the labor ministry—was a model of propriety. Except, it turned out, she was the head of the whole darn operation.

It was a miracle Rebecca came out normal. She graduated university with honors, entered the Royal Air Force, became one of Britain's first female pilots and now flies for TransLondon, staying as far away from her rogue family as she possibly can. Her phone is unlisted. Her address a state secret. When they want to reach her, they contact TransLondon, where she never takes their calls and always sends their letters back unopened.

Ben described Rebecca as naïve, impressionable and sweet. He couldn't come up with a single bad habit or annoying quality, no matter how hard I pressed. Disgusting.

As for Merona, he arrived in Fairbanks with too much money and charisma and started Merona Air almost a year ago. Even so, I never had the slightest inkling he was up to no good.

In the middle of the dance floor Miss-Not-a-Darned-Thing-is-Wrong With-Her was dancing with Merona in a none-too-innocent fashion. Jo was similarly plastered all over Tony, swaying to a local garage band. Ben went to get a pitcher of something and was waylaid by a couple of girls in two-sizes-too-small low-rise jeans, overly bleached hair and shirts that covered the bare minimum. Hard, six-pack bellies and belly rings proudly on display. Justine and Jaye were squeezed up against each other in a corner booth, heads together, holding hands.

Which left Mac with me.

"Abbey." He touched my hand lightly. A zing ran up my arm, and I shivered. He moved his leg closer to mine so we were touching, and I stopped thinking. He rested his hand on my thigh, and I didn't mean to, but I jumped.

"There's something I have to tell you," he said.

"Look. If you've decided you want Molly and this," I waved a hand from him to me, "was a big mistake, I don't want to hear about it."

"I—" he said.

"This isn't the time or the place."

"Ab," he began.

"Hello," The voice from above interrupted.

Merona and Rebecca stood arm in arm, waiting for us to close our mouths or get a grip or respond like normal human beings.

Mac came to first, slid out of the booth and took Merona's outstretched hand. "Good to see you, Frank. And you must be Rebecca. Nice to meet you."

"Abigail. Very nice to meet you," Rebecca said, ignoring my stare. "I've heard so much about you."

Okay. I know she wasn't getting her information from the Fairbanks Gossip Network, because that doesn't include cheechakos. In other words, she couldn't have heard any of the really embarrassing stuff, could she?

"All good, I hope."

Barf. But I had an investigation to complete so . . .

"Why don't you two join us. I feel terrible that I haven't had a chance to welcome you properly, Frank, and now you, Rebecca. Please. Sit."

They sat as directed, ordered drinks and Rebecca took over what was supposed to be my interrogation. "Word has it, Abigail, Ben is staying with you. Is he really?"

"You've been talking to my mother. Right?" I asked.

She looked confused. "One of Frank's pilots lives out your way," she answered.

"That would be Jeff Casey?"

"Right. So, how do you two know each other? You and Ben."

"Funny story," I said. Hey. I'm the one who's doing the interrogating here. "We were eighteen. He was up here for a Star Trek convention. He came as Number One. I was Deanna. When he decided to do his sabbatical in Alaska, naturally he called me."

Mac, meanwhile, was taking an inordinate amount of interest in the salt and pepper shakers. Trying not to snort as far as I could tell.

"Coincidence, don't you think? Ben and I being here at the same time. It almost looks as if he's followed me," Rebecca said.

At last! Rebecca's dark side. I'd have to point that out to Ben later.

"Funny, he thought you were following him," I answered.

"Ab," Mac started.

"Sorry. I didn't mean anything," I said, even though I did.

"What really brings him all the way to Alaska?" she asked, her voice dripping with disbelief.

Liking her less and less was all I could say. Maybe her appeal is like some kind of Star Trek cloaking device that only works on men.

"eBay," I said, without elaborating. The more talking she did the better.

Suddenly I had her full attention. "eBay? Isn't that some computer program for shopping addicts?"

"Wrong program," I said, continuing with the keep-it-short plan.

Merona jumped in. "Why all the interest, Becks? You'd think you were still interested in him."

She shot him a Keep Quiet look and continued, "What was that about eBay?"

"Ask him yourself," I said, as I looked across the room at Ben, who was headed our way with alcoholic reinforcements. "Here he comes."

I stood. Rebecca followed, pivoted on one foot like a professional ballerina and beamed up at Ben as if he were the second coming. "Benjamin," she said. In one swift move, she liberated the tray, slid it onto the table and clasped him to her in a welcome home hug that came this close to being pornographic.

In a move any choreographer would envy, Ben pried her off of him, slid into the empty side of the booth and pulled me in behind him, thereby ensuring Rebecca wouldn't end up sitting in his lap. Which left Mac on the opposite side of the booth. Whatever Mac was going to say would have to wait.

Rebecca tossed her purse under the table, never taking her eyes off of Ben. "Dance with me, Ben."

"I, ah."

"He can't," I said. "Hurt his back. Fell out of bed this morning."

Ben gripped his shoulder and groaned. "Hurts like the devil."

"I thought it was your back," Rebecca demanded.

He moved his hand to his back and said, "Hurts all over, bloody clumsy of me. New bed."

"Frank," Mac interrupted. "I've been meaning to call you about a panel for the Aviator's Convention."

Rebecca had no choice but to let Merona gently pull her into the seat beside him. The conversation dragged on and on about load capacity and stall speeds and all things air related. Ben seemed perfectly content to learn something new, but I could feel Rebecca fuming. She'd taken to tapping out notes on her water glass between sneaking peaks at Ben.

Finally enough was enough, because she said, "It's getting late. Early day tomorrow. We really must be off." Merona went along, and they were gone before we knew it.

"Well. I learned a lot about bush planes, but nothing about what's going on with Merona," Ben said.

"Au contraire," I said. "Something about you being in Alaska has Rebecca unnerved. We learned that much."

"She thinks I'm stalking her. That would unnerve anyone."

"Maybe." I sipped the fizzy drink Ben had deposited in front of me earlier and thought about that, then realized what Mac had done. "Mac, you're a genius. Asking Merona to be on your committee. Now you can get some answers," I said.

"Such as?" he asked.

"What is his relationship with Rebecca? How did they meet?"

"Ah, I don't think—" Ben said.

"No, you're right. I'll do it. Put me on the panel, too, and I'll grill him. It'll be less suspicious that way." Because everybody in Fairbanks knows how curious I am. "Let's go home so we can work on a plan."

I retrieved my bag and threw it over one shoulder. "Agreed?"

The Northern Lights flittered across the sky in neon reds and greens and oranges as we headed for home.

We'd no sooner reached the front door when Jo and Justine made up an excuse to drag me away so they could hear everything that had happened with Rebecca and Merona at The Whaler.

Once safely ensconced in my bedroom, Jo unscrewed a lipstick and polished her lips perfectly.

"Jo, it's eleven o'clock. Tony'll be kissing that off in an hour."

"Exactly," she said. "Do you have that mascara I like?"

I tossed my bag on the bed next to her. Only it wasn't my bag. "Jo, Justine, where's my purse?"

"There," they said, pointing to the purse on the bed.

"That's not mine."

I almost killed myself getting down the stairs in a panic. "Mac, have you seen my purse?"

"Right there. I picked it up at the bar"

He was right. My slightly scuffed, Coach bag was there. I grabbed it and made myself dizzy, racing at breakneck speed up the spiral staircase to tell Jo and Justine the news. Only, I was late. When I got there, I found them sprawled on my bed with the contents of the mystery purse dumped in their laps.

"What are you two doing? That purse isn't mine," I gasped.

"We know," Jo said.

"It's Rebecca's. You have a problem with that?" Justine demanded, as she stuffed an Elizabeth Arden lipstick back inside along with a wallet and paperback novel.

"Ah. Maybe," I said. "I mean, I wouldn't like it if Rebecca ransacked *my* purse."

"And she'd never do that to you, would she?" Justine said.

I shrugged, wishing I wasn't in a good-girl phase of the moon.

"'Cause that would be wrong," Justine said.

"Extremely," I said.

"Shut it, you two. I think I found something." Jo waved a wad of paper that looked familiar. Like shipping manifests. "These are copies of packing slips from eBay transactions. Every one with a different user name."

"English, Jo."

"She has packing slips, but her name isn't on them. Get it?" She pushed the papers across the bed to me.

"So, you're saying her name should be on each slip. Right?" Justine asked.

"Not necessarily," Jo said. "Sometimes I buy something on eBay and have it sent to as a gift."

"Back to square one." I leaned against Justine, disrupting her perfect lotus position.

"Not necessarily," Justine said, rattling the contraband purse under my nose. "We haven't gone through her wallet. Or her checkbook for that matter."

"Wait," I said, as she pried open the bag and popped open Rebecca's wallet, checking for hidden pockets.

"We should copy these papers, just to be on the safe side," Jo said, ignoring me.

"I thought Merona was the bad guy here," Justine said, "not Rebecca."

"Did you catch those Jimmy Choos she was wearing? Pilots don't make that kind of money," Jo said.

"They could have been a gift. It could have been—"

"Where there's smoke. That's all I'm saying," Jo said.

"I'm with Jo on this one," I added.

Justine shrugged. "Fine. So we watch both of them. What can it hurt?"

"Don't say that," I snapped. Because really. You know how that whole thing works.

It was past midnight when we descended the stairs. Tony and Jaye had left a note and set of car keys on the table. There was no evidence of Mac or Ben. I could only assume they were tucked into their individual beds. How I managed to leave Mac and Ben alone, I'll never know. Maybe if Jo and Justine hadn't sucked me into their Sassy Sisters Investigation routine . . . As it was, I had no idea how things played out, leaving a whole new avenue of investigation I was going to have to pursue in the morning.

I considered my options as Jo and Justine pulled out in Justine's yellow Beetle convertible. Option 1: Eat the leftover cannoli and go back to bed where I belonged. 2: Skip the cannoli, find Ben, show him the purse and eBay forms, so we could put our heads together and figure out what it all meant. Or 3: Same as above, only with Mac, not Ben.

I headed up the stairs, munching on a cannoli, purse in hand, rapped once on Mac's door and turned the knob. Nothing. He must have locked it accidentally. Light was spilling out from under the door, so I knocked again. "Mac? Are you awake? Mac?"

The door slid open a scant few inches. Mac stood in front of the opening. "Forget something, Abs?"

I held up Rebecca's purse. "I need to show you something," I said with a mouth full of blueberry cannoli.

He didn't budge. "Nice purse, but I have an early flight. We can talk tomorrow." He said nighty-night and closed the door. I heard the lock turn. So. Not accidentally locked in the first place.

I suddenly remembered the gift Ben had given me earlier. I skipped down a flight of stairs, retrieved it and ripped off the paper to find a shiny, Magic 8 Ball watch. I love Magic 8 balls! I shook it and asked my question. Will I ever figure out Ben and Mac? I turned it over and read the reply: "Better not tell you now". I tried two more times, to no avail. I got: "Cannot predict now" and "Ask again later". I guess when the 8 Ball isn't telling, it means business. Never one to know when to stop, I tried again and came up with: "Don't count on it".

I should remember, when it comes to Magic 8 Balls and men, stick with Sicilian Tactic #45. Know when to leave well enough alone.

Chapter 14

I sat on the stairs and demolished the rest of my cannoli before going back up and knocking on Ben's door. "Ben, it's Abbey," I whispered. "Open up."

"Can we talk in the morning, Abbey?" Ben said through the closed door.

"Fine, but we found Rebecca's purse."

"Good night, Abigail. Sweet dreams," was all I got in reply.

"I'm not planning on tearing your clothes off, Ben. Just open up."

"I promised," he said.

Ah ha! I knew something was up.

"Okay. I get it. You're afraid you won't be able to resist me if you let me in."

"I'm not falling for it, Abigail."

"I'm sure the 8 Ball has something to say about it. Lucky 8 Ball, will Ben fall helplessly under my spell? Let's see. It says, 'You may rely on it'. See Ben. You're doomed."

"Not if I'm on this side and you're on that."

"Did you know the 8 Ball has sixteen replies?"

"It has twelve, Abbey."

"'My sources say no. My reply is no. Without a doubt'."

"That's three."

"'Ask again later. Reply hazy, try again. It is certain'."

"'Reply hazy, try again' is not on the 8 Ball."

"I'm looking right at it. It says, 'reply hazy, try again'."

The door opened and Ben reached for the ball, allowing me to pull us both into the bedroom and lock the door behind us.

"I have something else you can't resist, Ben," I said and then slowly proceeded to show him.

It's not what you think.

Ben and I were stretched out on his bed, he in pajama bottom shorts that revealed his adorably bony knees, the contents of Rebecca's purse between us.

"I can look for a pattern in the eBay ID's," he said. "It's possible Merona is involved in an eBay scam of some sort and Rebecca is onto him. In that case, she could be in danger."

"We're getting ahead of ourselves, Ben. We don't know if Merona's the guilty one. Rebecca, on the other hand, I'm not so sure about. I know you're an Assume-The-Best kind of guy, but maybe her family rubbed off on her, or maybe she likes thousand dollar shoes too much and got tempted."

"You're wrong, Abigail. She never would—"

"How do you know? You're thinking with your—"

"And you're acting like a petulant—"

"Am not. You're the one who refuses to listen to reason—"

The door banged open. I swear I'd locked it. Mac stood in the frame looking all kinds of dangerous.

"We had an agreement."

The deadly look he shot Ben made me feel like we'd been caught on the bed naked instead of just pilfering Rebecca's purse.

"You locked me out," I accused, resorting to Sicilian Tactic #4.

He eyed Ben's shorts, lack of other attire and turned back to me. "And you came here?"

I wracked my brain for another appropriate Sicilian Tactic and came up empty. I shook the 8 Ball and asked, "Magic 8 Ball, will Mac please go to bed and forget this ever happened?"

"No doubt about it," I said, as I waved the 8 Ball between Ben and Mac. Then I squeezed past Mac and said good night before either of them started wondering why the hell they put up with me in the first place.

I listened for fireworks from below, and hearing nothing but two doors soundly closing, I fell into bed on what felt like the longest day of my life. Four days until February 14th and I was beginning to wonder if I was going to make it.

I should have asked the 8 Ball, but I was so exhausted I fell asleep, clothes, 8 Ball, unanswered questions and all.

Chapter 15

Countdown to Valentine's Day:
Three days to go

Why does falling asleep in your street clothes seem like such a good idea at midnight, when common sense says you'll regret it in the morning having slept on buttons, zippers and inseams all night? Now I was up, all stiff and creaky, at the crack of dawn, feeling like I'd been pasted and wallpapered. The sky was lost in a deep winter sleep and yet I was wide-awake, ruminating on what I would say to Mac when I saw him. One thing was certain. I didn't have to worry about avoiding him, because now he was officially avoiding *me*.

I changed clothes, ran a brush over my teeth and hair (different brushes—I wasn't that sleepy) and left for AVA without benefit of shower, breakfast or common sense. Mac was scheduled for an early flight and I needed to get to him before take-off.

I arrived to find the hangar hopping with activity. I'd made great strides in organizing AVA since Gran turned the business over to me last year, but the hangar chaos stubbornly eludes me. We have plenty of room until one of the planes needs maintenance and then we're climbing over tools and carts and shoving boxes to one side. As close to a hazard you can get without the FAA stepping in.

Mac and our part-time loading crew, Jason and Jennifer, were knee deep in grocery orders going out to Bethel when I walked in.

"Hey, Abbey," Jen said and waved at me from behind a mountain of boxes.

Anywhere in Manhattan, Seattle or Chicago, Jennifer would fit right in. In Fairbanks, her lip and nose rings, and ten earrings are enough to garner looks, even without the dreads. She completes the look with pilled wool sweaters over cargo pants in winter, holey T-shirts and cargo shorts the rest of the year. She works like crazy, is dependable as hell and brings an energy to AVA I can't help but admire.

"Hey, Jen. How's school?"

"It's cool."

It's always cool. "What about you, Jason? School okay?"

He grunted. Jason grunts a lot.

Okay. Mac next. "You left bright and early."

"We're running behind about ten minutes. Can you go over the manifests so Jason and Jen can finish?" he asked, all business.

"Sure," I said, taking the clipboard from him. In his defense, he didn't say it in a snotty way. Just professional.

"Why don't I go along for the ride?" I suggested. Going along for the ride is code for fun. Laughing, catching up, delaying gratification, and sometimes, instant gratification. But that's all I'm saying on the subject.

"Can't. Load's too heavy," he answered, without even checking.

So, I checked. Sadly, it was true. After factoring in last night's six cannolis, we would be overweight by an extra hundred pounds or so. That he didn't look disappointed was frustrating.

Unfortunately for him, he couldn't run forever. I'd catch up with him in exactly six hours, just in time for an early lunch. "See you later," I shouted over my shoulder, leaving them to it. I had other balls to juggle besides Mac's.

Work. I meant work.

The numbers on my computer screen were swimming before my eyes when Jaye dropped a stack of mail on my keyboard. "Justine asked me to deliver these."

He picked out a brochure from the pile for the Mountain Goat, Mac's dream plane, and scanned the glossy photos. "You should think about getting one of these, Ab. That Super Cub is starting to cost more to fix than the price of renting a new one."

He was referring to the chaos in the hanger this morning, where the patched-together Super Cub was taking up space we have plenty of other uses for. "I can look into some extra hangar space next week, if you like," he said.

Any pilot in Fairbanks would have hung upside down covered in nothing but frosting if it would mean laying hands on a Mountain Goat. "No promises," I said. "Jaye, have you and Justine talked with Juliette since she left?"

Jaye is the most laid-back guy on earth, so when he sighed, I looked up. "What?"

"Juliette loves being with her grandparents, and they're putting a lot of pressure on Justine to move closer."

"You must be on crack, Jaye. Justine couldn't wait to get away from all that muckety-muck, tea party crap. "

"Guilt is a powerful thing, Abbey."

"What about you? Would they even let you stay in England?" I asked, hoping to heaven the answer was no. I didn't know what I would do without Jaye. Not just because he's a great pilot. He's Radio AVA, the voice of reason in a sea of madness.

I needed to think fast.

"Justine," I shouted, as I made my way to the lobby where I knew she was updating our billing system. "Did you know the radiation fallout from outdated nuclear facilities in the former USSR is a serious health threat to the U.K.?"

I was going to have to put in a call to my mom, the best selling, bad news travel expert, but for now, I'd punt. "In Vinnie's latest book, The United Kingdom of Catastrophe, she says eating beef in England is like buying a ticket to the Mad Cow Lottery."

Justine closed the laptop. "I should ring them up immediately," she said.

"Don't forget the beef by-products. They're everywhere. In soup, sauces, frozen dinners, cat food, cookies, ice cream, pudding, margarine, cake!"

"Cake?" Jaye whispered as Justine picked up the phone. I'm sure her mom was going to find all this enlightening. "You're bad," he said.

Hey. I have a business to protect. Sicilian Tactic #46: You do whatever it takes.

A delivery guy came and went with such stealth I might have missed him if it wasn't for the FedEx box Justine was tearing into as she chatted with Juliette on the phone.

I figured the package was history, except Justine couldn't go all smash-happy when she was on the phone with Juliette. Which meant, the Mr.

Potato Head she'd extracted from the box was safe for the time being.

I snatched the toy from her, because I could tell this gift wasn't directed at Mac. A quick search produced a card that showed it was Rebecca asking Ben out for a drink—as soon as possible, because she couldn't wait to catch up with him after all this time.

Blugh.

Justine kissed the phone, hung up and said, "Give it," as she yanked the card from my hand. "Rebecca? What does she want with Ben? I thought he was dog's dinner to her."

"So? Do we bash some brains in now or later?" I asked, eyeing the junk drawer where the hammer resides, ensuring easy access for gift smashing emergencies.

"That depends. Rebecca or Mr. Potato Head?" Jaye asked, trying and failing to hide a sly grin.

"I'm meeting Jo for lunch. Let me know what you decide."

Jo and I love the Cosmos Diner. Not for the food, ambiance or service, but for its location on 2nd Avenue, at one time one of the most interesting streets in Fairbanks. During the oil pipeline boom of the 70s, it was called Two Street and teamed with pipeline workers and prostitutes.

"You won't believe it," Jo shouted at me as we found a booth and tossed our parkas on the seat beside us.

"Your sex change operation was a success?"

"Close, but no."

"Umm, you dumped Tony for Patrick Dempsey?"

"You act as if it couldn't happen?"

"No. It could. Definitely. It could."

"The pregnancy belly came this morning."

"By rocket ship?"

"And it's perfect. I tried it for an hour and thought I was going to die. My feet ached. My back ached. I couldn't walk without tipping over. Tony is going to hate it!" Swear. She was positively glowing.

"I have a better idea," I said. "Why don't you wear it."

"What'll that accomplish?"

"Your feet will hurt, your back will hurt and when you're miserable, who else will be miserable, Jo?"

"You're evil under that nice-girl-next-door exterior. You know that?"

"Hey. You're the one who hatched the pregnancy belly plan in the first place."

"Well, I'm not gonna wear it. I want him to back off, but I'm not about to torture myself in the process."

"Which means the abstinence thing didn't fly, huh?"

"Duck," Jo hissed furiously. "Mac just walked in with Molly!"

God help me. I ducked under the table, making believe I'd dropped something, hoping Mac and Molly would move to the far end of the restaurant and miss us entirely. I was mid-Academy Award winning performance, scanning the floor for the imaginary fork, when I heard Jo say, "Hey," first to a pair of hiking boots and then to leather knee-high boots with spiked heels (Ridiculous in this kind of weather), and I jammed my head against the bottom of the table.

Mac leaned over so we were eye-to-eye under the table. "Hi, Abbey."

"Fork," I said as I unfolded myself as quickly as possible and yanked my head to free my hair from whatever it was that was making it stick to the table. I checked my head for bald spots and gave Mac a frosty hello. What the hell was he doing here with Molly, anyway? Lucky we didn't have Justine's hammer, because from the look on Jo's face, I wasn't sure she could be trusted with a blunt object.

"Jo, have you met Molly?" I asked knowing full well she'd missed Molly's visit to AVA the day before.

"I haven't, but so you know, Molly (said like she really meant belly button lint), it's pretty tacky to go after Mac when you know he's got Abbey. And by the way, the chocolates were delicious."

She stood, towering over Molly. "Oh. And so you know. If you're even thinking about hurting my friend, I'll make you regret it." Sicilian Tactic #53: Scare the Heck Out of Them. "Now scoot before I forget my manners."

To me she said, "Let's go," before she dragged me out of the Cosmos building and down the street while Mac led a speechless Molly in the opposite direction. My eyelashes were freezing from the tears running down my face. I'm not sure if they were tears of sadness at Mac getting back with Molly before the body was even cold or from laughter at Jo's wiseguy routine.

Whatever. Jo wasn't done trashing Molly. "If she thinks she can march into town and stomp all over our toes . . ."

I shook my head and shrugged in an I don't know move. I didn't know anything anymore.

"I mean, what happened to sisterhood? The code. You know. You don't go after another woman's man?"

"It could be an innocent lunch," I said.

Jo smacked me on the side of my head. "And I could be Oprah, but I'm not."

"Well, you really couldn't be Oprah," I said, brushing frozen tears from my face.

"Why not?"

"For one, you're not just white. You're ghostly white."

"A detail."

"Two. You hate public speaking."

"I could learn."

"You're five inches taller than she is."

"I was speaking metaphorically, Abbey."

"Oh. Metaphorically."

"Yes, and you've lost the point entirely."

"There was a point?"

"Forget it."

"Okay."

"And, Abbey?"

"Yeah."

"You've got a big old wad of purple chewing gum in your hair. It suits you."

A weaker woman would have folded, realizing she'd just run into her significant other's ex with a disgusting wad of gum in her hair. I, on the other hand, had no intention of wasting another second thinking about hair yanking (his), accusations (mine), and head bashing (his). I had no intention of doing any more crying over spilled milk, as Vinnie likes to say. There are a lot of cows in the world.

Damn that Mac. Three days before V-Day. Maybe the vision was wrong and I wasn't going to marry him. I was going to kill him.

We walked the few blocks to one of our favorite restaurants, Hot Tostadas, with me on autopilot and Jo leading the way. The wind pushed against our fur-trimmed parka hoods, our scarves flying behind us, and I remembered what every Fairbanksan knows: Get out of the cold before you frostbite your nose, ears, hands or toes.

As we entered Hot Tostadas, the yeasty warmth spread through me like a hot bath, relaxing away a large part of the Mac/Molly run in. Jo pulled out her cell phone as we settled into a corner table deep in the maze-like recesses of the restaurant. "I'm going to call and tell him what a slimy cave dweller he is."

I pinned her hand to the table. "No, you're not."

"Then you call."

"What would I say, Jo?"

"That he's a slimy cave dweller. Or, you could ask if he's heard about Sicilian Tactic #72, and that you're gonna do it to him if he's not careful."

"I don't remember a Sicilian Tactic #72."

"He doesn't know that, does he?"

"That's Sicilian Tactic #31: Fake 'em out."

"Whatever."

As I focused on the menu, my thoughts slid to Mac and Molly, chatting about nothing or everything, and me here with Jo. On the outside.

"Abbey. How soon do you think it'll be before Vinnie calls and asks what I was thinking, not slapping the pudding out of Molly?"

I dunked a huge tortilla chip into the avocado dip a waiter had dropped between us and rolled her words around in my head until something clicked. "You know how I hate it when guys ask, 'Are you on your period?' every time a woman gets angry or a little crazier than usual? Well, don't hate me for saying it, but Jo . . ."

"What?"

"Maybe you're P.G."

"Politically correct?"

"Expecting, Dumbo. With child. Pregnant," I said. For my own safety, I leaned back in my seat. Less chance of her snatching the remaining hair from my head.

"I know."

"You know you could be or you know you—"

"I've been thinking about getting the test. But I'm not sure I want to know. Then I'd have to figure out, do I tell Tony? Or do I jump off a cliff?"

"The usual, right?"

"It's not funny."

"I know. But it could be wonderful."

Jo would be an amazing mom. Once she got past the fear, I knew she'd be really happy. I was as sure as I know her middle name and that the first boy she kissed stuck his tongue in her mouth and made her gag. She was ten, he was twelve, and it put her off kissing for two years, but she's been making up for it ever since. "The sooner we do this, the sooner we can deal with it."

"If I buy a test, the cashier at Fred Meyer will tell the cart guy who'll tell his dad, who probably works at the university, and he'll tell one of the kids on the basketball team and then Tony'll know and I won't have a second to myself to think."

"Wait. You could buy the test for me," she said after we'd ordered and our waiter was well out of hearing range. "Then Tony would never know." As if it were the most logical solution in the world. The one little flaw being that half of Fairbanks, the half including Mac, Ben and most of my friends, would think I was baby mama.

Jo caught on quick. "It would serve Mac right."

"You think?"

"Fine, forget it."

In the end, a plan was hatched. I got Jennifer to fill in at AVA while Jo and I picked up Justine so she could buy the test. Justine doesn't care what anyone thinks.

I really admire that.

"Take the bloody test already," Justine shouted through the bathroom door. "None of us has eaten lunch. Abbey's worrying herself sick over Mac going off with that Molly—"

"I am not."

"And we're both standing out here reduced to screeching like idiots through bleeding doors."

We were back at Jo's store where we'd pasted hastily lettered signs to both doors, reading, "Closed this afternoon due to an acute case of temporary insanity." Justine's brilliant idea. Too bad Jo was being obstinate.

She slammed open the bathroom door, looking pleased with herself. "I've decided."

It seemed impossible that she would have made such a life changing decision in five minutes. And didn't her saying "I've decided" mean the test was positive? I held my breath.

"I'll take the damn test when I'm ready and I'm not ready. So live with it."

"Let's talk about something else for a while. I'm so sick of thinking about being pregnant, I don't want to hear any words that even start with a P."

I leaped in to change the subject. "Ben got a pah . . . (package? parcel? present?) delivery today. You'll never guess who from."

"Rebecca," Jo guessed.

"How'd you know?"

"You said she was showing a lot of interest in him at the bar. Who else?" She gave me a *duh* look. "What did she send?"

"A Mr. Pa . . . (Potato Head wouldn't do). One of those egg-shaped thingies you stick eyes, ears, noses, and mouths on," I said, faithfully avoiding all P words.

"So, is Mr. Potato Head a gonner, Justine?" Jo asked, ignoring her own rule.

"She stayed the execution," I said. "Now, does anyone want to go over Rebecca's purse again, 'cause I have to return it to her after I leave here."

"Like I said before, let's copy everything: her driver's license, the eBay papers, notes, receipts, phone numbers," Jo said, getting into the swing of things.

We dumped the contents of the bag on Jo's desk. Nail file, lipstick, hairbrush, eBay papers, wallet, change. Nothing new or interesting from what I could see.

Justine snatched the empty bag and rummaged through it. "Wait a sec. I think I found a hidden pocket. And there are keys inside."

"Jackpot."

The keys didn't look familiar. Not post office box keys, generic house keys or padlock keys.

"Why don't we make impressions," Jo suggested. "I might have something here that'll work."

"We could use soap," Justine offered.

"Do you have one of those art plaster kits?" I asked.

"Let's spread out," Jo said. "Justine, you take the children's section; I'll take housewares and tools. Abbey, you take arts and crafts."

Fifteen minutes later we'd scrounged together two of the three items on the list, plus a Polaroid camera for taking a snapshot, if nothing else worked. Another thirty minutes later, Justine was rubbing a blister on her thumb from holding the match too long and Jo's desk and computer were splattered with candle wax. On the bright side, we also had a reasonably accurate impression of both keys, as well as a couple of photos.

While Justine rubbed Neosporin on her sore thumb, Jo got busy scraping candle wax off her desk and I placed everything back in Rebecca's bag. I'd about finished when the back door of the shop slammed open and Tony surprised us.

"Temporary insanity?" he joked.

He snagged the back of Jo's hoodie and held her in a passionate embrace.

Justine turned a furious shade of red as we rushed to the bathroom to hide the evidence. Luckily Tony and Jo missed the Laurel and Hardy routine, because I could imagine him saying something like, "You gals having a makeup emergency?" and then Justine tripping him while I pushed. Crisis averted.

Jo's bathroom was functional at best. And made for one. Justine elbowed me in the ribs as she squeezed past me and grabbed the test off the sink. I pivoted in a circle, the only possible maneuver in the crowded space. Where to hide it? The only storage space was in the medicine cabinet or under the sink. Neither ideal locations. All Tony would have to do is look for a roll of T.P. and that would be that.

"You could hide it in the small of your back like a detective does with a gun," Justine said.

"With my luck, it would fall down my pants and come flying out right at Tony's feet."

"Well. Do you have any better ideas?"

"You could stay in here and guard it. If Tony notices you're gone, I'll say you're having a make-up emergency." I have no trouble throwing around sexist jargon when it suits my purpose.

"Fine. But don't leave me in here forever."

"I'll be back as soon as he's gone," I said and headed back toward the office, hoping Tony and Jo were done with the lovey-dovey stuff already. Uh-oh. Loud voices assailed me as I reached the hallway.

"I told you I'm not wearing that thing, Jo. Non capisce?"

"In plain English, fuck off."

"Nice, Jo."

"You agreed."

"I was kidding. Like if I said, 'I'll eat my car if the Jet's win.'"

"That's not how—"

"You're not gonna win this one, Frodo." He fingered the top button on the front of her shirt and pulled every so slightly, enough to give her a thrill. "See you at home," he said. (An invitation she couldn't refuse.)

I came around the corner as he disappeared out the back.

"Did he call you Frodo?"

"I like it," Jo said, bristling up like a prickly cat.

"Okay." Frodo isn't bad. It's more creative than Sweetie Pie. More interesting than Cupcake, unless you're a dog, that is. "I like it, too."

Jo shook her head and grabbed a Diet Coke from the mini-frig behind her desk. "That was close."

"Too close," I said, as I snagged Jo's soda and took a sip.

"We're getting better at this Sassy Sister's Investigations stuff," Jo said.

"Luckier. Speaking of which, while Tony was trying to see if you two could spontaneously combust, something occurred to me."

She nodded.

"We could make real copies of the keys. At the hardware store."

She shot me an accusatory look. "I spent an hour melting soap and wax? We're idiots. It's Justine's fault. Where is she, anyway?"

"Oh, God," I said, rushing to the bathroom. I opened the door and said, "He's gone," as if he'd left this very minute.

"So, where is it?" Jo said, peering around Justine into the bathroom, not finding the test.

"In the loo," she said. "I put it where he'd never find it." She lifted the toilet tank lid with a flourish and extracted a dripping, plastic grocery bag.

Jo took the bag, holding it between two fingers like it was a slimy fish.

"Here, let me." I pried open the bag with a fingernail and checked inside for moisture. "It looks like it survived."

"I'd love to stay and review how brilliant we all are, but I don't have time to fanny around all day," Justine said.

"Me, too. I still need to get the keys made and bring the purse back to Rebecca before she misses it.

"I'm off then. Work to do," Justine said.

Speaking of work. "Justine, that reminds me. If any pac . . . boxes arrive, have mercy on them. There's always a chance one of them could be for me."

"I'm not screwing up, Mom."

I had to work not to shout, "What happened to, the 'you don't need the cow' business? What happened to, 'marriage is a trap'?"

I really shouldn't be taking calls from my mother when I'm driving; I might accidentally on purpose drive into a light pole.

"What's going on, Mom?"

"Your grandmother called. She says Mac is the best thing since sex on the beach. So fix it, already."

If I knew what to fix, I might have a better chance.

"Gran didn't say that, Mom.

"What? You know everything, now? Besides, that ex of his isn't gonna wait for you to make up your mind. Put two and two together, Abbey. You lose."

I took a corner faster than was technically safe, but my mom does that to me.

"You gotta get rid of that Ben person," she demanded. "He's ruining everything. You need to figure out what you want, Abigail. Just remember, you're your mother's daughter."

Scary thought. I stared at the red light shining above me on the empty, ice fog filled street and wanted to bang my head against the steering wheel. Sometimes my mother has that effect on me, too.

"Straighten up, Bunny."

After Mom's words of wisdom, I needed a hot bath and a margarita, because I was more confused than ever. The good news? As a counselor, I know that being confused is a good thing. When you're confused, it means you're open to seeing things in a new way. Ready to take chances. Make changes.

If only I knew what they were going to be.

Chapter 16

If necessity is the mother of invention, then I needed to create a whole new tactic thing. The Vinnie Diversionary Tactics. More specifically, ways to avoid Vinnie-related urges to pull my hair out, to move to Fiji, where they don't have cell phones, or to drive myself into light poles. Beginning with Vinnie Diversionary Tactic #1: Use Caller ID Stupid. It's there for a reason.

Vinnie Diversionary Tactic #2: Always assume the worst, so as not to be surprised by unadulterated and unprovoked Mom attacks. And of course, Vinnie Diversionary Tactic #3: Try to remember, Vinnie thinks she's saying it for your own good. Really. She may not be trying to reduce you to tears, but just in case, don't give her the satisfaction.

I fumed as I sat at the green light, dreaming up Vinnie Diversionary Tactics, until, finally, the Lincoln behind me, driven by an elderly gentleman wearing a fuzzy, beaver hat and heavy Mr. Magoo glasses, honked. Okay. Which way? Straight ahead would take me to Merona Air, where I could do what I was supposed to be doing—digging up dirt or trouble or whatever. South meant Rebecca's hotel. Maybe I could persuade a bored maid to let me into her room on some brilliantly subtle and creative guise so I could snoop.

Despite all of my Vinnie Diversionary Tactics, I couldn't seem to quiet the recording of Mom's voice in my head.

I jammed the steering wheel to the left, cutting off a string of cars in the next lane. One crude hand gesture later (the other driver, not me) and I was flying across town, as if I only had three days to live.

I'd had enough of Mom, Rebecca and Merona. Men, too. Enough

already!

Home in record time, I took the stairs in twos, dropped my pack on the entryway floor, stopped in the kitchen long enough to fling the refrigerator door open and see that my choices for something icy-cold came down to ginger ale and milk. I hastily poured the soda into a well-worn jelly jar and pounded the stairs to the third floor, barely spilling a drop before I reached my bathroom, with its dual shower heads, carpets as soft as silk, one large bay window above the Jacuzzi, and a discreet doorway leading to a separate room reserved for the toilet and one small hand-washing sink.

I pushed through the door, about to set my ginger ale on the closest horizontal surface, when the shower door slid open and Ben stepped out. All soapy and smiling.

I dropped the soda and screamed like a school girl. Hey. Don't judge. You would have, too. For one, Ben was supposed to be out solving profound and telling questions about human behavior and capitalism. Not standing in front of me looking like a Greek God, making no attempt whatsoever to grab for a towel (albeit, tucked away in a hand-made grass basket across the room) as he should have been. Not standing in front of me. His interest and intent showing.

Don't tell me you wouldn't look, too. Never mind. While I was taking him in like he was a chocolate éclair, Ben was checking me out like I was his favorite toy.

If he moved one inch closer, I might just scream again. To save myself. My insides were mush and the tingling I was feeling down in Rio was nothing good girls talk about. In fact, it had nothing to do with being a good girl at all. I couldn't drag my eyes away. Luckily I wasn't moving. Luckily I hadn't ripped off my own clothes and lunged for him. Not that it wasn't right up there on the top of my To Do Before You Die list. I was pretty sure it would be great. I could almost feel his hand moving slowly up the inside of my slightly parted thighs when he said, "Abbey, would you please hand me a towel?"

"What? I mean. How? I. What?"

"Abbey."

"Where? No. When. What? God." Shut up, Abbey. "Ben." That was better. "Don't come any closer." Not good. "I mean, I thought you were out. Working." I needed to clear my mind and this wasn't helping one bit. Rats. "You need to. I mean, I need to." Turn around, Abbey and shut up, for God's sake. "Where's . . . okay, never mind."

I turned away. To recover my sanity. And a towel.

"Towel?" I said, as I tossed one over my shoulder.

Ben came up behind me. I sensed him before I felt him. So close the hairs on the back of my neck and arms went crazy. So close I could feel his breath. So close droplets of water touched my hair. I turned and that was all it took. Our lips met and I was back in that space where all senses overflow. One hand went to my jeans, ready to shuck them, along with any semblance of modesty, when I could have sworn I heard the front door slam downstairs.

Ignore it, I told myself. And I did. The kiss deepened, his intention hardened, and I definitely needed to get those jeans off. Now. I think a groan or a moan escaped my lips and I pulled him closer to me, if that was even possible. And God, it felt good.

I definitely heard a door this time. The refrigerator. Despite my desire set on go, my mind on numb, my body on fire, self-preservation mode clicked in. I moved back, wishing we could stay this way all day, before I made the only decent choice I could. I turned the doorknob, to make my second escape of the day. Third, really. If we're including the Mac and Molly incident earlier.

The door didn't budge. Steam from the shower must have swollen it shut. Either that or, in my haste, clumsiness or brain fog, I'd forgotten how to work the damn door knob. But that didn't really matter, did it? I couldn't get the blasted door open and conceivably that noise downstairs was Mac. In the kitchen right this very minute.

Then, confirming the worst, Mac's voice drifted up from the bottom of the staircase. "Abbey? Are you home?"

Maybe if I didn't answer, he'd think I was out. 'Cause why would I be home in the middle of the day? My car. Damn. He'd know I was home by my car, and it was only a matter of time before he'd be up here for the living proof. I could play sick. Groan a few times through the closed bathroom door. But Ben's new rental car was down there, too. Eventually he'd figure out that Ben wasn't in any of the other rooms and by process of elimination, he'd put two and two together and I'd be screwed. I may have been lusting after Ben seconds ago, but I wasn't quite ready to produce the video: Abbey does Ben. Front page news.

"Abbey." The voice was coming from the first landing, now, and the door still wouldn't budge for all my twisting, pulling and head banging.

I sank to the floor and mumbled, "I'm lost. Screwed, really," forgetting that Ben was still there and minutes ago I'd been well on my way to at least one of the above.

If Vinnie were here, she's say, "Make up your mind." But screw Vinnie. (Vinnie Diversionary Tactic #4.)

"Abbey?"

Closer. Closer. Doom eminent, I looked up at Ben, now towel-clad, a wicked grin firmly in place. Totally gorgeous, too. Maybe I could just lay down and die, gloriously caught between two delicious men. Not such a horrible way to go.

Out of the blue I was on my feet. Miraculously the door was open; Ben came in for a kiss so intense, I swear, I lost my balance. Then, in a flash, I was on the other side of the closed bathroom door trying to stay upright, as Mac hit the third floor landing.

"There you are. I've been trying to reach you all afternoon," he said as I collapsed into his arms. Not in a prima-donna-Freudian-I'm-too-delicate-to-handle-stress way—more like in an I'm-tripping-over-my-own-two-feet sort of way.

All I could think was: Don't come out of the bathroom, Ben. Stay in there. My new mantra. Stay. Stay. Stay.

"Something tells me you're up to something, Abbey." Mac set me on my feet, breaking my concentration. Mantras require concentration, that much I know is true.

Stay in the bathroom. Stay in the bathroom. Stay. Stay. Stay. Stay. Stay.

"Abbey?" Mac gazed at me the way he sometimes stares at the New York Times crossword puzzle.

Newer mantra. Get Mac away from the bathroom. I grabbed his wrist and pulled in the direction of the stairs, aimed a mental "stay" at the bathroom door for good measure, and led Mac down to the relative safety of the living room.

"Ab, where's Ben?"

Okay. Not so safe after all.

"Who?" Quick thinking!

A grin spread up from Mac's mouth until it reached his eyes. "You know. Ben."

I shook my head, shrugged, turned one hand up.

"His car's in the yard."

"Hmmm. He probably went off with some eighteen-year-old university research bunny slash hanger-oner."

When he intensified the New York Times puzzle look, I added, "In her Miata, top down. Have to be cool, even at 40 below zero."

This time, he was the one to shake his head. Mac's learned early in life that all good things come to those who wait. "I've been looking for you. To explain about lunch."

I'd just had a close encounter of the juicy kind upstairs with Ben, so who was I to criticize a little lunch date? I held up a hand. "Don't," meaning, it's not necessary, but which I could see from the deep ridges lining his forehead, he took as, "Don't bother trying to explain away your shitty behavior, you dog."

"I deserve that. When I saw you and Jo, I took advantage of the situation and let you think Molly and I were together."

Okay, news.

"I ran into her outside. I'd finally run out of excuses. It was just going to be five minutes and a cup of coffee. That's it."

"My mom says you want her back."

He broke into a laugh, this close to being a snort. He reached out and rested the back of his hand on my forehead. I pushed it away. "What are you doing?" I asked, even though I knew.

"Checking for fever. You're listening to Vinnie, now?"

"Well. She says Molly's willing to give you what you want and apparently men like that in a girl."

"I suppose the men who wants girls do, but, Ab, I want a woman, not a little girl.

"Easy for you to say. My mom says—"

He placed a hand across my mouth to keep the words from tumbling out. "I swear, Abigail Vertuccio, if you quote Vinnie one more time, I'm throwing you over my shoulder and taking you to the hospital for an emergency Vinniectomy." I opened my mouth, and before I could speak, he added, "I mean it."

I pushed his hand aside for the second time and noticed his wristwatch. "Don't you have a flight pretty soon?"

"Damn," he said, before making for the door, but not before getting in a quick peck on the corner of my mouth.

"Go. You'll be late." I waved him off.

"I love you," he said, quickly, and was gone just as fast.

Saved by some weird twist of fate. Then his words sank in. He loves me.

I am such a shit.

Before Ben could appear downstairs, looking all edible in his Ben-smelling jeans and T-shirt (or in his altogether) and turn me back into mush, I headed out the door. This time, all business.

Thinking about Mac loving me and Ben's nakedness was definitely counterproductive, at least for the time being. I was going to have to play my hand one day soon, but today was not that day. I hopped into my car with every intention of steering in the direction of the investigation, truth, justice and the American Way, when I realized that, damn it all, I really did need to talk with Ben. To find out what he'd been up to all day, to tell him what I'd been up to. About the key and about my plan to go by Merona Air on a pretense and snoop around.

But there was no way we could talk here.

After ten minutes ruminating on how I was going to keep my self-respect and pants on if I went back in there, Ben knocked on the car door.

"That was close," was all he said as he slid into the seat beside me.

Did he mean, Mac finding us in the bathroom? Or did he mean, "That was close. We almost did it?"

True in either case. So, I nodded.

"But it worked out for the best, didn't it?"

Did he mean, it worked out for the best, because we would have regretted acting like Free Love Barbie and Ken? Or did he mean, it worked out for the best because Mac didn't catch us and we escaped? Or that it worked out for the best because our relationship wasn't going anywhere, so why start something we had no intention of finishing?

"Didn't it?" he asked.

Yes and no. Time will tell. Beats me. "So, why were you in the shower in the middle of the day, anyway," I asked. Sicilian Tactic #2: Change the subject.

A sheepish look crossed his face. Ice crystals clung to his eyebrows and hair. I started the engine and turned up the heat, waiting for his reply.

"I had a close encounter with a boxer and a rosebush."

I didn't recall seeing any bleeding wounds, gaping holes or long angry scratches on any part of him while he was nude and open for inspection. Although, my attention was drawn to areas where any chance of rosebush contact was minimal, unless he'd been taking a leak on said rosebush and/

or boxer. Unlikely in February. At least to anyone from Fairbanks.

"So, you were peeing on a rosebush and the owner of the house—a boxer—pushed you into the bushes?"

He didn't bother to glorify it with a look. (I would have.) "The boxer was a canine. The rosebush was under Merona's living room window."

"So, I was close."

"Everything was fine, until someone let Bruno out." He cocked his head and squinched his eyes in a smart ass expression I took to mean, "Get it now?"

I gave him a blank look in return.

His face turned hot red and he turned away. "When Bruno found me crouching under the window, he licked me into the rosebushes."

I snorted a laugh that made him cross his arms over his chest. I swallowed a second snort, while choking back gigantic belly laughs. Not easy.

"It's possible he mistook me for a rosebush."

"And peed on you?" I couldn't help myself. The laugh came without thinking. Spit flew from my mouth, inadvertently hitting Ben in the face. Truly, I was trying to be good. It's just that I could see it. The look of surprise on Ben's face turning to apprehension as Bruno the boxer rushed toward him like a dieter to a donut. If I didn't stop laughing soon, I was going to wet my pants and then who'd be laughing?

"We should march right over and tell Merona that he needs to train his dog."

The laughter did accomplish one thing, besides bringing out Ben's dark side. I was no longer obsessing about Ben up against my jeans. The whole The-Dog-Peed-On-Me story took care of that scenario.

"Careful, Abigail. Your time may soon be at hand."

Right. Whatever. Time to get busy. I shot him a, "You coming or staying?" look. The one my mother liked to use on me when I was too slow out the door. Vinnie's get-moving routine usually involved a lot of foot tapping, one hip swung out as far as it would go and The Look. I could have tapped my toe on the gas petal, but it was unlikely he'd have heard. And sitting didn't cut it for the hip out part. But The Look worked. "You want to ride along? I have to drop off Rebecca's purse."

"Let's go Mercutio."

"If I'm Mercutio, that makes you Romeo and we're in big trouble. As far as I know, they both came to bad ends."

He thought about it. He had his hat off and was messing up his freshly washed and combed hair, still damp and smelling like ripe peaches and peppermint. "We're not coming to a bad end, Abbey. I'm certain of that," he said, taking my mittened hand in his.

I revved the engine, reclaimed my hand long enough to shift into first and moved the car down the winding, snow-packed driveway and onto the highway, heading for the next leg of our journey. The rest, I'd deal with later.

The ride was companionable in its silence, each of us lost in thought. I couldn't begin to imagine what his thoughts were. Me. I was back on Ben's Bruno adventure. As we reached the turn off to Metro Field, I elbowed Ben through his heavy parka.

"Ben. Why were you at Merona's today? I mean, besides peeping in his window and seducing his dog."

The crinkles in his forehead deepened before he looked over at me with a question in his eyes. "I was waiting for you."

"Me?" Now it was my turn to be puzzled.

"This is the first you're hearing about our meeting, isn't it?"

"What meeting? Don't tell me you had another psychic event, because you're not—" Then I stopped myself when he waved a plain white envelope in front of me. I pulled over to get a better look, and when I was certain I hadn't parked in front of Jo's Aunt Millie's house or the house of the person who Zambonies the ice at the university (Tony's buddy), or Gran's mail carrier or in the middle of a covert Alaska State Trooper operation or in front of any house even remotely connected with Vinnie or the old town Fairbanks gossip network, I took the note and read it quickly.

"I didn't write this," I said, after looking it over a dozen times.

"I know that, now."

"I never asked you to meet me at Merona's house." I repeated.

"I know." He pushed one hand through his hair as if that would solve the problem or at the very least clarify things a bit.

A light bulb came on. "Who would want you to go to Merona's? Or maybe the question should be, who wanted you away from what you were doing? Wait. Where were you?" I asked, more accusation than inquiry.

"At university. Nothing to do with Rebecca or Merona at all."

"This doesn't make sense." I looked up and down the street as if the answer was waiting for me on the icy sidewalks and snow-covered yards.

"Unless it was a trap. Maybe Merona and Rebecca think you're onto them, so they made sure you'd be at his house at a certain time. Oh. My. God. To take care of you." The very idea of Rebecca or Merona, or anyone for that matter, hurting Ben made me crazy. Well, we'd see about that.

"Then they let the dog out to wee on me as a warning?"

"Ha. Ha. Wait and see, Mr. Romance in a Rosebush."

"Seriously—"

"Wait, who gave you the note?" I turned it over again, looking for clues.

"I found it on my windshield."

"Odd."

"Abbey, if Merona wanted to hurt me, he wouldn't send me to his own house. That would be daft."

The windows of the car were well on their way to fogging over and I flipped on the windshield wipers. In case someone did see us, they wouldn't be able to add steaming-up car windows during an afternoon tryst to their list of things to gossip about. At least not today.

"I may have sussed out part of the problem," Ben continued, drawing my attention back from steam, lust and quiet places with no witnesses. He slid out of the car, reached across the car hood and tugged on a tiny corner of something that apparently had slipped down between the window and hood, snagged it, then jumped back into the car, brushing ice and snow off the damp envelope before handing it to me.

I held it by one corner and said, "If only we could lift the fingerprints."

Ben said, "Do you have cellotape? Any kind of powder?"

Brilliant idea. "Check the glove box," I said, forgetting about what he was about to unleash: registration and insurance (miraculously on top), scissors, sunglasses (only slightly scratched, one arm bent), baggies, pepper spray (1994 vintage), a half-eaten Milky Way (slightly white around the edges. Hmm, still good), tissues (some new, some questionable), one lipstick (Hot Mama), and, voilà, clear packing tape.

He continued digging, past a pair of pliers, a mini-first aid kit (three Band Aids and a packet of cream), seven pennies. No powder. "What say we just rip her open?"

"There's one more place to look." I leaned as far back as I could, fumbled under the back seat until I found a cosmetics case from my last trip to the beach (well, the river—optimistically called a beach). My summer kit had all the basics: sunblock, chewing gum, lotion, cards, deodorant and an unopened tin of baby powder.

"Try this."

Ben had the good grace to refrain from commenting on the sheer volume of junk I had tucked into every available crevice in my car. (Who knew when I might need that half-eaten Milky Way?) Instead, he opened the envelope, careful to hold the note by the edges, and confirmed that it said what we knew it would. "Ab, meet me at Merona's house ASAP. Love, Ben.

He held the note as I sprinkled the fine powder over the surface, brushed it off, then proceeded to lay strips of tape neatly across the paper in rows. I couldn't wait to see if it worked. I pulled back one of the pieces of tape until it came free and held it up to the light. "Holy Christmas. It works! I can't believe it. I see a fingerprint. Well, half of one. Ben, it worked." I hugged him for dear life, dumping the open baby powder in his lap. "It really worked!"

Somehow my lips were this close to the corner of his lips. Our eyes met. I breathed in peppermint and peaches again. If we kissed here, the whole town would know. I was sure of it. Even with the windows completely iced over.

He pulled back the fraction of an inch I needed to regain my equilibrium and smiled a smile that settled in my soul—one my heart recognized as true happiness. "You were right," he said.

About the kissing?

"It worked."

The note. Right. I pushed back into my own seat while he brushed baby powder from his pants, creating a fragrant cloud around us. Then he carefully placed the evidence into one of the sandwich bags from the glove compartment. "We're getting pretty good at this."

Now all we had to do was get samples of Rebecca's and Merona's fingerprints and we'd be all set. Not as hard as you might think. People are always touching things, aren't they? We could steal a fingerprint-laden coffee cup, like in the movies. (Can you lift fingerprints from take-out cups?) I wedged the baggie into my purse, and without warning, the world spun around into another vision.

I've had some strange visions, but this one threw me. Odd times weird. There was Molly, all done up in 50s housewife attire, pearls included, up to her elbows in Betty Crocker recipes and trays of cookies. Enough to feed an army. Her eyes desperately gleaming like alternate-universe Donna Reed.

I opened my eyes to the slow rhythm of Ben's breathing, as he waited patiently, one hand on my knee, relaxed. No worries. No questions.

"That was freaky," I said, but didn't bother to elucidate. It wasn't worth thinking about, what with the vision clearly being a product of some subconscious, unresolved, maniacal obsession about Mac and Molly, and how she, unlike me, was just waiting to captivate (or was it capture?) him by giving him everything he ever wanted. Hence, the metaphorical cookies.

"Abbey, why don't you let me drive?"

Why not? Who knew when or if the cookie vision would strike again.

We did the over and under routine, ultimately crawling all over each other on the way to our new seats, and for my part, getting a pleasant little surge along the way, even though I was now a hundred percent certain I'd be hearing all about this in one way or another, probably sooner than later, from a friend of a friend of a friend, who heard it from . . . well, you know.

The phone rang. I wrestled it out of my parka pocket, hit talk and before I could answer, got an earful from Jo. "If you were going on a stakeout, you should have invited me along. I could have helped, you know."

I covered the mouthpiece and whispered, "Jo," even though she was talking loudly enough for everyone in the neighborhood to hear.

No use defending the indefensible, I told her about the duplicate notes and finished with the hugely successful fingerprinting operation. "I've got the fingerprints right here!" I shouted.

"Shut up," she said. "That only works on some hokey TV show."

"Tell her, Ben," I said before I remembered that if she didn't already know about Ben being with me, she didn't need to hear it now.

"Your new partner? More fun on a stakeout, is he? You can get in a little make out time when things get slow. At least, that's what I hear. Maybe I should officially resign from Sassy Sisters. Or is it a done deal?"

Oh. God. Was she winding up or down?

The scenery whizzed by as Ben steered us closer to the airfield, with Jo rattling on and on about every perceived slight done to her by yours truly over the years. I was about to interrupt her diatribe (Somehow. I hadn't figured out how exactly), when she abruptly did an about-face and ended the call. "Gotta go. Tony's back."

When we arrived, I rubbed my sore ear, slung Rebecca's purse over one shoulder and slid out of the car, nearly dinging Merona's Landrover in the process. Next to it was a cherry red Miata. Rebecca's rental?

"Not her style. There," Ben said, as he pointed to a deep gray Volvo.

"Try that one."

This called for a little investigating. I needed to break in, that's what I needed. "Ben, be the look out, okay?"

"Consider it done."

He took his post at the corner of the building, keeping the front door of Merona Air in view. I should have gotten right to the job at hand, but instead I watched him as he bent to tie his already-tied shoe. Next he did a pocket check for not-lost keys. Then he dropped his keys and took way more time to collect them than was necessary. Basic Spy School 101, but very sweet.

The car was a bust. I was about to break out the fingerprint kit, when something cold and reeking of snowball smacked me on the back of my head. I straightened, closed the Volvo door quietly and arrived at Ben's side half a minute before Rebecca drove around the corner in a hardtop Jeep, skidded into a parking spot and jumped out.

I hissed in Ben's ear, "Volvo, eh?"

"Ben. Abigail. Lovely to see you." Swear to God, she purred. "Are you two here to see Frank?"

"No, I'm Dorothy, here to see the freakin' wizard," I whispered into Ben's collar.

"Don't ever think—" he whispered, but I didn't hear the rest because Merona saw us, bounded from behind the busy counter of the air service and hustled across the lobby, "Vertuccio. You come by to see how the big boys play?" Then he added something that sounded like, "Har, har," to put a polite twist on the cutting remark and stretched out a hand to Ben.

"Heard you were having a going-out-of-business sale," I sniped. "Did I get that wrong, Frank?" Pompous ass. With that red bulbous nose and soft middle he reminded me of Bad Santa. One too many Heinekens, and I say this not out of spite or bitterness.

He held his hands up, like I was the sheriff and he was the bandit.

"What can I do for you today, Sweetheart."

I cringed and bit back a sharp retort. I slid Rebecca's purse off my shoulder and was about to hand it over to her when I noticed a corner of the baggie with the lifted fingerprints sticking out. I palmed the bag, but not before Rebecca caught me. "What was that?"

"Your purse. I accidentally picked it up the other night," I stuttered, making the truth seem like a lie. "I realized I had the wrong one when I went to pay for my gas today."

She reached for the proffered bag. "I meant, what did you remove and put in your pocket just now?"

My fingernails suddenly needed attention and I fiddled with a cuticle and dropped the purse, scattering the contents across the lobby floor. An errant tampon rolled past the line of customers waiting at the counter. A lipstick made it as far as the front door. The eBay receipts lay strewn across my shoes. (Sicilian Tactic #30: Distract them, before someone ends up dead.) I stooped to gather them up, but Rebecca got there first. (Me, I would have gone for the tampon.)

"Are you into eBay, Rebecca?" I asked, donning a nonchalant tone I didn't remotely feel.

Merona bent over her shoulder, looking at the papers, but Rebecca had the receipts back in her purse in seconds.

She eased a hand through Ben's arm. "Ben, we really must catch up. I'm dying for a decent cup of tea before my aerobics class. Frank and Abigail don't need us here," she said. "Frank, we'll be back in an hour," like it was a fait accompli.

Ben did a visual check to see how I felt about it. I shrugged. Who knew what he'd find out.

Right, and I'm Saint Dodo Head, Patron Saint of Screw Ups.

And by the way. Rats. I hadn't told Ben about the key. Too late now. As Ben and Rebecca slipped away, an impatient customer pounded his fist on the counter. "My flight is scheduled to leave in fifteen minutes, not in an hour. Can't you people get anything straight?"

The young woman at the counter—Birdie, her name tag read, all of 5'2" and 90 pounds tops—took a step back before reassuring him the flight would be leaving right on time. In one hour.

I would have suggested he take his business elsewhere. Oh yeah, that's what happened last year when he pulled the same routine on me at AVA. Birdie, on the other hand, offered a sincere apology, which did nothing to placate him.

Finally Merona stepped in. "John, a pleasure to see you again."

"Merona. When I threw my business your way, I thought I would be getting professional service. I see I was wrong." Mr. Obnoxious waved toward Birdie. "This one here should be serving burgers and fries, not handling important business transactions."

"I'm sorry my girl got your departure time wrong, John. It won't happen again."

Enough, already. I was this close to Sicilian Tactic #47: Tell them where to go, when Birdie took a breath, shut down the computer, then carefully unpinned her red and white Merona Air name tag and placed it on the counter. To Mr. Obnoxious she said, "I don't know how your mama raised you, sir, but my mama always says, 'Don't let no man reduce you to his level,' and I don't plan on disappointing my mama," before disappearing behind the Employees Only door, slamming it soundly behind her.

You go, Birdie, was all I could say.

"Merona, what are you going to do about my flight," Mr. Obnoxious demanded, oblivious to the fact that Merona was now left to handle the flight single-handedly.

That didn't stop a heavy flow of passengers, loaded down with packages and bags, waiting to be checked in. From the looks of it, Merona was about to explode.

"Merona," the customer insisted, "what about my flight?"

I wanted to smack both of them upside their pointy heads—especially after Merona's, "Did you come by to see how the big boy's play" remark. On the other hand, if I offered to help, I'd have access to his computer. Would any bona fide spy let an opportunity like that slip away?

"Frank, why don't I help out until you can get someone to fill in," I said, as I slipped behind the counter as if I belonged there.

He took in the mounting chaos, clearly torn between wanting to tell me where to stick it and the truth—he needed me. Wordlessly he booted up the computer Birdie had switched off before her hasty departure. I peered around him in time to see him peck out his user name, Merona Air, and password: "Unbeatable". We'd see about that.

He made a quick announcement to the customers, which boiled down to, "Keep your pants on," then gave me a crash course in the Merona Air reservation system. Easy, being the same one we used at AVA.

His office phone rang as we were finishing up. "Go on, Frank. I've got it," I said.

Minutes later the crowd thinned out. With no sign of Merona or a replacement, I peeked through the crack in the office door to ensure he was still on the phone, then hit the keyboard. File. Open. My Documents. At least a hundred files came up. I scrolled down, past personnel files, flight regulations and shipping manifests. At this rate it would take all day, which wasn't an option. Any minute now Merona would be coming through that door.

Whoops. Merona slammed the phone down. No sooner had I closed the files when he came up behind me, powdering me with sugar as he waved a half-eaten donut in one hand.

"You're off the hook, Vertuccio. My graveyard shift girl agreed to come in early. She should be pulling up in five."

No, "Thanks for your help." And, of course, no mention of what a jerk he'd been to Birdie and how he deserved everything he got.

I gathered my parka, mittens and purse (this time the right one) and headed for the door.

"I heard Jo's niece is looking for a part-time job. She worked at Bradley Air in Anchorage. I can have her call you if you want," I offered, all neighborly like.

"Sure, have her give me a call."

I jumped in my car and sped off. Not so bad for a day of amateur sleuthing. Because now I had a way into Merona Air—if Jen agreed to a little espionage in the line of duty. And best of all, I got the password to his computer. And who knew what Ben was getting out of Rebecca.

As Jo would say: Score!

Chapter 17

The feeling of elation was short-lived, replaced by the same old worries: Ben and Mac. And what was up with my two best friends? Justine smashing everything in sight; Jo playing chicken with Tony. I needed help. But who to ask? Clearly not Jo, Justine or Ben. Not Vinnie, for obvious reasons.

I slammed on the brakes as a larger-than-life Hummer sent me swerving toward a ditch. Damn, I hate it when people drive their too-expensive SUVs, phone plastered to their ears, acting like they couldn't possibly waste the three minutes it takes to drive from the library to the post office without multi-tasking. Okay, so I do it, too. Seems I have a whole set of double standards these days. Like, I get to eat the last peppermint patty in the bag, but I'd better not find that bag empty. I can leave dirty dishes in the sink all week, but I don't want a boyfriend who does. On a larger scale, I can have a nearly naked encounter in the bathroom with Ben, but Mac better not be having lunch with Molly.

Before all this blasted insight came over me, I'd been about to whip out my cell phone (still driving) and call Ben to find out what happened between him and Rebecca. (I mean, what he found out from Rebecca.) Maybe I'd go with Sicilian Tactic #54: Act like you know exactly what you're doing even when you don't have a clue. Then there was always Vinnie Vertuccio Mandate #1: Eat the whole cake. For crying out loud, life's not a damn wedding rehearsal.

And speaking of weddings. Note to self: Remember to keep far, far away from Mac, despite his blurting out the L word (especially after his blurting out the L word), despite my guilt over lustful scenes of the Ben variety. Because late last night, while I was tucked into bed, innocently minding my own business, the Abbey Meets Her End vision hit me.

I was floating through time in a dress only fairies could have produced: all black, except for when the light shimmered over it and it turned deep violet. Woven entirely of delicate ribbons with silver and gold thread. Not a bit of white fluff, or lace in the entire spaghetti-strapped, up-to-the-thigh confection. Completely scary.

I was smart enough to know I'd better not mention the not-a-scrap-of-white-in-it wedding dress vision to Jo, or she'd stop believing I was in serious danger of matrimonicide in three days. And I could not afford to lose my an ally in this battle. I really couldn't.

I had my cell phone in hand, ready to bite the bullet and dial Ben, despite the latest wedding vision being on replay, when suddenly there was a loud crunch and I was slammed forward into complete darkness.

The road from Merona Air to AVA is sometimes lonely and deserted; other times it resembles a speedway. Today I wasn't alone. Someone was holding my wrist, hopefully checking for signs of life and not there to steal my Magic 8 Ball watch. A warm, concerned voice spoke, but when I attempted to open my eyes and focus on the face connected to the voice, a mysterious, powdery substance floated down from my eyelashes and crumbled on my tongue, choking me. Donut dust?

"Can you tell me your name?"

I choked up some dust and croaked. "I don't think so."

"Good. What is it?"

I thought it over. Someone was shaking my shoulder. "What year is it?"

"Tuesday."

"Good. Are you married?"

"No." Wait a minute.

"Good. Do you think you can stand up if I help you out of the car?"

I was still on, "Are you married?" I was beginning to make sense of things. The powdery stuff? Air bag. My rescuer flirting with me when I was half dead? No. Probably wanted to know who he could call to take me off his hands.

"What happened?"

He shook his head quickly. "Looks like a hit-and-run."

An Alaska State Trooper took his place, followed right behind by a way-too-loud ambulance and a couple of guys dressed in white, looking like they should have been driving a nut house van. A lot of fuss for nothing. So maybe I had closed my eyes briefly after he'd said "hit-and-run," but I was sure there were no major breaks, no debilitating sprains or cracked skulls to speak of. Lucky for me the Troopers didn't take me away and put me in with the rest of the terminally stupid. I blame myself. For being on the phone and not paying attention, mostly.

I was still covered with powdery residue, my head throbbing, when I arrived at AVA an hour later than I'd intended, hoping I could slip in without anyone noticing my new look.

"What in bloody hell happened to you?" Justine shouted the second I stepped into the (fortunately) empty lobby. "You look like you fell into the dust bin."

I must have been slow with a comeback, because Justine's look softened; she rushed over and eased my dusty parka off my shoulders before any words could make it from my throat to my tongue. I didn't put up a fuss as she led me to a chair and shoved a cup of hot coffee in my hand.

She peered into my eyes and repeated her question in a soft voice. "What happened, Abbey?"

"Air bag. I'm fine. Really."

"You look like dog's dinner." Back to the Justine I know and love.

"Thanks."

"No. Actually, you do," she said, pressing the undrunk coffee on me.

"Really, thanks. A hit-and-run and now a visit from the fashion police. Go figure."

"When you say 'hit'?"

"A. Car. Hit. My. Car. And ran away."

She raised her fist, ready for a fight. "Sodding bastards. How could they?" She felt my head for signs of fever. Not a usual side effect of traffic run-ins, but sweet.

"I'm fine." She pulled one of my eyelids down and stared into my eye while I swatted her hand away. "I'm fine."

I moved to escape her motherly ministrations, half-heartedly, but found the effort not worth the pain. Growing up in Vinnieland, it felt good to be babied, actually.

"Lucky them, I wasn't there. I would have smashed the—"

"You would be covered with fluffy dust, too. It happened so fast."

"Who would do this?" She was pacing now. At some point, she picked up her hammer and was dropping its head into one hand, over and over. She spun around and pointed the hammer at me. "It's you messing in this business with Ben." Thud, thud, went the hammer. "Someone doesn't like it." Thud, thud, thud. "They're sending you a message."

I rolled my eyes. Ouch! "Justine, you've been watching too many 'Murder She Wrote' reruns. No one is out to get me." I shot her a big grin (double ouch) to let her know she was taking things way too seriously. "Besides, I haven't found anything. Zip. Nada. Zero. So—"

"But do they know that?" she countered with an ah-ha look.

"They? There's no they, Justine."

"Then why are you running around spying on Rebecca and Merona? Why did we spend hours copying a key for no reason?"

I sighed. I was sighing a lot these days. "You know why. I told Sam I would."

"And I'm the bloody Queen."

"Are you calling me a liar?" I squinted, giving her the best Vinnie look I could muster. Not my best effort, because even my eyebrows were starting to hurt.

"Lying to yourself, I think."

"Oh, no. The key. I forgot to tell Ben about the key. I was just dialing him when—"

I stopped myself too late.

"You were ringing Ben? Driving? If you have a death wish, I can think of easier ways."

I tried to ignore the hammer she was waving around at me. "I need to tell Ben about the key."

"What key?" Jaye came in through the hanger door, took one look at me and added, "I'll take a half-dozen powered and a half-dozen glazed."

Justine elbowed him in the ribs. "It's not a joke, Jaye. Someone is getting tired of her poking about in their business, and now someone hit her."

I took a cleansing breath. "Hit-and-run."

Jaye dropped the smile in a flash. "That's nothing to take lightly, Ab. Justine could be right." Behind his back, she apparently couldn't resist shooting me a nanny-nanny look. Very mature. "What do you remember?"

"Nothing."

"All right. What were you up to today that could have given them cause to worry?"

I frowned and added a shrug for good measure. "I helped Jo hide her pregnancy kit. Tony could have found out and got mad I was butting in."

"Jo's pregnant?"

Oops! I should just keep my mouth shut when I'm concussed. "False alarm," I lied.

Justine kicked me in my rapidly swelling ankle. "Ouch!"

"What else?" Jaye asked.

"Well, I did snoop through Rebecca's purse and find what could be considered incriminating evidence, and then I returned the purse to her today and I don't know how, maybe she's obsessive compulsive, but she noticed I'd been snooping."

When he looked at me like any idiot would have burned the evidence and scattered the ashes over the Chena River, I added, "Bad idea, huh?" He nodded. "Then I got Merona's computer password and opened up one of two of his files."

"A regular Charlie's Angel," Justine said.

"Anyone else want to get you?" Jaye asked, innocently enough.

"Well, Mac. But I don't think he'd try to kill me."

"Might. If he knew what was good for him," Justine added.

"Is it safe to say the motherly Justine has left the building?" I directed to Jaye.

A smile crept into the corners of his mouth and he squashed it like a box of candy on Justine's desk. I knew who's side he was on. Had to be.

"If you'd just stayed away from That Ben, none of this would have happened," Justine insisted.

I touched her arm. "Justine, I'll be more careful. Very careful."

"Promise. On your mother's life."

Too easy. "I promise."

It was only after I'd sworn six times I'd be good that I noticed random bits and pieces of metal and plastic all over the counter.

"A portable DVD player, and I'm assuming a charmingly romantic photo montage of their many happy times together," Justine answered my unspoken question.

"Good thing Mac's a saint," I said, hiding how good it felt to have her on my side.

"Good thing it wasn't Molly's head," she countered.

"You're an angel, Justine."

"And you're mental. I don't know why Mac bothers, frankly."

Okay, enough already. I hoisted myself up and propelled my dusty butt toward the door, forgot my coat and came back. "Gotta go." Then left again before Justine could remind me of all the reasons I should hang onto Mac like a tick on a moose, because I knew every single one. But then something clicked. Why should I be the one who had to hang on? Maybe he was gonna have to hang on to me.

When I was far enough away from AVA so Justine couldn't see me and pull a full-on hissy fit, I parked and dialed Ben's number. The phone rang as I considered Justine's theory. If, and I do mean if, someone intentionally hit my car, I may have stumbled onto something. But what? Maybe we left bits of wax in the crevices of Rebecca's key. Or maybe she really is obsessive compulsive and she noticed the receipts were out of order.

Of course, could be Merona had a system to warn him when employees snooped in his computer files. That would be bad.

Where was Ben anyway? I hung up and my phone immediately rang.

"Ben?" I answered, anxious to hear his voice.

"Mac."

"Rats," I said and then to cover up my mistake, rambled on about being in an accident, about Justine's theory, about SUV-driving-car-phone-talking lunatics, and smashed DVD machines. I'm pretty sure I ended with, "I'm going home, 'cuz I'm covered in donut dust."

I guess Mac had heard enough, because he said, "Meet you there," and hung up.

Double and triple rats.

Chapter 18

In February the sun sets around 3 p.m. in Fairbanks. So when I finally pulled up beside Big Ellie at around 6:30, it was dark out. I was relieved to have made it home without further incident, but something wasn't right.

1. There was no sign of Ben and he still wasn't answering his phone,
2. No sign of Mac, either, and
3. A light was on in Big Ellie, and I damn sure didn't leave it that way.

I edged my way around the front of the car, slipped on the ice and righted myself quickly, only to discover my muscles ached, like the loser in the WWW championships. I threw open Big Ellie's side door, ignoring the little voice inside my head that reminded me of all the times I'd yelled at the heroine in a movie, "Don't go in there, you idiot," when she arrived home to find her apartment door ajar and was about to do something stupid.

I was hoping I wouldn't find a burglar, with a nothing-to-lose expression on a Hell's Angels body, when I stopped in my tracks, opened the door a crack and peeked inside. I put my ear to the opening. Hearing nothing, I pushed the door in and took the first step. Nothing. No breathing. No flash.

No complete stranger stretched out in my comfy arm chair, reading a dog-eared copy of Lady Chatterly's Lover. No burly biker type standing over me with a menacing look on his taut, expressionless face. No hyped-up crackhead clutching my dusty, battered VCR. Not even a Sassy Sister in a too-tight, black ninja outfit.

I slumped into a chair and sighed. Jumped up and checked the closets and shower. Whew! Coast clear. Except the burglar had been busy. The heat was up, my coffee pot, now half full, sat out of place on the kitchen counter, cold to the touch. A plate with nothing but crumbs rested in the sink.

I caught a whiff of vanilla lingering on the air, but it was no help. There was no evidence of illegal entry with intent to bake. No crusty baking sheets, no gooey mixing bowls, no lovely snickerdoodles cooling on racks, waiting to be eaten. There were the crumbs, but a burglar who leaves crumbs surely wouldn't have rinsed out the dough-encrusted mixing bowl. Would he?

Think, Abbey. What would someone want with Big Ellie? Did the snack mean someone had been waiting for me? Or had I left that plate in the sink, the coffee pot on the counter and forgotten about it? I looked around for evidence of burglary. Except for the kitchen, nothing was out of place.

Who would have broken in and left with nothing? Ah-ha! Maybe one of Sam's friends. What? They couldn't find a terrorist to torture? No hidden bombs to find? No felonious felons to locate. No white collar criminals to crack. I pulled my hand through my hair in a gesture I'd picked up from Ben and shook my head. I didn't need more trouble than I already had, and this was beginning to look like trouble.

I know I should be happy the intruder was gone. But what would really make me happy was not being in this mess in the first place. I'd be happy if I knew who the burglar was. I'd be happy if I knew where Ben was. I'd be happier still if Mac would stop throwing around the L word.

Like happiness was an option.

A second inspection of Big Ellie's tiny interior turned up nothing else. I sank back into the aforementioned easy chair, picked up the dog-eared copy of Lady Chatterley's Lover, which I actually do possess, and mindlessly riffled the edges of the pages. I would have loved it if something had fluttered to my feet, like in the movies, but that was not how it was going to be. All I had were more unanswered questions. Frankly, I had to resist the urge to scream.

I blame it on Alaska. If I hadn't returned to Fairbanks in the first place, I wouldn't have met Mac, and if I hadn't met Mac, then Ben wouldn't be such a problem now. If I hadn't returned to Alaska, I wouldn't have met Ben or Mac and I'd still be on the road in Big Ellie, with no worries other than figuring out the location of the next decent rest stop. If I hadn't returned, I wouldn't have met Justine, who needed rescuing by Sam, who then asked me, in return, to save her brother. And if all that hadn't happened, Big Ellie wouldn't be sitting here just waiting to be burgled.

I needed to talk to Ben.

What with the hit-and-run, spying and the arrival and departure of Big Ellie's surprise guest, my head was throbbing out the beat of a song I couldn't remember. I trudged up the path, the one Mac keeps meticulously free of ice and snow all winter long, and felt a pang of guilt. If the sky fell on me right this very minute, I would deserve it.

I really would.

When I pushed open the front door to the house, my shoulders rebelling from the minor exertion, I was greeted with an eerie silence. Mr. Peanut stirred briefly, and that was only after I called out, "Is anyone home?" into dead air space.

I moved past Mr. P, up the spiral staircase, checking each room, in case Ben had crashed early. (And no, I wasn't wondering if he and Rebecca were back in her hotel, lying in a mass of tangled limbs, dopey in their post-coital bliss.)

No sign of them. I mean, him.

No Mac either, but I wasn't expecting him, given his car wasn't outside. I reached for my cell phone. The dead battery signal mocked me. I would not be defeated. I tossed my coat and bag on the landing and headed for my office, plugged in my phone and low and behold, there was a text message from Mac.

"Have emergency. Jo on her way over. Love, Mac."

There was the L word, again. I'd really have to think about this new development. But later. Now I couldn't remember the last thing I'd eaten or when. Not counting a mouth full of airbag fluff. Chocolate cake with chocolate frosting and Chunky Monkey ice cream sounded great, but when I reached the refrigerator and threw open the freezer door, I knew Ben & Jerry's was just a pipe dream.

I don't know how long I stood in front of the fridge with the door hanging open, trying to decide if the veggie lasagna from last Thursday was safer than the pizza from who-knew-when, when the front door slammed open and Jo bounded through, shaking snow out of her hair and stomping her icy boots with a vengeance.

"I brought food," she said as she removed one delicious smelling item after another from her bulging backpack. Way better than maybe-safe lasagna or probably-moldy pizza.

The spicy aroma of Jo's homemade Italian meatball subs was enough to make me stick out my tongue and beg. (When it comes to food, I don't have any class at all.) I came up behind her, slipped my arms around her waist, rested my head on her shoulder and hugged her. "I love you, Jo. Thanks."

"Justine was right. You must have a concussion."

I held onto her as she unwrapped the subs, the smell making me this close to delirious, the whole Big Ellie incident fading from my consciousness. "Why? Because I appreciate what a great friend you are?"

"Because you're about to cry over a meatball sub, now get off me before I—"

Her threat was drowned out by the phone ringing. She picked up without a word. Hey, she was closer and the rule is, the closest one to the phone answers. It doesn't matter whose house it is.

"No. No. He's not here," she said, her tone all frigid, like it was a telemarketer or something. "When?"

I shot her a, "What's going on?" look, which she ignored.

Her forehead crinkled into a frown. "You what?" She rolled her eyes dramatically, shook her head, then snapped, "Right, bye," and hung up a little harder than was absolutely necessary, I thought.

She blew out a quick breath. "That," she said, as if she'd just tasted something awful, like scum or kitty litter, "was Molly."

Wait for it, I thought.

"She wanted to know where Mac was. She said she was expecting him at her place, but he's late."

I took a bite of my sub, then licked sauce off my fingers one by one, before I answered, "Liar."

"Me?"

"Molly. Why would Mac tell me he'd be right home when he had a date with her?" I mumbled with a mouth full of meatball. "She's playing us."

Jo handed me a napkin, barely disguising her disgust at my talking-with-mouth-full routine.

I noticed she was looking everywhere but at me. "What?" I asked.

"So. Where is he?"

I was trying to eat, damn it. My head still hurt, my back hurt, I was exhausted. Mac was throwing around the L word like loose change, and I didn't want to think. I wanted to eat. I took my sub over to the sink, the better to catch globs of flying sauce, and bit down into the tastiest food on planet earth. Yum.

Jo pulled me by the back of my shirt over to a chair and shoved me down into it. My knees caved. Lucky she didn't go for the sub or she might have come up against the Sicilian in me.

"Ab, since when do you eat over the sink like a hung-over frat boy?"

"I just realized something, Jo," I said, my voice tinged with sadness. "Despite the God-like subs, you're not very nice."

She sat down beside me and reached for the second sub. "Bite me. Now about Molly and Mac's date."

"There is no date. It's not a date." I banged my hand on the table, sending the saltshaker skittering into her lap.

She raised her eyebrows and gave me a look that made me want to pluck every hair out of her eyebrows one at a time—by hand. Only for a second. The fact that I might have a slight concussion was beginning to sink in.

"Still," she continued, "he could be at her place and who knows what might happen. She's gorgeous and sexy and determined. She could seduce him and then what would you do?"

Ridiculous. "Why would Mac go over there in the first place, Jo? He told me he loves me."

"He's a nice guy. She needed her lawn mowed."

"It's snowing."

She held the back of her hand to her forehead and feigned feminine distress, like she was in an old Greta Garbo movie. "She told him if he didn't come over right away, she was going to throw herself into the river."

"For all the good it'd do her. The river's frozen."

"Okay. She told him she was sick and needed a ride to the hospital." There was that "emergency" thing.

I was savoring the warm marinara sauce lingering on my tongue. I took another bite, chewed, lingered and swallowed, before answering. "I really don't think—"

"That's right." She grabbed the half-eaten sub from my unsuspecting hand. "You're not thinking. She's a vampire. She could be screwing him senseless right this very minute and you're eating cake." She shook the sub for good measure, spraying bits of sauce onto my hair and eyelashes.

Whoa. Cool down, Jo, and give me back the damn sub. And cake? I'm eating meatballs. Oh yeah, Josephine. Napoleon. Get it. But I didn't say a word, 'cuz I've never seen Jo this crazy before and I wasn't taking any chances on what alternate universe Jo might do next.

Saved by the bell. The phone rang, and I snatched my sub out of Jo's unsuspecting hands. Then I reached over and picked up the line. The closest-to-the phone rule be damned. "Yes. Okay. Right." I hung up and sat across from Jo. "Molly. She said not to worry about Mac. He's pulling up right now."

"God."

"She thought I'd want to know," I said flatly.

"So what we have here is a case for Sassy Sister Investigations," Jo said, as she furiously scrubbed the table within an inch of its life. I held my sub away from her maniacal machinations. "We have to get over there and put that bitch in her place."

"We have to get a grip," I said. "You're acting crazy." A light bulb went off in my otherwise scattered brain.

"Have you used that pregnancy test yet?" (Sicilian Tactic #30: Distract them, etc.)

"Why? Am I looking fat or something?" she shouted, then did an about-face. "Wait a minute. This isn't about me. It's your happiness on the line. Blow it if you want, Miss Smarty Pants."

I wasn't about to tell her my happiness was never going to depend on a man because I wasn't stupid and she wasn't listening.

"Okay. Okay." I was a counselor once upon a time, and I firmly believe in humoring the insane when necessary. "I'll go over and see what's going on. Will that make you happy?"

Her face lit up like the Northern Lights on Christmas Eve.

"I'm going with you." She jumped up, ready to head out on her mission, with the zeal and tenacity of an Olympic sprinter.

I grabbed her sleeve and yanked her back. "Oh no you don't. If I go, I go alone." I aimed a stare worthy of Vinnie at her. "You stay here in case Mac calls or comes home." She was about to protest. "Or else you go and I'll stay here and wait for Mac."

She nodded unhappily and agreed to stay put as long as I swore on Jim Morrison's grave not to let Molly get away with a thing. Not a single, solitary thing.

I drove on autopilot, yet somehow the car safely reached the tiny Ester neighborhood where comfortably worn cabins lined the winding snow-covered roads. I reached Molly's street in record time, and even from a block away, I could see Mac's car. My heart clutched in my chest, before I reminded myself I wasn't going to get upset. No problem. If he was there and not at home checking to see if I was bleeding from the head, it had to be important.

I could see it now. Molly with a bottle of sleeping pills and Mac saving her life via a blood-boiling race to the hospital. A monstrous polar bear trapping her in her bedroom and now she can't get to her heart medicine, unfortunately located in the bathroom medicine cabinet. Or, having scaled a ladder to get her car keys off her roof, where her kleptomaniac cat had left them, she was now lying in a crumbled heap in the snow—Thank God she had her cell phone handy!—and could not get up.

I perused the perimeter. No sign of crumbled Molly. No sign of bear carnage. No sign of cats with keys or anything else peculiar, if you didn't count Mac's car in Molly's drive. I knew there was no going back when I slid out of my car, climbed her front stairs and found myself crossing Molly's threshold, hoping no one from the Fairbanks Gossip Network was lurking in the vicinity. And who leaves the front door wide open at 20 below zero or whatever the heck the current temperature was, anyway?

Something told me this wasn't going to be good. Clairvoyance, street smarts or reading too many mysteries? Don't ask.

No Mac in the entryway. No Molly, either. I tip-toed down a narrow hallway, taking in her eclectic decorating style. A Mapplethorpe juxtaposed with a Starry Night print, a Michael Graves lamp resting on a Victorian end table. Interesting. Also interesting was the steady of stream of water I heard coming from the end of the hall.

Following the sound of the water, I reached a closed door and pressed one ear against the cool, smooth wood, contemplating my next move—telling myself I wasn't crazy for being here in the first place—when I heard what sounded like, "Oh, God. Oh, God. Oh. My. God."

But really. It couldn't have been.

Chapter 19

Good God Almighty. It was Molly Does Niagara Falls. From her supple breasts to her zaftig thighs. A Goddess in Syran Wrap, clinging to Mac like he was left over pork chops. Her outfit, if you could call three feet of Saran Wrap an outfit, left nothing to the imagination, except possibly, if you were the guy, imagining how you were going to unwrap her, and if you were me, how to squash her like a bug.

It all went down in slow motion. I walked through the door. Mac wrestled with Molly, fighting the stubborn cling wrap with one hand, grabbing for his shirt with the other. His hand sliced the air like a bullet in "The Matrix." I watched, horrified and fascinated, as Molly slithered one hand down her thigh, hiked up the plastic and leaped up on Mac, wrapping her legs around his hips.

In his defense, not that I was ready to defend him, he didn't look all that into her, not even when her naked thighs made contact with his waterlogged jeans.

His mouth was moving but the words hung in the air, unheard. Molly's smile was almost diabolical as she ground her body into his, hanging on like a world-class gymnast. I swear I could hear the scraping sound of her pelvis against his jeans above the deafening sound of water rushing over and around us, even though I still couldn't hear the words Mac was desperately shouting at me.

I was about to shout back, "What?" when I was spun around abruptly, and came face to face with Jo, spitting fire bolts. She shoved past me, slogging her way through the treacherous water, heading for Molly and Mac. She raised one hand, and for a second I thought she was going to wave to Mac, which made no sense at all. Then her balled up fist connected with Molly's left eye and there was Molly, lying in a puddle on the floor and Jo shaking her hand, shouting, "Son of a Bitch," with Mac standing there, looking like he couldn't figure out what the hell had just happened.

Me? I turned to go, and the lights went out. I guess Mac in the bathroom with the cling-wrap girl was the straw that finally broke the concussion's back.

For the second time in one day, I didn't end up in the hospital or psyche ward, although the ambulance guys couldn't figure out what was so funny that I couldn't stop laughing for the life of me.

Later, when I thought about the whole Mac and Molly scene, I could understand how a nice guy like Mac might have fallen for Molly's desperate pleas to race over to help with her runaway plumbing, if in fact that was the excuse she'd used. Nothing funny there. I could understand how his sweater came off. It was wool, wet and heavy and probably smelled like wet grouse. But the cling-wrap? God. If she had shouted, "Ride me big boy," as it appeared from all accounts she was leading up to, I would have popped a blood vessel. And Jo. Coming on like an avenging angel. Oh my God, my side hurts. Ow. Ow. Ow.

So, I find my boyfriend half-undressed in the bathroom with a naked ex-girlfriend, who was about to have her way with him whether he liked it or not, but I couldn't wrap my head around it. I had a sudden flash.

Forget Molly. Forget Mac. I'd had a bad feeling all evening, and even Molly in Saran Wrap couldn't get my mind off of the fact that I needed to find Ben.

When Jo and I finally extricated ourselves from Molly's—no death or dismemberment involved—and arrived home, the house was still empty and frankly, I had gone from curious to freaked out.

Mac showed up right behind us and I left him in the kitchen with Jo, where she proceeded to grill him. Why'd you go over there? The water. Why was your shirt off? The water. And on and on.

"Who's on first?" I asked.

Jo turned her back on Mac long enough to snap at me. "What?"

"Never mind. You go on shouting at Mac; I'm going to bed." I shot a pointed look at Mac. "Alone."

You might think I was giving up on Mac a bit too quickly. But there was plenty of time to deal with him later.

Sicilian Tactic #48: Everything in its own time.

No need to be hasty. All the time in the world to plot their demise.

I was going to bed. Actually I was going to lay down long enough to make Jo and Mac think I was in bed, then I was going to sneak out to find Ben.

Chapter 20

You love New York style cheesecake, right? Wouldn't dream of living without thick crust pizza with everything on it? Then you understand about Mac and Ben. Each entirely different yet indispensable flavors. Each satisfying in their own way. But how do you choose one and give up the other? Which would go? Think about it. Creamy, rich cheesecake will never melt in your mouth again. Or hot, gooey pizza. Whichever. You have to choose. Ben. Mac. Ben. Mac.

I found myself exploring my options, as I drove toward Rebecca's hotel, trying not to consider the possibility that Ben could actually be there at this time of night. I didn't have far to go in a town all of eight square miles. Five minutes from home and I was pulling up outside the Marathon Inn, considering how a real spy would approach the problem. Dial Rebecca's room on the off chance Ben would answer? Nope. Rebecca answered and let's hope she didn't have Caller ID. Plan B. Call the front desk and ask if Rebecca was entertaining this evening. Unfortunately, they couldn't possibly divulge such personal information. Well fine. It's not like I was asking for the color of her panties. Plan C. I didn't have a Plan C, and I couldn't bring myself to dress up like a maid, break into her room or set off the fire alarms. Sicilian Tactic #49: Work inside the law unless they give you no other choice.

I sat in the parking lot with the engine idling, frost forming on the windows. Chewed my fingernails and checked my voice mail. Bingo. A text message from Ben. "Tried to ring. Lots to tell. Home soon."

That was more like it. Something going right. I turned the heater up, backed out of the lot and hit the road toward home and Ben. (I know, kick me.) Especially since I knew Jo was gone and Mac was safely tucked in bed, dreaming of flying, unhindered by the laws of man and nature.

The first thing I noticed as I arrived home was that every light in the house was off, save one. Ben's room. I should have bought a lottery ticket on the way home, what with the way my luck was holding.

I closed the car door quietly. Opened and closed the front door quietly. Slipped off my coat and kicked off my boots. I was all set to race up the stairs (just as quietly), when I found myself gently swept up into a kiss I could only give in to, being as that kiss was all I'd been dreaming about lately.

I could have died happily, except that Ben pulled away, making me long for the heat of his sturdy chest. He pressed a finger to my lips and led me gently toward the circular stairs, our current heading being bliss. He ascended the stairs, one step ahead of me, never releasing the steady pressure of his hand on mine. Five steps up, he turned and pulled me to him, continuing where we'd left off. I moved my body close enough to his to feel his heartbeat and up the kiss from delicious to got-to-have-him. He pulled back again at the exact moment I knew I'd never make it as far as his room. All I could think was, "This is going to happen and it's going to happen here. Now."

I found myself moving again, the staircase now the location of my exquisite frustration. Each time we stopped, his kisses grew longer and deeper, his lips lingered on my fingers, the palms of each hand, the curve of my neck.

Oh, God. How many more stairs were there! He was taking me to the place I wanted to go, but slowly. Way too slowly. I was about to rip the shirt right off of him. I was. I sneaked open a couple of buttons, slipped my hand in and got the response I was hoping for. That created some urgency. We took the rest of the stairs in a flash. Once inside his room, we crashed against the wall, forgetting about sound, sense and reason. When he eased one hand along my thigh and brought me this close to heaven, a moan escaped my lips, or maybe from his. I reached between us aiming for the top button of his jeans but lost focus temporarily when I heard a loud creak.

The bedroom door flew open, Ben swung around, revealing my now-bare breasts for all the world to see, including Mac, who was wrapped from neck to knees in Saran Wrap, saying something I never thought I'd hear him say.

"Is there room for one more in here?"

Chapter 21

Countdown to Valentine's Day: Two days to go

Put a mirror under her nose."

"Don't be ridiculous. She's not dead."

"What are you? Doctor Who?"

The voices were far away, accompanied by an unexplained pounding in my head. If I stayed perfectly still, maybe they'd both go away.

"She's awake."

"How would you know?"

"Her breathing changed. Abbey? Abbey?" Someone said, followed by a shoulder shake and a finger prying open one of my eyelids.

"Ouooch!"

"Not dilated."

"Good, then you can let her sleep."

"I don't—"

"Let's go." A door slammed shut and just like that, I was alone. The last delectable remnants of my three-way Saran Wrap dream fading from consciousness.

"Good morning, Sunshine," Jo said, when I'd finally dragged myself into the kitchen wrapped in my ratty, terry cloth robe with the teacups on it, looking like the first-place winner in the Miss-I-Don't-Give-a-Damn-What-Anyone-Thinks-About-The-Way-I-Look competition.

Justine looked at me like I was day-old deviled eggs. "Love the look.

Suits you."

It was too early in the morning for me to deal with Cranky Justine. What time was it anyway? I glanced at the oven clock: 7 a.m.

Justine, who, for reasons I couldn't begin to fathom, was dressed in black leather from head to toe, her hair tucked neatly into a coordinating biker's cap.

"What are you supposed to be?" I asked, sweetly. "Barbie's bitch?"

Jo sent us a menacing glare that screamed, "Desperate Housewife on Crack."

"Enough you two," she said, threatening us with the business end of a rubber spatula. "I have pancake goo and I'm not afraid to use it."

"She started it." I pointed at Justine.

Justine bumped things up a notch. "Ben rang," she said. "Sorry he missed you. He'll see you at the office later."

"Why didn't he come home last night? Did he say where he was?"

"I'm not his mother."

In that getup she didn't look like anyone's mother.

"How's Juliette?" I asked, remembering the important stuff. I mean, Justine always has my back, even when she is a bitch on wheels.

"She returns today. Homesick."

"Thank God," Jo said. We all had been a bit worried that Juliette might be hypnotized by the adulation of her doting grandparents and never want to come home again.

"I'm flying out this morning to meet her in Seattle. Then right back tonight."

"Dressed like that?" I scanned her up and down, wondering if she meant to scare Juliette into never leaving again. Too late I realized how it sounded. "I mean—"

Jo jumped between us before Justine could pop me one. It was then that I noticed they were twins in black, right down to the biker boots.

"All right. What's up with you two."

They looked at each other and shrugged.

I waited a beat, but when no one filled the silence, I had no choice. "Don't make me sic Vinnie on you."

"Nothing serious." That from Jo.

I trained an evil eye on one then the other, to see who'd crack first.

Jo said, "Look, you're going to find out sooner or later, so—"

"Later, from the looks of it."

"We may have broken into a hangar at the airport. "

"You—"

"Merona's."

"What?"

"We didn't steal anything, so you can just stop looking at us like we're Bonnie and Clyde," Justine said.

More like Curly and Moe.

"What'd you find?"

"What'd we find? That's all you have to say?"

"Please. Like it would do any good if I threw a hissy fit."

"Nothing."

"Excuse me."

"The place was empty."

I shook my head. "No one rents a hanger so they can leave it empty," I said, thinking of the overcrowded space at AVA and Jaye's pleas to expand into the hangar next door.

"Well, empty except for a few planes. Nothing suspicious."

"What hangar was it, anyway, and how'd you get in? When did you go?" I asked. "Did anyone see you? Was there an alarm?"

"Now she has questions," Jo said, as she flipped a golden-brown pancake into the air high above her head. "No one saw us. If there was an alarm, it didn't go off. About an hour—"

"We used the key," Justine interrupted. "Rebecca's."

"Really?"

"We figured it wasn't a post office box."

"Or a door key."

"Definitely not a padlock key."

"Yeah, yeah. I get it. Not the key to a graveyard gate."

"Then it hit us. It could be a hangar, and from there it was easy. We went from hangar to hangar until we found one that fit."

"At the crack of dawn, obviously," I said.

"Obviously," Justine answered. "Too bad it was a total waste of time."

"It wasn't a waste of time," Jo said. "We found out that Merona isn't selling stolen goods.

"Or if he is, he isn't using that hangar."

To recap the day so far: Ben was okay, even though I couldn't help but wonder what was keeping him away all this time. And Justine and Jo had gone off the deep end.

I sent them packing, assuring them I was well enough to be left on my own, and would be back at my desk within the hour to fill in for Justine in time for her flight to Seattle. I checked the house to see if Mac had left already, and he had. I found myself gloriously alone with a little free time before I had to be anywhere or see anyone. I flew through my morning ritual: teeth, hair, shower, clothes, and then gave into a pressing urge to visit Ben. His room, anyway, the next best thing to being with him.

In the short time he'd been here, his room had taken on a decidedly Ben aura. The desk housing his briefcase and laptop was littered with brightly colored sticky notes. A pile of fresh laundry sat at the foot of his neatly made bed, ordered into stacks of jeans, T-shirts, socks and boxer shorts. I sat on the bed and held up a Vote for Pedro T-shirt, sniffed for any lingering scent of Ben. None. I scooted to the top of the bed and laid back against his pillows and closed my eyes, remembering my Ben-on-the-stairs dream, minus the whole Mac in Saran Wrap part, willing my brain to drift back to the unrealized details.

The phone rang, blasting me out of Ben's imaginary arms, just as he was about to—"

"Hello. No, he's not here." I searched the night stand for paper and a pen to write a number on. Some old friend of Mac's looking for him. I wrote the number without looking down. "Got it. Great. I'll be sure to tell him," I said and hung up.

Wide awake. Dreamland well beyond my reach, I got up. I had to get to work. There'd be plenty of time for fantasy later.

Although I hate to admit it, AVA and Gran's dumping it on me, changed my life for the better. The mom and pop bush air service keeps my feet on the ground during the best of times and keeps me from jumping in Big Ellie and running away from life at the worst of times.

It was actually good to be back at my desk, doing the routine, day-to-day tasks that keep me from ruminating on my problems. The other good thing about being back was that I could ask Jen about going undercover at Merona's. Lastly, I realized, as a mail truck screeched to a halt outside my office window, was that I'd get to open any deliveries before Justine smashed them to pieces. What with her winging her way to Seattle.

I love opening packages. Especially when they're for me and this one was. I looked it over. The return address was unfamiliar. With Jen covering the counter, I took the package to my office and tore into the plain, brown wrap. I pushed aside crumpled newspapers until my hand touched something smooth and soft. A classic Einstein Rocks T-shirt. Odd. I have the same shirt, crumpled in the bottom of my laundry basket at home. Or not.

"Someone's messing with you," Jen said, over a cup of coffee and a sugar donut, when I mentioned how my T-shirt had arrived in today's mail.

"You make it sound sinister," I said, although all evidence pointed to exactly that.

"What's sinister?" Jaye appeared in the doorway, sloughing off his jacket as he spoke. "Someone bothering you, Abbey?"

I held a hand up to protest, but Jen, not into sugarcoating things, answered for me. "Someone broke into her trailer. Maybe her house, too."

"Big Ellie. Not a trailer."

She humored me. "Broke into Big Ellie. Then they stole one of her shirts and mailed it back to her. Crazy, right?"

I shook my head again when I saw concern darken Jaye's eyes.

"It was a joke."

"Abbey," Jaye said, weighing his words carefully before he spoke. "No one I know would think this was funny." He turned and paced, returned, rubbing his hand against the stubble on his chin. "You were in a hit-and-run. And how did they get the shirt?" His eyes held mine, forcing me to take him seriously.

"Someone was in Big Ellie yesterday, but I'm sure they didn't get into the house."

"Bad enough," Jen countered.

"It's only a shirt," I said.

Jaye was silent, his forehead wrinkled into a frown as he paced. Back and forth, back and forth.

"Someone wants you to know they can get to you anytime they want. I think you need to take this seriously, Abbey."

"Relax. It's not like they sent me a pipe bomb."

"What about the accident? Explain that one."

I rolled my eyes, pulled both hands through my hair and got up to return to work.

"Abbey," Jaye called after me.

I turned back. "Yeah?"

"All I'm saying is, would it hurt to be careful?"

I am careful. I mean, I'm not stupid, after all. The first thing I'd do when I got home was lock Big Ellie. It's not really breaking and entering when the owner leaves the door unlocked. The second thing was to look for my dirty Einstein T-shirt. If it was no longer laying crumpled in my laundry basket, then I might worry. For now, I had bigger fish to fry. I still had to ask Jen about going over to Merona's—when Justine returned that is. Okay, I needed a real To-Do list.

I reached into my purse to retrieve Mac's message and put it in his mailbox, only to realize that in my rush to leave Ben's room, I'd picked up his day planner. I ran a finger across the rigid spine, wondering if Ben was thinking about me, when a flash spun me out of my reverie.

It happened so fast I couldn't process all the images. Barrels, piles of rags. Damp. Gray. Concrete and steel. Ben. Laying on the barren floor. I knew without a doubt he was trapped, despite his phone messages. If they really were from him at all. The place was deathly quiet, smelled musty. I picked up the planner; another flash hit me. I gasped for air. When I opened my eyes, Jaye was beside me, his hand on my shoulder, gently shaking me.

"What do you see?"

I looked at him, ghosts of the images lingering behind my eyes. "Ben needs us."

No need to convince him. "Where is he, Abbey?"

"Someplace large. A warehouse, or maybe a hangar. I can't be sure."

"Close your eyes," he said, his voice soft, lulling me, soothing. "See it, Abbey."

Sometimes it does work that way, relaxing into it. "It's not working, Jaye," I said, minutes later. "The clock's ticking and we have to find him and it's not working." We were going to find him if it was the last thing I ever did.

"Abbey, we could call out the National Guard, knock on every door in town and it would still take a week."

"It's not like I'm giving up."

"I'm not suggesting you are. I'm saying, relax and find him."

His hands moved into the dip between my neck and shoulders, pressing, kneading. "Relax. Think about Ben. Where is he, Abbey?" He continued the massage as I gripped Ben's notebook. Nothing. Nothing was happening.

I opened my eyes again, turned a page with phone numbers and addresses I didn't recognize: Oxford, Cambridge, Wales, Scarborough. No flashes. I kept flipping pages as Jaye worked to calm my nerves, both of us hoping for a breakthrough.

Something caught my eye in the middle of a page of doodles and phones numbers: H42. Maybe nothing. I traced the ink with my finger, and for no reason at all I was reminded of the time Jo and I had sneaked into one of Gran's hangars and almost got ourselves locked in for the night. Terrified more at the thought of being caught than about having to spend a night in the dark. And then I knew.

I leapt to my feet so fast Jaye had to take a step back to keep from crashing into the wall.

"Hangar 42."

Hangar 42 doesn't really exist anymore. Actually, it exists, but as a rusted out shell of a hangar, taken out of service when Harden's Field was replaced with the newer, more convenient Metro Field. Hangar 42 was left to decay and sink into its current state of disrepair. That no one had torn it down was a testament to procrastination in the face of too much to do and too little time.

I knew the old dirt road to Harden's Field may have suffered from years of disuse, but I was unprepared for the reality. When we reached the edge of the air field in Jaye's 4 x 4 pickup truck, the road was covered with a foot of deep, crusty snow, save for a two sets of wavering tracks, giving credence to my theory that we were on the right path. If we went slowly, stayed in the icy grooves before us and kept a steady pace, I was thinking we just might get out there without having to call in the reserves. I could tell Jaye was thinking the same thing by the way he carefully maneuvered the truck, gripping the steering wheel with both hands, his eyes never straying from the road ahead.

Meanwhile, I had time to think of all the things I should have done. I should have called the police. At the very least, Mac. I'd remembered to pack the bolt cutters, but I should have brought an extra blanket for Ben and some hot coffee in a thermos. I should have—

"We're here," Jaye said as we drove up to a set of rusty overhead doors. The truck tracks turned and exited in the opposite direction, leaving behind a trampled hodgepodge of footprints and a snow-covered car with rental plates. I yanked the bolt cutters from behind the seat.

"Ben, are you in there? Ben, Ben," I shouted, my voice cracking with fear.

The cold froze the tears in the corners of my eyes as I rushed forward and pushed, then pulled, on the smaller door to no avail. I pounded my fist on the metal, yelling, "Ben," again and again. I thought I heard something inside and tried again, only harder. Meanwhile, Jaye approached the overhead door and found the problem. A thick, heavily rusted floor bolt was in place, and though he yanked on it as hard as he could, it wouldn't budge. He picked up the bolt cutters from where I'd thrown them on the ground in frustration and worked the tool around the heavy bolt. After several aborted attempts, he snapped the bar in two with a satisfying thunk.

I came up beside him and helped push the heavy door back on its rollers. We grunted from the exertion, sweat pouring off us even with temperatures dipping to 20 below zero, then rushed inside. Me calling out to Ben, Jaye scanning the interior for any sign of him.

"There are two doors in the back," he said, as he pointed to an area that must have housed a storeroom or office at one time. I raced toward one door while he went for the other. I approached the door that still sported a Wein Air sticker, leaned back and threw my weight against it. Jaye came over and while I pushed with my shoulder, he gave it a good kick; the door caved in, landing me on top of Ben in a shower of rotting, splintered wood.

I groaned, spitting out wood chips, and rolled off of Ben. I dusty, nose-dripping mess, but I didn't care. It felt like I'd won the lottery.

Ben look up at me, smiling as if he'd known all along I would be arriving at any moment.

"I do love a powerful woman, Abigail Vertuccio," he joked, as he hobbled to his feet and proceeded to brush splinters from his hair and eyelashes.

I couldn't think of a single thing to do but leap into his arms and hug him like my life depended on it. It didn't matter that he smelled like sweat and moldy newspapers.

When I finally gave him some breathing room, he looked at me with a hint of mischief in his eyes and asked, "What are the chances of a hot bath, Ab?"

I felt myself blush. Hoping against hope Jaye wasn't right behind me, I shook my Magic 8 Ball wristwatch for the answer.

"Seems this is your lucky day. The 8 Ball says, 'Outlook is good.'"

Chapter 22

Aren't Valentine's day cards supposed to be for children? Over-size cardboard versions of Big Bird and Batman. Shakily scissored, paper hearts in red or pink. But no, it seems Valentine's Day is alive and well, thanks to every hopeless romantic willing to shell out $4.95 on up for a four-color piece of prefab, romantic gobbledygook. Who knew?

Not that I'm not romantic. But I prefer my romance with a twist. A crazy tune. A homemade cake, possibly decorated with gorillas acting all kinds of love-sick, revealing the true nature of romance. Not in an irate-feminist-don't-fuck-with-me way, more in a I'm-so-cool-and-funny-way-even-though-I-know-Valentine's-Day-is-a-made-up-holiday-designed-to-separate-me-from-my-money kind of way. Even a poorly written, but not too soppy or heartfelt poem would be acceptable, if done right. For example. I am so blue without you, I'm getting the flu. So what can I do-oo-oo.

You get my drift.

Better still, we could eliminate Valentine's Day altogether. Think of the money we'd save. Think of every person (face it—woman) who spent months longing for a diamond engagement ring and instead received a dozen roses on Valentine's Day. Or the woman who was expecting a romantic weekend at some sleepy little inn on the coast, including long walks along the beach (not to mention the beyond romantic lovemaking), but who ended up with tickets to Englebert Humperdink. Then there's the person (again, insert woman) who would have been thrilled with Englebert tickets, who got, "What? Yesterday was Valentine's Day?" from her significant other, while he scratched his balls and downed a brew in front of The Game.

Consider how Valentine's Day has done more to ruin relationships than any Mustang impulse purchase, and you, too, may take up the battle cry, "No more Valentine's Day massacres!"

I personally gave up Valentine's Day when Rob, my ex, decided he had to confess to waking up in bed with one of my best friends (former best friends) on Valentine's Day. End result? Marriage over. Valentine's Day ruined forever.

And now this. A Valentine's Day card waiting for me when I arrived home all grimy and exhausted from kicking in doors and sitting on filthy hangar floors, after rescuing Ben. A card from the last person on earth I needed to think about right now. Vinnie.

Deep breath. Okay. Fine. She may be the most annoying person I know, but she's still my mother and I haven't learned anything if I don't know you have to respect your mother no matter what. Even when it makes your eyes twitch and your stomach knot up into a ball so tight you may never straighten up again.

I slid a finger under the flap of the hot-pink envelope and whipped out the card. I shouldn't have been surprised, because how could anything Vinnie does still surprise me? She's so Vinnie. And yes, it really should be an adjective.

Picture a cowboy bar. Wood dance floor. Smoky, dark interior. Center stage is the Marlboro Man, muscles rippling from his sculpted shoulders to his museum-quality six-pack, right down to where his jeans should have started but didn't, dancing with an equally hot mama with Dolly Parton-size implants. Cowboy hat and knee-high cowboy boots her only accouterments.

Across her Dolly-like chest, in cherry red lip liner, it said "Abbey." Next, Vinnie had lassoed the Marlboro Man, again in cherry red, and left the tail leading to the inside of the card, where, when I flipped open the card (after considering and dismissing the idea of tossing the whole thing in the trash) she'd written in an overly dramatic script, "This is what (or should I say who) I'd like you to be doing on Valentine's Day. But you know me. I'm a realist, so have fun washing the dog, doing the laundry and reading War and Peace or whatever it is you do for fun. Love, Mom."

Arrg! I still have relatives in Sicily. Would it be a crime to call up Cousin Vito, who for his own reasons can't take too much Vinnie, and ask him to take care of the problem? So, if she ends up . . . oh, never mind. I don't have time for daydreaming, and okay, I'm feeling a tad bit guilty here. In reality, I wouldn't hurt a single hair on her pain-in-the-ass, obnoxious, narcissistic head. Honest.

Uh-oh. Freeze frame. Scan to a second envelope lying on top of a stack of unopened mail. I peeled back the flap on that one with gritted teeth and pulled out a card with a photoshopped picture of Mac pasted on the body of a strolling minstrel singing an Adam Sandler-esque poem. I know this because he wrote on the card: "Imagine an off-key, repetitious, sing-songy tune to the following:

> I know you don't want to hear it
> But I had to tell you, anyway
> Before I burst from keeping the words in
> Like a seal that ate too many fish
> You never know who you're going to love,
> And there's no use fighting it,
> You don't have to marry me
> If you can't take waking up to my face
> You don't even have to acknowledge me
> But I'll be here beside you
> Every day like a puppy who's craving a biscuit
> 'Cause I love Abbey, even when she's really crabby.
> And that's all there is to it."

"Bad news, kid?"

I surveyed the remnants of Mac's card, now a pile of crumbled, torn pieces, before I looked up at my new tormentor. What the hell? Tony? I shrugged and tossed the pieces in the trash. "Water bill."

His forehead wrinkled up imperceptibly. "Where is everyone?" he asked. "I knocked but no one answered."

I'd been too busy plotting revenge against Vinnie and escape from Mac. Ben, I presumed, was still resting up after his ordeal. Who knew where Jo was.

"Earth to Abbey," Tony said, as he tapped my shoulder. "I need a favor."

Good. Something tangible. Something I could control. "Sure, Tony. What is it?" I said, turning my full attention on him.

"I need a Valentine's Day present for Jo."

Great! Valentine's Day again. What did I look like? Macy's? Dear Abbey? I mean, do I look like I give a flying fig about Valentine's Day?

"Abbey?"

Do I look like someone who wants to hear another single, solitary word about Valentine's Day?

"Uh. Abbey?"

Do I look like someone who's going to throw an entire Valentine's Day cake with ten tons of butter cream frosting at the next person who even mentions the V word?

"Maybe I should come back."

I shook my head and dragged myself back from the edge.

"No, no. What can I do?"

He hesitated, probably going over his options. Could he make it to the door in time if he bolted now?

"I'm trying to decide between a trip to Costa Rica or a Jacuzzi."

"It's February, Tony. It's not rocket science."

"Like I said. Maybe I should come back." He turned to go.

"No, no. Why the big ticket items? You buy a new SUV without telling her?"

He took his time before answering. "It's Jo. She's acting crazy."

I raised an eyebrow.

"Crazier than usual," he qualified.

Hmm. "How so?" I didn't like to go behind Jo's back with Tony, but truth? Curiosity won out.

"For starters, the phone calls. All hours of the day and night. Sure, she says it's her mom or her sister." He did a hands up. "But who talks to her mom in the closet on the portable?"

"You think she's having an affair?"

"Madonna mia! She's having an affair!" He slammed a clenched fist on the desk then slapped his forehead. "I'm an idiot. Of course—"

"Wait a minute." I grabbed the back of his shirt as he was charging the door. "Slow down. I thought *you* thought she was having an affair. I don't think that," I said. "She'd never do that."

He turned on me. "Then why'd you say it?"

"I didn't." What was the use? "What else? You said she was acting crazy."

He paced, making me dizzy, then turned in an ah ha fashion, pointing a finger. "She blows up over everything."

Nothing new. "Define 'everything.'"

He went over a laundry list of mistakes, real or imagined, Jo had blown up over during the past few weeks, including his using her favorite lipstick to leave her a note on the bathroom mirror.

"Who cleaned the mirror?" I asked, after he stopped to take a breath. Another shoulder shrug.

"Okay then. Seems reasonable enough."

"There's more. Weird stuff showing up on the credit card. She's buying wedding dresses. A ton of them."

"Tony, she runs a thrift store. Think June. The wedding month. It's coming up. What doesn't make sense to you?"

"She's gonna sell a hundred and eight wedding dresses?"

I sighed. "Why don't you just ask her?"

"What? And sleep in the car? No thanks." In a voice that resembled an adolescent squirrel, he added, "You were spying on me. I don't tell you how many basketballs or shower towels to order for your team." He swung his hip out and put a hand on it. "Do I?"

I almost choked, but managed to spit out a single word. "Tony?"

"What?"

I pointed over his shoulder to the open door at an about-to-boil (even her hair looked angry) Jo. I guess it's true what they say after all. Loose lips sink ships. Never let them see you sweat? It takes two to tango? I didn't know, but I had a feeling Tony was about to regret the day he was born, and I couldn't bear to watch.

"Bye. Have fun. Don't forget to write," I said. And I was out of there.

Chicken? Maybe. But I was still in one piece. All in all, a good thing.

For all I complain about Vinnie, she's taught me a thing or two. I slid down the hall and waited. Jo's heat turned into a slow burn. Deadlier than the fireworks I was expecting.

"Someone's been going through my files." She pushed out a sharp breath, barely containing herself.

Tony didn't move.

"You think imitating me is funny? You think I sound like a demented chipmunk? Maybe you should have thought about how uncomfortable it is sleeping in your car, before you started spying on me."

She was circling the room now, around and around, in a red-headed blur. "Don't deny it. You filed my phone contacts folder under P. So there."

I was familiar with Jo's filing system—put the file you use most in front. Obviously. But it looked like poor Tony didn't know that.

"What were you looking for, anyway?"

When he continued to hop from foot to foot, like a seven-year-old who needed to pee, a pathetic and stunned look on his face (Okay, I peeked again) she continued. "My files are an open book. What possible reason—" She stopped suddenly as the color rose in his cheeks. "Oh my God. You think I'm having an affair!"

Tread carefully, Tony, I thought, hoping against hope I could save him telepathically. Whatever you do, don't say, "Well, are you?"

"Well?"

"Well, what?" Jo spat.

"Are you?"

Her words flew like torpedoes. "You *do* think I'm having an affair." She turned to go, then turned back. Stone cold. "How could you?"

If Ben hadn't been awake before, he was now. The neighbors a mile away were awake now.

"Don't give me your Saint Jo routine," Tony shouted. "You're in the closet talking with God only knows who, at the crack of dawn, and Abbey said—"

She turned back to him but stopped. "No, she didn't. Abbey knows me better than some people do, apparently."

I could have sworn she was going to slap him. He must have sensed it, too, because he took both her wrists and held them. Not in a Spread-'em-you're-under-arrest way, more like in a Stay-calm-you-looney-tune kind of way. We know you're a nutcase and we need you to calm down because we're taking you to a nice, safe place.

She wrenched free and backed up. I scooted farther down the hall, in case she came charging out. When she didn't appear, I scooted back in place. They were faced off, nose to nose.

"You could be having an affair," Tony insisted, arms crossed defiantly.

"I could be Tracy Chapman, but I'm not," Jo countered.

"Come off it."

"I could be Bill Nye the Science Guy, if we're talking crazy. Or better yet, the old man who's building that house out of beer bottles."

"Get real," he said, but I could see he was fighting a losing battle.

"You get real. How can you think that?" she said, covering her mouth with one hand, looking defeated, suddenly.

"Look at your friends, for one. Abbey has two guys. Maybe you can't handle her telling you all the juicy details and want to check it out for yourself." Then, as if he'd just discovered penicillin, he added, "It's that old boyfriend of yours. Isn't it!"

Jo looked like she'd been slapped. "Don't you dare compare me with

Abbey. I'm not afraid of love and commitment. I married you, didn't I? I'm not the one playing two guys against each other."

There was more. But when I heard "afraid of love" and "playing two guys," I took off. How could she? She knows I'm not afraid of anything. I stomped down the hall, not knowing where to go or what to do. I turned back. I'd tell her I am not . . . I turned around. Why waste my breath? I forced myself to walk. When I reached Ben's room, I pushed open the door, looked over at the bed where I found a lump under the covers and Ben's scruffy head peeking out the top.

I moved to the side of the bed, yanked back the covers and shook his shoulder until his eyes drifted open. "I'm not afraid of love, am I?"

I didn't wait for his answer. I undid the top button of my favorite red wool sweater, pulled it over my head and threw it across the room where it landed cattywompus across a lampshade on Ben's desk. I bent to pull off a boot and Ben's hand closed around my wrist.

"What's wrong, Abbey?"

His hand was warm; his voice was soft and liquid with sleep. His eyes, filled with concern, held something more. Something molten. My insides responded to both. I chucked the boots and went directly for the zipper on my jeans with my free hand. "I'm not afraid of love. I can make a commitment."

My jeans pooled around my ankles, where they tangled up, and I sank to the floor in a heap. Meanwhile, Ben swung his legs over the side of the bed and slid down beside me, still holding my hand. "What's this about, Abigail?"

That didn't slow me down for a sec. Just the opposite. He smelled all warm and toasty, like grilled cheese. His face was close enough for me to feel his warm breath, and that hand kept reminding me of how good it would feel on other parts of my body. I wrestled the jeans over my uncoordinated feet, pushed Ben back and rolled myself on top of him.

Did I mention that he was naked, save for a pair of banana covered boxer shorts, which I figured weren't going to be that hard to navigate. Negotiate. Whatever.

I leaned forward to show him the kiss of a woman who can commit. He lifted his head and I got a nose full of forehead. Ouch. He was on his feet in a move Spiderman would envy, and when I followed, he placed one hand on each of my shoulders, holding me back. He dipped his head, peered thoughtfully into my eyes and said, "I'd rather our first time, and mind you, we both know there will be a first time, but Abigail, I'd rather it not be a revenge shag."

I attempted to answer, but he put a hand over my mouth gently.

"And it won't be with a divided heart. It won't be because of something someone said to make you furious."

"Uncle Bertie."

He moved his hand long enough for me to get in an "I'm not—," then covered the lie with a hand and added, "We stop here until you choose."

Hormones. Temper. Craziness. Call it what you will. I didn't register a single word. "I know you want me," I said, stupidly.

Uncharacteristically, he rolled his eyes. His expression was the one you use when your friend is drunk and there's no talking sense into him. "Okay, I see I'm going to have to get hard arsed."

Huh?

"Play hard ball."

He came in close and moved one hand below my rear, setting off a whole slew of internal fireworks. Good. He'd come to his senses. He lifted me up. The bed! Thank goodness. I felt nervous, scared. About to cross a line. Wait a sec. Everything went cold. No Ben contact. I was on my feet in the hallway. With Ben on the wrong side of the closed bedroom door.

Playing hard to get. Right. But what he didn't know was that his bathroom adjoins a tiny guest room currently crammed with Gran's keepsakes and excess gear. I hit the door, shoved aside piles of dusty boxes and squeezed through the opening to Ben's bathroom. I had to get my clothes, if nothing more, I rationalized.

Ben was in the shower. And me? Now the daughter Vinnie would be proud of, I was taking my shot. I slipped out of my panties and tank top and stepped around the shower curtain. No one was going to say I was a frigid, chicken-shit virgin. Re-virgin.

Water streamed over Ben, caressing him wildly, as he rinsed soap from his hair. I inhaled sharply at the sight. His response at finding a nude Abbey next to him was a bit disappointing.

"Persistence, thy name is Abigail," he said before he captured my hands, which were headed toward victory.

"Abigail, Abigail, what am I to do with you?"

I leaned in and said, "I think—"

He escaped the shower in one swift move, before I got to the "You know" part, dripping his way to the bedroom. I followed, dripping my way behind him. I found him leaning against the bedroom door. Déjà vu.

"Haven't we done this already. Give it up, Ben. It's fate."

"Or madness."

"It's inevitable."

"Possibly a full moon."

"Meant to be."

"It's—" Before he had time to finish, the door opened, smashing us onto the floor with him on the bottom, me on top, and Jo staring down at us from the hall, with Tony right behind.

"Oh, Lord, save me!" Jo said when she saw us on the floor, not playing Twister.

"See," Tony smirked. "What'd I tell ya!"

I heard a "hmmph" as Jo soundly elbowed Tony in the ribs before she gave him a hard shove.

Still on top of Ben, conveniently covering all his best parts, I signaled her to turn around so we could untangle our limbs, cool our (my) libido, find a sheet or a towel or some clothes, and regain our composure.

Ben rolled me off of him and made like a gazelle for the bathroom. Me and the bathroom and Ben hadn't been working out so well lately.

"Abbey!" Jo shouted.

"You don't have to shout," I said, as I crab-walked my way to Ben's dresser where I found and slipped on a pair of pajama bottoms and a vintage Stones T-shirt.

"Then talk to me."

I couldn't think of a thing to say other than, "Some friend. Saying I can't commit. Thanks a lot."

"Oh, and we're moving in."

Still under a Ben-induced brain fog, I sputtered, "Where? Who?"

"Me and Tony. Tony was right. You're a danger zone. So we're moving in."

Tony appeared over her shoulder and I sent him a "What the hell is she talking about?" look followed by, "What the hell are you getting me into?"

"Tony said he came over here to warn you that you could be in danger."

Good 'ol Saint Tony had the decency to look embarrassed.

"He said you wouldn't listen to reason."

If I could just get my hands on him for two minutes.

"He's right. You need protection."

"I need Excedrin."

Ben exited the bathroom and handed me the bottle of painkillers.

"I wasn't being—"

He interrupted. "It's brilliant that you're concerned, Tony, but it's all been a terrible misunderstanding."

"Right, like you two on the floor."

He doubled over as Jo's elbow connected with his stomach this time.

"He meant—"

"Don't get me wrong. It's no one's business if you two—umph!"

Did he have a learning disability? Or did he enjoy getting elbowed? The next blow was going to be to the groin, if I knew Jo.

"Enough said. We're gonna protect you 24/7. No one is going to get near you, 'cuz we're going to be with you every minute."

Great.

Ben took one of Jo's hands in his and spoke softly. "Jo, no one's in danger here. I know it looks bad. Me disappearing like that, but I bungled it." The open disbelief in Jo's eyes, and the hope in Tony's, was obvious. "I saw Hanger 42 written on a note at Merona Air, and on a whim went over to do a little investigating on my own. After I was inside, the bolt slid closed and I was trapped inside. Apparently, I'd dropped my phone outside and couldn't ring anyone. There was nothing dodgy about it." He stopped to gauge her reaction. "Truly, Jo. If I thought Abigail was in danger, I'd ring Sam this minute and have her on the next flight."

Jo visibly relaxed, expelled a breath she'd been holding.

"Good. It's settled. You and Tony can go home."

Me. I was struck with a sudden case of smart-ass. "Tony, thanks so much for worrying about me."

He ducked his head, ignoring my sarcasm. "I'll go start the car. Meet me outside?"

Jo nodded and he was gone. She glanced from Ben to me, and back again. "Maybe I should stick around after all. Maybe you two need protection of an entirely different—"

"Go." I pushed her through the door.

"I mean, you never know—"

"Now." I had my back to hers, forcing her down the hall, one step at a time.

"You never know when your clothes might fall off and you—"

"One more word and I'm telling Tony where to find your test."

"That's blackmail," she said, eyes wide.

"Really? I thought it was me. Getting rid of you."

We'd reached the spiral staircase where pushing was no longer an option.

"Fine. I'll leave, but you have to promise me one thing."

"I'll floss daily, Mom."

"No, really. I want you to be safe," she said, as she made her way down one flight.

"I'm safe, already. Ben told you what happened."

She tossed something up from the landing below. I caught it one-handed. Looked into my open palm to find a flat, round disk, with the letters "ribbed" as bold as you please written across the top. Smart ass.

"Hey, Jo," I shouted after her. "What do you need with a boatload of wedding dresses, anyway?"

That said, I skulked in the hall outside Ben's door. I wasn't ready to think about what Jo thought of me. I wasn't ready to consider I might be a commitment-phobe. I didn't want to think about how Vinnie-like I'd been. Oh my God. That part alone was enough to make me freak. I had to clap a hand over my mouth to contain a low, steady, rhythmic groan, reminiscent of the much-maligned alley cat. I was really getting into it, contemplating my misspent youth, when I heard Ben calling me.

"Abbey has left the building," I said.

The door didn't budge. "With Elvis, I presume?"

"No such luck. She's on her way to Siberia. Forwarding address unknown."

The door remained tightly shut. "Siberia, huh?"

"Yep. Siberia. With Vladimir Ruchenko. Don't ask."

No knob turned. No squeaky hinges squeaked. I should leave. Siberia couldn't be any colder than Fairbanks. Could it?

"No. Right. Vladimir Ruchenko. The infamous Russian KGB agent, of course, known for any number of involuntary disappearances."

"Now in the business of voluntary disappearances. What with the cold war being over and all."

"Preying on misguided individuals who may feel they've made irreparable social blunders, although they have not."

"Or maybe they have, but have friends too decent to say so."

"Abigail, you've done nothing—"

"Don't you worry about me, Ben. I'll have a new identity, complete with fake ID before morning."

I could imagine Ben, on the other side of the door, combing through his hair with one hand, pulling his pants on with the other.

The door opened a crack. He hadn't been putting on his pants after all. What he had done was shove the dresser in front of the door. Was I that dangerous? Powerful? Irresistible? Right. Reality check.

"Look, Ben, I'm back. I've defeated my evil twin and sent her packing." I held up two hands. "See. Unarmed and innocent. Let me in."

"Brilliant tactic, but how can I be certain you're not the evil twin, and the good twin is locked up in the basement as we speak."

He slid the dresser aside, sank to the floor, his back to the door and leaned his head against the wall. I followed suit on the other side of the door. If some cosmic photographer had happened by at that exact moment, I imagine we would have looked like a set of perfectly matched bookends. Then Jo's words about love and commitment reared their ugly heads, and I angrily shoved them aside. Better to concentrate on Rebecca. Something I could do something about.

"Ben, the receipts in Rebecca's purse? I got it. They're selling drugs on eBay"

Breathing. Hair rustling. More breathing coming from his side. This had to be hard for him. He trusted Rebecca.

"Listen, Ben. What made you think Rebecca was in trouble in the first place?" And not causing the trouble, but I didn't say that part.

Easy question, apparently. "She's very responsible," he answered quickly. "Predictable, really. Hair appointment every six weeks. Teeth cleaning every six months."

Rah, rah, rah, Miss Goody-Two Shoes. "Enough already. I get it."

"When Merona came along, she simply took off with him. Not like her at all."

"Maybe it was love at first sight."

"You can be in love and rational."

You can? "Maybe total randiness."

"Maybe. But again. Not her usual behavior."

"So, she was acting differently. And you assumed she needed help?"

Big sigh. "Sounds daft when you say it."

"Love does that to a person." I held my breath.

"Merona's the one we need to look at, Abbey. He shows up in Fairbanks with more money than God and starts Merona Air. Where did the money come from?"

"Who knows. A rich aunt. He's a gigolo on the side?" I offered. "Rebecca was the one with the incriminating receipts. She's the one we should be concentrating on. But, hey. Maybe it's not drugs," I said, giving her the benefit of the doubt. "She could be selling black market Russian caviar, diamonds and mail-order brides."

"The eBay receipts were for mail order brides?"

"She could be back in the family business, fencing stolen goods for the family. Better yet, she could be selling things that don't even exist. Wait. I've got it. Laundering the money through a hefty investment in Merona Air."

"I think that's a bit—"

"You're biased. It's right in front of your face. Check the receipts for yourself."

He stood, then peered at me through the crack in the door. "Abigail, I'm studying how eBay's success depends on the trust factor. I'd be sorry to think Rebecca or Merona were misusing that trust for personal gain." He took a long minute. "But—"

"But we have to find out."

"Not you. I've put you in enough danger already. This is getting serious, and I'm not willing to take any more chances with your safety. You're out of it, Abigail."

The little hairs on the back of my neck bristled and my cheeks flamed. I had a choice here. Sicilian Tactic #22: Retaliation, best served cold. Then there was #8: If you can't convince 'em, confuse 'em. But no, I'd come close to crossing over to the Vinnie side recently, so I stopped myself. One, two three, four, five, six, seven, eight, nine . . . one hundred. Calmer now.

"You told Jo there was no danger. You told her the lock fell. No one was out to get you, and you—"

"Lied."

My eyes popped open. He lied? That changed everything. "Open this door right this minute!"

When he opened the door for me, I moved across the room to his bed and got into a cross-legged position—sex the farthest thing from my mind, in case you were wondering. He sat on the opposite end of the bed, his hair still dripping from the shower, all seriousness.

"Truth. Now."

"Okay. I got a message on my cell phone that you were at Hangar 42. Hurt. When I arrived at the hangar, it was deserted. I searched everywhere, and when I reached the office, someone pushed me from behind. My head hit the floor and that's all I remember. He stopped for a breath before he continued. "I didn't wake up until I heard you pounding on the door."

I fell forward until my face touched his sheets. I needed to stay calm. At least until I knew who's head I was going to have to smash with Justine's hammer.

Ben rested a hand on my head and said, "We'll figure this out, Abbey. But in the meantime, we need to keep you safe. Don't forget about the car accident."

I looked up. "You think it was intentional?"

He nodded solemnly. "I think we unnerved Merona and this is his way of telling us to back off."

"The shirt, too?"

"What shirt?"

I forgot. Ben didn't know about Big Ellie or the shirt.

"What shirt, Abbey?"

I filled him in. The short version.

To his credit, he didn't lock me in the bathroom and call Jo.

"If my calculations are correct, we currently have two break-ins, one hit-and-run and a kidnapping between us." His knee brushed mine and I remembered something other than foul play. "I know you, Abbey. You need to take this more seriously."

Oh, I was taking it seriously. Just wait until I got my hands on Merona and Rebecca.

My phone rang. "Justine! You're back," I said, surprised to find I'd missed her cranky presence after only one day without her.

"You need to get down to AVA, Abbey. Right now."

I didn't waste time asking who, what or why. "On my way," I said as I clicked off and made for the door. I hit Jo on speed dial. "Jo—"

"We're in the car. Justine called. See you there."

I repeated the routine with Mac's voice mail, slipped on my parka and grabbed my car keys, with Ben right behind. Once on the road, I ran over a curb, slid through two yellow lights and cut off a teen in an oversize gas-guzzler who shot me the finger, before sliding to a stop in front of AVA, just as Tony and Jo hopped out of their 4 x 4.

"What's going on?" I asked.

Tony shrugged; Jo did a hands up; Ben opened the door and ushered us inside where we found AVA looking completely . . . normal. Normal, with the exception of Juliette, who was sleeping peacefully, tucked into the overstuffed couch in a far corner of the room and an irritable Justine being patted repeatedly by a placating Jaye.

"I am not overreacting."

"I didn't say—"

Overreacting to what? I looked at Jaye but his eyes remained neutral.

"Abbey, are you wearing pajamas?" Justine shook her head. "Oh, never mind. I was waiting for our bags at the airport and I overheard two men talking. They were British, so of course, I listened."

"Of course. What did they say that has you so upset?"

"They mentioned your name and Merona air, but when they saw me looking, they lowered their voices. But I still heard, 'Take care of it' and 'Don't you worry.'"

So nothing.

"Not important in itself, I admit. But when I arrived back at work, I found this note.

She unscrunched the crumpled note and read. "Back off before you regret it."

Not a very creative threat. The note was made of cut out letters and looked like a first grader's art project, being as it was done with faded pink construction paper and globs of Elmer's glue.

"It's addressed to you, Abbey," Justine said, as she shook the note at me.

"That's it," Jo said. "You're going to have to learn to pee with me standing right beside you, because I'm not leaving you alone for a minute."

"You can stay with us, Abbey." The image of me peeing in front of Jo must have been too much for Jaye. "I'd feel much better if I knew you weren't going home right now," he said.

"They may have a point," Tony added.

"Abbey will be safe with me," said Ben. "I won't let anyone harm her."

"You? You got yourself kidnapped and locked in an abandoned warehouse," Justine snapped. "You can't be trusted with doggie do."

Jaye said, "Maybe we're—"

"I'm not overreacting," Justine said, "Abigail needs to back off, and if that's how you feel, maybe you should—"

I covered my ears. Argh! Please, God. I'll choose between Mac and Ben, fall in love, make a commitment, stop telling little white lies, call my mother every Sunday (even if it kills me) if you'll please, please save me.

"Abbey?"

I came back to the scene at hand: Justine, looking like she wished something from Molly would show up so she could demolish it.

"What?"

"What do you think?" Ben asked.

I surveyed their concerned faces and thought about it. What did we have to lose if we did back off?

We had no proof who was behind any of this. Someone was trying to scare me, but so far there was no permanent damage. We could call the police, and if they weren't interested, there was always my rat of an ex-husband, Rob, now a special investigations state trooper, who still harbors a bit of guilt over his horny toad behavior with my now-ex-girlfriend, Suzette. And if not Rob, then Sam. She's British Intelligence, for crying out loud.

We'd back out. Back off. Whatever. I'm not Nancy Drew, though I secretly yearned to be for most of my teen years.

"Okay. We back off," I said, not bothering to relate the whole convoluted mind journey that brought me to my decision.

Jaye let out a sigh of relief. As did Tony. Jo and Justine weren't as easily convinced.

"You mean it?" Justine

"Promise?" Jo

I nodded. "Girl Scouts honor."

Jo shot me a look. "You were a Brownie for two minutes. You don't have Girl Scouts honor."

"Well then. Sicilian honor." Sicilian Tactic #33: Lie for crying out loud.

"We can't trust her," Justine told Jo.

"I'm wounded." I placed one hand over my wounded heart.

"Well. Can we?" Jo demanded.

"Of course. Absolutely, positively."

But before I could swear, "On my honor," one more time, a vision hit me. So strong I had to grab Ben to keep from falling flat on my honorable ass.

Chapter 23

I'm fine," I said, before anyone had a chance to ask. "I have to make a call."

They looked confused, but let me go into the office unimpeded. God only knew what they were thinking. I made the call, fiddling with a pen, the one with the rotating airplane on top, which reminded me of the day I met Mac. I'd arrived back in Fairbanks to help Gran run AVA after years of running away from Fairbanks and all the bad memories it held, and Mac, well, he'd taken my breath away. Simple as that.

One, two, then a third ring. I was about to hang up when a recorded message came on.

"It's Abbey. Please call me. We need to talk."

At times my visions are gray and distorted like the frame of an old View-Master. But now, more often than not, they're like watching a movie in hi-def. As for recurring visions? I look at them kind of like emotional baggage clogging up the psychic airways. This time it was two little words that set me off. "I promise." In the vision Vinnie was pushing me down the aisle. Wedding vision turned nightmare.

In truth, I knew no one could force me to utter the dreaded words "I do" while stuffed like a sausage into a pristine Vera Wang creation. Okay. Maybe in a Stephen King movie. Or if someone was dangling Jo over the edge of a roof and I knew for a fact they would make good on their threat to throw her off unless I took the oath. Then I'd do it.

Other than the above, I couldn't think of a single reason I would end up living a life of involuntarily servitude. Ah . . . marriage.

Either way, I wasn't taking any chances. Stranger things have happened.

My phone rang, sending Brad into the stratosphere, like Glenda the Good Witch.

"What is it, Abbey? I'm busy," the voice demanded without benefit of "Hello" or "How are you?" or "Is everything okay?" No, "How's Mac?" No, "I love you and miss you."

"Hi, Mom. How are you?"

"Busy. Like I said. I was teaching Rocko to surf and he hit his head on the board. I'm patching him up. So what's so important? Speak."

Good question. When I first saw Vinnie in the vision, for one bizarre moment (it had to have been a ripple in time) I thought talking with her would explain everything. I should have known that would be like trying to talk to the dog that bit you. "Forget it, Mom. I meant to call Mac."

"What's so urgent you need to talk with Mac? Where is he? Es mi hija. La Virgen," she snapped.

If my rusty, high school Spanish served me right, she'd just told Rocko I needed to get a life.

"Nothing, Mom. Nothing. Gotta go."

"Not so fast, Missy."

I wanted to hang up on her so badly, but call me gutless. Besides, she'd only call back anyway, more suspicious than ever.

"I heard you have two balls in the game."

I was pretty sure there was a sexual innuendo in there somewhere. In that case, though, wouldn't it be four balls?

"I heard someone was in the shower and got the shaft."

Definitely not sexual. Because as we all know, I got nothing. "Mom!"

"Maybe I should come up there. Rocko, no. Later para es. And help you."

"No!" I shouted before I realized I was yelling. I turned the volume down. "I mean, no need, Mom. I'm fine."

"Freaked out—"

"Not insecure, not neurotic, not emotional. Gotta go, Mom. A plane's coming in. Late. Oh no, the landing gear's stuck. Hear those fire trucks? Whire, whire. Woo, woo. Call you real soon. Give Rocko my love. Take care." Sicilian Tactic #30.

I was lifting my head off the desk (Was it only 7:30 p.m.? It felt like midnight. Calls with Vinnie are so exhausting.) when Jo appeared in the doorway.

"We found another package for Mac. It must have arrived when you were climbing Big Ben."

"Very funny. Have Justine smash it. I'm busy." Busy trying to get Vinnie out of my head.

"She already is. Can't you hear the pounding?"

"I thought that was my head."

"Talked with Vinnie, huh?"

When she finds me looking like this, it's obviously Vinnie-related.

"Time to snap out of it, Ab. We need to come up with a Plan B."

"B?"

"Yeah. Plan A is you and Ben mind your own business. Plan B is what we do if the bad guys don't realize we've implemented Plan A."

I nodded. "And keep coming after us? Is that what you're saying?"

"Exactly. We need to figure out what we stumbled on that got their panties in a bunch. I mean . . . maybe someone saw me and Justine trying all the hangar locks."

"Then *you* would have been rear-ended and Justine would have spent the night at Hangar 42, not me and Ben."

"True." She stretched her arms over her head, as she's prone to do when nothing makes sense in her world, bent forward, doubling over to place her hands flat on the floor beside her shoes. "What? It helps me think."

"I didn't say anything."

"Improves the blood flow."

"Good." I did a weak stretch in solidarity.

"You could use some improved blood flow, you know."

"My blood's doing just fine on its own, thanks. And what's that supposed to mean, anyway?"

"You running around with Ben. Not thinking."

Who was she to judge? She's been through more men than—

"You're thinking with your hoo-ha, Abbey. Face it."

I turned my back to her, afraid of what I might say, but she came around to press her point, face-to-face. "I've been quiet long enough."

"Not nearly long enough," I countered.

"All right, Abbey. I'll leave it for now; this isn't the time, but—"

"I heard you, Vinnie."

"Not Vinnie. Vinnie would be saying 'Right on' and 'Go for it, Buns.

Get all you can get while you still have your looks.'"

"Maybe she'd be right," I said. Lordy. The second time I'd agreed with Vinnie (albeit it to annoy Jo) in one week. Scary.

Jo placed the back of her hand on my forehead. I pushed it away with more force than I'd intended. "No fever."

"Ha. Ha. Let's get back to Plan B. Maybe we should fingerprint the warning note."

"It's in 8,752 pieces by now. Justine's on a rampage. She's ordering a kevlar vest for you on eBay as we speak."

"Wow. Under that Navy Seal Special Ops exterior, she's a real cookie."

"Tell that to the video camera she demolished."

"Rats, I've been wanting one."

It would have been nice for catching special moments on tape. Like Jo laughing in that robust, throaty way she has when someone is saying something particularly outrageous. Or one of Ben twirling his Magic 8 Ball, as if it held all the real magic in the world. Mac climbing into the cockpit, looking more cocky than Tom Cruise in "Top Gun." Which reminded me of Molly, and there I was back to reality, again.

"Was there a note from Molly in the package?"

"Why? What do you have in mind?"

"We could fingerprint it, too, Columbo."

"And that would help, how?"

"We fingerprint everything that comes in, besides the mail, of course. But everything else: gifts, notes, threats. For all we know, the gifts aren't even from Molly."

I heard myself say "we fingerprint everything," like I was checking off items on a to-do list: mow the lawn, buy groceries, take out the trash, pluck eyebrows, fingerprint all incoming threats. "Then we'll be able to eliminate the suspects one by one."

She shook her head until her red curls took on a life of their own. "How's Justine going to take it when she finds out?"

"Plan C. Don't tell Justine about Plan B."

She closed her eyes and chewed her lips thoughtfully.

The idea was looking better and better. "We dust Big Ellie, the latest package, my room, the car. We already have a set from the note Ben found on my windshield. Now all we need is a used glass or cup from each person on our list."

"Weren't we going to do that before?"

"I know. I know. I was right there at Merona's." I slapped my forehead in frustration.

"That's okay. One step forward. Two back."

"I guess." I reached out and pushed a hair from her eyes. "And, Jo?"

"Yeah?"

I could tell she was already far, far away, cooking up all the devious ways she would get those prints, but it was important she hear me on this one.

"You're crossing a line, Jo. I'm not Vinnie. You don't have to worry about me." I said it softly, but with a big Back Off, right out there where she couldn't miss it.

It was just like the winter when I'd trudged down the snowy bank of the Chena River, ice skates over one shoulder, slipping and falling, Jo right behind, until I made it to the river's edge. After lacing up my boots, I eased out over the watery surface of the mostly frozen river. Jo didn't scream or call me stupid; when reason didn't work, she simply dragged me off the ice like a caveman bringing home supper. She never told my mother. She never cared that she was risking our friendship to save me from myself. For two weeks I blamed her for rescuing me from a situation where I clearly didn't need rescuing.

Now she nodded. Agreement reached.

But knowing Jo, it was far from over.

"Get out and stay out," I shouted at Jo and Tony's retreating backs. Of course, that was after I'd heard the satisfying thunk of their car doors slamming. Thank God for Jaye, who'd convinced a travel-weary Justine that Juliette's need for her own bed outweighed Justine's need to make certain I wasn't going to run right out and get myself murdered, kidnapped or tattooed, at the very least. Which left Ben and me alone.

"Ben, you can go home, too," I said, hoping he'd take the suggestion. The memory of my throwing myself at him earlier was still burning a hole in my stomach. "I have to check messages, but then I'll be right behind you."

"Not a problem, Abbey. I'll nap on the sofa," he said, already stretching his lanky frame across the sofa, arms relaxed behind his head, legs dangling loosely over the edge. "By the way, Abbey, how did you know before about Uncle Bertie? That it meant angry?" he asked, his voice dripping with sleep.

"www.englishslangforbuddingalaskananglophiles.com"

His eyes popped open. "Catchy."

"I also learned bollocks, shag and randy."

"Ah, all much beloved in the U.K."

"See? I have the terminology down, so you can leave now, secure in the knowledge that I can hold my own, or at least confuse the heck out of any scoundrels who come my way."

"Very good. However, there's one small detail."

"Which is?"

"We came together, Abbey."

Okay. Back to work. Which boiled down to two cups of coffee I didn't need, Jen saying yes to going to Merona, his taking the bait, then one quick call to offer a job to Birdie, who agreed to be at AVA at 8 a.m. tomorrow morning. One message from Mac, who was stuck in Coldfoot waiting for an engine part. The rest of the messages took me less than ten minutes, consisting mostly of thinly veiled requests for clairvoyant insight I had no intention of giving.

Frost was clouding the office windows and exhaustion was making me stupid by the time I finally shut down the computer and found Ben sound asleep, mouth open, making soft snuffling sounds like a baby, his expression as innocent as Juliette's. I wondered if he was back in the U.K. in his dream, squeezed into a crowded booth at the local pub surrounded by gaggles of adoring undergrads, right in his element.

I took a step back, not wanting to intrude. His black lashes resting on his cheeks reminded me of Juliette's, too. I wanted to reach out and check his breathing like you do with an infant in a crib. So sweet. And someone had tried to take him away from me.

Just thinking about Ben lying on the floor of that hangar made the Sicilian in me want to use every single one of the Sicilian Top Ten Methods of Revenge, handed down to me by my great Uncle Carmine in a secret ceremony when I turned thirteen. Apparently the age in Sicily where one is old enough to protect the family honor and take on the responsibility of ancient vendettas. Secret handshake and all.

I pulled the worn and crumbled list from my wallet and read. Oh. My. God. I couldn't do any of those things. For one, they involved body parts, hot substances and you don't want to know the rest. I wanted revenge, but I was thinking more along the lines of their car stereo programmed to play "Sugar, Sugar" into eternity. Or booking a private island for a month—on their credit cards, of course. Better yet, making certain the culprits got a cell with Crazy Eddie, who liked to yank people's fingernails out as a hobby.

Holy mother of mercy. Mom was right. Vinnie Mandate #2: Vengeance does serve a purpose. I knew exactly what Rebecca and Merona were up to. And it wasn't mail order brides.

Suddenly the roller coaster was pulling into the station and I didn't have an ounce of energy left to plot devious strategies. I stood in front of AVA's front door, contemplating the cold and snow and icy roads, inertia mingling with exhaustion. I needed to go home, but couldn't find the energy to take the simple steps necessary: left arm into left sleeve, repeat with right. Pick up keys, zip parka, lift arms, slide on hat. Too much effort.

I threw the lock on the doors and doubled back to my office. The couch there may be hard, the old leather cushions patched badly with brown duct tape, but it was here, not seven miles up a snowy road. I used every last bit of energy I had left to pull my parka over my shoulders before I fell back on the couch, into a deep, deep sleep.

Countdown to Valentine's Day: One Day to Go

Once upon a time, there were three bears. Papa Bear was talking about buying a Cessna C-34, while Mama Bear was going over the expense to productivity ratio. Meanwhile, Baby Bear was chillin' outside with two friends, who Mama Bear swore were trouble. Of course Baby Bear wouldn't hear it. In truth, they were all part of an organized crime ring, hiding out deep, deep in the forest. Baby Bear had a tattoo on the back of his neck that I couldn't quite make out.

"Coffee?"

I pried one eye open (the other was securely glued shut) to find two blurry figures hovering over me. This called for getting up, but when I tried, I fell back into my dream. Baby bear's tattoo. I could almost read it now.

"Abigail."

That wasn't right. Why would my name be tattooed—

"Abigail!"

I opened my eye again. Still there. They were coming into focus now. One tall and dark. Definitely male. One short, pert, female. Shit. Shit. Shit. Mac and Birdie.

"Pajama party?" Mac asked, as I managed to push sleep aside and force myself into a sitting position, eyes firmly shut. I guess he'd already found Ben asleep in the lobby.

The vintage Sanitary Ice Cream clock, shaped like a big moo cow, wagging tail and all, read 7 a.m. I'm sure I'd told Birdie to be here no earlier than 8.

"Drunken orgy?"

"Go away!" flew out of my mouth before I could wrestle it back.

Through my eyelashes, I could see Birdie filling out forms on the customer side of my desk, making believe she wasn't hearing every single word.

"Aren't you in Anaktuvik?"

"I have a surprise for you. But you have to open your eyes to see it."

I reached for his hand, pulled him close and whispered, "Get Birdie out of here. I don't need to greet my new employee on her first day with morning breath." I blew him a kiss, so he'd know how bad it was.

"If you're not up in five, I'm getting the ice cubes," he whispered. "Come on Birdie. Let's give Sleeping Beauty here time to wake up. And, Birdie, in case you're wondering," he joked, "yes, it's always this crazy at AVA. Will that be a problem for you?"

I listened as Birdie explained to Mac about how he didn't know from crazy and how her meemaw once took Birdie's daddy to court for running down her prize-winning Blushing Maiden rose bushes and how the judge, who'd courted meemaw in high school, gave daddy community service. Daddy, not to be undone, showed up at the Skocum County beautification project in Meemaw's rattiest terry cloth bathrobe with two-inch round pink curlers in his hair and bunny slippers on his over-size feet, scandalizing Meemaw and the entire Ladies' Auxiliary. Meemaw went after him with her garden rake, and chased him clear down the middle of Main Street.

The tail end of the story drifted off as they exited the office. Ben walked in, looking about like I felt. I was going to make a crack about how I didn't used to get so creaky after sleeping on a couch, when I remembered something.

"Ben, I was wrong. Rebecca and Merona aren't drug dealers. They're identity thieves." I wasn't going to give him a chance to contradict me, so I plowed on without taking a breath. "Don't you get it? They're stealing IDs on ebay. All you need is a name and social security number and you're good to go. Then you can get credit cards, IDs, anything. They make an eBay sale and then ask for the customer's social security number, saying it's to verify identity. Sure, most people won't give it out, but enough will. Do. If that doesn't work, all they have to do is collect email addresses, make up a phony eBay Web page and get the information that way. It would look legitimate, and I bet a lot of people fall for it, too." I stopped and waited a beat. "Okay. You can talk now."

"I thought we were backing off?" He sat next to me. I got up and crossed the room. I still had that morning breath thing to think about.

"Figuring it out does not affect the backing out plan. Don't you want to know what's going on here?"

"I was planning on finding out on my own, Abbey, but I can see there's no stopping you."

Our eyes met across an uncrowded room. Was that music I heard? I broke eye contact and stepped into the functional, if not roomy, bathroom in the corner of my office to brush my teeth. It could become very important that I have fresh breath soon. I wondered: If I peed, would he hear me?

Ben peeked his head in the doorway, one hand resting on the door frame, looking completely edible. And me with a mouthful of toothpaste. I had no choice but to swallow.

"I'm off," he said. "Jo asked me to meet her at her store this morning."

"Really?" I ran the toothbrush under the water and returned it to its cup. "What for?"

"She didn't say. But you're absolutely not to know, I'm told."

I absentmindedly ran a hairbrush through my tangled hair, now a rat's nest. "Ouch. And you're sure it was Jo. Not Merona talking like a girl. Or a set up. You think you're meeting Jo, but by tomorrow you're in cement boots, six feet under in Abyss Lake?"

"It was last night." He took another step forward, occupying the only free space in the tiny room. "Jo found me in the loo while you were trying to disabuse Justine of the notion of getting one of those prison tracking bracelets for you."

"And she wanted to meet you today and wouldn't say why?"

"Other than not to tell you, she said nothing."

"Abbey." Mac was in the bathroom doorway now. "I think Birdie's ready."

Trapped. We were trapped in the tiny bathroom like rats, with no back door. I could see the photos in the morning paper. Me and Ben being loaded into the coroner's van on stretchers. The headline. Clairvoyant Didn't See It Coming!!!

"I'll be going now," Ben said, as he easily slid around Mac. "Mac, good to see you."

"Same here," Mac replied before he turned back to me. Maybe I was overreacting.

He took in Ben's retreating back, then me in the bathroom. I wondered if this reminded him of anything.

If it did, he wasn't saying.

"Birdie's ready, Ab."

I moved past him without incident, but then he tugged the back of my shirt, moved closer and whispered into my neck. "This wouldn't be about Molly, would it?"

It might have been. If I'd thought of it. Unfortunately. Well, I wasn't going to apologize, what with there not being even a square inch of Saran Wrap anywhere in sight.

"Because nothing happened." He lightly kissed the nape of my neck, sending familiar chills down my back. "And nothing was going to happen. Not ever."

"Are you ready for me, Abigail? Or should I wait outside," Birdie asked after she entered the room and caught Mac pressed up against me, a fistful of my shirt in his hand.

I pulled away, expecting resistance and stumbled forward into Birdie as Mac released his grip on me. "Birdie, I'm so glad you're here. We're all looking forward to working with you," I said. Fast thinker. Right?

"Thank you—"

"I only have three things you need to remember. One. We hire professionals and treat them as such. Two. If you have a problem with someone, talk to them about it. And three. Don't put up with any crap. Not from customers, not from coworkers, not from me. Just like it was at Merona's, I'm assuming," I said, although we all knew different.

"At Merona's it was, 'Anything goes in business and keep your mouth shut. The customer's always right, no matter how obnoxious, inebriated, or addle-brained.' But other than those, it's exactly the same."

"Good. Then we're in agreement."

Birdie straightened her shoulders and pulled herself to her full height. A broad smile crossed from her button mouth to her almond-shaped eyes and, swear, she looked like she was about to salute.

"Yes, Ma'am, I believe we are."

"Oh, and Birdie? If any packages come in, don't smash them. That's Justine's job."

It took me no time at all to realize that hiring Birdie was pretty damn smart. She already knew all the systems we used at AVA. She had a work ethic that would make her mama proud. Inside information on Merona (which I was going to have to mine later) and bonus, a family of characters straight out of "The Dukes of Hazard", the DAR, and "Designing Women", along with the unending supply of stories she had no problem sharing about all of them.

By the time lunch rolled around, I could have sworn Uncle Jimbo would never have forgiven Aunt Billy Jean for leaving the top down on his '78 cherry Mustang convertible during a hail storm, even though Birdie said he came around as soon as Billy Jean set out a healthy serving of her prize-winning country fried steak, gravy and biscuits.

Meanwhile Birdie's niece, Mae, and her friend, Betty-Lou, had bigger fish to fry. Like how to get out of a year's worth of detention for painting fishnet stockings, hooker makeup and come-and-get-me boots on the life-size statue of the Virgin Mary that graced the entryway of St. Joseph's Girls High.

To make matters worse, several Skocum High School students with an entrepreneurial spirit photographed the Virgin Mary in her new outfit, ironed the image onto T-shirts in St. Joseph's school colors and were currently making a killing on the Internet and in back alleys all over town. Mostly to St. Joseph students, who'd taken to wearing them under their school uniforms.

At one point, I suspect a customer almost wet herself when Birdie regaled her with a story about great-aunt Muffy from the Atlanta Wilkeses, who tried for all she was worth to keep up on the modern vernacular, but who still thought cool meant she needed a sweater, phat meant overweight, metrosexual meant there was a new bus route to 6th Avenue, and jiggy was some off brand of Jell-O. Not that she'd ever had Jell-O, because when she went in for her brow lift, the hospital served it to her and she told the unsuspecting nurses aide she'd rather eat chocolate covered dog turds than something that looked like congealed vomit.

Birdie's family may be slightly nuts, but her mama was golden. The kind who told her she looked like a goddess when she dressed up in striped leggings, ballet tutu and old army boots. Unlike mine, who told me I looked like a chicken when I got upset.

When Birdie was five, she stuck her hand in great-grandma's 80th birthday cake; her mama immediately followed suit and made it into a family tradition. My mom would have yelled at me about it until she turned eighty. She'd still be kicking and it would be "See, Abigail. No one else one decided to stick her hands in the cake. See how much nicer this is." And I'd respond by cutting a huge piece and saying, "Here, Mom. Eat up."

I mean. Don't they say cholesterol kills?

God. I should be ashamed. I am ashamed. Jealous of Birdie for getting the good mom and daydreaming of knocking mine off with birthday cake. Truly pathetic. There are faster methods.

Stop it!

After a quick welcome lunch, I left Birdie with Justine, heaven help her, and took off to track down my first set of fingerprints. Molly's being the most logical choice. Our one big assumption was that the packages had actually come from her, but what if our perpetrator was using her to lull us into a false sense of security? What if the next package wasn't so benign?

Hmm. I should look into getting some bomb-sniffing training for Cupcake. I wonder if Mac would go for it? Either way, it wasn't going to be me going after Molly. I still couldn't shake the image of a mostly naked Molly trying to devour Mac like a black widow spider. Nope. I was going over to Jo's store—to plot strategy, bitch and moan about Molly, share some of Birdie's funnier stories and to find out what was up with the pregnancy test these days. Definitely not in that order. I mean, if Tony (not all that observant) noticed something funny was going on with Jo, I needed to check it out.

At least Mac wasn't planning our wedding. There were no telltale signs of covert wedding operations around the house or office. No hidden crepe paper wedding bells. No tux rental in the back of his closet. No new underwear for the honeymoon. He hadn't been sweeter, more solicitous or romantic lately.

Nothing was out of the ordinary, except for Jo, a hit-and-run and a kidnapping.

"You're up to something," I accused Jo, seconds after arriving through the back door of her shop, hoping to surprise her into confessing.

"You're on crack," she replied, then shook her head before she went back to pricing a handful of mood rings.

"Before, I thought all your craziness was pregnancy related, but phone calls in the closet? A million wedding dresses? Luring Ben over here for a secret meeting?"

Jo spoke slowly, like she was explaining quantum physics to a toddler. "Did you ever hear the old saying, you can't get everything you want?"

"You're not answering my question."

"Exactly."

"Fine. I'll ask Ben."

"Fine. Good luck with that."

She turned her back on me. I recognized her don't-mess-with-me side. It doesn't show up often, but when it does, she wins, you lose. I was looking around the store, contemplating my next move when a customer dressed in a full-on cowgirl outfit walked up to Jo. "I'm here to pick up my two wedding dresses."

She gave me a funny look, then added, "Don't I know you?"

Jo practically vaulted over the counter to get to the dresses and press them on the cowgirl. "Here, Kat. Why don't you take these in back and try them on."

"I could swear I know you," she insisted, pointing at me as Jo leaned into her, gently pushing her toward the dressing room. But Kat wasn't having any part of it. "I'm Katrina, Reverend Baylor's sister."

Jo sighed. "Kat, this is Abbey. Abbey Vertuccio. Remember from high school?"

"Oh. Right. Abbey." She reached out and shook my hand, then waited. "Anything? You see anything?"

"Ah. No. Not really," I lied.

"Not really? What?"

"Nothing."

"That dog won't hunt. Give."

Fine. "I saw you in a '78 Crown Vic with a guy who looks like Tony from the Sopranos. That's all."

"Shit. That's Bob's brother. Trouble since the day he turned two. I'd better get home and hide my party dresses. Did you happen to see when he'd be arriving?"

I shook my head and in no time at all the door was hitting her in the backside and Jo and I were alone again.

"She forgot her dresses," I said, hoping Jo would fill in the blanks. No such luck. "Anything you want to tell me about, Jo?"

"Lots. Not that you'd listen." She busied herself with a ball of tangled necklaces only tin snips could undo.

"Fine. Forget it." But pushy Kat gave me an idea. I casually reached out to touch Jo on the arm. She slapped my hand away.

"Get off of me. I have a shop to run and you have fingerprints to find. At least I thought so."

I tried again.

"No fair," she said, as she squeezed behind the glass counter, safe from sometimes clairvoyant fingers. "So? What are you waiting for. Go already."

"I'm going, but I'm not done with you, Jo Beth Callahan-Caroni. Not by a long shot."

She pushed out one hip, stuck out her chest and threw down the gauntlet. "May the best man win."

I sat in my car, parked in the narrow alley behind Jo's store, figuring out my next move. The engine was only one step ahead of the 30 below zero cold beyond my windows; the ice fog was so thick I could barely see to the street corner.

As I sat there wondering why Jo had a zillion wedding dresses in the store, I couldn't help but think of Valentine's Day. It was creeping up on me and I couldn't shake the feeling of dread. Wedding or no wedding, I sensed that change was coming and I wasn't ready for it. Not now. Maybe never.

I didn't want to become someone's property or appendage. When I wanted to leave, I didn't want to have to ask for permission. Maybe I wouldn't leave, but having the option was crucial.

Now Jo. She may be the one person I know who's been in love with her life since day one. Even when things weren't right with Eddie (Serious Ex-Boyfriend #1). If I were acting weird, no one would notice. But Jo acting crazy was making me almost as worried as I was about the arrival of V-Day.

Fingerprints were one thing, but Jo was now officially my top priority.

"Ben?" I said after he picked up the call. "I have something to handle with Jo. Can you take Cupcake over to Molly's for an emergency appointment? Tell her it's a favor for Mac. You can say his house key is missing and he thinks Cupcake swallowed it. She'll see you if she thinks she can get her hands on his house key; meanwhile, you can steal her—" What could he steal? Not the doggie thermometer. "Well, you'll figure something out."

He had to agree. How could he not? When you save someone's life, doesn't it belong to you? That's not right. If you save someone's life, you're responsible for him. That puts a different light on the whole subject. But the only thing he had to fear from Molly was Saran Wrap, and I was guessing she didn't keep a ready supply at the veterinary clinic. So, no worries. Now

I could focus on the task at hand.

I turned off the car and tried the back door to the store. Seriously. Jo was going to have to stop leaving that door unlocked. Someone could sneak in. I listened a minute, and hearing nothing, closed the door softly behind me. I headed for the bathroom, looking for the pregnancy test. The room was exactly the way we'd left it the day we hid from Tony. I opened the medicine cabinet, checked behind the bottles of lotion and first aid supplies. No stick with a bold plus or minus sign hiding inside. Next I lifted the lid on the toilet tank, shushing myself as tile hit tile with a dull thud. But the tank was empty, except for a corroded red brick displacing water at the bottom.

I headed for the round, aluminum trash can that was squeezed between the sink and toilet and pulled off the lid for a look inside. I couldn't bring myself to plough through the trash with my bare hands, or to dump the contents on the floor. Hoping against hope, I checked under the sink, found rubber gloves and a trash bag, and got to work pulling out tissues, Q-tips and old newspapers, transferring them to the large black bag. I was in the process of extracting something sticky from the bottom of the can when trouble struck.

"What do you think you're doing, Abigail Vertuccio?"

Busted. Before I could frame an appropriate response, Jo whisked the can out of my hands, pushed me out of the bathroom and down the hall.

"That's it, Abbey," she shouted. "This is war."

That was a half second before she shoved me, none too gently, out the back door, into the foggy, friendless alley.

Sex is the real problem. It's behind every fix a woman lands in. Take Jo. She's worried she could be pregnant. Or by now she knows. Either way. It's sex. Take Justine. She thinks Molly wants Mac and that Molly doesn't give a damn how much that hurts me. Again. Sex.

Maybe the real culprit isn't sex. It's men. If you'd just pick right, everything would be perfect. Like delicacies in a bakery showcase. An enterprising clerk in a stiff linen apron asks, "Would you like a serving of Computer Geek, Ma'am?"

"Yes, please." Computer Geeks: patient, willing to spend untold hours in pursuit of their goal, understand that proper input gets proper output. Never gives up.

"How about a bit of Superior Court Justice on the side?"

"No thanks." Too judgmental. Obviously.

"Maybe a little Psychiatrist?"

"Really. No thanks." Analyzing every move until the word "spontaneity" loses all meaning? Forget about it.

"I have just the thing for you," our aproned friend says, as she delves deeper into the case and pulls out a sample of University Professor. "I think you'll enjoy this one."

University Professor: infinite love of learning; if they don't know something they research it in detail until they've mastered it perfectly. Can anyone say Kama Sutra?

"Yes, please. I'll take one for now and one for later."

"Before you go, why don't you try a little Pilot. You'll never fly so high—"

Pound. Pound. Pound. The car window shook as Jo pounded me out of my reverie. I could almost smell the fresh-baked Pilot. I cranked open the window. About an inch. I'm no fool.

"You're going to die of carbon monoxide poisoning, you idiot."

I could see the headline: Bakery Sex Scandal Kills Prominent—

Pound. Pound. "Get going or I'll sic the cops on you."

All right already. I cranked the window the rest of the way down and rolled down the alley. Maybe the carbon monoxide was getting to me.

Back to AVA to regroup and get some work done while my brain unfogged. Not that I wasn't close to being obsolete with two powerhouses like Justine and Birdie on board. AVA would be fine, whether I popped in or not. AVA has a niche market that Gran carved out years ago. There was a big glitch last year from an unsuccessful saboteur, but since then we've regained our market share. We're not rich, but the staff is well paid, I have a house and car and Mr. Peanut, thanks to Gran. Beyond that and Big Ellie, I don't need much.

I gunned the engine and took a hard turn onto University Avenue toward AVA. Maybe I needed a new challenge. Something at least as exciting as jumping in Big Ellie and taking off cross country. Bungee jumping? Skydiving? Mountain climbing? The obvious answer was flying, what with all the planes at my fingertips. Only how secure would you feel knowing you were flying with a pilot who was one clairvoyant flash away from taking everyone down in a crumpled heap of flaming metal?

When I arrived at AVA, the lobby was littered from one end to the other with rucksacks, rolling suitcases and boxes of every size, some packed meticulously, others with tape slapped on as an afterthought. I zigzagged my way to the office and watched as Justine and Birdie moved behind the counter effortlessly, like it had all been expertly choreographed, labeling luggage, handing out boarding passes and soothing weary travelers.

People were gathered amicably over cups of coffee, bagels and donuts from the coffee cart. A sleepy-eyed teen in an AC/DC shirt lounged across two chairs, earplugs insulating him from the husband and wife team who were religiously reciting every line of an "Above the Arctic Circle" brochure.

A warm feeling came over me. Familiar and safe. Bordering on contentment. I half expected Justine to shout something caustic across the room, in keeping with her usual don't-get-all-fluffy-on-me attitude. Instead, when I caught her eye, she smiled quickly and returned to her customer.

You know those times when everything is exactly right?" That's what I was thinking when I tripped over a red, sausage-shaped bag, almost landing flat on my face, except for a burly guy in overalls and a goatee who snatched me up before my nose hit pay dirt. And still, the mood persisted. Peace. This was peace. Like I really could fly.

I settled down behind my desk and leaned back. Flying was ridiculous. But maybe that's what you do. Start with the ridiculous and go from there. It's not like anyone needed to know about it. And hey. If it didn't work out, at least it wasn't going to be sex that brought me down.

The message light on my phone was blinking furiously. I picked up, punched in my password and hit play. Jen's voice came on—a whisper really. "Hey. Good news. I'll call you later. On my break."

Hmm. Good news must mean she got Merona's prints. Go, Jen!

The phone rang as soon as I hung up."

"Abbey, it's Ben."

"I recognized your voice. Where are you?"

"I'm leaving Molly's now. Woof!"

"Woof?"

"Sorry. Here, boy." His voice was muffled, like he'd covered the phone after the "sorry" part.

"Is something wrong with Cupcake? Did you get the prints?"

"Wait. Let me pull over." A horn blared, a car door slammed and then Ben came back on. "That's better. Bad enough driving on the right without ringing someone as well."

"So. What happened at Molly's?"

I dumped a box of large paper clips on my desk, fighting a case of serious impatience.

"Not exactly as planned. But I did get her prints on my pen, so all's well—"

I twisted a paper clip into the shape of a snake. Or a rabbit. "What didn't go as planned?"

"Cupcake was at puppy training camp, so I stopped by the animal shelter to take a photograph of a puppy to bring to Molly."

The paper clip figure was beginning to resemble King Kong, now. "Vet by photograph?"

"When I arrived at the shelter, I found the perfect candidate. With the biggest brown eyes."

This was obviously going to be a long story. I began a paperclip Empire State Building and waited.

"He can sit, roll over, heal, fetch and play dead. They let me feed him."

Uh, oh. I set my sculpture aside. "So, Ben. You got the photo of the dog and went over to Molly's. Right?"

"Yes. Yes. I did."

Something wasn't right.

"Molly saw me in the waiting room and she was very gracious. When she wrote out the prescription, I lent her my pen."

I shook my head and rolled my eyes. "Prescription, Ben?"

"I couldn't leave him there, Abigail. They said it was his last day. If I didn't take him, it was going to be kaput for Mr. Potato Head."

"His name is Mr. Potato Head?" I started demolishing the Empire State Building.

"It was Liberace. I changed it. He has a rather large head."

I sighed. I couldn't help it. "And what's Mr. Peanut going to say about this? Who's going to pick up the bloody pieces of Mr. Potato Head after Mr. Peanut gets done with him? And don't you think two Mr. P's is confusing?"

"You're right. We'll call him Harvey."

I hit speakerphone and held my head between my hands.

"I'm not naming a dog after an giant bunny in a 50s movie."

"Woof."

"And that would be Harvey?"

"Yep. We're on our way home," he said. "Meet us there and I'll do introductions."

I practically flew through the lobby on my way out, hit the road, tires spinning, and arrived home seconds before Ben pulled up, smiling like a proud papa. He opened his car door and got out, followed by what looked like a bear cub. Okay. Maybe not. But it was at least as big as a bear cub, from where I was standing. My eyes traveled from dog to Ben and back again. What was Mr. Peanut going to do about this? First Ben invaded the house, followed by Mac and Cupcake—even if he was off at camp. I wouldn't be surprised if Mr. Peanut packed up and moved into Big Ellie at the first opportunity.

"If Mr. Peanut—"

"I know."

"If they fight—"

"I agree."

I gave him the look. "Okay, then. We'll see how it goes."

It turned out our new visitor loved cats. While Ben and I rested on the sun room couch, Harvey let Mr. Peanut snarl and hiss and do a fat-tail-and-ears-back routine, giving Mr. Peanut his fill of threats, scare tactics and bullying without moving a muscle. When Mr. Peanut got tired of all the threatening and harassing, Harvey curled up into a furry ball next to Ben's feet on the floor and snuffled peacefully in his sleep.

"Crisis averted," Ben said, as I watched Harvey's chest rise and fall.

"He's not going to enjoy an eight-hour plane ride back to England, you know. Did you consider that when you took him?" I said, playing devil's advocate.

Ben leaned forward, stroked Harvey's soft ears, neck and head. "That may not be a problem, Abbey."

What did that mean? Was he saying he wasn't planning on taking the puppy back with him?

"Ben, you know I can't keep him when you go home."

His eyes searched mine. For what, I didn't know. "Never mind. Let's wait and see how it goes. Either way, I couldn't leave him there with only one day left."

Softy. Of course, he couldn't. And Mr. Peanut seemed okay. As long as I remembered not to cozy up to Harvey in front of him, there was a good chance Mr. Peanut wouldn't seek revenge by peeing in my laundry basket or ripping my sheets to shreds.

Ben went about the business of unpacking Harvey's doggy supplies from the car, filling brightly colored matching ceramic bowls that read,

"Woof" and "Woof Woof," with bottled water and organic dog food, which, I think, was pound for pound more expensive than breakfast cereal, ensuring that it was all safely set up on the far end of the kitchen so as not to offend Mr. Peanut. He then proceeded to unpack every dog toy known to man with the exception of the castle dog house Mac and I had made fun of the day Cupcake arrived.

Mr. Peanut was going to be in kitty heaven, stealing Harvey's cache of new and interesting goodies. A squeaky stuffed alligator was right up Mr. Peanut's alley. Then there was the ball on a rope, the oh-so-soft doggie bed, the doggie quilt to match, and of course, the doggie pillow. So much to choose from and so little time. I could almost see Mr. P rubbing his paws together. But then Ben pulled out an equal number of enticing kitty toys. Plush orange carrots, blue striped fuzzy mice, balls of all colors and sizes and Mr. Peanut was a catnip goner.

Ben left the two of them to sort through the loot and sank down beside me on the sofa. "Not so bad, huh?"

It was now or never. I had to ask Ben the question I'd been wanting to ask for two days. "Ben," I started, gathering up steam. "I need a favor. And you can't say no."

I caught Harvey surrendering a green plastic pork chop to Mr. Peanut and smiled before returning my attention to the problem at hand. "Because you owe me."

"Anything." He took my hand, and now I felt like a jerk about the whole you-owe-me part.

"I need you to protect me on Valentine's Day." I caught his startled look and added, "Not that kind of protection. And not all day. Just from around noon to three. That should do it."

"What kind of protection are you talking about, Abigail?"

I took a deep breath and stood over him. "I need you to make sure I don't get married. Keep me away from any churches, synagogues, prayer halls, ministers, priests, rabbis, and especially from Mac. No. Don't look at me like that. I'm not crazy. Just promise. You owe me!" I did it again. Rats.

"Yes. Of course."

"Yes?"

"Of course. I'll do it."

I expelled the air I didn't realize I was holding. I sat, head back, eyes closed. "Thank you." When I opened my eyes again, he was grinning like a Cheshire Cat.

"What?"

"Nothing really."

"What?" I insisted.

"Well. For one, spending the day with you on Valentine's Day, isn't a favor. And two, Jo asked me to do the very same thing. Not protect you, but keep you occupied. I believe her exact words were, 'So she won't crack up over the whole stupid wedding thing.' Apparently, she can't do it because she and the basketball team are planning a big surprise party for Tony's two-year anniversary at the university. "

I punched him in the shoulder. "And she couldn't tell me? Her best friend?"

"She thought you'd never go near a big party on Valentine's Day. Too close to a wedding reception and all," he replied, rubbing his shoulder where I'd connected.

"That's ridiculous," I said, even though I knew that's exactly what I would have thought. "It's not in a church, is it?"

"Not even close." Good. I was safe.

"But, Abbey?" he asked in all seriousness.

"Yes, Ben," I answered, equally serious.

"Who's going to protect you from me?"

Hmmm.

Chapter 24

Ah. Blissful domesticity. A crackling fire roared in the fireplace. Mr. Peanut nestled against my hip, while Harvey was spread-eagled across Ben's lap. I stared into the fire, spellbound. All we needed now was a little Ben asking for a story and a little Abbey, sucking on a bottle and the scene would be complete.

God! What sorcerer had me in his clutches?

It must have been the big, fluffy snowflakes landing softly, right beyond the window. That and the Dewar's spiked hot cocoa. The thick, wool blanket wrapped around my shoulders. The rhythm of two, breathing as one.

Magic! And not the good kind. Scary. I sat up, nearly splashing my cup of lukewarm cocoa all over Mr. Peanut, who rewarded me with a scowl before moving on to a more reliable source of heat. Ben.

"Something wrong, Abbey?"

"I can't sit here all day," I snapped. The best I could do on short notice. Mr. Peanut readjusted his position, trying to edge Harvey off Ben's lap in the process. "I have to—"

"You have to."

Was that a mischievous grin on his face?

I stood, sending my mug crashing to the floor. Harvey opened his eyes briefly and closed them again, satisfied that nothing important was going on.

"I have to clean up this mess. Then I need to cook. I'm starving. I need to chop something. Fillet. Frappe. Fry. Something."

"You are a nutter," Ben mumbled.

I raised a defiant chin and opened my mouth to rebut his wildly unfair accusation.

"A delightful one," he interrupted. "Now, since you have flipping and frying to do, I'll head over to the university to see what I can find out about identify theft." He rose, setting Harvey and Mr. Peanut in the warm spot he left behind.

"You think I'm right?"

He leaned in, kissed the tip of my nose, then the corner of my mouth. It was looking like he wasn't about to answer any time soon when the doorbell rang.

Saved by the bell. Or as they say back in dear old England, saved by the bloody bell.

I threw open the front door and Jen materialized, stomping her boots and rubbing her gloved hands together. "My car heater went out," she said, as she did a warm-up dance. Tiny icicles clung to the ring in her eyebrow, the inside of her nostrils and her deep-brown eyelashes. I pulled her inside before she could turn into an ice pop, and checked her over for visible signs of frostbite. "Any pain or numbness?"

"I'm fine. Just cold," she said, shivering like she couldn't stop herself.

Ben took over. He wrapped her in a warm blanket, settled her in front of the fire next to Harvey and Mr. Peanut, then pulled her mittens off one at a time, checked each hand, then carefully removed each boot and each sock, warming her frigid toes between gentle fingers. She closed her eyes and sighed at the comforting warmth of his touch. A feeling surged in my chest. A cup of pride seasoned with a teaspoon of jealousy. Okay, Abbey. Make up your mind. First you want him, then you don't.

Campbell's tomato soup, nice and hot, the heel of a warmed loaf of sourdough bread, napkin, spoon. Jen's snack was ready and I was back from the edge. I set it down beside her. Her eyes opened slowly and she gratefully bent to inhale the spicy aroma.

"Careful. It's still hot."

"It's perfect."

Then she telegraphed me a smile that said she had news. Details at ten.

I crossed over to the window and peered out at her car. A beat up old Jeep on its last legs. "Hey, Jen," I said, pointing out the window at the Jeep. "Don't I pay you enough?"

"Watch it! That car's a classic!"

A classic heap of junk. But what did I know?

"Aren't you going to ask me what I found?" she asked, between bites of the crusty bread.

"I give. What did you find out?"

She inhaled deeply. "Well. First there was the letter from the bank. Merona blew a gasket when he called them. You should have heard him. 'I damn sure do have money in that account, you incompetent moron. Oh, yeah? Well, I happen to play golf with the president of your institution, young man.' Like that." She gulped some soup and continued. "He'd hardly hung up when he got a call from one of his credit card companies saying he was over his limit and did he want to rectify it? He about went ballistic. Seems he's bouncing checks right and left, Abbey."

She noticed Ben's sympathetic look, and added, "He's a grade-A jerk, Ben. He yells if his secretary forgets the cream in his coffee. He fired Sadie when she had the flu. Worse, he's obsequious to the most obnoxious customers. But here's the thing. I hate to say it, but I think he's innocent."

Well, if Merona was innocent, that left Rebecca as the big bad wolf in Dolce and Gabbana clothing. I wondered how Ben was taking it.

"There's more," Jen said. "Two English guys came in looking for Rebecca."

I shot Ben an Ah, Ha look.

"Tall, very Hugh Jackman. The one with the great butt asked me what I was doing after work, but I had to come here so I blew him off. But man, I wouldn't have minded—"

"Anyway."

"They asked for Rebecca," she said, after which she zoned out. Probably daydreaming about Mr. Firm Butt.

"Then?"

"Right. She wasn't around, but earlier I overheard her tell Merona she was going to the gym. When I mentioned it to the boys, they took off," she grinned, "but not before I got his number."

"Jen, you need to be more careful," I warned. "If these guys are who I think they are, they run one of the most profitable car theft rings in the UK."

"Wow!"

"Not wow. Dangerous." I pointed a finger at her. "Stay away from them," I said, channeling Vinnie.

"I'm not a child, Abbey."

"If you say so. Just be careful."

"Right. As soon as you are."

Great. I'd created a monster.

In no time at all, Jen was warmed up and ready to hit the road. Ben offered to drop her at home before he started on his identity theft research. Turns out he wasn't humoring me. Turns out he thought my conclusion was "brilliant," although he wasn't ready to indict Rebecca, just yet. First things first. Learn what we're up against, then go from there. He didn't deny it was strange Rebecca's brothers showing up like this, what with a thriving business waiting for them back home, and why would they venture this far outside the profit zone?

I mean, really. If they weren't here to help Rebecca (And why would they be? She'd disowned them, or so we were told), were they here as part of some elaborate scheme to scam Merona? From what Jen said, maybe they were well on their way to achieving that goal and they were in town to make sure Rebecca didn't get creative with the proceeds.

I chewed thoughtfully on a piece of hard sourdough bread and checked the time. Rebecca should be at the gym by now. The brothers, if my gut instinct was right, would be arriving shortly thereafter. It was 5:00 p.m. now. I needed to move it.

There was only one gym in Fairbanks and I have a membership. True. I've never used it. It was one of those, "I'll wash your hands, you wash mine" deals. The owner wanted a discount on some shipping and Gran took a lifetime family membership in return.

Preparing for every possibility, I packed sneakers, a headband, sweats, a bathing suit so old the seat was threadbare, a huge towel (in case of a sauna scenario), deodorant and called it good.

My plan? Eavesdrop, of course. I needed: tape recorder, batteries, waterproof bag. And before you could say, "You have the right to remain silent," I'd have the evidence against Rebecca and her brothers, and they'd be right where they belonged—dining on bread and water and clanging tin cups across strong, metal bars. Oops. 5:15.

It occurred to me I could use a disguise. The only thing that came to mind was one of Gran's bathing caps, circa 1951, Pepto Bismal pink with rows and rows of rubber ruffles, which Gran keeps on a mannequin she acquired when Nordstrom deserted Fairbanks ages ago.

When I arrived at the gym, the muscle-bound young man behind the desk, wearing one-size-too-small biking shorts and top, was appalled that we'd had our membership for years and this was the first recorded visit by a Vertuccio of any size or shape in the gym's history. He insisted on giving me the mandatory first-timers training on the equipment. So I didn't sue the gym when I flew off the abs machine and landed on my unexercised rear.

Seven minutes after I attempted to bribe him, unsuccessfully, with a mangled twenty if he'd let the rest of the training slide, I found myself pumping iron on a contraption right out of the middle ages. Sixteen minutes later, I spotted Rebecca straddling a scary-looking gym thinga-ma-bobby.

I turned abruptly and hissed at my tormentor. "Luke, if I don't stop soon, I'm going to die, and who do you think I'm gonna sue? " I asked, putting every bit of menace in my voice I could muster.

He didn't look convinced.

Two guys were heading for Rebecca. I had to get rid of this guy.

"I won't go on any other equipment without you. Promise." I waved the twenty, just in case.

"Keep to the sauna, pool and Jacuzzi."

I handed over the money. "Deal."

Luke turned to his next victim: a milky-white, grandpa with a snug Harley sweatshirt stretched over a generous beer gut, who looked like he was about to expire.

Jeb and Jeb, as I've taken to calling Rebecca's brothers, were getting away. After a brief word with Rebecca, they headed down the hallway toward the locker rooms. My guess was they weren't here to increase their heart rates, but what better place for a private conversation than the Olympic-size pool?

I slipped down the hall after them, chucked the sweats in favor of my vintage swimsuit, found and slid into the Jacuzzi closest to the pool and waited. Bingo. Jeb and Jeb were coming out of the locker room; Jeb One was wearing trunks; Jeb Two, Speedos. Jen was right. Nice butt.

I ducked underwater, like a crocodile on the hunt, eyes above the water—a pink, rubber-ribbed crocodile. They didn't seem to notice. Jeb One pulled a cigarette and lighter from the inside pocket of his swim trunks and lit up. Jeb Two snapped, "I don't want to get kicked out of here on a technicality. Get rid of that, you Prat." Jeb One took a drag, blew it in Jeb Two's face before he squashed the butt against the wall and tossed it in the air. It flew over my head and landed with a tiny splat beside me, where it bobbed like an errant rubber ducky. No problem. They didn't know me from Adam. Or did they?

Probably not in Gran's cap. I affected my best southern accent, every bit as folksy as Birdie's and flashed the boys a big smile. "Now don't you worry yourself about this." I palmed the butt and stuck it under my towel. "I won't say a word. I know how it is to be—," but they weren't listening. Or weren't interested in hearing about my addiction to Peppermint Patties and how that lead me to getting busted right in the middle of church services. Or so my story was going to go.

Instead, they snagged a spot twenty feet to my left and sat on the side of the pool. Jeb One dangled his gnarly feet over the deserted deep end; Jeb Two stretched out along the edge like an actor in a old movie.

As soon as their backs were turned, I reached inside Gran's stars and stripes beach bag for the tape recorder and hit record. Was twenty feet too far? I climbed out of the hot tub with the stealth normally reserved for 007 types, dried off slowly, moved closer to the boys and laid the bag with the tape recorder on the nearest lounge chair.

"Would you boys mind my bag for me while I make a quick trip to the ladies," I asked, then didn't wait for a reply. A quick count to a hundred and I returned unnoticed to the Jacuzzi. Not a minute too soon.

Enter Rebecca. Hair pushed back in a sleek French twist, not a drop of sweat anywhere, and The Jebs acting for all the world like beloved brothers who hadn't seen their sister in years.

I went into crocodile mode and ducked under the water. When I couldn't hold my breath another second, I checked. Still there. The Jebs sucking up to Rebecca. Her nodding.

"Abigail?"

I looked up. A pair of sneakers and jeans, and yep, Ben. He bent over, hands on knees. I grabbed both his hands and yanked as hard as I could, pulling him head first into the water. He sank, then sputtered and righted himself. I put one hand on top of his head and pushed him under, then sank down under the water after him, covering his mouth with my hand. When I was certain he wasn't going to run for it, I let go, jerked my thumb skyward and mouthed, "Rebecca." Whether he understood or not, he nodded. About thirty seconds later, I saw the flaw in my plan. One. The splash had been huge. Two. We couldn't stay down there all day. Three? I looked up from below the surface to find Rebecca and the Jebs hovering above us. And if I could see them . . .

I tried for a sigh and was rewarded with a mouthful of chlorinated water. I could explain my being there. But Ben? In street clothes. In the Jacuzzi? Hmm.

"In for a swim?" Rebecca asked in a crisp British accent, one that was beginning to annoy me, when we finally broke the surface. She eyed Ben, probably figuring he was the weakest link.

I whispered to him, "You have the right to remain silent. Nothing you say is going to get us out of this."

"Sorry. I don't have more time to play. Enjoy yourselves," Rebecca said right before she led the Jebs across the room and out the door without us having accomplished a single thing. If you didn't count looking like complete and unadulterated idiots.

"That went well," I said, once fully clothed and sitting across from Ben at The Brown Mouse café sharing a hot fudge sundae and an order of fries.

"Good try, though."

I rifled through my bag for the hundredth time. "Rebecca must have palmed the tape recorder when I wasn't looking."

"Or it fell out."

"Still defending her, I see." I slid out of the booth so fast I sent the salt and pepper shakers skidding into his lap. "I'm going home. You can get Rebecca to pick you up."

Two women in the next booth looked over. Great. Now I had a call from Vinnie to look forward to. Gossip be damned, I stalked out with Ben trailing behind.

"Be reasonable, Abigail."

Reasonable? The one expression guaranteed to land any American male in the dog house for the foreseeable future. Ben was from the UK, but still. I held up a hand. "I'll forget you said that."

He got my meaning. "Said what?"

Crisis averted, we drove home in utter silence. I wasn't mad at Ben. I was mad at myself. A bumbling screw-up in the detective department. Not too successful in the relationships department, either, but let's not go there.

Home felt like a refuge on an otherwise bleak and dreary evening. I left Ben to his own resources and decided I wanted to forget about spying for the rest of the night. I wanted a jacuzzi bubble bath. Thank you, Gran, for springing for one of life's little necessities (when you live in Fairbanks, Alaska, that is).

Jim Morrison was belting out "Backdoor Man" as I sang along, eyes closed, oblivious to the world. I inhaled vanilla scented bubbles, lifted a handful to my mouth, opened my eyes and blew.

"Ah!," I screamed.

Ben was above me, one hand over his eyes, the other holding out the portable phone. "It's for you. Sam. She refused to wait."

He couldn't see my eye roll, but added, "She threatened me with bodily harm if I didn't bring the phone to you immediately."

He peeked between two fingers. I know he did. Another time I may have tried to get him where I wanted him, but not with me looking like a drowned rat: red eyes, drippy nose, wet hair. "Get out, Ben."

"She says if you don't talk to her now, she'll only keep ringing."

"Fine." I grabbed for the phone. The events of the day had finally gotten to me and I snapped. "I'm in the tub, Sam. Is there such a thing as privacy in your world?"

"I heard."

She's not even from Fairbanks. I could see how Vinnie or Gran would have heard. But Sam?

"Ab, remember when I asked you to keep Ben out of trouble for me?"

"I remember."

"Because he has an overactive imagination and goes off half-cocked?"

I guess. But since she'd only asked me to watch over him as some misguided setup, I figured I was off the hook.

"Anywhere in there did I say, 'Get Ben kidnapped?'"

"Ah. No?"

"Involve him in Sassy Sisters Investigations?"

Um. "Not specifically."

The familiar sound of a helicopter, whoop, whoop, whoop, sounded in the background. Sam could be up to her eyes in bad guys and I'd made her stop everything. How selfish was that?

"Abbey, you're causing problems."

"I don't—"

"You showing up in the wrong places is bollocking up the works."

"Huh?"

"Ben showing up at the hangar. And you, following James and Ewan."

"Who?"

"Rebecca's brothers."

"Oh, the Jebs."

"Who?"

"Never mind."

"Putting your own employee at Merona Air?"

Did she know the balance on my checking account, too?

"I need you to keep your promise, or—"

"Or what?" What could she possibly do from Chechnya? Egg my house?

"Ask Ben. He knows."

Oh. God. Ben was still here. More than I could say for the bubbles. "Would you please hand me a towel and then GET OUT!"

Once safely wrapped in a fluffy beach towel, I closed the toilet lid and sat. "What have you got up your sleeve, Sam?"

"I know you, Abigail Vertuccio. You'll agree with me one minute and forget all about it when that curiosity of yours takes over. When you want to do something, you look for reasons to do it. I need you to look for reasons to stay out of my way."

I sensed the, "There will be consequences if you don't" in her voice.

"And if I don't?"

"I happen to know someone with the Alaska State Troopers who would love to take protective custody of you for a day or two."

It had to be Rob The Rat, didn't it? What else are ex's for if not to drive you crazy.

"You wouldn't."

"He said he'd get a kick out of seeing you in an orange jumpsuit."

The dog.

"He said he owes you one."

"He owes me one? He's the one who—"

"Earth to Abigail."

I knew a losing hand when I saw one. "Answer me one thing and I'll back off. Is identity theft involved and is Rebecca the crook I think she is?"

"Stay out of it, Abbey. Think of Rob's smug face when he slaps the handcuffs on you."

I'd had Rob slap handcuffs on me before, but we weren't going anywhere and I wasn't wearing orange. Or anything for that matter.

"You with me, Abigail?"

I tossed the phone into the hallway where I figured Ben was politely eavesdropping.

"We'll see, Sam," I shouted. "We'll see."

Sicilian Tactic #50: Never doubt it for a minute. Blackmailers will pay.

Chapter 25

VALENTINE'S DAY

7 a.m.

Chubby cherubs drifted across a thunderous sky, while multi-colored sprinkles rained down on wedding-dress-clad little girls as they danced in circles, their heads thrown back, mouths open wide.

I awoke with a start. If I didn't know better, I would have sworn Cupid's army was camped out on the foot of my bed. I closed my eyes and lay back down. Or maybe I had ghosts.

"Ah hem."

I snuggled deeper into the covers. My plan was to sleep all day.

The covers rustled at the base of the bed. Someone tickled my toes. I jerked up so fast I connected with a not-so-ghostly chin.

"Cut that out or I'll exorcise you," I threatened.

Back to sleep, where Cupid, dressed in commando boots and pith helmet, had me by my big toe, while another cherub took aim at the blood red bull's eye painted across my bare bosom.

"Wake up, Abigail!"

"Ah, shit," I moaned. "It's Valentine's Day, isn't it?"

"Watch your language, you bloody twit," Justine reprimanded.

I opened my eyes in time to avoid the pillow Justine hurled toward my head, but not in time to avoid the facts. Today was Valentine's Day and there was no getting around it. My friends were camped out on my bed and there was no getting around that, either.

"What is this? A V-day intervention? Am I supposed to stand, hand on heart, and pronounce 'I, Abigail Vertuccio, am a Valentine's Day-phobe?' Fine. I'll get a sponsor. I'll go to the meetings. Anything if you just get out and leave me alone."

I clutched the comforter in my fists and squeezed it against my eyes. "Are you still here?"

"Jo thought since it was Valentine's Day, you'd freak—"

"I did not —"

"Justine wanted to be here in case Molly—"

"I tried to stop them—"

"Right, and I'm Pope whoever."

"I made you a Valentine's Day cake, but Auntie Jo said we'd eat it tomor—"

"Don't worry. Auntie Abbey will eat your cake, Jules."

"Telling a child she can't give a cake to her aunt is—"

"Good God!"

"Language, please."

I checked beneath the covers. Thankfully, not naked. Good. I leaped out of bed, if you could call the creaky, crab walk I managed a leap, did an end run around the herd of imbeciles (omit Juliet from that description) who were still perched on my bed, and escaped down four flights of stairs. Mittens, hat, parka, out and across the snowy yard in my slippers—ten yards to go and I'd be safe. I yanked Big Ellie's door handle. Nothing. I managed to get my mittens off with my teeth and pulled the handle, again. No good. I shook the door. Kicked, crunching my slippered toes. Screamed. Turned and trudged back across the icy yard, back inside, mittens, hat, parka off.

"All I want to know is which one of you cretins went and locked Big Ellie? And where are my keys?"

Tony, Jo, Ben, Justine and Jaye, now scattered around the kitchen, kept sneaking looks at each other, like a bunch of school kids refusing to rat out the genius who'd glued condoms all over the principal's car. (True story. Better saved for another time.)

"I know, Auntie Abbey," Juliette said as she stretched one hand high over her head.

Jaye snatched her up in an affectionate hug. "It isn't nice to tell on Mommy, Sweetheart."

Ten different Sicilian curses wrestled for top billing on the tip of my tongue and I would have blasted Justine to Barrow and back, except for Juliette's precious, open-hearted face smiling over at me from the snug harbor of Jaye's arms.

I smiled at Justine, as sweet as apple pie. "I'll talk to you later."

"We all know your first instinct is to run, don't we?" was her reply.

"It's not good to run away, Aunt Abbey. It scares Mommy. I don't want you to go," Juliette whimpered. Her quivering little chin sealed the deal.

"Auntie Abbey isn't going anywhere, Jules. I'd never go anywhere without telling you, honey." Then it hit me like a brick. Whether I'd known it or not, I had someone, try though I might to avoid it, who I simply could not walk away from.

"As for you, Justine, I was going to Big Ellie to . . . to get my reading glasses; so you didn't have to scare Juliette over nothing." No reason I had to cop to the whole truth. I'm grown. I can do what I damn well please.

"I'm not scared, Aunt Abbey. I'm a big girl."

I could tell from the confused look on Jaye's face, he didn't know whether to get Juliette out of the firing zone or keep her there as an emissary of peace. But then one look at Justine told him what side his bread was buttered on and he made his decision. "Time for school, Sweetie."

After ample juicy kisses and zerberts all around, Juliette left with Jaye, which left Justine free to knock some sense into me.

"Ignore Justine, Ab. She's exhausted from digging up road signs and beating them into submission," Jo said.

Tony snorted, flexed his muscles and made like he was swinging an imaginary sledgehammer. "Toothpicks, anyone?"

"English please. What road signs?"

"The twenty road signs from here to AVA. Molly's messages of eternal love and devotion to Mac on Valentine's Day," Tony blurted out, ignoring Jo's jabs and Justine's evil eye.

"Great." I sank into the first available seat—of the wingback variety, clearly designed to intimidate rather than comfort. "And so it begins. The St. Valentine's Day Massacre, in living color."

"You're dating yourself, Ab. It's high definition these days," Tony corrected.

"The St. Valentine's Day Massacre in high def," I corrected. "I feel much better now."

He placed a hand on my shoulder. "Hey. It's not that serious. Marriage ain't the end of the world." He caught Jo's menacing look and added. "It's pretty good. Actually great. That's what I meant. It's great!"

Tony the Tiger in action. Grrr!

"Thanks, Tony. I'll take it under consideration."

He released a breath. "I gotta get ready for the team meeting. Happy Val...ah...I mean, bye."

"So. What really happened to the signs, guys?" I asked, after Tony made his escape.

Jo ignored me as she pulled several cups of cofee from a bag along with lemon-filled cheese Danish, thankfully not dyed pink or shaped like doughy hearts. Only after ensuring my two hands were full, coffee in one, scrumptious Danish in the other, did she launch into an account of Justine's early morning Valentine's Day exploits.

"You should've seen it. She plucked every one of those signs out of the ground with her bony little fingers and demolished them. It was great."

"So...what? Her pickup is toothpick central?"

"Not hardly. We dumped them on Molly's front porch."

Justine was beaming like she'd just scaled Mt. McKinley.

"Eager beavers, aren't we?" I said, having a hard time containing my sheer admiration.

Justine's about ten years ahead of me in the strong-woman department. Maybe I should sign up for lessons. "Thanks, Justine."

"Really?"

"Really. You're amazing." I snatched her into a big bear hug, before she could back away, and held on. "You're a great friend and I love you."

"Someone has to keep that Molly bitch in her place. Now unhand me, you wanker. You'll muss my hair."

Not that she has much hair to muss. About an inch, tops, but I held my tongue because hadn't she just smashed all those Valentine's Day messages? Hadn't she dragged a sleeping Juliette out of bed at the crack of dawn so they could be by my side on the one day she knew I could use the morale support? Even though she thinks I'm a complete twit for worrying about some stupid, neurotic, impossible vision?

"What hair?" That was not me. I swear. It was Jo.

"Hey, it's not that I don't appreciate you all coming over. The coffee. The Danish. And Juliette. But you can go now. I'm okay," I said.

Doubtful faces greeted me all around. Given no choice, I spilled the plan. "Ben's going to stay with me." I did a graceful Cinderella pirouette, only losing my balance once. "So you can go. I'm good."

"You won't dig up the key to Big Ellie and take off? – Justine.

"You won't suddenly have a vision you're drowning in an ocean of white tulle and freak?" – Jo

"If I do, Ben will do CPR."

"You won't—"

"Whatever it is, I won't."

Please let them leave and I'll do anything. Give up pizza and hot fudge sundaes. Dress up like Elvira and do a striptease on Rob's doorstep. Anything. Anything. Anything. If you make them leave, I'll—

"Okay, we're outta here," Jo said, tilting her head toward the front door—apparently the signal for the rest to follow. Thank God, because I'd been this close to promising to call Vinnie once a week from now until eternity. Thank you. Thank you. Thank you.

"It's just you and me, kid," Ben said, doing the most pathetic Bogie ever, the house thankfully empty.

"Please, don't say, 'This is the beginning of a beautiful friendship.'"

"I was about to say Happy Valentine's Day, Abigail Vertuccio."

I slouched over my cheese Danish, inhaling the fragrant aroma, across from Ben at the kitchen table where it was clear he was hiding something behind his back.

"Aren't you going to eat before everything gets cold?" I asked, with a mouth full of pastry, which I promptly washed down with a slug of lukewarm coffee. Maybe frat boy table manners would distract him. It was worth a try. I wiped my mouth on my sleeve.

"Charming, Abigail, but it's not working."

I shot him my wounded puppy dog look—the one with the blinky eyes.

"Not working, either."

Rats. "Okay, what is it?" I asked, as if he were offering me candy-coated slugs or chocolate-covered buggers. He slid an envelop under my napkin, took a quick bite of his pastry and pushed his chair back.

Acid rose in my stomach and shot up toward my throat. I choked as I spit out the words. "You're leaving?"

Of course, he didn't budge. I was acting like a five-year-old being left at kindergarten for the first time, so what else could he do?

"I was going to the loo, but if you'd rather, I could wait."

Holy, I don't know what, Batman. Heat rushed to my cheeks and I hid behind my cup (thankfully, grande). "No. You go. I don't mean, go. I mean, you can go, like in leave, not GO."

"I can go, but not go."

He held up a hand and laughed. "I'll just go then," and exited stage right. If this were a play, they'd have to shoot the heroine to put her out of her misery.

Ben's card peeked out from under my napkin. So far, the first two cards I'd received this morning hadn't been too great. Vinnie's sarcastic, Mac's too adorably loving and loaded with expectations. I could hear Vinnie now: "Three strikes and you're out, Abbey."

Gran would have said, "Third time's the charm, Abbey. Never forget that."

Thank god for Gran. For every, "Don't let your head get too big" comment from Vinnie, Gran was right behind making the universe a softer and gentler place.

I should call her, wish her a Happy Valentine's Day. I reached for the phone, dialed, waited until Gran shouted, "Buns, you read our minds. Al and I were sitting here talking about calling our favorite grandbaby."

"Your only grand and not a baby," I admonished.

"Did I ever tell you the story—"

In the background Al shushed her, telling her I didn't want to hear some boring story about two old farts. Gran whispered in return, "Call yourself an old fart, but leave me out of it.

"Buns? You still there?" but she didn't wait for my answer. "Last year, we were on the road playing back up for some Stones wannabes. I was sick of the hot weather, wishing for 50 below zero, ice fog, fires in the fireplace and you, Buns. You know what he did? Hush, Al. He told the band he was through. We were packing it in and going home. Said he could play music anywhere, as long as he was with me. Well, you did, you big softy."

I felt like crying it was so sweet; still, I managed to squeak out a "What happened, Gran?" since they sure as heck hadn't come home.

"The feeling passed. I remembered I could be home in five hours, any time I wanted. I remembered what 50 below zero feels like. Not the fantasy."

"That easy?"

"You just change the way you look at things, Buns, and everything turns out."

Leave it to Gran to not only live the love story of the century, but to have the wisdom to recognize what she had.

8 a.m.

I usually call Gran first thing on holidays, then Vinnie. Still. If it was 8 a.m. in Fairbanks, that made it noon in Jersey, which meant I had a 50/50 chance I'd catch Mom with some hunky guy from the beach and she wouldn't thank me for the obligatory holiday call. On the other hand, if she called me before I called her, I'd be made to suffer for eternity. Kind of like the fingers-in-the-birthday-cake thing.

Luck won out. Her answering machine picked up. "If you're calling to say you're sorry for working out of town on Valentine's Day and not taking me out for a romantic dinner, don't bother leaving a message. And hey, don't think I'm callin' you back."

Sheesh. I didn't know who the poor guy was, but he didn't know Vinnie too well. Unless he was busy executing a moon landing, there was absolutely no justifiable reason for doing a no-show on Valentine's Day.

I left the usual holiday message, blessing my lucky stars it wasn't me on her naughty list, and hung up. No sooner than I'd sighed with relief at dodging the bullet, the phone rang. Vinnie. Maybe I could make believe I was the answering machine.

"You don't say 'hello,' anymore, Abigail? You some movie star who doesn't have to say 'hello?'"

"Hi, Mom."

It's easier to go along. It's not wimpy, it's self-preservation. Because she knows people. Uncle Carmine for one. He loves me, but if he had to choose between me and Vinnie, self-preservation would mean he'd go with Vinnie. I get that.

"Happy V-Day."

"You said that on your message."

"Gran says 'Hi.'"

"Where's the old broad now? Singing backup for a Spanky and the Gang reunion tour?"

"She's very happy. No one stood *her* up on Valentine's Day."

"What'd you say?" She shouted.

"I said noma snuffa foophle haven." Sicilian Tactic #55: Pretend you don't know what the heck they're talking about.

"What the—"

"We're breaking up, Ma. I can't hear you."

"Damn phone."

I disconnected, crossed my fingers and counted to ten. Then I checked my watch. I'd hung up on my mom and, so far, had lived to tell the story. I wanted to remember the exact time. 8:02 a.m. One minute three seconds so far. Four seconds. Five seconds. Six seconds. Two minutes seventeen seconds, eighteen seconds, nineteen seconds. And no call back from Mom. Amazing.

"Abigail, what are you doing?" Ben asked as he watched me clicking off seconds and jotting the time down on my Little Kitty note pad. Five minutes seventeen seconds.

"Nothing. I'm doing nothing."

My face was turning red. I could feel it. I ducked my head behind the note pad, hoping he wouldn't notice.

"Working on your puzzle? Five minutes, seventeen seconds? The time you'll need to find the next clue?"

Turns out Ben's Valentine's Day card wasn't a card as much as a scavenger hunt. As long as no weddings were involved, I was all for a Ben Diversionary Tactic. Getting my mind off Vinnie, off marriage, men, love, commitment and any plans beyond surviving this day was beginning to sound pretty darn good to me.

9:00 a.m.

What do Naked Peter, a knuckle buster skull ring, a Mr. Peanut bank and a poster of Jim Morrison have in common? Before today, I would have said, nothing. Now I can say they are Ben's idea of those things I couldn't do without on Valentine's Day. Though I had to scour the entire house, top to bottom, to find them. There was one last present he was saving for after Valentine's Day, he said, and he wouldn't tell me why, though I prodded, bullied, pleaded, bullied some more and bargained with all my might.

"You might as well pick up your messages," he said, "because I'm not talking."

While I'd been busy digging dust bunnies out from under the beds, sticking my nose between towels in the linen closet, rifling through books in the library, going through Ben's underwear drawer (well, he could have hidden something there) and playing childhood games at the crack of dawn on the worst day of the year, the phone had been ringing off the hook. From the looks of it, half of Fairbanks wanted their own personal Valentine's Day forecast, and since Madame Zora was closed for the holidays, that left me.

"Hi, Abbey, I was wondering if can you tell me what Doug is getting me for Valentine's Day, 'cause if it's a ring, I need to make an appointment to get my hair done. What'd ya think, Ab? Will a trip to Hawaii make up for the new Harley? Happy Valentine's, Abbey. I bet you're getting a lot of calls from people wanting to know how it'll go today. Don't worry. That's not what I'm calling about. I wanted to say hi, see how you're doing. You still seeing that cute pilot? Cuz if you're not . . . well, do you see it working out for me, Abbey?"

Then there were the slew of friends and neighbors and friends of friends and neighbors who'd heard the whole story about Mac and the vision and were calling to lend a helping hand.

"Abbey. Is that you? I guess I got the machine. This is Lori. You know. From high school. Have you heard how I joined the Wiccans! Well, I did. Don't hang up. I'm not that kind of witch. Anyway, (sounds of pages flipping and a baby making googly sounds in the background) Lilly says hello. Where was I? Oh, yeah. I was going over my spells and when I heard you were worried about getting married, I mean, who can blame you? Look at me. If I hadn't married Mike right out of high school, who knows? (Waaa!) Hold on a sec. Okay. She's eating now. Thank God for breasts. As I was trying to say, I have a spell for you. It's to ward off demons. But close enough. Right? So. If I heard right and you want to ward off Mac, you'll need . . . Oh, wait (more page flipping) you have to remember to get naked under a full moon for this one. Is that okay? Because it won't work if you don't."

I fast forwarded to, "add a half cup nutmeg, bake on high and make sure he eats a big serving."

Ben came in right around the "naked" part.

"Baking Naked? Sounds like a best seller."

Not a bad idea. I fast forwarded in time to catch Uncle Carmine's rumbling baritone. "Heard you were having trouble with some gabonz. You tell me where he hangs and I'll see he don't bother you no more, Cookie. (Pause) If you call, use the cell. Capisco?"

"Should I be scared?" Ben quipped.

"Are you the one giving me trouble?"

"Not with half of Fairbanks plotting my demise if I cross you."

Half of Fairbanks was looking out for me, and I hadn't lifted a single finger in the name of love, so obsessed was I with the impending Valentine's

Day Massacre.

I headed for the kitchen to heat up my coffee and think. There were probably a million Valentine's Day cards and candies on sale right this very minute all over town. Half price. First priority. The Sassy Sisters.

"Ben, I screwed up. I forgot to get something for Jo and Justine for Valentine's Day. Any ideas?"

He came up behind me. For a second I thought he was going to give me a bear hug, but he veered off, lifted himself onto the kitchen counter and sat, arms crossed over his chest.

"What?"

"Tony's anniversary party. They really want you there, Abigail."

I stuck my chin out and pouted, looking like Juliette before an early bedtime. I lifted myself up onto the counter beside him and said nothing. His shoulder bumped mine and I knew I was toast.

"Fine. I'll go."

"You won't regret it."

"Under one condition." I paused to give him the full dramatic effect.

"And that would be?"

"When the time comes . . ."

"Right."

"When I'm suppose to . . . you know."

"Get married."

"Don't say it!"

"Say what?"

"We'll be *doing it*. Agreed?"

He looked at me like I'd suggested we sign a mutual suicide pact. As if I'd asked him to give his Magic 8 Ball collection to the Goodwill.

"Am I hearing you—"

I whispered exactly what I wanted him to be doing at the appointed hour and he blushed wildly.

"Agree or it's no deal."

He looked around. Checking for escape routes, no doubt. The window? How quickly could he make it to the front door?

"Agreed?" I captured one of his hands to seal the deal, before he could find a way to talk me out of it.

9:30 a.m.

I stood by the door, nervously tapping my feet.

"We have three choices. One. We say to hell with Sam and spend the morning lifting fingerprints." He didn't run away screaming, so I continued. "Two. We jump in Big Ellie and head for Chena Hot Springs to avoid Valentine's Day altogether." I took that frown as a no. "Or three. I don't have a three."

"Three. Help Jo." He slid his hand into his pocket, came out with a list and waved it at me. I crossed back into the kitchen where he was still perched on the counter. His knees brushed my pajama bottoms as I grabbed for the note. He swung off the counter and stuffed the list back into the side pocket of his battered 501s.

"So, you wanna play, huh?"

He backed away slowly, never taking his eyes off of me. "You always win, Abigail, but not this time." He pointed a finger. His eyes dark. His brow furrowed. All serious.

"Okay. Okay. If you feel that strongly about it."

I backed away from him, bumping into the kitchen counter.

"I do," said Ben, relaxing.

I reached behind me. Yes. Pay dirt. I made my move and before he knew what was happening, I blasted him with water from the sink hose. His hands flew up to stop the flood, leaving the list unguarded in his pocket. While we struggled over the hose, I slipped a hand into his pocket, but I wasn't fast enough. He moved to one side causing me to lose my balance. As I crashed into the kitchen table, I latched onto Ben and we both slid to the floor in a puddle of water.

For a minute, the full body contact threw me and I lost sight of my mission. Ha. Exactly what he wanted. I flipped him over and straddled him. What mission? Oh, yeah. The list. The pocket. My lapse cost me precious seconds, allowing him to get back on his feet, smirking as he hovered above me. He was gonna regret that smirk. Trust me.

Except he crumbled the note like a ball of Wonder Bread and popped it in his mouth. "Af oo fam mer moo—mile," he said, as he pointed to his mouth. Then he made a big show of gulping. "Fy sfwear."

I held two hands up in surrender, rushed out of the room and up the stairs to Ben's room. When I returned, I found him smoothing the gummy paper on the kitchen table, trying to make out the instructions where the ink had smeared. I sneaked up behind him, his favorite Magic 8 Ball in hand, and held it over the sink of greasy water where last night's dishes were soaking. The phone rang, but I ignored it.

"Hey, Ben?"

He turned. His eyes widened at the hostage scene unfolding before him.

I held my free hand out to Ben. "Hand over the list or the 8 Ball gets it." Vintage, first edition, mint condition.

"That's—"

"I know. All original."

His eyes searched mine (and not in steamy love story way) for signs of sanity and found none. "It's—"

"I know. Mint."

He clapped one hand over his eyes. "You're mad."

"Exactly."

"One inch closer to that water, Abigail Vertuccio, and I'll really do it, I will. I'll. Call. Vinnie."

My cell phone vibrated in my pocket. Vinnie.

"You wouldn't."

"I'll tell her you're stripping on the weekends."

"Ha. She'd love that." I laugh in the face of fear.

"I'll get her to come up here. Tell her you need her."

Uh-oh.

"Send her a ticket, why don't I. One way."

How important could the list be, anyway? I set the 8 Ball in his open palm and sat. "I wasn't going to do it. You didn't have to stoop to Vinnie."

He sat beside me, leaned in and brushed my ear with his lips. "Seems I did."

"Thanks for the vote of confidence."

"Thanks for giving my 8 Ball back," he said with the grace of someone who could afford to be generous, having won the battle.

But not the war.

10:00 a.m.

"Let's move it," I snapped as I yanked my parka over my teacup PJs, retrieved my keys and backpack from the entry table, where the newspaper was lying in the trash. But wait a minute. Why was today's newspaper in the trash? I'd been so busy trying to get the list from Ben that I'd missed it.

While Ben wrapped himself in an unwieldy Dr. Who scarf, I pulled the paper out of the trash. In the middle of a full-page of V-Day messages was a photo of me, Mac and a cherub shooting a love-poisoned arrow (okay, maybe not poisoned) straight into us. Underneath, it read: "Mac and Ab sitting in a tree. You know the song. Signed, M."

Ben, who'd finished arranging his scarf so he wouldn't trip over it, noticed the paper and said, "You look beautiful in that photo," before putting an arm around me.

M for Mac? Mac knew I wasn't one for corny public displays. Holding hands? Yes. A friendly hug. I'm good. Not this. Not on Valentine's Day. M for Molly? No. If Molly had placed an ad, it would have been her and Mac in the photo. M? Mom? Yes, yes, yes. This had Vinnie written all over it.

"You don't look upset. Jo said you'd bust a—"

"Nope. Don't care."

"Truthfully?" he asked. All joking aside.

Seems they all figured it was Mac who'd placed the ad. Only I knew the truth and I wasn't going to let Vinnie get to me, again.

"Let's get a move on," I said.

I'd had about all the Vinnie I could take for one Valentine's day.

Chapter 26

N ew Sicilian Tactic. Figure out the whole Mom thing, before it's too late. And while I was at it, figure out the whole men thing, too. And don't expect being clairvoyant to help. Look how that's worked out. Starting with my senior prom, a strapless dress and no idea ahead of time that my boobs were going to be on display for the entire senior class to see. Followed by a marriage, an affair and losing the friend he cheated on me with.

Being clairvoyant is sometimes like bad TV reception. You tune in to the "Three Stooges," and end up watching Jillian in the gym with the "Biggest losers." No help at all.

And don't expect any help from Vinnie, either. Right after I married Rob and the I-do's were barely cold, Vinnie practically leaped out of her pew to tell me about a good Sicilian shrivel-his-balls-into-crusty-dog-pattys curse, for when he ran around on me.

Being Sicilian and a Vertuccio, I know from curses. When Jo and I were little, we heard a lot of Vinnie's curses. Followed by loud Italian expletives, followed by rude Italian hand gestures.

"I want to be like Vinnie when I grow up," Jo would say—all awestruck by my Mom's dark beauty, hot temper and quick wit. "If I was Vinnie, all the boys would want to die because they'd love me so much, but I'd tell them all right where to put it," she'd say. Vinnie's adoring groupy.

When Vinnie made us solemnly swear we would never take crap off a man, Jo stood with hand over heart and repeated the oath, eyes shiny, secretly thrilled to be inducted into Vinnie's Take-No-Prisoners Club.

Fortunately, Jo's infatuation with Mom died out when Matthew Frye, who Jo secretly worshipped, let it slip that Vinnie was the most magnificent woman he'd ever seen. Thank you, Matt, or I don't know how Jo and I could have remained friends. I really don't. I needed an ally, not a Vinnie groupie for a friend.

Once Vinnie's spell wore off, Jo and I started our own Take-No-Prisoners Club with the following by-laws:

1.　Never again fall under Vinnie's power. That one was for Jo. I hadn't been sucked in by Vinnie since I was six, but a good rule all the same, in case I was ever hospitalized, incapacitated, drugged or otherwise in a weakened state, making me vulnerable.

2.　Watch out for hormones. If you're positive the guy you secretly worship has screwed half the girls in school and are equally positive you can change him, count to a million and chalk up your misguided belief that he's misunderstood to hormones. Yours.

3.　The word "yes" will get you nothing but trouble. So, remember to keep your mouth shut for heaven's sake.

4.　Buff up, so when a man offers to carry your groceries or change your flat, you won't make it about needing a man around the house because of all of those big, strong muscles.

5.　Remember. It's all about controlling our own destiny. It's not about losing yourself to some guy along the way.

6.　Have a healthy disrespect for authority. One that got us into trouble a time or two. Or three. Or four.

7.　Keep your eyes open for possibilities. Which was how Jo eventually came to run her thrift store and how I bought Big Ellie, long before I could think of any practical use for her at all.

8.　Go all the way. Not with Frankie or Eddie or Nick. Give life your best. Better to risk failure than not to try at all.

9.　Get over being your own worst enemy. Trust yourself; be supportive rather than critical, acknowledge your skills, abilities and beauty. Say, "I can" for God's sake.

10.　Trust your gut. Or in my case, my clairvoyance.

Our Take No Prisoner's club got us through acne, cramps, puppy love, cliques and into adulthood until I broke Rules 2, 3, 9 and 10 without a second thought and picked Rob, a player in high school.

"But he loves me," I said.

He may have dumped girls like a trash truck dumps its haul . . . "But he's grown up now," I whimpered. "I'll love him so much he'll never look at anyone else."

I turned off my self-preservation switch and look where it got me.

New rule: Pick a man you admire and respect. Someone you trust. Can talk with. Someone you're a better person for being with.

Okay. Mac, 4 out of 4. Ben, 4 out of 4. Add in sexual attraction? Mac, 5 out of 5. Ben, 5 out of 5.

Life would be so easy if I had a crystal ball. Because we already know about being clairvoyant. It isn't the walk in the park people seem to think it is.

Chapter 27

10:30 a.m.
Still Valentine's Day, damn it.

W hile your pajamas are charming, Abigail, I wonder . . ." Ben's voice trailed off.

He was right. If I had to leave the safety of home and hearth on V-Day, it wasn't going to be in teacup pajamas. I shucked the PJs and traded them in for the black on black look: jeans, Black Sabbath T-shirt, pilled and moth eaten wool sweater, thick hunter socks with a bright orange rim around the tops, a clove of garlic—for emergencies of the romantic kind. The most unwedding-like outfit I could think of. No Scrumptious Slut lipstick, no Drop-Dead Gorgeous blush. Parka used when chopping wood, topped off with an old, wool hat with flappy ear covers. Yep. Totally marriage-proof. Now I was ready.

Ben watched as I clutched the front door, hovering half in, half out, reluctant to take that first step.

He hit the auto start button on my key ring and the car roared to life.

"Ready as I'll ever be." I guess. I took in a fortifying breath and sighed. It wasn't like me to be a scaredy-cat. But clairvoyance and romance are damned serious and often scary. Anyone who isn't scared when they're teetering on the edge of a cliff—"

"All set?" Ben's voice jarred me back to him and I took a step. So far so good. Two steps, then three. I looked around for signs of trouble and found nothing but rows of towering spruce trees with their boughs bent over by heavy ropes of silvery ice, Big Ellie, right where she should be, looking like a relic from the ice age, Family Circle-style footprints crisscrossing the snow-covered yard, a snow angel, a lone tree branch brushing against a porch rail and ptarmigan scuttling through the brush.

"I'm ready," I said, feeling anything but as I crossed the icy path and slid into the driver's seat.

"Did you remember the CDs Jo wanted?"

I tapped my pocket and nodded. "The Best of the Animals, AC/DC, Beatles Live, Emmy Lou Harris, Nirvana, James Taylor, Ami Mann, The Funkadelic 70s.

"Ack!" I hit the brakes, sending Ben bouncing forward, barely avoiding the windshield. Lucky we were barely crawling along, still in the driveway. "Crap!"

The car heater cord whipped around behind us like a kite doing a death spiral. Ben jumped out of the car and returned with the frayed cord. "Third one this week, if you include the two I executed earlier."

"You demolished two cords this week?" I snorted. This day was going to get better. It had to.

He waved the broken cord at me. "Do you really want to have this conversation, Abigail?"

Maybe not. "You win. Get in."

Add to list. Buy new cord.

"Where to?" I asked, once we crowned the winner of the lifetime award for the most decimated heater cords. Me, of course.

Ben unfolded the list, flattened it on one knee and read, "Rescue punch bowl from Aunt Liz."

No way was I asking Jo's great-aunt Liz for that punch bowl without fortifications. Fresh Boston cream donuts. Flowers. Possibly a trip to Lisbon? Because, to hear Liz tell it, that bowl was left to her by her grandmother, who swore she got it as a gift from the governor. Jo swears great-gran left it to her, not Liz. Being's how possession is supposed to mean something, any fool could see how I wouldn't be anxious to get in the middle of this one. Ben didn't know any of this, but God help her, Jo did. And she was still willing to send him into the tiger's den without consideration of life and limb. And I thought she liked him.

"What else?"

"Pick up cake from Conti's Bakery."

I could see it now. Me and a big, fancy cake. One tire losing traction. The car sliding. Squealing brakes. Jo's cake with the miniature basketball team on top slipping to the floor in slow mo, my back seat a sugary mess.

"Let's swing by AVA first." In answer to his questioning look, I added, "For a packing box. If that cake doesn't arrive in perfect condition, we're toast."

"Point taken."

We drove in silence. I shook off one of my heavy wool mittens and hit play on the stereo. "I honestly love you," rang out. I hit a second button, "Can't live, if living is without you." Double yuck. Changed that. "Reunited and it feels so good." Damn Valentine's Day. Nothing but love songs. At the second "reunited," I could have sworn I heard doggy accompaniment. "Reunited and it feels so, woof."

I checked between my knees. No dog. A quick glance over my shoulder revealed nothing as well. Poor Ben. Stuck with a madwoman on Valentine's Day.

I quickly navigated to AVA and arrived, waves of guilt flooding me as I crossed the threshold into the busy terminal. I needed to get back to work and pull my weight, even though, from the looks of it, Birdie and Justine were handling things beautifully. Then there was Jen to feel guilty about. I wouldn't blame her if she quit and never came back after this spy mission at Merona's.

I came around the counter and greeted Justine, who whispered "Another package arrived for Mac," as she worked her computer, smiled at customers and sent them on their way before turning her attention on me. "I didn't have time to deal with it, yet."

Meaning, she didn't have time to blow it up, bulldoze it or flatten it like a tortilla.

I checked behind me for Ben, who was wedged into a seat between two extremely agreeable young things: streaked hair, low cut jeans, flat bellie's, bra straps and tattoos peeking out of deep V-neck, clingy tops, overstuffed backpacks between spread knees. Big bright smiles, with lipstick a little too red and breasts a little too close to Ben's arm. One hand dangerously resting on Ben's thigh.

Not jealous. Oh, good, he moved it. Take that you temptress.

"Earth to Abbey. About the package?"

"Oh. Right." I tore my eyes off of Ben and his groupies. Back to Justine.

"Tasty morsels. Aren't they?"

"What?"

"The girls." She tilted her head in their direction. "Hard to resist, huh?" Then she did a head to toe once over of my outfit and added, her voice filled with sisterly disdain, "Unlike someone who appears to be dressed for a lumberjack competition."

The whole lumberjack, mountain girl outfit was intentional, so there was no need to feel insulted, was there? Besides, who could possibly want a girl when a woman was available?

Ignoring Justine's pointed stare, including the "tasty morsel bit," I headed for the storeroom to corral a box and be on my way. Birdie came in behind me and corralled me, first.

"Abigail, I don't mean to be sticking my nose in where it don't belong, but Justine told me about Ben being kidnapped and your car accident and how you all suspect Frank Merona."

"Okay."

"Lord knows, he's a hard one for even a mama to love, but he can't have done it, Abbey. I'm as sure as I know my grandpa sneaks Southern Comfort during Sunday church services."

"What makes you so sure, Birdie?"

She counted on one hand. "He's at Merona Air 24/7, and wouldn't do an ounce of dirty work himself, if you paid him. Then I heard him saying how AVA was giving him a run for his money. Like he respected that. If he respects anything. And last week he told Rebecca to keep those two no-account brothers of hers out of Merona Air. Said he didn't want the likes of them around. Might as well have called then trailer trash; you could have blown her away with a feather when he said it."

"When did you hear all this, Birdie?"

"Yesterday. When I went back for my last pay."

Ben came up as quietly as a feather on the north wind.

"Ben. Where are the girls? They had to go restuff their bras? Check their belly rings for signs of a weeping infections? "

A broad grin spread across his face, like a cat with cream. A dog with chocolate. A gambler rolling sevens. A man who caught a girl—make that a woman—being jealous.

"Better not say it." I said, holding a hand over his grin.

The grin widened under my fingers. The corners of his eyes twinkled. "I mean it, you." I aimed a finger between his eyes with my free hand.

"Blu re?" he shrugged his shoulders, gave me a disarming look and mumbled under my hand.

"Funny." I removed the hand as he captured it and gave my palm a quick kiss.

"We'd better be off then, hadn't we."

"Roger that," Birdie said, in a stagy British accent. If she'd only known what "roger" meant on the other side of the pond, she would have been going to church twice this Sunday.

"Thanks, Birdie. I'll see you bright and early on Monday," I said, knowing full well she and Justine would have the computer up and the coffee on before I hit the door at 8 a.m.

Birdie opened the office door and peered into the lobby. "Your fan club's waiting, Ben. Maybe you two oughta sneak out the back. You can't be too careful where love-crazed girls are concerned."

Maybe it was the love-crazed music blasting from every stereo in town today, including the one at AVA, but enough already.

"And, Birdie? Can you please turn off the love song marathon on the stereo? Don't you think we've had enough pain for one day?"

10:45 a.m.

No one could say I didn't do everything in my power to protect Jo's blasted anniversary cake. I took Conti's cake box and set it inside a box from AVA before lovingly wedging it into the back of the car between the spare tire and a bag of clothing I'd been meaning to drop off at the Goodwill. Not even Santa Claus could have packed it with more care. When I was absolutely certain it was as safe as I could make it, I asked Ben, "Where to next, Obiwon?" deferring to the man with the list. This was after we'd exited AVA through the back alley, in order to avoid any encounters of the groupie kind.

"Being with you, Abigail, is always new and exciting."

"I'm not the one drawing girls to me like honey," I said, seconds before my feet hit an icy patch and I careened under the car, smacking my head on the open car door. I clutched my forehead and moaned. Could this day? I won't say it. Won't think it.

Strong arms lifted me back onto my feet. Soft lips brushed my owee and warm arms held me close. "Poor Abbey," Ben said as he rocked me and patted me like a baby. "We'll get through this day. We will," he reassured me.

His voice was so sure, so warm I almost believed him.

Believe him or not, we had things to do, places to go. We couldn't stand around all day, although, Lord knows, I wanted to. Get ice. Get the precious punch bowl. Gifts, too. Carefully thought out, last-minute gifts for . . . everyone. Pick up Tony's suit, etc., etc.

"We may as well get the hard part over with next." I wiggled away from Ben long enough to scoop up a handful of snow, form a ball and hold it against my aching head. "It's not like we're actually going to get the punch bowl," I complained.

While Ben drove, I explained how Jo's mom had managed to orchestrate a shaky joint-custody agreement of the bowl that made no one happy in the end. Jo got the bowl July through December. Which meant, there was no way Liz would hand over that bowl to Jo.

"It's only a punch bowl," he said, innocently as we pulled up to Liz's house.

"It's détente," I replied, as I brushed chunks of calving snowball from my lap. "Liz could scare off a horde of combat fishermen in Seward. And that's before breakfast."

"Why don't I keep the car warm and you go in after it, since you know her?"

I shoved a chunk of snowball down the front of his shirt. It was rewarding to see how he shrieked like a little girl before he leaped out of the car, shook off his jacket and did the best snow-ball-in-the-shirt end zone dance I'd ever seen, all the while threatening me under his breath. Priceless.

I leaned out of the car and shouted, "Why don't you use that charm of yours for the greater good?"

If I hadn't been holding the rest of a snowball to my wounded head and moaning pitifully, I think he seriously would have tossed me into the snow bank and driven off leaving my frozen carcass along the side of the highway like road kill. Dumped. Just like I'll be when he goes back to England or Britain or the UK, or whatever the hell they like to call it there. Well, shit. Screw him.

"Abbey?"

"Huh?" I jerked my head up and turned back to Ben.

"The bowl?"

"On second thought, I think we should just zip over to Freddies, buy a punch bowl and call it good," I said. "Maybe Jo won't notice."

"It's possible."

"Possible Jo won't notice or possible we could find a look-alike or possible Liz will be falling down drunk and hand over the precious punch bowl willingly?"

"We're getting old here, Abbey."

"You're a regular Chris Rock today, aren't you?"

"Chicken?"

"Easy for you to say. You've never met Liz."

"I suspect you'll march in there and work your magic on her like you do everyone else and come away with whatever your heart desires." He cracked my door open and held a hand out to me.

"Magic?"

"Later, Abigail."

"Hey, you brought it up." I held his arm to prevent escape. "What magic?"

He wiggled free. (I had mittens on, which explains it. Otherwise, no way he would have escaped my clutches.)

"What magic?" I yelled after him, as I trudged through ankle deep snow.

He headed for Liz's porch, reached for the shovel leaning against her battered railing and started flinging snow over his shoulder onto the snowy lawn.

"I'll be a minute here, Ab; why don't you go inside and warm up?"

"What f-ing magic are you f-ing talking about?" I shouted.

"If I wanted to listen to Eminem, I would have brought the CD!" someone shouted. "Is that you, Abigail Vertuccio, acting like your mother isn't going to hear every embarrassing detail? I'd get inside like the guy with the cute butt suggested if I were you."

Whatever magic Ben was alluding to had failed me once again.

I looked up into Liz's enormous double-D bosom, popping out of a one-size-too-small white satin dress, which could have passed for an evening gown, if not for the 6-foot wedding train draped over one arm and a white tulle bridal veil perched precariously atop a head full of fat, pink curlers. My mouth must have dropped open, because she snapped, "Have it your way," before she slammed the front door in my face.

Ben set the shovel next to the porch and came up beside me. "So, no punch bowl?"

"Magic, my ass." I stomped my way back down the slippery path and landed, for the second time in one hour, on my ass.

I laid back into a snow pile and sighed. Ben watched my helpless female routine for a few beats then sank down beside me. We had about sixty seconds before our butts froze to the walk and stayed that way until next May. I knew it. I wasn't certain he did. It was one thing to freeze your own rear at 20 below zero. Not so nice to freeze his.

"Fifty seconds and Liz will be stringing fairy lights around us and congratulating herself on having her Christmas decorating done," he said.

Sigh.

My jeans crunched like two parting strips of Velcro as I freed my rear from Liz's walk. I rewrapped my scarf around my neck and contemplated her front door. Did I dare try for the punch bowl after gaping at her chest like a horny boy at an all-girl mud wrestling show? And what was it with the dress?

In one last ditch attempt—so I could tell Jo I tried my best—I hunted through my pockets with frozen fingers until I found my cell phone, got Liz's number from information and dialed, remembering to keep metal from skin, so Vinnie would not have to hear about how I froze my cell phone to my ear in broad daylight.

"Hi, Liz. It's me." I waved toward the front window where I assumed she was watching from behind her peephole. "What's with the wedding dress?" did not cross my lips. Jo would have been proud. "Jo's giving Tony a party and—"

"Tell Jo to check the calendar. February is not July, August, September, October, November or December. Got that?"

She hung up; I redialed.

"Any idea where I can get a duplicate bowl in exactly . . ." I checked my watch, "two and a half hours? Liz? Liz?"

I pocketed my phone. "What do you say, you distract her and I slip around back and steal it?"

Ben placed a comforting arm around my shoulders and steered me toward the car, all the while distracting me with tiny pecks on the cheek. "This calls for a new plan," he said, as he opened the passenger door and settled me safely inside.

"Offer her sexual favors if she'll give us the bowl?"

His scrunched up eyebrows said it all.

"You could offer to . . ."

"What?"

"I don't know. Dress up as a delivery man and strip? Do a lap dance?

Promise to make her breakfast in bed for a month. Wait. Let her eat breakfast in bed off your stomach for a month."

His laughter peeled out against his better judgment, I suspect, and he shook his head before getting into the act. "Paint her toenails?"

"Exfoliate her back hair?"

"Flip her pancakes?"

"Butter her buns?"

I was going to pee my pants if we didn't stop. "No more, I give up." I help up two hands in surrender. "Let's just wing it. Jo'll be so busy, maybe she won't even remember the bowl.

A plane roared overhead, drowning out the better part of what sounded like, "That's what I love about you, Abbey. Your never ending optimism," while Ben kissed my forehead in a way that wasn't at all brotherly, but wasn't quite throw-me-in-the-backseat-for-a-quickie, either.

Reality check. Did he say that's what he loves about me? Or that's why he loves me? Just what I needed. Another unanswered question. But I wasn't about to ask.

Because I'd already made a fool of myself enough for one day.

Chapter 28

1:00 p.m.

"A quick stop at the bookstore for gifts and we'll be done," I said. Optimistic, I know. "Turn here. Left. No. Your other left. Ack! Stay on the right side of the road," I shouted.

I dropped my head into my hands, then thought better of it. Best to watch the road when Ben was driving. Not that he wasn't a good driver, if only he'd stay on the right side of the road.

He pulled into a parking space across from the bookstore, hopped out and came around to open my door. Fur flew and for a second I thought I was trapped in one of my mom's old fur coats. Just as fast the blur was gone. What the heck was that?

"Harvey. How'd you get here?" Ben asked.

So, I wasn't crazy after all. That was barking I'd heard.

In the time it took me to remind myself I wasn't crazy, Harvey shoved past a woman wrestling with the door, her arms piled high with packages, and was inside the bookstore.

"Harvey," Ben whispered, as we entered the store.

No sign of him.

"Let's try upstairs. The café is up there."

We took the stairs in twos, bumping and tripping over each other and laughing like two kids. "It's not funny," I said.

"Not in the least," he replied, trying to hold back a laugh.

I grinned back. "Really? A dog in the bookstore without his owner?"

"A man with a woman without an umbrella."

"What are you talking about?"

"What are you talking about?" he laughed.

When we reached the top of the stairs, I pointed to the stacks. "You take mental health, I'll take serenity. Mental health is that way."

"There's a serenity section in this store?"

"Nope. That's just what I'm looking for. Hey, did you hear that?" I definitely heard scruffling sounds, like those of an eager puppy sneaking up on an open deli case of tasty treats. I dropped to my knees in a cloud of dust, sneezed, wiped my nose on my sleeve and crawled along, peeking under tables and chairs, in search of our four-footed deli bandit. Nothing but a row of fake fur diaries. I snagged one for Juliette. No blankety-blank dog. I was sure the bandit was close. I could hear his snorty breathing. Past the mystery section. My knees were throbbing, but I scored a used Janet Evanovich for Jo, in like-new condition.

Woof. I steered my creaky knees in the direction of the "woof," past home improvement and a volume on antique airplanes for Jaye. Before I could reach either Harvey or the section on Southern witticisms for Birdie or the art section for a book on tattoos for Justine, I bumped into two legs of the human variety and looked up to find the cuter of the two Jebs.

"Shit. I mean. Jeb. Fancy meeting you here."

I stood, brushed myself off, sneezed again and tried to bluff my way through the encounter. "I thought you and Rebecca did all your shopping on eBay."

If I could have stopped myself, I would have. But I didn't have time, because Harvey came tearing down the aisle, fur flying, and launched himself at Jeb's ankle, sunk his teeth in, then held on with every fiber of his being. Jeb yelped like a wolf in a trap, jumped up and down, shouting curses I didn't understand and tried to shake Harvey off without success, which landed them both in a heap on the floor with Harvey snarling and shaking his head like he'd just caught the fattest, juiciest rodent he could ever hope for.

Maybe he had.

"Lady, you can't have that dog in here," a voice demanded. Whoever it was snatched Harvey off of Jeb One, lifted me to my feet and steered us toward the stairs, then out the door, with me cursing up a blue streak while he pushed me into a car face forward, directly into Ben's unsuspecting lap.

"Soopy. Bly fidn't peen foo." I tried to get my mouth of out Ben's— never mind. Anyway, I couldn't move. "By toot fis uck."

I didn't know who extricated me from Ben's crotch, but next thing I knew I was sitting upright in the most disgusting place I'd ever been—the back seat of an unmarked police car.

Now I got why the parking lot was so full. It was all the unmarked police cars, with several cruisers along the periphery. I *thought* that guy behind the bakery counter looked familiar. A cop. And the bookstore behemoth who lifted me off my feet? Another one.

Harvey didn't like the back seat any more than I did. He squeezed out of my hands and launched himself at the metal grate between our captor in the front seat, turning up the bark to tornado warning level.

"What the heck is going on here?" I asked Ben, in case he knew any more than I did.

"I'm not certain. I was listening to Rebecca's brothers talk about how they were about done with their work here, when Inspector Morse here pulled me out without a word." He shot the officer in the front seat a withering look. "He won't talk."

"Officer. Why are we being held? I demand an answer," I shouted over Harvey's howling.

"Abbey, all I know is I was told to keep you here until this operation is over and that's what I'm doing. So sit back and relax, because it could be a while."

I recognized that voice. "Joey, is that you? Joey Costa from fifth grade? God. What's going on?"

He shrugged, then turned to face me. "I'm not supposed to say, Abbey. But you must have pissed someone off pretty high up because as soon as you showed up, word went out to get your, and I quote 'pain in the ass' out of there before you messed everything up. That's all I know."

I pressed my face against the wire screen and pleaded, "You must have heard something. Come on. Remember when you stole Mrs. Nelson's keys and froze them to the hood of her car? I never told, did I? (Sicilian Tactic #34: You owe me and I've come to collect.) What's going on?"

Harvey woofed in agreement and scratched on the metal barrier for good measure.

Joey sighed. Scratched his stubbly chin. "Sorry, Abbey. I would if I could."

"You can." Sicilian Tactic #46: Do whatever it takes to get what you need. "Remember the Captain Bartlett Inn, prom night and Sonia Johnson's lace panties?"

"God."

"Black. Lacy. Panties!"

Harvey was sniffing a blob of gelatinous goo. I picked him up before tongue hit goo, pulled out my cell phone and waved it at Joey. "You still married to Carrie MacIntyre from high school? Does she know about the panties? Hmmm. What's your phone number?"

Ben took my phone and dialed 411.

"I could ask her and clear this right up."

"Information?" Ben said. "May I have the number for Carry MacIntyre Costa? Yes. Thanks much."

"You didn't hear it from me. Right?"

"Woof."

"I didn't hear a thing."

"Rumor has it someone in MI6—that's something like the British FBI—put the word out that if you showed up, we were to stop you by any means necessary.

Damn that Sam.

I sat back onto the hard plastic seat to think about Sam, MI6 and the Jebs. I sure didn't want to think about how many desperate, drunk, drug-addicted scummy criminals has graced this seat before me. I wriggled the door handle to be sure it was truly locked, that it wasn't all a big Valentine's Day joke concocted by Jo or some other well-meaning friend. No luck. We were locked in. The smell. Not really a smell. More of a stench. Terrible. Vomit, old pizza, year-old cigarette butts mixed with farts and burps. My imagination was taking over and if I didn't get out of there soon, I was going to scream. When Harvey licked the seat, I did scream.

"Look, Abigail." Ben gathered Harvey up into his arms, out of harm's way, and pointed to the side door of the bookstore where a couple of serious looking guys, undercover cops I figured, were piling into matching unmarked cars.

"What—"

The car radio blared and a dispatcher said something in code that only Joey seemed to catch. "You're outta here. Need a ride?"

They'd arrested the Jebs! Did that mean Rebecca was winging her way to prison in the back of a squad car, too? And what about Merona? I had questions, but no answers. On the bright side, now I wouldn't have to worry about hit-and-run drivers, kidnappers, or people breaking into Big Ellie. What a relief.

If only it wasn't Valentine's Day. If only I didn't have much more serious stuff to worry about than kidnappings, stalking, and breaking and entering. I needed all my strength, cunning and survival skills today. What with a wedding to avoid and all.

"You going to Jo's anniversary party?" Joey asked.

"Forget about the party. You'll call me as soon as you hear something, won't you?"

"*If* I hear something."

"Good."

"Woof."

"What I want to know is, how could she?"

Ben, the soul of patience, shrugged, as I ranted on.

"I helped her. I gave her a job at AVA. Not that she needed one, being British Intelligence and all, but, hey, I trusted her. I dropped everything and went all the way to Mt. McKinley to help you because she asked. Not that you needed help."

I ignored the road in front of me to see if Ben was getting it and fumed. "Why didn't she tell us? I know why. She thinks we're complete incompetents."

"We did manage to bring a dog to a—Red light!!!" he screamed.

I jammed on the brakes and slid on an icy patch, stopping only inches from the bumper in front of me. "It's not like we did it on purpose. It was an accident.

"We could have helped. Instead, I have mystery goo on my pants. It's disgusting. We got to sit in the back of a squad car while she gets all the glory and now half of Fairbanks thinks I've been arrested. Oh, God. That can't be good for AVA, can it?"

Ben waved my cell phone at me, "No calls from your mum. So I think you're safe."

I wrenched the phone from his fingers to see for myself. "You're right. Not yet. But soon. Oh, and I shoplifted. I'm a criminal." The evidence was right there in a heap in the backseat where Joey had so thoughtfully deposited the gifts I'd pilfered, along with Harvey, in his haste to get rid of me.

"They're reserving a cell for me as we speak."

We hit another light. I stopped short and buried my face in my mittened hands.

"We'll turn around. Go back and pay, Abigail. No harm done."

"What? Are you crazy? And be late for Jo's party?"

Chapter 29

1:47 p.m.

"Maybe I should drive? You seem a bit distracted," Ben said shortly after I ran over a curb in the parking lot of the university, barely missing an octogenarian who was exiting the handicapped ramp with a walker.

"I missed him. What more do you want?"

Valentine's Day makes me crabby. What can I say?

"Besides. We're here and on time. Now Jo can't bitch and moan at me all day long."

He shot me a less than patient look.

"What?" Sheesh. In one day, I'd confronted Liz, crawled all over a dusty bookstore, been thrown into a filthy police car and was about to face a party on Valentine's Day; the way I saw it, I was being nice.

"The back door, right?"

I pulled around back after Ben nodded his reply. He hopped out, pulled his hood over his head, headed for the gym door and yanked. Nothing. He cranked on the oversize handle again, but it wouldn't budge. "It's locked. I'll call Jo."

He made a call from his cell phone, nose red, his frozen breath hanging in the air. "Jo says to hold on to your . . . Never mind. She'll be here in a few minutes."

I wanted to pretend it wasn't almost 2:46. Be any place but here. What was I doing here, anyway? Mac wouldn't have made me come here? Mac! I hadn't heard from him all day. Where was he? Not that I wanted him to call, but why hadn't he? No way was I going inside that place without knowing exactly where Mac was and that where he was, was not in there. Well, you get it. All day I'd been depending on Sicilian Tactic #35: Ignore a problem if you can't deal with it. Oh. Wait. That's an Abbey tactic. Time to face the music.

I popped open the car's hatch and scooted Jo's anniversary cake forward. Ben came around to help and we slid the cake onto the roof of the car, waiting for Jo to arrive, while Ben held it steady. Who knew? A cake-addicted streaker could race around the corner and abscond with it, leaving me and Ben open-mouthed and wishing we were on the next flight to Tahiti. I left Ben to it and went around the corner to get the word on Mac.

Going with the obvious first, I removed my mittens and dialed his cell. No luck. I blew warm air into my hands and shivered while I waited for an answer to my next call.

"No, Abigail, he's not here. He left a message that he was going out of town for the day," Birdie said. "Justine thinks he has a job interview. I told her he'd never leave AVA. Ouch!"

"Abigail, are you at the party, yet?" Justine must have yanked the phone away from the offending blabbermouth. "We need to talk," she demanded.

Before I could answer, Jo leaned around the corner of the gym and shouted at me. "Abigail Vertuccio, get your butt in here, before you freeze your tits off."

Thank God. "Gotta go, Justine."

"Don't think you can avoid—"

"Hanging up now."

"Abigail—"

"Bye now." So far so good, but then I turned the corner to find Molly and Ben chatting like old friends, with Harvey barking his head off at Molly's heels. On closer inspection, Molly was chatting, Ben was nodding politely, not getting a word in edgewise, while Harvey was looking like he wanted to take a bite out of Molly's leg, if only Ben would let him.

"We'd better get the cake," I said to Ben, ignoring Molly completely. I reached down to give Harvey a good scratch. You gotta love a dog with good taste.

"Hello, Abigail. I was just telling Ben about—"

"The cake," I repeated to Ben, giving Molly the deep freeze.

He came over to help. Unfortunately, Molly followed. Was she brain dead? Did she not recognize a cold shoulder when she saw one?

"I was just telling Ben how I might be moving to Portland; Mac has always loved it there and I hear he was offered a job—"

Ben let go of his side of the cake for a second. Shock? Surprise? Joy, at the idea of Mac moving away and leaving the playing field wide open?

"Ben. The cake," Jo shouted from the open doorway. He regained his grip on the box and we crab walked slowly to the entrance with Jo navigating.

"Careful with that. Watch out for that patch of ice. Pay attention, Abigail. Molly, could you step back, please."

"Here, let me help," Molly offered, ignoring Jo as she grabbed for the free corner next to Ben.

"No thanks. We've got it, Molly."

But before, "You can go now," reached my lips, the ground flew out from beneath Ben's feet and the next thing I remembered was Ben hurtling toward me. We hit the ground while Jo heroically tried to save us from the fifty-pound anniversary cake that was coming straight for our heads.

Molly stood above us mumbling about how the cake was surely ruined and how disappointed you must be, Jo, and on and on. I would have slapped her, but I had too much on my mind, what with worrying about Jo murdering me with a silver-plated cake knife. Besides, there was Ben, who sustained the majority of the cake-related damage, to worry about.

The twisted and broken box lay open on the icy sidewalk. Bits of icing and cake clung to Ben's hair, nose, toes, and all places in between. His eyes were closed and he wasn't moving. Harvey softly licked frosting from Ben's chin, wishing him awake. Molly was nowhere to be seen.

I leapt into action. I put my cheek to his lips. Thank God, he was breathing. Death by cake was not something I wanted to have to explain to Sam. I took off my coat and tucked it under his head, then moved back in and whispered into his ear. "Ben," I urged softly, as I shook his shoulder. "Ben. Wake up."

"Abbey, I'm going for help," Jo said as she ran for the door.

Ben's eyelids fluttered open and the corner of his lips turned up when he saw me.

"Can you move?" I asked as I gently wiped icing off his cheeks before it froze in place.

Ben's whisper, "I think so," was drowned out by, "Here, let me help," from Mac, who came out of nowhere, with Molly right behind. Ugh. Molly, again. Probably she brought Mac here, hoping he'd find me in a compromising position. I'd bet money on it.

"I didn't expect to see you here," I said, as Mac helped Ben to his feet."

"Obviously not," Molly said, all sugar and syrup. "Or you wouldn't be licking frosting off another man in broad daylight would you?"

"What?" I said before I remembered it was better to ignore her.

I turned to Ben. "We should get you inside. Here, give me your hand."

Mac helped Ben to the door, ensured he was safely inside and returned to me.

"Where have you been all day?" I snapped.

He wiped a dollop of frosting from my nose and licked his fingers, his eyes never leaving mine. Harvey snuggled next to Mac's feet, happily licking up cake off the shattered box.

"Well, we all know about Abbey and Ben now, don't we?" Molly sniped.

Would she never go away? Did I have to dip her in wax and ship her off to a candle factory for her to get the message she wasn't wanted here?

Saved by the best friend. Jo bounced over with a UAF security guard and a spare jacket in hand. Unfortunately, she overshot her target by a foot, skidded into Mac, who slammed into Molly, and they all went down.

Jo didn't lose a beat. She shot to her feet and directed the guard toward Molly. "Get her out of here, will ya, Hank?"

Then she waved her arms at Mac and shouted. "Aren't you supposed to be somewhere else today? Now go away."

"But I got a message—" he started.

"Get lost. Scram. Vamoose. What are you waiting for?" Then she dragged me by the sleeve into the building and that was the last I saw of Mac for I don't know how long. I wasn't sure where he went. Later I checked by the buffet table. I scoured the dance floor. I perused the locker rooms and the bathrooms. Wherever he was, it wasn't here.

Just what I wanted. I suppose.

Chapter 30

2:10 p.m.

I'd never entered the university gym through the back door before and it was darker than lunchtime in Barrow, Alaska, in January.

"Why is it so dark in here, Jo?" I asked, but got no reply.

We were surrounded by rows of discarded bleachers, worn out hockey equipment and more I couldn't identify due to the low light. I followed Jo through the maze toward a huge set of double doors that surely opened onto the gym and the party. I sucked in my breath.

I was about to ask if she'd heard about the Jebs, but we reached the gymnasium and it was now or never. Time to face the music. I entered the room and all the air whooshed right out of me. My heart pounded; I gasped for breath, feeling like I was drowning. Sweaty palms. Lightheaded. Oh, God, was this what a panic attack felt like? Are you supposed to put your head between your knees? Or was that for killer hangovers? The walls were closing in. Like certain death, like doomsday, like the apocalypse.

"Snap out of it, Abbey. It's a party, not Armageddon."

"Help!" I managed between gulps of air.

Jo pushed me forward; I pushed back. She bent one knee, put it behind mine, unfroze my locked knees and shoved. It was either fall on my face (my numbers were already over the limit on that one today) or go into the Abbey-Ain't-Getting-Married-Today-No-Way-Not Now-It Ain't-Happening Valentine's Day Party.

I knew this thanks to the life-size photo on the wall of me with a big black circle around my head and a red slash from my hair line down to my chin. No way you could miss the words, "The First Annual Abbey Ain't Getting Married Today, No Way, Not Now, It Ain't Happening Valentine's Day Party" written in bold letters below.

I remembered that photo, taken on the day of my first-ever skiing lesson. One Jo talked me into. Like today. I'd have to think about that. Was there a pattern here? Anyway. The photo was taken at the bottom of the bunny slope only seconds before I crashed through the sawhorses and into my unsuspecting ski instructor. Jo captured my wide-eyed terror for all posterity and now the life-size Oh-No photo was there on the wall for all of Fairbanks to see.

"Ha, ha," I said to Jo. "Very funny."

How was I going to get that photo and shove it down Jo's throat?

"We thought so," she replied, good-naturedly.

I wanted to know why she wasn't she screaming at me about the punch bowl? Why wasn't she hitting me over the head with chunks of Tony's anniversary cake? "We?" I asked. "Did Justine put you up to this?"

Oops. Justine swooped down on us out of nowhere. "I bloody never. It was her idea. Tell her, you cow," she snapped, right before she punched Jo in the shoulder.

"Where did you come from? I thought you were at—"

"I'm here now, aren't I?" Justine pushed through the doors and shoved me into what looked like Cirque de Soleil meets The Nutcracker Suite. Or Oz. Except everyone was wearing a wedding dress. Truth. Even the men. Wait a sec. Especially the men.

And not a spec of red, rose, pink, blush, rouge in sight. Above us a sea of fairy lights twinkled as bright and beautiful as a star-filled sky. Below the party was roaring.

"Is that the basketball team up there?"

My eyes must have been playing tricks on me. I pointed to center stage where twelve beefy guys in wedding dresses (Tony's entire basketball team) crowded around a lone microphone. The captain, who had "Love Slave" spray-painted down the train of his dress and across his bodice, roared, "Welcome one and all, to the We're No One's Love Slave, Valentine's Day party. Yeah!"

"He's ad libbing. I never called it that," Jo corrected.

Another of the basketball players was done up in a short, filmy Goth-like dress, with black net stockings and a thick, leather-studded dog collar, along with the requisite leather ball and chain attached to one ankle.

Another went with a classic meringue, except for the KISS makeup and knee-length, hot-pink wig. Not to be outdone, a third went for the Elvira look: sleek, sexy and scary. The ultimate anti-bride. If you didn't count me.

My mouth gaped open as they strapped on guitars, plugged into their amps and launched into an off-key version of "Love Hurts." Across the gym I spotted a group of little girls—all decked out in poofy white dresses and matching veils—twirling and dancing to the music.

"Hey. That's Juliette!"

"Justine said it would be okay, this one time." She looked over at Justine. "Hey. Where'd she go?"

I twisted around and followed Jo's gaze. "Check the buffet."

Across the room, bizarre brides of every variety cluttered around long picnic tables draped in black.

"Anyone for a piece of Can't Buy Me Love Pie?"

Yikes. I jumped out of my skin when Justine reached around me with a slice of the custardy confection.

I've seen Justine dressed in many different styles: eighteen and pregnant, bare-belly above low-rise flared jeans, cut-off Beatles T-shirt, peace tattoo, tongue ring and feisty attitude. I've seen her in gypsy shirts and bangles, in a geisha outfit and half naked, but never, not even when she married Jaye did she wear an honest-to-goodness bridal gown like the one she was wearing now.

It was all too much. I felt like swooning, like the heroine in an Audrey Hepburn flick waiting to be rescued by a roguish Cary Grant. No. Too dated. It would be a 90s film. I'd be Reese Witherspoon, waiting to go from black and white to color. No, that wouldn't work. I looked up to find I was on the floor trying to adjust my eyes to the light.

"Look what you've done now. She fainted," Justine scolded. "I told you—"

I got up and shook Jo and Justine off as I swayed gently on my feet, regaining my balance. My sanity was way beyond reach. Because no way could I believe what my eyes were telling me. "That's not really the basketball team up there, is it?"

Yep. There was another one, decked out in a white and black wedding gown, leaping into the air, shrieking out a song I didn't recognize, making love to his guitar. And another: right next to him, rocking along with a life-size blow-up doll adorned in a life vest and a "Help Me, I'm Drowning" sign plastered across her rubberized Dolly Parton chest.

Someone wake me up. I had to be dreaming. Only I wasn't.

"She needs food," Jo said as she pushed me toward the buffet. "Here. Have some donuts."

Only, the donuts were I Don't Donuts and they were nestled next to platters of Divorce Court Cannoli, Prenuptial Agreement Apple Upside Down Cake, Til Death Do Us Part Pizza, Ball and Chain Burgers, Wedding Bell Blues Blintzes and Marry Me Meatballs.

Passing up the Screw Until Death Do Us Part Punch, I pushed aside a bride of Frankenstein and a shotgun wedding bride to get to the Save Me Scotch and downed a shot. Only then did I finally notice that half the women in the room were wearing "Not The Bride" signs. Holy Heaven.

I needed one of those. Bad.

"Auntie Abbey!"

Juliette crashed into my legs, all flying tulle and crushed ribbons. "You're here!"

I couldn't resist brushing the curls out of her eyes before snatching her up into a big bear hug. She wrapped her legs around my waist and held on as I spun her around in circles. Her favorite thing. Then she wiggled down as quickly as she'd arrived, hitting the floor at a run.

"Walk, Juliette," Justine commanded with a smile.

We watched as Juliette scooted between a gaggle of Not The Brides, back to her friends—happy to be playing dress up at the grown-up's party.

I wrapped my arms across my chest. For protection? Warmth? I wasn't sure. Maybe a little of both.

"I can't believe you let Juliette dress up like a bride, Justine," Jo said. "I mean, you won't even let her play with Barbies, so what's this about?"

"It's all in fun, really. Isn't it?" And she shrugged.

"And," I put in, "Juliette loves to dress up. Last week she was a fireman. A month ago she wouldn't take off her Spiderman pajamas to go to school."

Across the room I could just make out the top of Juliette's head, crowned with a woven braid of daisies, and smiled. "If I could have a child exactly like Juliette, I'd almost want one," I whispered.

Jo nodded her agreement.

"Now that you mention it," Justine said, "what ever became of that pregnancy test, Jo. You never would say."

"What pregnancy test?"

Tony! Oh, my God. Tony. Wearing a wedding gown. Unbelievable. And where the hell had he come from? Oh, shit.

"What test?" I asked, inanely. "Oh, you mean the post office test Sarah Radcliff was telling us about."

He came up beside me and smirked. "Good try." Then he turned to Jo, and in a tone I hope never to have directed at me, repeated, "What pregnancy test, Jo? And before you start in, don't patronize me. You've been crazier than a New York City cabdriver lately, and now Justine's asking you about a pregnancy test."

Poor Jo. Caught like a rat in a trap. Like a firefly in a mayonnaise jar. Like a salmon in a net.

"You talking to me?" Jo demanded as she stuck a finger smack dab in the center of Tony's chest. Good move. Going for Sicilian Tactic #4: Take the offensive in any defensive situation, you'll recall.

I could see Mount Tony was about to blow, so I did the only thing a best friend could do. "It's my test, Tony. Not Jo's."

I had his attention now. Damn, I had the attention of everyone around the buffet, as well. Great. Just great. Now my mother would hear I was pregnant. Mac would hear I was pregnant. Oh, brother. Tony rubbed his chin, but then said, "Good try, Abbey, but I'm not buying it."

"It was my test," Justine said. "I wasn't ready to share the news, so if you could keep your voice down, I'd appreciate it."

"Thanks, Justine. But you don't have to throw yourself to the wolves for me. Tony has no right coming in here like a bull moose and—"

But she didn't get a chance to finish the thought, which surely would have included in-depth details, diagram included, of where Tony could stick his imperious, chauvinistic, ill-conceived, self-destructive and downright-foolish-in-the-first-place tone, because in one quick move he tossed an astonished Jo over one shoulder and added a swat to her rear as an afterthought.

"We're going to finish this one. Right now," he said.

Jo was hanging over his shoulder, her Not The Bride sign swinging in the breeze. Tony was a vision in Carolina Herrera, trailing a ten-foot long train. I hoped someone was capturing this for posterity. My big question? How do you suppose she got him into that gown in the first place?

"She won a bet," Justine said, keeping one eye on Tony as he shoved Jo into a broom closet behind the bleachers and one eye on Juliette, who, along with the rest of the princesses, were back at the buffet table shoving handfuls of chocolate-covered cherries (Wedding Balls) into their mouths with alarming speed and dribbling gooey red and white juice down the front of their dresses, their hands smeared with melted chocolate.

Justine replaced Juliette's candy with a plate of apple slices, cheese cubes and cherry tomatoes, patting her lovingly on the shoulder; I helped myself to a drink while she filled me in on the details of the bet.

"They were watching the second "Tomb Raider" movie. Jo said Lara Croft was going to kill her son-of-a-bitch boyfriend who wanted to destroy the world. You'd have to see the film to understand. Tony said, no way, she didn't have the guts. If Jo won, Tony and the entire basketball team had to appear wearing wedding gowns. Meringue preferably. If he won, she had to say 'You're right' at the end of every argument for a month. As you can see—"

"Well, all I can say is, Thank God for Tony she won."

Because Jo would have gotten even. No doubt about it. Painted his toenails, bleached his nose hairs, shaved his butt. All while he was sleeping.

I bumped Justine's shoulder. "You wanna go rescue her? Fake a flood in the locker room? An orgy in the stairwell?" I knew I wasn't going anywhere near those two alone.

Justine took Juliette by the hand. "We're off to find Jaye. She's had enough for one day; haven't you, darling?"

Then it hit me. My window of opportunity. Jo in the closet and Justine dropping Juliette off with Jaye meant I could make my escape and no one would notice. With seventeen minutes to countdown, I could be in North Pole before anyone suspected a thing. If I got a move on it.

A chain of Bride, Not The Bride, Bride, Not The Bride, snaked around the room as I made my break for the back door. I took a wrong turn at the end of the buffet line and was blocked by the string of gyrating, jerky bodies. The whip end grabbed my hand, sending my drink crashing to the floor. He dragged me behind, bumping me into assorted brides along the way. I thought I was trapped, until unexpectedly the chain snapped in two. I went one way, it went the other and I was free.

Good thing the kids were leaving; the chain was looking more than a little inebriated. I plotted a new getaway route; ten steps past the curtain of fairy lights, right at the basketball hoop, twenty paces past the Make-A-Baby-Bleachers (as we used to call them when I was in school), then if time allowed, peek into the closet and see who the sole survivor was—Tony or

Jo—then out through the back. Easy.

"Abbey. Gawd. I haven't seen you since you were in diapers."

Marilyn Monroe. Swear to God. An old friend of Vinnie's. Unlit cigarette hanging out of her mouth, big hoop earrings, glass of something alcoholic in one hand, plate of wedding cake in the other, wearing a distinctly Ab Fab chic wedding dress with hot-red bra showing through her lacey bodice.

"I heard all about you, a Geisha and a priest. Sounds like something Vinnie would do," she snorted.

What sounded like a good time in the making was really a poorly executed stakeout by Sassy Sisters Investigations; but I didn't have time to explain it to her.

"See any futures lately, Abbey? Because I've been kind of wondering if you ever get the lottery numbers on that radar of yours."

"Abigail, there you are."

I swung around and found myself face to face with Ben.

"Ben!" I said, a little too enthusiastically. "This is Marilyn. Marilyn Monroe."

"The—"

"Not the real one, but close enough. Right?"

"It's lovely to meet you, Marilyn. Forgive us; we're impossibly late to meet—"

"Jo. We promised we'd—"

"Help with the big surprise."

"The finale!"

"Right. The finale."

I shot Ben a look. Enough Already! "Male strippers. You don't want to miss that, do you? They should be arriving. God. Right now. Gotta go."

Over my shoulder, I shouted, "Nice to see you. Stop by AVA anytime."

I crossed my fingers, hoping against hope that I could get to the back door—forget about the closet—before I was waylaid again. Twelve more yards. But no. There was Kiki Johnson, coming our way. I poked Ben and hissed. "Problem at three o'clock."

The closest door to us was the girls locker room. It would have to do. We dove between an Elvis and a Liberace bride and were through the doors and in the dark before Kiki noticed a thing.

"Whew," I said, leaning heavily against the door, my eyes closed to the dark room.

"Whew, indeed," Ben said, copying my back-to-the-door move.

"We can hold them at bay here for a while, then make a break for it," I plotted out loud.

Ben wasn't paying attention. "Do you hear something, Abbey?"

Only the muffled sound of music, laughing and general partying coming through the door. "I don't hear anything." Unless you count my heart, Ben's breathing and the swish of my jeans against the side of his as I turned to him.

"What time is it?"

I felt rather than saw him check his watch. The light from the dial glowed softly against his face. "2:35."

"Twelve minutes to go. Better start now."

"Abbey."

"We agreed. You and I would do it."

He placed a hand on my shoulder, effectively maintaining a zone of sanity. "*You* agreed, Abigail."

"You didn't say no and there's no time like the present." I held his hand in mine, moving us a fraction of an inch closer. Not enough to send him running.

"I heard it again." He turned his head toward the showers.

"You're imagining things. There's no one here." I edged forward, forcing him to take a step back, but not before his lips accidentally brushed mine. I could have sworn I heard him inhale deeply before he took that step. Then he had a change of heart, apparently, because he swept me into his arms and I didn't know where we were going, but we weren't going back.

A raucous laugh cut the air and I jumped. I held onto Ben, listening for footsteps, the rustle of clothing, any sound at all. Silence again. Ben finally whispered, "Where are the lights?"

I didn't know, but I reached for my key ring and flicked on the emergency flashlight. A weak beam pierced the darkness enough so we could explore the space in front of us. Rows of benches cut through the center of the room, the walls on each side were lined with lockers. I knew the layout. Beyond this room were the showers and equipment room.

We crept forward, secure that no one could surprise us now, until we heard what sounded like, "Oh, God," coming from the back. We pressed on gingerly until we hit a dead end. The equipment room was locked. Was the sound coming from a vent? We scanned the floor, ceiling and walls for possibilities. Another, "Oh, God" led us to a tiny hole in the back wall of one of the stalls, and when I straddled the toilet, leaned against the wall and peeked through, all squinty eyed, I found I had the best view in the house to the inside of the men's locker room. It seems the entire basketball team (and friends) were busy watching what could only be, no matter how you looked at it (I mean considered it), a porn flick.

I must have come in on it in the middle, because the flirtation and foreplay were over. On screen, two nubile, scantily clad beach bunnies with ample talents were frenching each other enthusiastically while an over-tanned Mr. Big Stuff was having his way with a well-endowed, real-life Barbie. If I closed one eye, I could make out two of the boys on the team elbowing each other, accompanied by low wolf whistles and generalized hooting by the rest.

Back on the screen, Mr. Big Stuff looked like he was gearing up for a grand finale. His head was thrown back and he had Barbie screaming, "Yes. Do it. Yes. Yes, Yes," looking like she'd just got the million dollar question right.

Ben tapped my shoulder. "What do you see, Abbey?"

When I didn't answer, he gently nudged me aside; I jumped and dropped my flashlight.

"Hey. I was watching that," I complained. I must have said it way too loud because the boys in the next room scattered like pigeons. In seconds the men's locker room was empty. The only sound was coming from the movie no one had taken the time to snag from the portable DVD player.

Mr. Big Stuff sure had stamina. The brunette was enjoying his ample—

Abruptly, Ben bumped me aside and I lost my concentration. Damn. I'd never seen a porn movie before. Ben took both my shoulders, turned me back toward the door, to guide me out of the stall. He must have been expecting compliance. I'm sure he wasn't expecting me to turn on a dime, making him crash into me. Better than porn, I thought. And he damn sure wasn't expecting the kiss. I'm not sure I was.

It went on and on and I don't recall who knocked it up from PG to xxx-rated, but we did and I was back to Plan A. Do it with Ben. Locker room and all. He wanted me. Lord knows I wanted him. Is there a rating higher than triple X?

2:39 p.m.

Before I had a chance to find out, there was a huge crash out in the gym that sounded like the stage collapsing, followed by all kinds of screaming. We raced to the locker room door, careful not to trip each other up on the way out. When Ben opened the door, we found the lights all over the gym had gone out. Thank God the children had been sent home earlier or I would have panicked right then and there.

"I'll go and see if I can help," Ben said, leaving me alone in the dark.

I followed Ben into the gym, but couldn't see a thing. Then I remembered my mini-mag light. But before I could go back for it, I felt a gentle hand on my back and a soft, southern voice saying, "Abbey. Thank God I found you."

"Birdie? What happened? Is everyone all right?"

I could barely hear her above the crowd. "Mac asked me to find you."

"Where is he?"

With a persistent hand on my back, she steered me in the direction of a door I hadn't noticed before, one adjacent to the locker room. We moved down a long, dark corridor until we reached the far end of the hall and Birdie pulled the door open. The outside lights were off as well, but with the snow reflecting the moonlight, I could see my companion now.

Only, it wasn't Birdie at all.

Chapter 31

M olly. What's going on?"

Where she'd been calm before, now Molly sounded panic-stricken. "It's Mac, Abigail. He's in the car. He refused to go to the hospital until I found you."

"What happened?" I searched the parking lot and spotted Molly's red Honda. I ran over, slipping and sliding, trying to keep from falling on the unplowed path, until I reached the car. The windows were tinted, so I had to open the door to see in. No Mac. I threw open the back door next and leaned in. Again, no Mac.

"Molly, where—"

It happened so fast, I didn't have time to wonder why Molly had suddenly picked up a Southern accent, why Mac would be in her car in the first place, why he would refuse help if he really needed it or why Molly was standing there, the mirror image of Audrey Hepburn in her Funny Face wedding gown.

I had no time at all to wonder any of this, because I felt a sharp pain on the back of my head and then the lights went out.

2:47 p.m.

"Rise and shine, Sleeping Beauty."

The room was dark except for the light shining in my eyes. Where was I? Molly was there—standing over me, ghostly in white, like an avenging angel. Was I having the wedding vision? My head ached, my neck felt like a front end loader had run over it. I was shivering from the cold. Not the wedding vision. I shifted on the cold, cement floor and realized I was slumped against Mac. It had to be, but I couldn't look. I had to keep my eyes on Molly, who was pacing now.

I recognized Hangar 42.

"Molly, what happened?" Sicilian Tactic #1. Play innocent.

"You're never going to marry Mac, Abbey," she said, pacing, pacing.

I leaned forward and tried to stand, but found I was bound around the waist by a rope, attached to the wall behind me. Panic rose in my throat. I sneaked a peek at Mac. He was breathing, but not moving. I fought against shutting down, drowning in fear.

"You have everything," Molly continued. "Why did you have to take Mac away from me? What did I ever do to you?"

Think, Abbey. Think.

I leaned forward, testing the line. I had maybe five feet of rope to maneuver with and that was it.

"Sit still, Abbey. I need to think."

I didn't know how far Molly was prepared to go, but it was all clicking into place. The break-ins, the hit-and-run, Ben's abduction. Not the Jebs. I needed a plan, because no one was going to be looking for me when the gym was in the middle of a meltdown. Orchestrated by Molly, no doubt.

"Mac," I whispered. "Mac."

"He's all right. Sleeping pills. You think I'd hurt him? I love him. If you hadn't barged in, everything would be perfect. If you would have taken the hint. But no."

She whirled around, whipping the train of her gown around behind her, pointing a gun at me that looked too small to do serious damage, but even I knew better.

"You couldn't keep your hands off him, could you? You had to have both of them. Poor Mac. Not knowing what a slut you are."

I couldn't look down the barrel of a gun, no matter how small. I closed my eyes, gripped Mac's hand in mine and prayed for guidance. There was no way I was going to escape by brute force, but . . .

I fell back in a dizzying faint, then held my head, moaned and slowly opened my eyes, gazing unseeing into the distance.

"What did you see, Abbey?" Molly demanded, as she waved the gun around wildly. "Tell me."

I shook my head.

"What?" she shouted, shaking all over. "What?"

I stared out of glazed eyes, sank against the wall, a dismal, defeated look on my face, and answered. Slowly. Reluctantly. "I saw you and Mac. In Portland."

"What else." She paced nervously, keeping the gun trained on me.

"Married. It was Christmas."

Her face lit up; she moved closer and kicked my boot. "Talk."

I hesitated. "Three kids. Two girls and a boy."

"A boy." Her hand dropped to her side and she loosened her grip on the gun. "Mac, Jr."

"You were pregnant."

She twirled in joy, and in that second, I swept my feet under hers, grabbed the hem of her oversize dress and yanked. The gun skittered across the floor, echoing through the empty hangar. Molly went down. I rolled onto her. She struggled, but the wedding dress was her undoing. I had her pinned like a corsage. True. I couldn't budge, but neither could she.

Molly wiggled like a fish on the line, a the steady stream of filth spewing from her wretched mouth. I was beginning to wonder how long I could resist smashing her head against the floor, when the hangar door banged open and Ben barged in, shouting like a Jedi warrior, with Harvey right behind, barking like a hound from hell.

My heroes.

They bounded in with such determination, they missed the entire I-had-Molly-trapped-already part, and launched themselves in the general vicinity of the white dress, where they landed on Molly in a bone-crunching (totally unnecessary) rescue.

"Abigail!" Ben shouted.

After he finally escaped layers and layers of white tulle, he smothered me in an exuberant embrace while Harvey covered Mac with slurpy doggie kisses and Tigger jumps.

"Thank God, I found you."

"Mac's hurt."

Ben rushed to his side.

"Sleeping pills, Molly said. Call 9ll."

"Already done. Let's get you free."

With one knee on Molly's back, Ben quickly extricated me from my bonds; then he went to work on Mac. When he was done, he lifted Molly to her feet, with her hands held firmly behind her as she kicked wildly and tried to bite him.

I was about to wallop her one when Justine crashed through the open door, ran full force across the hangar and leaped on top of Molly, taking her down again, kicking and screaming, the beautiful dress now splattered with red from where Molly's nose hit the cold, hard cement floor. I can't say I was sorry.

"Abbey. Thank God I found you," Justine cried.

Two rescues in one night! Not that I needed rescuing. I pretty much had Molly down in the first place. But two rescues. Three, if you include Harvey. I wanted to cry.

"You'll pay for this, Abigail Vertuccio," Molly shouted as Justine twisted her arm behind her back for good measure.

A siren blared in the distance, moving closer and closer until my ears hurt. Before I knew it, one of Fairbanks' finest had Molly in the back seat of a squad car.

"This isn't over, you bitch," she screamed. "Wait and see."

A second officer took Ben and Justine aside to take their stories. Justine gesticulated wildly, talking over Ben, about how she'd managed to track and capture the innocent-looking-but notorious Molly, thereby thwarting her evil plot to get rid of Abbey and marry an unsuspecting Mac.

I held Mac's hand while an ambulance screamed up to the hangar. Two paramedics rushed to his side and went to work. Checking for all kinds of things I didn't want to think about. Only after Mac had successfully answered questions, like what day it was and how many fingers they were holding up, did they load him into the ambulance. I kept pace every step of the way, squeezing his hand.

"You're going to be fine, Mac," I said. "They're just taking you in so we won't sue them. You're fine," I said. For my own benefit more than his, I knew.

He squeezed my hand and closed his eyes. "There's something I need to tell you, Abbey."

"You can tell me later. Just rest."

"No. I want you to know it was always you."

"I know that already. So be quiet and rest."

"You may not be marrying me today, Abigail Vertuccio. But someday," he said, right before he fell asleep.

It was the drugs. Exhaustion. Shock. Had to be.

Chapter 32

I'd already lost count of how many times I tripped today, so it was no surprise when my foot caught on the ambulance steps and I landed flat on my back. It happened right after they finished loading Mac and I was stepping up to ride along. The next thing I knew, two guys in white were bending over me, and Ben and Justine were looking like they were about to faint.

"Don't look at me like that. I tripped. It's nothing."

"She has to go to the hospital, too," Justine demanded of the ambulance drivers, totally ignoring me.

God, I didn't want to go to the hospital. Not as a patient, anyway. I hate hospitals.

"I'm fine. Just clumsy, that's all. Nothing to worry about."

"Don't believe her. She's been terrorized by that Molly woman. She's suffering post traumatic shock. She's exhausted. She needs a doctor," Justine ranted. "Lord, I should have brought my hammer."

The ambulance guys gave each other a look before they went through the same routine with me as they'd done with Mac. "She looks good, but don't worry. We'll take her in."

"No," I said, with less force than I'd planned. "I need to go home. Besides, you can't make me." Nah-nah.

Ben saw the light and intervened. "We can take turns staying with her."

Justine started to argue, but he persisted. "Someone needs to go with Mac and make sure he's okay. I'll take the first shift with Abbey. You and Jo can take the next two. I won't leave her alone for a minute."

He placed his hand over his heart with such sincerity, I almost believed him. "Promise."

"She needs to be in the hospital."

"I'm fully trained in First Aid and CPR. I'll ring the hospital at the first sign of trouble."

"Well . . ."

"I'll drive her there myself if she even blinks."

"Not if your car is frozen."

"I'll plug it in. You can call as often as you like."

"But."

"They can't make me go," I insisted, in case Ben's plan failed.

"All right, but if anything happens to her . . ."

I had visions of hammers and Ben's lovely head.

"You coming?" the ambulance driver interrupted. "Because we can't stand around here all day."

Chapter 33

"How did everything get so screwed up, Ben?" We were headed for home with me in the passenger seat, Ben behind the wheel navigating the icy streets, ignoring the rantings of a concussed woman.

"Everything will be all right, Abigail."

"Mac's in the hospital. Molly's sworn an oath to get even with me. What's right about that?"

"For one thing, you're safe. Mac, too." Ben put a hand on my knee and smiled. "See? The glass *is* half full."

"God. Did you ever think maybe the whole glass is half full thing is a conspiracy to keep us from starting revolutions?"

"Good comeback."

He navigated around traffic and pulled over, so he could take my hand. "Abbey, I thought I'd lost you. When I saw Molly take off with you. I mean, I made a complete cock-up of this whole thing, running around like some amateur spy. Dragging you into it."

"I was the one—"

"If you had been hurt—"

"I'm fine."

"But I was reminded of something."

"Hmm?"

"I won't lose you, again. Ever."

I closed my eyes and rested my head against the cool windowpane, turning his words over in my head as we got back on the road. I didn't open my eyes again until we were coasting down Gran's windy driveway, know pretty soon the onslaught would begin. Jo and Justine would arrive first, of course. Then the calls would follow. Gran. Vinnie. And more. I knew it was only a matter of time before everyone in Fairbanks heard about the V-Day attack—every detail included, from Molly's wedding dress right down to the triple rescue, if you included Harvey. And by the time three people passed it on, the story would go that it was my wedding day and how sad it was that I was laid up on my honeymoon. Hope you feel better, and by the way, can you tell me about____. Insert usual human condition everyone wants to know about.

Ooh! An idea. What if I told everyone the clairvoyance was knocked right out of me? Then I'd be free.

Ben was faithfully plugging in the car when my cellphone rang. Caller ID said it was Vinnie. I let it ring. Later for stinging accusations, recriminations and Vinnie tactics of the usual variety.

Ben came around to my door, took my phone and tossed it on the dash. "Abbey, I know the timing isn't good, but I need to tell you something," he said. "I have to go home."

"We're already home," I said.

It was so quiet, I could hear the trees rustling.

"Here. Let me carry you in."

"I can walk."

"I insist."

I shook my head. Ow! "I'm fine."

"I'm going to carry you."

"Wait. I have an idea, Ben. Let's hop in Big Ellie and get the heck out of here."

"Brilliant. We won't have Molly to worry about because Jo will kill me, but not before Justine gets me with her hammer."

"Seriously. If I stay here, they're going to drive me crazy with all their mothering. Do you want me to go crazy?"

He laughed. "Some would say—"

I put a hand over his mouth. "Danger, Will Robinson!"

"Really, Abigail. They'll be frantic."

I headed to Big Ellie on my own steam and climbed aboard, even though my muscles were screaming for me to turn around, go inside and sink into a nice, hot bath.

"Come on Ben, the bus is leaving."

He hopped in beside me, most likely questioning his judgement, but what could he do in the face of Hurricane Abbey?

"Where are we heading?"

"How far is Mexico?"

I started Big Ellie and was rewarded with a satisfying roar of her engine.

"We're going to have to come back some time."

"Do you know something I don't know?"

And there it was. That wolfish grin. The one perpetually lurking beneath the nice-boy facade.

He zipped my parka up to my chin, pulled my hood up so that the ruff tickled my cheeks, slid my gloves on and kissed me like he meant it.

"I know one thing, my dear Abigail. Resistance is futile. Absolutely and utterly."

That was when it hit me. That was the exact moment I got it. I was in way over my head, and being clairvoyant wasn't going to help me one little bit.

Epilogue

Three months later

I don't get it. Why would Molly send Abbey a necklace and gold heart, with 'Love Conquers All' on it?"

Jo wound the chain around her fingers and stared past the window at a pair of donut-shaped clouds floating our way. Making me hungry, actually.

"The note said, 'To Abbey, from M.' Only Mac didn't send it and you called your Mum. Right?" Justine aimed at my back.

I was trying to ignore the whole conversation, but failing.

"Love conquers all isn't Vinnie's style," I shot back. Hearts and flowers, in general, were not a Vinnie thing. Unless you're picturing "Love" as a demented cupid wrecking havoc on the vulnerable and conquering the strong and willful. Then, yes. Vinnie was an option.

"But she never said anything about a necklace."

"Love the conqueror! That sounds like Molly," Jo interrupted.

"How the sodding hell did we let this happen, that's what I want to know. We caught her up to her armpit in trouble and now she's escaped," Justine ranted, breathless.

"She was never charged."

"And do they even call to warn you?"

I knew the answer.

"No. We have to read about it in the bloody newspaper." She shook the newspaper for emphasis.

"They probably wouldn't have convicted her anyway. Mac didn't actually see her drug him. I didn't see her hit me."

"The hit-and-run? The break-in? The T-shirt? If the Jebs didn't do those things, which I'm certain they did not, now that they're shipped back to the U.K. on identification theft and fraud charges, then it had to be Molly, for God's sake," Jo put in.

Before I could shout, "Of course, it was Molly, but apparently we don't have enough evidence," Justine let out a bloodcurdling scream and I nearly hit my head on the roof.

I gripped my seat and briefly cranked around so I could see what the heck was going on. "What the hell?"

"God, your driving. It's—"

"I could have crashed, for heaven's sake," I shouted, turning back to concentrate on the view in front of me.

"Next time you turn, look first. You nearly—"

"I did not."

"What were you saying about evidence?" Jo interrupted.

"Anyway, she's gone and all we can do now is be thankful she didn't do any more damage than she did," I said.

"We can watch our backs is what we can do," Justine said with finality. "And make sure we have a hammer."

That, too.

With that we settled in for the ride as we headed back to AVA.

Eventually, I interrupted the silence. "Otherwise, all's well with the universe, wouldn't you agree?"

I caught a hint of a smile gracing the corner's of Jo's mouth and added, "I mean, Jo's happy. Not pregnant as feared. Tony's just happy to get his old Jo back, now that you're not sneaking around arranging non-Valentine's Day parties to pacify me. Jen's back at AVA and Birdie's making Justine's life easier, right?"

"Which reminds me," Jo said, "did you hear about Rebecca and Merona?"

"That's old news. Merona's back on his feet financially. The Jebs are history, blah, blah."

"They're getting married!"

"Shut up!"

"To each other?"

"It's true. Rebecca may have been cozying up to Merona at first to help catch her no-good, low-life brothers in the act—at Sam's request, I might add—but I guess she saw something in him she couldn't resist."

"His money."

"More like a kindred spirit, I'd say. Both ruthless in their own way. I mean, ratting out your own flesh and—"

"And Sam. She could have told us Rebecca was a good guy."

"So to speak."

"Regardless."

Justine sucked in her breath, gripped the edge of her seat and squeezed her eyes shut.

"Geesh, I didn't do anything. It was just a bump."

"Ignore her, Ab. Since Molly kidnapped you, she keeps seeing Molly behind every bush and trash bin."

"Have your laugh, but . . . ah!" Her scream swallowed any words of impending doom.

"Let's head home before Justine has that baby right here," Jo said.

"I'm only three months along, thank you very much."

"Hard to believe. All those pregnancy tests for Jo and then—"

"I know." Justine temporarily forgot she was terrified of my driving skills and beamed a beatific smile our way, cupping one hand lovingly over her non-existent belly. "I'm thinking of naming him Tobias."

I caught Jo choking back an "uck" sound before she said, "Lovely."

"Or, Duncan."

"What about Ben or Mac?" Jo asked.

"Stop asking already. I haven't decided," I complained. Would they ever leave me alone about who was the man of my dreams?

"I was talking about baby names, but clearly you have men on the brain," Jo said.

"Do not."

"Um."

"What's that 'um' for?"

"Nothing."

"Not nothing."

"Let's not go there," Jo said.

"Let's," Justine said. "I'll review. You're in love with two men. Don't deny it. Both are intelligent and gorgeous. Each, God only knows why, wants you. But what do you do? You let them both go."

"Not exactly."

"You didn't pick one."

The light was softly falling and if not for unrelenting friends in the back seat, it would have been magical.

"Who would you choose, Justine?" Jo asked, swinging Molly's necklace around and around.

Justine closed her eyes. "I think Ben's unique. Like Abigail."

"You mean weird, right?"

"Quirky."

"But Mac's steady. He's the parking meter Abbey's hot air balloon is tied to. That was how you put it, Abbey? Wasn't it?" Justine asked.

"A hot air balloon that can't travel. What good is that?"

"So you're saying I should choose Ben?"

"No. I'm just saying, you're underestimating Mac."

"If Ben were a food, he'd be tiramisu. Mac would be hot apple pie."

I nudged Jaye who'd been sitting beside me, silently riding shotgun, and whispered, "It doesn't bother you? Justine's calling Ben tiramisu."

"Don't start trouble, Abigail," Justine said. "Jaye knows tiramisu is not for me. I fancy hot fudge sundaes. That's Jaye."

Jaye had the grace to blush from his bangs all the way down to the delicately freckled skin on his neck. But that didn't stop him from smiling all the while.

"Almost home," he said as we approached AVA, but Jo and Justine were back to their debate—oblivious.

"Mac's giving Abbey space to figure out what she wants."

"Ben went home to settle his affairs, but he's coming back. He's not waiting—"

"Well, Mac made believe Valentine's Day didn't exist this year, all because of Abbey's hysterical-fear-of-marriage vision. And he dances like a dream."

"Ben surprises her."

"Abbey doesn't like surprises."

"Abbey needs surprises."

The wheels slammed down on concrete in a perfect landing and we raced across the runway toward the hangar, with Jo and Justine still arguing. We slowed to a stop and Jaye opened the door of the Cessna; Justine rushed out and threw herself onto the ground dramatically.

"Thank God, we made it."

Jaye laughed and patted my shoulder.

"Good flight lesson, Abbey."

Justine, still knees to the ground, muttered, "Never again. Never again."

I'd only had the controls for about ten minutes of the entire flight, so I think Justine's reaction was a bit much.

"Never again, Abbey. I mean it," she repeated.

My first lesson with Jaye and I hadn't gone into a trance. Hadn't hit another plane. No visions of Ben or Mac. No drama, if you didn't count Justine's white knuckles, screaming and the whole throwing-herself-on-the-ground-in-thanks routine.

The three of us—Justine, Jo and I (Harvey, too)—strode toward the office. I was imagining us walking in slo-mo, our hair flowing in the breeze, thinking how great it was to have friends like Justine and Jo, when Jo elbowed me.

"Do you see that? Is that?" She held one hand above her eyes and squinted. "It looks like . . ."

"Sam," Justine snapped. "Bollocks!"

Harvey rushed up to Sam, happily yapping at her heels. (Yep. I ended up with Harvey.) She crouched down on one knee and rubbed his nubby head, while Justine pulled herself up to her full height and stared Sam down.

Getting right to the point, Sam said, "I need a favor, Abbey."

"Oh, no you don't," Jo said, all Mama Bear protective and Papa Bear suspicious. "You've caused nothing but trouble around here."

"Say no, Abbey," Justine demanded. "Whatever it is."

Jo looked like she was ready to sit on me if it would keep me out of Sam's evil clutches. Justine looked this close to taking a hammer to Sam's head.

Me? I grabbed Jaye and headed for the Cessna. Maybe Sam would be there when I got back. Maybe not.

I asked my Magic 8 Ball watch—because we all know how being clairvoyant works. "Will Sam turn my life upside down again?" (Not to mention Mac and Ben.)

I closed my eyes. No use finding out the bad news any sooner than absolutely necessary.

"Without a doubt," Jaye read.

Rats. Time for Sicilian Tactic #56. One Ben came up with right before he left for the UK.

When you're cornered like Butch Cassidy and the Sundance Kid, whether it's by love, the Bolivian Army or a spy in Banana Republic clothing, don't just stand there.

Jump, already!

Acknowledgements

When you live in Alaska, you learn it's okay to depend on others. The person who offers to jump start your car when it's 40 below zero when you leave your lights on at the mall. The neighbor who loans you a space heater every time you forget to plug in your car. Friends who keeps you from going crazy when you're stuck inside for two weeks when it's 60 below zero and all you want to do is eat chocolate and sit in front of the TV watching Ace of Cake DVDs.

Friends are especially important when you are writing a book. They refrain from reminding you that you weren't this grouchy before the #@*#@! book. At risk to their personal safety, they tell you when you've gone off the deep end and need that vacation to the Lower 48. Stat. They read your early manuscripts and only laugh at the funny parts. They are tireless in their support and optimism.

Many thanks to Amy, Sandi and Laurel, who did all of the above. To my family, for all your support and love, my heartfelt thanks.

Look for more Abigail Vertuccio escapades

and

Sicilian Diversionary Tactics in

Alaska Virgin Air

by Izzy Ballard

from
40 Below
INK

STAYED TUNED
FOR

IZZY BALLARD'S

NEW NOVEL

Temptation, Alaska

COMING IN 2012

from

40 Below
INK

About the Author

Izzy asked us to be perfectly clear on one point. She adamantly denies any resemblance to Abigail Vertuccio, even if Izzy did happen to grow up in New Jersey to a flamboyant mother of Italian descent.

Although a wonderer at one time, she landed in Alaska because "Alaska is a place where everyone and anyone fits in, and that's not such a bad thing." That and she can't get enough of the humongous Alaska skies and the midnight sun in the summer. In the winter, she writes and prays summer will arrive before cabin fever forces her to jump in her motor home and take off for Reno.

If you would like to contact Izzy or view all of Abbey's Sicilian Tactics, please go to: www.IzzyBallard.com.

* We should clarify that Izzy doesn't really have a motor home, although sometimes she wishes she did.